PROLOGUE

"So long as men meet in battle, there will be bloodshed. Bloodshed will ever keep up barbarous passion. To break this fierce spirit, a radical departure must be made, an entirely new principle must be introduced, something that never existed in warfare—a principle which will forcibly, unavoidably, turn the battle into a mere spectacle, a play, a contest without loss of blood…machine must fight machine.

"But how to accomplish that which seems impossible? The answer is simple enough: produce a machine capable of acting as though it were part of a human being—no mere contrivance, compromising levers, screws, wheels, clutches, and nothing more, but a machine embodying a higher principle, which will enable it to perform its duties as thought it had intelligence, experience, reason, judgment, a mind."

— Nikola Tesla, 1910

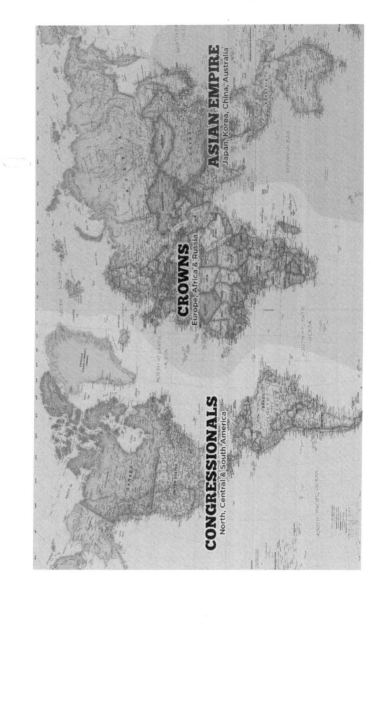

NIKOLA TESLA

TWO MONTHS EARLIER
NEW YORK CITY, USA

Nikola Tesla sat alone in the small rented room that served as both laboratory and living quarters. He had a clean, sharp look about him. He was thin, intense, and women said he wore clothes well.

The components of a large DC generator lay strewn before him, an exploded semicircle of magnetic coils, steel shafts, and oiled bearings. He was a handsome man, and his penetrating gaze encouraged problems to open themselves up to him.

He consulted a diagram, then hummed a tune as he lifted and inspected the heavy armature coil. The song was old, a Serbian hymn his father particularly enjoyed. As the viscous lubricant ran down his wrists, he wondered what his father would think of the work he'd accomplished.

Milutin Tesla was a priest in the Serbian Orthodox Church, and never understood his son's preoccupation with machines. But there are many ways to be close to the divine, and Nikola chose to know God by learning how His universe worked.

The knock at his door brought his attention back to the earthly. He checked the time. Seven o'clock. That would be

Mrs. Harrison with his dinner.

"Mr. Tesla?" she called out. "I have your dinner."

He smiled. Just like his machines, the universe operated like clockwork.

"Please come in, Mrs. Harrison." He grabbed a towel and cleaned the grease from his hands as she let herself in.

Mrs. Harrison entered, carrying a silver tray. She was a large woman, but threaded her way through the boxes and machines that littered the room. The devices came in all matter of strangeness. Some were shiny, angular, and protruding, while others were dark, hulking masses of steel. Once she'd seen lightning flying about the room as if dancing with an invisible partner.

"I do believe they have multiplied," she said, laying out his dinner. "What on earth is that creation?"

Tesla crossed the room to her. "That is an antenna for sending wireless communications through the air."

"Really? Goodness! You *are* a clever man, aren't you?"

"Thank you, Mrs. Harrison, you're too kind." He waited for her to finish and leave.

"Yes, rather clever," she continued. "In fact, I'd wager such a bright fellow would have no troubles in paying up his back rent, would he now?" She finished unloading the tray, and stood surveying the disheveled room.

"You will have your due money very soon now, Mrs. Harrison. That I do promise."

"Yes. Well, a promise is quite nice, but-"

"Do you know of Thomas Edison, the inventor?" he asked.

"Mr. Edison? Why, of course. Bringing the electricity to people's homes. Astounding."

"Well, Mr. Edison has hired me to redesign his generators," he said, waving his hand at the disassembled machine. "And I am quite close to my goal. After which I will receive a sum sufficient to pay all debts, and much, much more. So…" He gently guided her to the door.

She let herself be led away. "Working for Mr. Thomas Edison, hmm? Very nice."

"Yes, so there's no need to-"

She stopped short, and Tesla ran into her. "Whatever is this device?" she asked, looking at a large wooden box. A glass camera lens peered from one side, and a thick bundle of wires led from the other, to a teletype machine.

Tesla drew in a deep breath. "It is… a mechanical brain. I hope it will one day allow machines to mine the earth, instead of risking men. Just an experiment at this point. Now, if you please. My dinner is going cold."

She patted him on the arm. "Yes, yes, I understand. Very busy for Mr. Edison. All right, enjoy your dinner, Mr. Tesla. And do let me know when your work concludes, will you?"

"That I will, Mrs. Harrison," he said, steering her out the door.

"A wife would be most helpful in ordering this room," she offered.

"I have no time nor inclination for such. I have my work to do. Good evening to you."

He closed the door and returned to his dinner. Broiled fish, vegetables and milk. He'd not realized the hunger that had crept upon him, but it was now undeniable. He began to sit, but then ran to the door, throwing it open and calling down the hallway.

"Mrs. Harrison! You have forgotten my napkins!"

She turned back. "Oh, I certainly did. I am sorry. I'll be sure to remember them tomorrow."

He frowned. "No, that won't do. I need to polish my silverware before eating, as you know."

She sighed. "That I do. Very well, I'll be right back. How many was it again?"

"Eighteen. It has always been eighteen!"

She nodded. "Right. Eighteen it is."

He started to close his door.

"Mr. Tesla, why that particular number? Why eighteen?"

He looked at her blankly.

"Because it is divisible by three, of course," he said, and closed the door.

THOMAS EDISON

The mansion known as Glenmont was a stunning twenty-nine-room Victorian example of the Queen Anne Revival style. It was a house of arches, turrets, stone patios, and five chimneys. Nestled within fourteen acres, the three-story creation spoke of success and opulence.

Thomas Edison had purchased the house as a gift for his wife, Mina. "While a great deal too nice for me, it isn't half enough for my little wife," he'd told others. The large grounds were frequently put to use for parties, sports and games, and to entertain visitors.

Sitting beside a roaring fire in the reception hall, Edison smoked a cigar and watched his youngest boy roll about on the rug. He'd nicknamed the boy "Dash" from Morse code, and it seemed to suit his temperament. Upstairs, he could hear young Marion and William singing some newly invented song.

His wife, Mina, entered the room and stood beside the comforting fire, rubbing her hands behind her back. "Is everything all right, Thomas? You look pensive."

"Hmm? Oh, I suppose I am," he said, tapping the ashes from his cigar. "It's this business with the generators." He rubbed his face.

"The distance problem you mentioned before?"

"Yes, quite. At this rate we can provide DC power to the home, but we'll need to build a substation every two miles to do it. The whole process becomes much more expensive."

"What about this Tesla person you hired? Isn't he working on that for you?"

"He is, and I have very high hopes in his results. The man has a head for power like no other. A bit bookish for my taste, but undeniably the right man for the job."

"So there you go. There's nothing to fret over, is there?" She moved behind his chair and rubbed his shoulders.

"Ah, that's lovely, thank you," he muttered.

He tried to quiet the panic in his thoughts. He had a successful business, hundreds of patents, and a family and home that any man would kill for. So why was he so worried?

Mina worked the knots she felt in her husband's shoulders. "So what's the worst that can happen? The project runs a bit expensive?"

Edison's smile turned sour. "No, that is not the least of it. Not by a damn shot."

She felt him tense. "I'm sorry, dear. I didn't mean to upset you."

He drew a deep lungful of smoke from the cigar. The acrid burning was darkly pleasurable.

"We've taken on other investors to build out the DC network. Very powerful men who did not become so by accepting failure gracefully."

She rubbed her fingers over his temples. "Well, either Tesla will come through, or they will learn to, won't they?"

Edison grunted. "Maybe they will," he said, watching the flames dance, reducing the wood to smoke and ash.

BETTER THAN THE CIRCUS

Tesla awoke to the sound of such clamoring and turmoil, he was certain the building must be coming down around him.

"Nikola!" a man yelled through his door, followed by a staccato beating against the wood. "Wake up, man! The Academy is waiting for you!"

Tesla blinked and sat up in bed. Groggy from the late night's work, he looked about his room. The DC generator was still in pieces, which vexed him. Some small, critical detail was eluding him. Perhaps if he—

"Nikola!" yelled the man again.

Tesla bolted straight up, still clothed from last night. "One moment, I'm coming!"

He found his overcoat and pocketed an apple for breakfast. Opening the door, he came face to face with Charles-Henri. The short Frenchman was red in the face, and his glasses were askew.

"Charles-Henri, did you run the entire distance here?" Tesla asked, throwing on his coat.

"*Oui*! Yes, I most certainly did. The entire Academy is waiting for you at the Royal Hall. Please do not tell me you forgot your presentation."

Tesla patted the man's shoulder reassuringly. "Of course not. I am not half the mad scientist others think of me. Come, let's go and educate." He headed out, charging down the hallway.

"Nikola! The oscillator?"

Tesla froze, then returned to his room. When he returned, he was carrying a small mechanical device.

"Right, off we go." Tesla led the way, and Charles-Henri caught up to him.

Ten minutes later the two bounded up the marble steps of the Royal Hall of the Academy of Science. Tesla threw the double doors open wide, and strode into the hall. A raised central stage was surrounded by a sea of benches. Three hundred scientists and reporters turned to look as he entered.

"Good morning, gentlemen! I am Nikola Tesla, and it is time we began the presentation."

As he walked down the aisle toward the stage, there was minor grumbling from the audience, but Tesla's work on oscillating vibrations was nothing short of thrilling. And besides, he was hardly the first scientist to behave oddly.

He leaped unto the stage and reviewed the audience. He knew many of the faces. His friend Samuel Clemens, who never missed his talks, sat in a front row. His novels, written under the pen name Mark Twain, were gaining quite a reputation. Tesla nodded a welcome as Samuel shook his head, smiling.

Farther back, he found George Westinghouse, the financier who was particularly interested in Tesla's work on AC power, sitting with William Stanley. A few rows away, Thomas Edison was whispering to J.P. Morgan. Tesla smiled at his current employer, but Edison didn't return the gesture.

A small table had been set up for his use, so Tesla sat his oscillator on it. Behind him another table held a steam generator, and various tools and devices from the previous speaker. He brought the steam generator over to his table, and lit the fire within to begin building up steam.

While the generator built pressure, an assistant brought

him a pitcher of water and a glass. He thanked the man, then turned back to the audience and raised his arms.

"Gentlemen, thank you for your indulgence. As you will soon see, the investment was a wise one. Now… resonance. Every object has a natural frequency at which it vibrates. If we know this frequency, and apply a vibration of said frequency to an object, we build up a wave effect that grows over time. Think of a snowball rolling down a hill and becoming an avalanche. The same happens within objects and can tear them apart from within."

"Such as the Angers Bridge?" someone asked.

"Precisely. The wind had already begun making the bridge vibrate, and when the French soldiers marched across, they added to the effect. The bridge collapsed, and two hundred men died. For this very reason, soldiers break step when they cross bridges."

Samuel Clemens chimed in. "I do hope we aren't felling bridges today, Nikola." The audience chuckled.

"No, I have something less grand in mind today. I see we have a full head of steam, so let's begin. I will attach the steam output to my oscillator thusly," he said, attaching a heavy hose to his device. "And now, to switch it on."

He activated the oscillator, and immediately a high-pitched whine sang from the device. Some members of the audience plugged their ears with their fingers.

"An unpleasant tone, to be sure. But watch how it can be put to use."

Tesla turned an adjustment valve, and the pitch of the sound dipped lower. He turned the dial the opposite way, and the pitch rose. Higher and higher it went, becoming almost painful to hear.

"Just a bit more!" he yelled over the sound.

He dialed the piercing tone higher, and the water glass beside him shattered as if detonated by explosives. A moment after the pitcher also flew apart into shards. The audience was shocked, then impressed.

Tesla turned the dial down until the tone was low and easier on the ears.

"As you see, oscillating vibrations are yet another tool man can harness and put to good work. In fact, I would go so far as to say-"

Crack!

The sound of splitting wood echoed through the hall. Everyone looked about for the source, but saw nothing unusual.

Tesla continued. "I would go so far as to say that through judicious application, controlled vibrations could be an untapped source of great power. There are innumerable applications, from mining to—"

CRRRACK!

Much louder now, the sound had an ominous quality, like imminent danger. Outside on the street, people were yelling, but the words were muffled.

Tesla's brow furrowed as he looked about the hall.

With a splintered roar, the main entry archway snapped, and half of it fell like a logged tree. The huge support beam crashed to the ground in a cloud of plaster dust.

Then the stage buckled, and Tesla fought to remain standing. Beneath him, he felt the heavy wood beams settling and falling apart.

"My God, the building's coming down," he whispered to himself.

The crowd panicked now, and everyone leaped to his feet, pushing toward the exit. Several men went down in the aisles as their peers flowed around and over them for safety. Here and there the audience held on to their wits and pulled the trampled men up to their feet. But mostly the large room held a spooked herd, bolting from a threat.

Tesla's friend Samuel jumped onto the stage, escaping the pandemonium. Tesla pulled him up to safety, then turned back to the oscillator.

"It's reached the natural frequency of the building!" he yelled above the turmoil.

"I should say so!" Samuel answered. "Disable it man, or your genius will turn to infamy. And worse, I will be dead!"

Tesla reached for the hose that delivered steam to his contraption. He turned and wrenched the fitting, but it refused to give way. "The heat has sealed it!"

Samuel stood rock still, feeling utterly helpless to assist his friend or himself. Then he saw the second table behind Tesla. He sprang forward to it, running his hands over the devices and tools. There must be something...

He found a huge iron hammer, suitable for driving railroad spikes. *And hopefully, smashing oscillators*, he thought. He grabbed the heavy tool and turned back. "Nikola!"

Tesla saw and understood in a flash. He whipped the hammer from Samuel's hands and heaved it back. With a full body swing, he brought the hammer crashing down onto the rumbling oscillator.

Clang!

The hammer bounced off, leaving a thumb-sized dent in the device's thick hull. The low, rhythmic vibrations continued.

Just then a new ripping sound tore from the east wall. Tesla glanced and saw a thick crack appear in the wall's plaster finish. Then the crack split wider, and became a running gash that leaped up the wall and above the large stained glass windows.

The sudden settling of the wall was too much for the old glass, and the windows shattered under the new weight bearing down on them. The audience was showered by a red, blue, and green rain of glass fragments.

Tesla turned back and set himself for another attack. He

drove the hammer down with all his strength. The head struck the oscillator squarely, cracking the outer hull. The high-pressure steam inside escaped violently, sending a scalding, shrieking white jet shooting over the terrified audience members.

And then all was quiet.

The low vibration ceased. There were no more sounds of splintering wood or plaster. The yelling of men calmed.

Tesla stared at his device, eyes wide. He remembered he still held the hammer, and let it slip to the floor.

Samuel looked to his friend. "Well done."

Tesla tore his eyes away from the wrecked machine. "I—"

A shrill police whistle cut through the room, giving the anxious men a jolt. Six uniformed officers pushed through the masses.

"What's going on in here?" one demanded. "We have calls from all the nearby businesses. Women going on about the end of the world. What's happened here?"

Samuel stepped forward, hands open in a genteel welcome. "Welcome, officers. What occurred here was nothing more than… than…"

"An earthquake," said Tesla.

Samuel gave his friend a sour, sideways look. "Yes, that's the answer."

Tesla stepped forward. "I was just giving a presentation on applied oscillations when the quake struck. Made a hell of a mess. Thank God you've arrived." Then he closed his mouth and waited.

Some of the audience voiced their disapproval, and called for Tesla's head, but the police decided against placing blame and turned to getting everyone out safely.

Samuel clapped him on the shoulder. "Good show, Nikola. Better than the circus."

Tesla turned, his eyes still wide. "I believe I need a drink."

"A capital idea!" Samuel replied. "And it's on me. The least I can do for such an entertaining morning."

Tesla and Samuel hastily found their way from the Academy and turned down an alley. They crossed Post Street, then turned west, through the grocer's area. New York had many fine taverns, but for Tesla, there was only one favorite, the Petal & Thorn.

Samuel checked his pocket watch. "It's not even ten yet. John will likely be sleeping still."

"A gamble we must accept."

They quickly walked the remaining six blocks. Above them, dark, swollen storm clouds gathered, threatening rain.

Samuel looked up. "God is unhappy with you," he said, smiling.

"He's not the only one."

Samuel followed his friend's gaze, and saw a rough, hulking man approaching. He looked like a railway worker, or maybe a professional fighter.

"Nikola Tesla," said the brute. "Good to see you." The smoldering hostility in the man's eyes belied the friendly words. He joined the men, standing uncomfortably close. "Going to be getting paid soon, am I?"

Tesla's face warmed, embarrassed to have his private issues made public to Samuel. "You will. Now if you'll excuse us." He walked around the brute, and Samuel followed him.

"That's good, very good," he called as they walked away. "Be seeing you soon then!"

They continued to the bar, and Samuel looked at his friend in concern. "Well?"

"That was Clay Bracken. He's a debt collector."

"Debts?"

"I had a bad run with the cards. A small matter."

"Hmm. Well, I'd wager he's good at his job. Do you need help?"

Tesla waved off the offer. "Not at all, my friend. But thank you."

They reached the bar just as the rain fell. The door was locked, so Tesla knocked, and they crowded together under the awning. "John Roberts! Please open, we need a drink!"

The two men stood in the doorway, waiting. Tesla raised his fist to knock again, but then a face appeared in the glass. John's eyes were red, and his face hung slack. Tesla wondered whether the barkeep had a late evening, or was the victim of a robbery.

John's bloodshot eyes slowly fixed upon the men. "Gods. My two best customers. At once. This cannot be a good sign."

Tesla knocked again. "Come on, John, let us in. It's been a trying day."

John grunted.

Samuel joined in, leaning over Tesla's shoulder. "Yes, we've narrowly escaped an earthquake, after all."

If John was surprised by this news, he gave no evidence of it. "An earthquake. Of course. You'd best come inside then."

He opened the lock and swung the door wide, standing aside for the men to enter. A bear of a man, he loved his liquor, beef, and women.

After they bounded inside his bar, John closed and locked the door behind them, then shuffled to his station behind the fantastic bar. It had been carved from a single large oak eighty years ago and had survived four fires, three bankruptcies, and now, apparently, an earthquake.

Tesla and Samuel settled onto high stools at the bar as John poured two whiskeys. Tesla found the warm wood paneling and rich jewel-tone tapestries especially welcoming today, and his nerves began to settle. The huge flagstone

14

fireplace was not yet lit, but the upcoming warmth of the whiskey would suffice.

John pushed the glasses to the men. As they reached for them, he pulled them back.

"I am going back to bed. These are on the house, but no more, agreed?"

"Absolutely, John," said Tesla.

"Agreed!" echoed Samuel.

"Very well." John slid the glasses forward, then turned and shuffled into the back kitchen, where he kept a spare bed.

"You are a prince, John Roberts," called Tesla.

The prince grunted and waved once over his shoulder, not looking up as he disappeared into the kitchen.

The two men sipped their whiskey, savoring the icy burn. Samuel let the silence hang, then offered, "A formidable weapon you've devised, my friend."

Tesla laughed. "It's incredible how many things that capture my interest become weapons, despite my not having that intention."

"Well, we all have our talents."

Tesla shook his head. "That was too close. The entire building could have fallen on our heads."

"I certainly had that impression, yes."

"I know what it was now. It's the building's skeleton. The main support structure is a mixture of iron and nickel. I found the frequency that would undo it at the smallest level."

"How on earth would you know the makings of the building?"

"Hmm? Oh, I did some work for the Academy last year. Experiments in grounding the site against lightning strikes, so I had to know the composition of the metal within. The alloy of iron and nickel has some special properties, which…" Tesla trailed off, lost in thought.

Samuel was accustomed to his friend going frozen,

transported to some other land in his mind. Sometimes his journey was short and he would finish his sentence at once. Occasionally, the delay was so great, Samuel would lose patience and wander off, to catch up with Tesla another day.

Today the trip was brief. Tesla's head snapped up, his mouth agape. "My God, that's the answer!" he exclaimed. He knocked back the glass of whiskey and gathered his overcoat. "I have to go!" He rushed out the bar and ran down the street, oblivious to the downpour.

Samuel sat alone. "Yes, clearly you must," he said to the empty bar. "Not to worry, I am happy to drink alone. I make very good company, actually."

He finished his drink and reached behind the bar for the bottle.

Tesla stood in Edison's reception hall, beaming and dripping wet. "It's a question of impedance, you see? By using a nickel/iron winding, and then changing the shape of the rotor like so, we gain the efficiency required!"

The solution had finally come, and it sprang into his mind fully formed. He'd sketched out the needed diagrams and confirmed the math before bringing it all to Edison, but he'd known he was right that moment in the bar.

Edison regarded the exuberant man standing in his home. *A tall, lanky, drowned rat*, he thought. *But maybe one with a solution.* He examined the documents Tesla brought.

Watching Edison's face as he perused the diagrams and formulas, he saw Edison believed in the solution as well. His money issues would very soon be laid to rest.

"Yes," said Edison. "I see now what you mean. It really is clever. Somewhat obvious, actually, but clever nonetheless. Well done, Nikola. I'll have my engineers begin making the modifications straight away."

Tesla grinned. "Excellent, Mr. Edison. Excellent!"

Edison straightened up and looked at Tesla. "Is there anything else?"

Tesla cocked his head. "Well, there is the matter of payment. You promised me fifty thousand dollars if I could solve your problem. You have your solution, so…"

Edison's face broke into a smile. Then he grabbed his belly and laughed heartily. He bent forward from the force of the mirth, then stood up, shaking his head.

"Nikola, you do entertain me. I never made such a promise."

Tesla's face grew warm, and he imagined his cheeks reddening. "Mr. Edison, you most certainly did. Fifty thousand. That was our agreement, and I have delivered my half of the barter. I very much need you to—"

"Son, I don't know what you think we agreed to. Honestly, I think you just don't understand our American brand of humor."

Tesla felt nauseated and fought the urge to sit down.

"Now, I am happy to compensate you for your work, of course. I believe two thousand dollars would be a fine payment for this level of work. How does that sound? I have that much right here, in the safe."

Tesla's ears rang with the rushing of blood in his head, and his vision narrowed to a tunnel vision. Edison was still speaking, but he couldn't hear the words. He could barely see him, even. Instead, he saw Mrs. Harrison's contempt and pity. He saw himself evicted from his room. Disgraced and humiliated. He saw his father's disappointed scowl.

"Are you all right, my son?" asked Edison.

Tesla held up his hand to ward him away. His jaw tightened hard, and he felt his molars grinding against each other.

"Nikola, please don't refuse my offer. If I wish it so, there

17

will be no electrical work for you in this city."

Tesla desperately wanted to strike this man who so casually mocked their agreement. He saw his hand of its own accord had become a fist.

But instead, he blinked back the fury, sucked a deep chestful of air, and unclenched his fist. Then he turned away and headed for the door.

"You keep your money. I have no need for it," he said and stepped out into the rain.

THE ROOSEVELT DOCTRINE

WASHINGTON, DC

The White House receptionist was exceedingly polite. "May I bring you anything, General? We have very good coffee." She smiled sweetly, genuinely wanting to make him comfortable.

General Sam Houston waved off the offer. "Thank you, but no, ma'am." His Tennessee drawl made her smile every time. *Sometimes one should not be comfortable*, he thought.

As the young woman returned to her clerical work, the general clasped his hands behind his back, looking around the small room. The receptionist's desk, an American flag in the corner, a comfortable couch, and three bookshelves. And the door, of course. Behind that heavy but nondescript door was the Oval Office. History was changed by the decisions made behind that door. He'd met the president five times previously, but every time was an impressive experience. He looked down, ensuring his uniform was straight, and his medals aligned. As always, they were.

He heard two men approaching, chatting amicably. He looked up to see the chief of military R&D, Dr. Bertram Gladstone, wearing his trademark tweed jacket. He didn't know the second man. The general's face broke into a smile, and he stepped forward to shake hands.

"Bertram, very good to see you again."

Dr. Gladstone was just as pleasantly surprised and clasped the general's hand tightly. "Sam! A pleasure, I didn't know you would be at this briefing too."

"I imagine the president wants an update on Beowulf, so here I stand."

"Of course, of course. General, let me introduce you to Thomas Edison. He's a brilliant inventor and scientist. I thought his perspective would be invaluable, and he was kind enough to join us."

The men shook hands. "Very nice to meet you, Mr. Edison."

"And you, General," Edison replied, impressed by the man's commanding presence. The general's large, strong frame, craggy features, and deep, rumbling voice often intimidated people. He gave the impression of power held in restraint.

Behind them the receptionist stood and crossed to the Oval Office door. She knocked and stuck her head inside, then turned back to the three waiting men. "The president will see you now."

The men filed inside the Oval Office, properly impressed by the trappings of power.

"Gentlemen!" a booming voice said. They turned and found President Teddy Roosevelt standing up behind the Resolute desk. He strode forward, welcoming them and shaking hands.

"Please, sit. I'm eager to hear the latest, and we have an important matter to discuss." He returned to his chair behind the desk and rubbed his face.

"All right… General? Where do we stand on Beowulf?"

"As far as the mechanicals go, we're on track, Mr. President. The new treads seem to be working much better, and the small armaments are in place. We've hit a snag with the main cannon, but Savannah thinks we'll have it resolved within the week."

"She's been a great asset. How's her father doing?"

"The colonel is hanging in there. He knows what's at stake. I don't think he's going to let his body give up until we get there."

The president shook his head. "Sad business. Let's just make something good come from it."

"Yes, sir. In fact, we're ready to begin field trials, with the exception, of course, of the central brain."

Bertram took a breath, knowing the focus was about to shift to him.

"So what's the story, Bertram?" asked the president. "I have a super weapon, but no brain to drive it."

"Initial testing looked very promising, sir. But since then, Hollerith has made... disappointing progress."

Edison leaned forward. "Forgive me, Mr. President, but this super weapon—"

Roosevelt looked at Bertram. "You've not told him anything?"

"No, sir, I figured that should come from you."

"That's fine." He turned back to Edison. "You know Bertram's R&D lab is hosted within General Houston's base?"

"I do, sir," Edison replied.

"Well, there's a good reason for that. That lab is working on some fairly exotic technology. Extremely sensitive work. We knew many of those efforts wouldn't bear fruit, but some will, and those can change the course of the war in our favor. Foremost among these projects is Beowulf. Basically, it's a super-tank. Massive, armed like a battleship, and tough enough to take on an army single-handedly."

Edison nodded. "Very impressive."

"It is, but you haven't heard the best part."

"And that is?"

The president smiled. "It's unmanned."

21

"I don't understand, sir. Unmanned because it's still under development?"

"No, no. When the Beowulf tank goes into battle, it will do so without a crew. You've heard of the new 'computers'?"

Edison nodded slowly, unsure of what he was hearing.

"Hollerith's team has been working on a mechanical brain capable of driving the Beowulf tank. Imagine… we can meet an enemy on the field of battle, and not lose a single man. It's an amazing time."

Edison sat back, processing what he'd heard. Machines were a large part of his life, but man was always their master. What the president described turned that on its head. He wasn't sure he felt comfortable with such a concept.

"It certainly is… exotic," he admitted.

Roosevelt laughed heartily. "I know, Mr. Edison. It's a radical concept, and it takes some time to come to grips with it. Hang in there." He focused back on Bertram, and the smile left his face. "This is unacceptable."

"I agree, sir."

"If your man doesn't deliver, this project goes nowhere. And I will not let that happen, not with the wolves at the door."

"I know that, sir." Bertram understood the pressures the president must be dealing with. War with Britain was coming. Everyone could feel it, like a cold fog rolling in off the Atlantic.

Roosevelt's temper flared. "You know it, but what do you plan to do about it? What exactly is your plan?"

Bertram felt his cheeks grow hot. His life had been academia, not politics. "Sir-Mr. President, we are aggressively pursuing all avenues of research-"

Edison interrupted. "Perhaps therein lies your problem."

Roosevelt's head snapped to him. "How so?"

"Well, the goal of any undertaking is not to explore all

possible avenues of progress, but to identify the single correct branch, and then fully and ruthlessly develop it to its logical endpoint. My friend Henry Ford is having great success applying this methodology."

Roosevelt froze. This line of thinking was more appealing to him. Don't spend months walking in circles, trying all approaches. Find one and drive it home.

"Action, action, and still more action," he said. "That's what I want, that's what I demand."

Bertram held his tongue, knowing he was on thin ice.

General Houston stepped in. "We know that, sir. And it will be done. On that point, Savannah told me of a new scientist, Tesla. She said he was doing remarkable work with electricity. Why don't we bring him into the program? Another set of eyes may see something previously missed."

Edison balked, raising his hands. "Ah, I don't think that's such a good idea, Mr. President."

Roosevelt raised his eyebrow. "Oh?"

"I just mean…the man is a loose cannon. He recently almost brought down a building with one of his experiments. I was in the audience at the time. He's naive and unpredictable."

Roosevelt laughed. "Perfect! Sounds like just the man we need in the War Department, right, General?"

"Yes, sir. Maybe we can channel that destructiveness toward the Crowns."

Roosevelt pointed toward the general. "Exactly! Make that happen."

"So, Tesla is cleared for the Rabbit Hole, Mr. President?"

"He is. Maybe he'll help us give that royal bastard king something to worry about. Lord knows I've lost enough sleep over this Einstein business."

Bertram saw his opportunity to step in. "Speaking of Einstein, I fear the bombs he's developing for the Crowns may be worse than we thought."

Roosevelt stopped smiling. "Worse? The damned things can tear a hole in a city. What's worse than that?"

"I ran into Professor Schwartz recently at a symposium. He knew Einstein, and he told me some technical details of the man's previous work that worried me. I did some research, and—"

"What's the bottom of it, man?"

"Mr. President, I believe Einstein may be close to building a radiological bomb."

Edison scoffed.

The general's craggy face grew dour.

"Radiological? You mean he has bombs that generate radiation?" Roosevelt asked.

Bertram nodded. "I do. The destructive force could be many times what we have seen so far, but worse, the radiation would contaminate the area for decades. And we know their zeppelins have the range to reach our shores. A few of these bombs dropped on a major city could render it uninhabitable."

Roosevelt's face blanched. "Dear God in heaven," he whispered.

Edison began to speak, but held himself still.

Roosevelt noticed. "What do you think, Mr. Edison?"

"Sir, I have no doubt that Bertram means well, but I find it extremely unlikely that any bomb can be made as he describes."

"I don't have the luxury in letting it go at 'unlikely.'"

"Of course not, sir. I'm just saying we should balance our concern against what is most probable. For example, in my military work, I've focused on the need for a telegraph network. If implemented, a network spanning the Eastern Seaboard could give us rapid news of enemy landings, and allow for coordinated counterattacks. This sort of development will bear more fruit than experiments into radiation."

Bertram frowned. Did Edison not understand the looming danger such technology presented?

Roosevelt thought about that. He realized Edison was speaking from passion, but these new technological dangers on the horizon were too great to dismiss. He'd rather be seen as too aggressive and proven wrong than the alternative.

"Thank you, Mr. Edison, for your perspective. I count myself as a fan of your work. Bertram, get him into your lab too. But we are not speaking of research. We need to cut the head from the snake."

General Houston nodded gravely. The drumbeat of war always reached this moment, when momentous decisions were made. "We have a three-person team trained for missions like this. They can be underway within a day. Of course, there is no formal declaration of war with England, as of yet…"

President Roosevelt pulled a document from the desk drawer. "There is now," he said, handing it to the general.

He scanned the paper, and his lips parted as he read aloud.

"The first duty of the United States Government remains what it has always been: to protect the American people and American interests. It is an enduring American principle that this duty obligates the government to anticipate and counter threats, using all elements of national power, before the threats can do grave damage. The greater the threat, the greater is the risk of inaction – and the more compelling the case for taking anticipatory action to defend ourselves, even if uncertainty remains as to the time and place of the enemy's attack."

The general set the paper down and considered his next words.

"Mr. President, are you considering a preemptive attack?"

"Those bombs represent a clear and present danger to this country, General. We need a new policy, and this is it. Call it the Roosevelt Doctrine."

General Houston nodded, deeply mindful of the

consequences of this moment in time. "Is the order given, Mr. President?"

Roosevelt leaned back and steepled his hands under his chin. Sitting behind the heavy Resolute desk, he often felt like the lonely captain of a vast ship. The desk was a gift to the Americans from Queen Victoria, made from timbers recovered from a British arctic explorer. A gift made in another time, before American riches created British envy. Before a time when death could rain from the sky.

"The order is given," President Roosevelt said. "Declare war against England. And assassinate Albert Einstein."

MAJOR ARCHIBALD THOMAS

Forty days at sea is not good for men, thought Major Archibald Thomas. His hawkish, attractive face wore a frown, etched deeper than usual. He stood on the upper deck of the HMS *Glasgow*, one hand on the railing for support against the heaving motion of the churning ocean. Overhead, the sky was darkening, threatening more rain.

One of the new steam-powered ironclads could make the journey from Portsmouth to America in twelve days, but those were all being retrofitted in secrecy. Still, the *Glasgow* was a ship of the line. Five decks, seventy-two guns and a crew of two hundred and twenty made a fearsome predator, even if she was a bit slow.

The king's orders had been specific in their hostility. Lead a battalion of seven hundred soldiers to New Haven, Connecticut, and kill anyone who prevents capturing the port there. Then march north and meet up with reinforcements to take Boston. A formal declaration of war would be made immediately before the attack.

He welcomed the thrill of combat, especially on foreign land. It had been three years since he'd been to America. His lips curled, thinking of the uncouth colonists. Red Bank, Pennsylvania. By the time he was done, the town was aptly named. He'd run many of them through and would have killed many more, but for the sudden signing of the Armistice.

Thankfully, things were now set right, and he'd have the chance to finish what he started. Loyalty was all, especially to the Crown. Those who wavered deserved what they got.

He'd had to pull strings with the king for this assignment. A battalion was typically commanded by a lieutenant colonel, but after the major explained his reasons for wanting the job, the king understood and made an exception.

Nearby, Captain Douglas checked his navigation. "Helmsman, make your course two-two-seven."

The young midshipman responded instantly. "Making course two-two-seven, aye." He leaned on the massive ship's wheel, and it shifted position slightly.

"Another day, perhaps two," said the captain. "We'll come in at night, and the moon will be a waning crescent. Good for landing."

Major Thomas nodded. "My men are damned unhappy belowdecks. They'll be pleased to have mud under them again."

The captain laughed. "I'm sure. The lower decks are awash in vomit."

"They are soldiers, Captain. Not sailors."

"Very true!" he said, chuckling again.

"Ship sighted!" yelled a lookout. He held an arm out, rigid, pointing at the horizon.

Major Thomas looked off the left side of the ship, but saw nothing.

The captain had a spyglass to his face, scanning for the new arrival.

"Yes… I see you," he said. "And you have a friend too."

He snapped the glass down. "American frigate and a smaller boat. Privateer maybe, or a packet ship hauling mail."

"Will you engage?" asked the major.

The captain scrubbed at his face, rolling the variables through his mind. He leaned over the railing and watched the white tips of the waves' crests. The wind was blowing from the direction of the enemy ships.

"Wind isn't favorable. They have the weather gage."

"How many guns on an American frigate?"

"Forty-four, but they're a tough hull. Admiralty frowns on engagement at less than two-to-one advantage." He mulled it over, rubbing his chin.

"Your decision, Captain," said Major Thomas. "I command only the army belowdecks, the ship is yours."

Captain Douglas craned his neck up to inspect his current set of sail.

"Of course," continued the major. "I'd hate for word of your timidness to spread."

The captain's head snapped back, but the major's grin told him he only meant to jest. He scanned the darkening sky. Heavy, steel-gray clouds hung low and imposing.

The major followed his gaze, not liking the look of the weather.

But the captain smiled. "I have an idea," he said, buttoning up his foul weather coat. "Beat to quarters!" he called out in a booming command voice.

A junior officer sprinted to the ship's bell. "Beat to quarter's, aye!" He rang the bell hard, five times, quickly. He paused, then repeated the alarm.

The crew sprang to their battle roles, clearing the decks of extraneous gear and equipment, securing it below. Down on the gun decks, crews primed the cannons with powder and loaded round shot into the hulking guns.

The captain nodded, pleased with his crew's efficiency. "Port guns, prepare to run out! Helm, make your course one-nine-oh!"

He turned to the major beside him. "We'll take them on, Major. And give your boys something to forget their seasickness."

Aboard the USS *Lexington*, Captain Franklin Jones studied the British ship through his glass.

"Ship of the line. Big bastard. Lot of guns." He handed the glass to Lieutenant Wilson, who eagerly took a look.

"Yes, sir," the junior man agreed, straining to make out details. "But she's got no copper."

No copper sheathing on the hull meant less protection from barnacles and weeds, which grew on a ship's timbers and produced drag in the water.

"A fair bet she's out of Portsmouth," said the captain.

"Which means a month of growth, at least."

The captain nodded. "Good for a knot or so. Good man," he said, clapping the young sailor on the shoulder. "We have the wind. Let's go get him. Signal the packet ship to hold back."

"Aye, sir."

Captain Jones turned and called out, "Starboard guns, make ready! Helm, three-three-five. Chase that Imperial bastard down!"

The *Lexington* turned and put on speed, cutting forward through the heavy swells.

Major Thomas watched the *Lexington* turn and gain speed. Behind it, the smaller ship was falling back. It didn't have the guns or the strength to join this fight.

The *Lexington* surged toward them, and the major counted twenty-two gunports along the side. Twenty-two timber panels that would be thrown open at the right moment, revealing two-ton cannons, each one capable of sending a thirty-six pound cannonball through their hull. The thought gave the major pause.

"Captain, I am no sailor, but doesn't the American have the superior position here?"

Captain Douglas was watching the *Lexington* maneuver intently. "Aye, that he does. With the wind behind him, he can press the attack, or move away."

"Well, he's certainly pressing," he said, watching the frigate quickly growing larger. Around its bow, white foam rose and churned as the ship cut through the rough, building waves.

"Steady, soldier. Watch and learn some navy tricks."

On the *Lexington*, Captain Jones gauged the distance to the enemy at four hundred feet and closing. Still too far for an accurate shot.

His lieutenant was studying them again through the glass. "She's got smashers," he said. The note of apprehension carried over the howling wind. "Three. On the forecastle."

The three carronades were high-efficiency cannons, designed for short-range fire. With a lower muzzle velocity, the shot created more wooden splinters when it hit, which often were more deadly than the ball itself. Their nickname was well earned.

"Not to worry, we're going for their rear. They won't get a chance to use 'em."

The captain could see the downwind *Glasgow* well now, even without a glass. She was heeled over against the wind, which brought her exposed flank up out of the water. A shot there, where the hull normally rested below the waterline, could be fatal.

The bucking waves were now pounding them hard. He held onto the railing and pointed as they gained ground.

"I want a shot there, below their line. Punch a hole in them low. When they change tack, they'll take on water, and slow more."

"Aye, sir!" called the lieutenant and shouted orders to the gun crews.

The *Glasgow* was big, but she was slow. The American ship was within firing distance now, and the major turned to Captain Douglas, expecting action. Surely, it was time for an attack or an evasive maneuver?

But the old sailor was content to wait and watch as a wicked smile began to form on his lips.

The *Lexington* pulled alongside the British warship, and Captain Jones gave the order. "Starboard guns, run out!"

The order was relayed to the gundeck below, and crews leaped to unlock the gunports and haul up the heavy panels.

But as they did, water roared into the gundeck. With the *Lexington* heeled over in chase, its attacking side was riding low. The weather had worsened considerably since they began their run, and the waves were crashing higher now, flooding into the ship.

Men were washed back away from the open ports, smashing into their mates who came forward to help. The chaos rose quickly as the foaming ocean rushed in, racing along the gundeck. Screams of anger and fear cut through the sound of raging water.

"Why haven't we fired?" yelled the captain. He ran to the railing, and looked over it. The ports were open, but then he saw the incoming water.

"Oh God."

"And there you have it," said Captain Douglas. "The weather has picked up, and he wasn't paying attention. Now he's in a pickle, all right."

He turned to his second-in-command. "Port guns, run out and fire!"

The order was yelled below, and moments later, thirty-six gunports sprang open. Crews hauled on ropes with pulleys, and the two-ton cannons were thrust forward. The *Glasgow* now had teeth.

"Fire!" yelled the gun chiefs.

Flintlock strikers fell, and the *Glasgow* heaved from the explosive force. A swift series of deafening booms blasted from the *Glasgow*, sending deadly fire toward the hapless Americans.

At the rail, Captain Jones looked up as the *Glasgow* opened fire. Along her side, white puffs of gunpowder smoke erupted from the thirty-six open ports. An instant later, the captain's world came apart, exploding in a hail of iron and shattered timbers.

The *Glasgow*'s gun crews were well trained, and most of their fire hit their targets, each one tearing a chunk out of the *Lexington*'s side. One of the rounds struck the *Lexington* just under the rail where the captain stood.

The explosive force punched through into the ship's side, throwing the captain back and sending him tumbling through the air. As he spun, an arm-sized splinter ripped through his side. He landed on the far side of the ship's deck, limbs askew and already dead.

Lieutenant Wilson had fallen to the deck, arms over his head. He stood, running his hands over his own body, searching for injury.

Then he saw the captain. A large section of the man's middle was gone, like he'd been bitten by a shark. The midshipman knew his captain was dead, and his training took over.

"I have the ship!" he yelled to the stunned crew. They nodded agreement, just wanting to be given orders.

He threw a look toward the *Glasgow*, and noted their position.

"Douse sail!" he commanded. "We need to fall behind them!"

The crew ran to haul on lines, running up the huge mainsail. With less sail, the *Lexington* lost speed, and the *Glasgow* slowly moved ahead of them.

"Not fast enough, dammit, we need more drag! Loose the drogue!"

Three crewmen ran aft and unfolded the parachute-like device from its storage rack. A heavy line was already attached to it. The men wrestled the unwieldy thing to the aft railing and slid it over into the sea.

The line played out quickly as it fell and splashed into the heavy surf. The ship's forward movement soon ran out all the line, and the drogue sprang open under the water, acting like a sea anchor.

The *Lexington* lurched from the sudden deceleration, and several crewmen fell to the deck.

Lieutenant Wilson smiled, though. He watched the *Glasgow* surge ahead of them, and saw his chance for revenge. With just enough forward momentum for a single maneuver, his ship had one last surprise for the British.

A crewman looked at his new commander. "Raking fire, sir?"

"Raking fire. Helm, come about to oh-seven-oh. Bring me right across her wake."

While a warship's sides were tough, the same was not true of her rear. Construction and weight demands meant thinner timbers must be used, which allowed for easier entry of a well-placed shot. But the real fear of raking fire came from the added damage a shot could do at that angle, working its way forward through the ship, gutting it from behind.

"Port guns, stand ready. We get one chance at this."

On the *Glasgow*, the attack was a magnificent sight. Nearly all their shots had struck home, and the damage to the *Lexington* looked severe.

"Very impressive, Captain!" said the major.

The older man shrugged. "Just tactics. And paying attention. If their captain had simply—"

He stopped, watching the *Lexington* slow, then turn towards them. It looked as if he meant to slide behind them. Then the captain's mouth gaped. He ran toward the helmsman, arms waving.

"Watch out, he's coming aft for raking fire! Hard to starboard, now!"

The *Lexington*'s hard turn put her right into position, and she cut directly behind the British ship. As the *Lexington* slid over her enemy's wake, her gun crews waited and watched. They saw the rear of the *Glasgow* slide into view, and gunners pressed their cheeks against their cannons, sighting down the line.

Lieutenant Wilson gave the order. "Fire!"

The Lexington opened fire, and iron roundshot burst from the ship. Most of the shots went wide, screaming along the outside of the enemy ship, terrifying the *Glasgow* crew, who heard death whistling by them.

But two shots found their mark, smashing through the aft timbers. The twin iron balls punched through the captain's quarters, destroying the richly appointed room and the two stewards inside.

Moving forward through the ship, the rounds tore into the lower quarterdeck. Eight officers died instantly in the hail of wooden splinters. The deck above buckled, throwing the captain and the major to their knees.

The cannonballs continued their way through the length of the *Glasgow*, ripping through a bulkhead, then blasting into the officer's quarters, killing four more stewards, before tearing into the middle gundeck.

Here, the open space, filled with cannons and gun crews, gave the heavy iron balls many obstacles to hit and ricochet against. Fifty-seven men died in that room, with sixty more injured.

Captain Douglas felt the twin shots ripping through his ship's insides. On his hands and knees, the horrible tremors and vibrations through the decking told him they'd been hurt badly, even before the screaming began.

"Get me a damage report!" he yelled, pulling himself to his feet. The deck had buckled, leaving him standing at an awkward angle.

Behind him Major Thomas struggled to stand also. "God, that felt like an artillery strike. Are we sinking?"

The captain shook his head. "We're gutted, but above the waterline."

He turned about, finding the *Lexington* sliding from behind them to their right.

"Time to end this," growled the captain. He checked the several crewmen who were sprawled around him. Finding one who still lived, he hauled the man to his feet. "You run forward. I want the smashers ready to fire at my signal. Do you understand?"

The man gazed blankly at his captain, a rivulet of blood streaming from one ear. Then he nodded.

"Good man. Go!" He pointed the man toward the bow and shoved him forward. The man stumbled, but made his way forward, stepping over bodies and around strewn gear.

The captain took the wheel himself and spun it hard to starboard. Without the crew trimming the sails, he quickly lost the wind, and the massive sails luffed, snapping back and forth with a disconcerting thunder. But he didn't care. All he wanted was to bring his forward guns around on the now almost-stationary *Lexington*. The *Glasgow* turned, swinging hard to the right. In two minutes the firing angle was sufficient. The two ships were barely a hundred feet apart now.

With hard, glaring eyes, the captain saw the *Lexington*'s crew racing around their deck, and he decided their fate.

"Fire!" he yelled. The order was relayed forward, and the three smashers opened up on the doomed *Lexington*. Its midship exploded in a shower of timbers and lethal splinters, sending bodies flying. The mainmast was struck down low, and a horrible splintering sound ripped across the water as the massive mast cracked and fell like a downed oak. The mainsail splashed into the rough seas, useless.

"Reload! And fire at will!" he called out.

A moment later the three smashers rang out again, and the *Lexington*'s quarterdeck disappeared, leaving behind a ruined and jagged crater. The force sent Lieutenant Wilson over the side, along with a dozen other officers. A few sank instantly, but many splashed about, helplessly treading water as their ship was destroyed.

The *Glasgow* gun crew reloaded and fired again. The shots punctured the *Lexington* under the waterline, and she began taking on water from two gaping holes in her side.

"She's hulled between wind and water!" a young crewman cried.

A fire broke out somewhere belowdecks, and black smoke poured from the ship's still-open gunports.

It was plain to all that the ship was finished. Men began leaping from the doomed vessel, taking their chances in the open ocean, rather than being burned alive. Soon the churning sea was littered with a hundred sailors, screaming for help and struggling to keep their heads above the waves.

Captain Douglas drew a deep breath and let it out. He looked down at his hands, unsurprised to see them trembling from the battle's drama. He jammed them into his overcoat pockets.

Major Thomas joined him, watching the *Lexington* list heavily to one side. Sailors were everywhere in the waves, swimming toward the *Glasgow*, begging for help.

"That's it then, they're done," the captain said to himself. He turned to a crewman. "Make ready to pick up survivors."

"Aye, sir."

"What?" said the major. "You're going to save them?"

The captain frowned. "They're a threat no more."

"That's not the issue, Captain." The title held a note of mockery now. "I am sent here to kill Americans, not to rescue them."

"All sailors have one mutual enemy, Major. The ocean waters. As long as we are not at risk, we have a moral duty to —"

"There's another American ship in the area!" the major yelled.

"A packet ship. A mail hauler. Hardly a threat. And look, she's turned tail and running. We'd never catch her anyway."

A junior officer arrived, breathless. "Damage report, sir. Your quarters are destroyed, the officer's quarters are seriously damaged, and we have various structural issues on the middle gundeck."

"Casualties?"

"Sixty-seven dead, sixty more wounded."

The captain sighed, and his shoulders hung low. "Very

well. Carry on."

The major squared off against the ship's captain. "Let me be clear with you, sir. You rescue those men, and I will see you hanged for treason."

The captain's eyes grew tight. "You can't be serious."

"I have the king's ear. And my report will paint a dire picture of your loyalty to the Crown. You know the price men have paid for being seen as disloyal to the king, yes?"

The captain froze, studying the major threatening him. He did seem the sort to twist the truth. The railing wasn't too far behind him. Wouldn't be hard to run him over it, just one more casualty on a bad day...

But no, despite the weasel's insinuation, the captain *was* a loyal servant to the Crown, and that unfortunately meant not murdering the king's officers, even this one.

His jaw tightened, staring hard into the man's eyes. "You hate them that much?"

"Don't discount the power of hate, Captain. I love hate."

Captain Douglas stared at a man driven by demons and decided he was too old for such fights.

He turned his back on the major and called out, "Set sail! Make course for New Haven. Now!"

He wanted to get below and check on his men. As he descended the stairs leading to the gun deck, the cries of the drowning sailors followed him down.

"IVBSRTH"

NEW YORK CITY, USA

Tesla returned to his room at Mrs. Harrison's. He shuffled off the soaked, heavy overcoat and hung it to dry. A puddle formed beneath it immediately.

Looking around his room, he wondered if financial hardship was to be a constant companion. A normal component of his life, to be endured and expected, rather than a problem to be overcome.

He fell into a chair and stared at the blank wall before him. What would he do now? Where would he go?

He briefly thought of returning home to Serbia. It would be good to see his mother again. A thin smile appeared when he remembered the sight of her emerging from the kitchen, carrying trays of plum dumplings. But the smile faded when he thought of his father, and the explanation of his failure. No, better to stay and persevere. Something would improve his luck. Something will come, and lift him up to—

"Mr. Tesla? It's Mrs. Harrison." She knocked at his door. "I heard you come in."

A grim smile twisted his lips. The machinery of the universe carried on, oblivious and uncaring of his woes.

Mrs. Harrison knocked again. "Mr. Tesla, I must have the back rent today, I'm afraid. Please come to the door."

He looked at the wire cores on the desk before him and wanted to ignore her. Simply dive into the solace of his work and be lost in mathematics and theory. But that would be ungentlemanly, and he was not raised in that way.

"I am coming, Mrs. Harrison."

He opened the door for her, and she pushed her way in. But seeing his face, she softened.

"Oh my, it's as bad as that then," she said.

He turned away and returned to his chair. "I would offer you something, but all I have is milk, and I'm sure it's gone bad by now." He slid back into the chair, waiting for her demands.

Mrs. Harrison stood, arms crossed, seeing the man's plight. He was no doubt brilliant, but was also probably lonely and certainly poor at looking after himself. Seeing the result of this combination of traits in one man made her sad. If she could, she'd have let him stay for free, at least until his fortunes improved. But she had four little ones to think of, and giving away rooms meant taking food off their table. Still, the man seemed to have such promise.

"So the work for Mr. Edison did not pan out as planned," she offered.

"The work, yes. The payment, no." He hung his head, staring at the floor.

"I see. And what will you do now?" she asked, coming to him and crouching low to see his downturned face.

Tesla thought about that for a hard minute. "I will have a whiskey," he said, holding up one finger. "But only one. As a tonic. And then I will continue my work. And I will succeed."

Mrs. Harrison patted his knee, and he did not shy from her touch. "A simple plan," she said. "But one I hope you see to fruition, Mr. Tesla."

She stood and headed back to the door. "For my part, I can give you four more days to work your plan. But this Saturday at noon, I will either have my rent, or you must be gone from this room. I hope you understand."

Tesla nodded. "I do. And thank you."

"All right then." She let herself out, closing the door softly behind her.

He sat, unmoving, for an hour. Then he stood and found his whiskey. He poured a small glass and crossed to the table that held the mechanical brain.

He sipped his whiskey slowly as he opened the box's top and studied the insides. Two dozen mechanical relay switches were bolted to the box's floor, connected to each other by a flurry of thin wires.

He traced a bundle of hairlike wires that led to the large glass lens, which stared outward like a baleful eye. Another single wire led out of the box to a teletype machine. The paper strip fed into it showed the message previously generated: "IVBSRTH."

He frowned, set down his glass, and returned to his overcoat. The apple was still in the pocket, forgotten. He set the apple in front of the glass lens. Then he turned on the device's power switch. A low hum filled the room, and the smell of ozone wafted up from the box. The relay switches came to life, many snapping from one position to the other. Then the teletype sprang to action, clacking out letters on the paper strip. When it stopped, he read the strip: "DSSCV"

Tesla turned the power back off and began pulling wires from the box. Looking around the room, he found a long coil of thinner wire, and began snipping off short lengths of it, then stripping the ends.

Two hours later he had a thick bundle of replacement wiring and an empty whiskey glass. He took a bite from the apple, then replaced it before the lens.

He slowly, carefully, replaced the wires that ran to and fro across the relay switches. Taking a screwdriver, he dialed a thick copper screw, and the heavy twin blades of the power amplifier shifted position, edging slightly closer to each other.

Satisfied, he flipped the switch back on, and the machine snapped awake again.

The relays worked, and the teletype banged out its message: "APPLE."

THE ELSTREE AERODROME

ELSTREE, ENGLAND

The Elstree Aerodrome was a sprawling complex of huge grass airfields, hangars, and administrative buildings. Along with the Borehamwood facility, it was tasked with building the king's zeppelin fleet, and work never stopped. Day and night, rotating shifts of engineers, fitters, carpenters, and electricians struggled to create the massive floating airships.

Within the zeppelin HMS *Artemis*, Albert Einstein lay on his back, peering up at the intricate workings of the bomb rack. His specifications had called for a design that would safely deliver nine of his new generation bombs across the ocean to America, then drop them precisely on command. What he saw above him was not satisfactory.

"Johan!" he yelled at the crew chief. "I scarcely know where to begin. The release catch is undersized. Each of my bombs weighs thirty-four-hundred pounds. I doubt this latch will hold them securely. The storage shelf isn't welded to the main frame. Bolts are not sufficient. It needs a full weld. And here, the drop guide rails are not a uniform curve." He banged a wrench against the rail for added emphasis. "You don't want one of my presents getting jammed in the rail, I can assure you." He slid out from under the machinery and stood, wiping grease from his hands with a rag.

With tired, heavy eyelids, Johan watched the scientist. *An intellectual with dirty hands*, he thought. *Like seeing a leprechaun riding a unicorn.* The thought made him chuckle, and he checked his clipboard to hide the reaction.

"Laugh now," said Einstein. "But I've just returned from Borehamwood Aerodrome, and their zeppelin is weeks ahead of you. Proper welds and all."

The crew chief yawned, not bothering to cover his gaping mouth. "We will be ready, Professor. Have no concerns of that."

Einstein had many concerns, but saw no reason to berate the man further. "Very well. Why don't you get an hour's rest, then we shall regroup, yes?"

Johan nodded. "Thank you, Professor. I have a cot in the hangar, and I've seen precious little of it this week."

Einstein clapped the man on the shoulder and saw the captain approaching them. "Go then. One hour, no more."

Johan nodded and made his exit as the captain joined them. "Captain," Johan said, slipping past him in the narrow corridor.

Captain Stevens watched the man go. "He's exhausted."

"They all are. The king's schedule has been… aggressive."

"Aye, that's one word for it," he said.

Einstein waved toward the bomb rack. "There are numerous problems. Some can be easily fixed, but some not so. The drop guide rails must be removed and replaced."

"Yes, I know. But otherwise, we are not so bad off. The hydrogen cells are filled, and holding."

"And the Blaugas?"

"Also safely stored under pressure. No leaks."

"That is good. That is very good."

"Our flight test today should be smooth. We're not ready for war, but it should be a lovely tour around the countryside. I expect we will have no water pressure, so no toilet service. But

45

we will survive that, won't we, Professor?"

Einstein grinned. "Yes, I believe we shall."

Just as at Borehamwood, security at the Elstree facility was tight. Royal Marines patrolled the grounds regularly, all deliveries to the base were thoroughly searched, and every person through the gate was checked, both against a list of approved persons and to verify they carried a bronze security medallion. Specially made for the construction of the zeppelins, it was stamped with the royal seal and bore the name of the facility the worker was assigned to.

Crouched within the tree line, Lucas pondered their plan to slip inside. Lean and wiry, he had the look of a runner.

A scientist named Einstein was in there, and today was his last day on earth. Lucas didn't know what the man had done to be marked for such a mission, but he didn't need to know. Despite his misgivings about assassinations, he only had to see it done.

He, Morgan, and Eliza had waited hours for the right time to approach the gate. The agency had given them the proper uniforms. Maroon coveralls with a black stripe along the legs. A long night at the nearby tavern provided the names and medallions they'd need. The three workers they'd killed were scheduled for work today. Now it came time for the deed itself. They either made it onto the base now, or the three workers would be missed from their sign-in, and a search would turn up a disturbing tale of three disappearances.

He brought the spyglass to his eye and watched the main gate. He counted five Royal Marines, but there were bound to be more within the guardhouse. As workers approached the gate, they were stopped. The list was checked, as were the medallions, and they were allowed to pass through. The marines stood out easily, with their scarlet jackets and white chest bands. They looked tired, but they were professionals and carried out their duties crisply, without the casual indolence a repetitive job can create.

"They're overworked, but paying attention," he said, handing the glass to Morgan beside him. Morgan raised the glass with beefy arms and took his own look. "Yeah... looks that way."

"What about guns?" asked Eliza, bending low and retying her boot lacings. Her years of gymnastics showed in her easy flexibility as she cinched them hard.

Morgan counted. "Handguns on all of them. Knives. Three have submachine guns. Look like Vickers."

"They are," confirmed Lucas. "Sustained rate of five hundred rounds a minute. And they never jam."

"Sounds like a party," quipped Eliza, tying her hair back.

Lucas grunted. "Truly. Well, let's go show our invitations. Ready?"

Morgan closed the glass and stowed it in his pack. "Ready."

Eliza touched her two blade handles with her fingertips, confirming they were in place. "I'm ready."

Lucas stood. "All right. Let's head out."

The group threaded their way through the foliage back to the main road, around a bend from the gate. They waited for a group of four workers to pass by and gain some distance, then they stepped out of the tree line onto the road and followed the group toward the main gate.

The three adopted the relaxed demeanor expected of workers off to the job. Fragments of a loud conversation drifted back to them from the workers up ahead. A friendly, but heated, discussion about cricket. The merits of overarm bowling versus round-arm. The three listened carefully, memorizing the useful trivia.

A few minutes later, and they were at the gate, with more

information about cricket than they ever desired. The workers ahead of them were checked and waved through. Lucas fixed a dour scowl on his face, and turned to Morgan as they approached the gate lieutenant. He affected an English accent. "All I mean is, first we get these damned flannel caps, now round-arm bowling? The MCC should stop mucking with things."

Morgan opened his mouth, realized he had nothing to say, and closed it.

Lucas turned to the gate lieutenant. "Am I right? I think I'm right."

"Name?" the lieutenant asked, ignoring the question.

"Ashdown. Walter Ashdown," said Lucas, studying the clouds above.

Morgan and Eliza took note of the marines around them. Eight total, with three Vickers guns between them. The black barrels could spit enough lead to cut them in two where they stood.

The lieutenant found the name and checked the time of expected sign-in. It matched, so he marked the name off.

"Medallion?" he asked, extending a black-gloved hand.

"Ah, right." Lucas dug in his pocket and handed it over.

The lieutenant verified the Elstree Aerodrome inscription, then flipped it back.

The process was repeated with Morgan and Eliza, and they were inside the base. The three walked on casually, but deliberately gained distance away from the gate.

"That was pleasantly non-painful," Eliza said, wiping sweat from her forehead.

Morgan playfully shoved her, knocking her out of step. "I'm a fan of luck, myself."

Lucas kept his head forward, but his eyes scanned the base. "We're not done yet. Let's keep the luck going, shall we?" He nodded toward a large hangar. "That's it. The *Artemis* should be inside there." He checked his watch. "Our spy said Einstein is scheduled to take it up for a test flight in three hours."

"Then we'll make sure he never comes back down," said Eliza.

Lucas nodded and led the group toward the hangar.

SAVANNAH BROWNING

Tesla hoisted a heavy pickax and drove it down into the packed earth, chipping loose a chunk of wet clay. He straightened and repeated the process. The morning air was cold, but beads of sweat formed on his brow. He was unaccustomed to hard physical labor, and the muscles of his lower back spasmed. He reached back and massaged them, surveying his surroundings. Before and behind him, a line of twenty men performed similar labor. They toiled in the wet ditch, five feet deep, opening a channel for the city to lay cables.

Edison's threat had been no idle display. For days Tesla spoke to financiers about his designs, or for simple work as an engineer. But repeatedly, he found doors closed to him, shut fast by Edison's whispered mentions of the inventor's rashness and inability to work with others. With his savings depleted, and hunger becoming a distraction, he had little choice but to accept what work he could.

Tomorrow was his deadline with Mrs. Harrison, but he pushed the unhappy thought from his mind. The city foreman was approaching, leading a horse-drawn cart carrying a huge coil of black cabling. He directed the cart near the open ditch and addressed his workers.

"All right, you men, that's deep enough. Sanders, take the end of this cable, and feed it into the channel."

Sanders found the end and played the cable out. The large reel was suspended on a central rod, and it spun easily. Tesla and the other men set their tools down and reached up for the heavy cable, laying it down at their feet.

A white logo was printed every so often, and Tesla turned his head to read it. The design read "Edison Electrical Company."

Tesla stared at the mocking logo resting against his wet, mud-caked work boots. In his mind he was back at Edison's home, being dismissed, dripping water on the man's rug. He closed his eyes. How did things turn out this way?

"God has a cruel sense of humor," he muttered.

"Does he now?" a soft, feminine voice replied in a lilting Southern accent.

Tesla's eyes snapped open and he startled, momentarily wondering if the Creator had answered him.

He looked up and saw a young, pretty woman standing above him. Her elegant, floral-patterned dress fluttered in the cool breeze, and the sun was behind her shoulder, casting her long blonde hair in a glowing, halo-like effect.

"I'm Savannah Browning," she said, reaching her hand down to him. "Come along, Mr. Tesla. We have exciting matters to discuss."

He hesitated, struck by the sudden shift in tone his morning was taking. Then he placed his hand in hers, and she helped him clamber out of the ditch.

Tesla joined her for a ride in her motorcar, and found he couldn't take his eyes off her as she drove through the city streets.

"Who *are* you?" he asked.

She laughed, a light, musical laugh that made him feel good, despite his confusion.

"I told you," she said, steering around a pothole. "Savannah Browning. My father is Colonel Browning, the military strategist?" Her Southern accent rose and fell in a charming cadence.

Tesla shook his head, not knowing the name.

"Well, you'll meet him soon enough. I'm taking you to Fort Hamilton."

"The army base?"

"That's the one."

She wove the car around a slow carriage and accelerated. "Be there in an hour."

"What does the army want with me?"

She turned toward him and looked into his eyes long enough that he grew worried for their safety.

"War is coming, Mr. Tesla. I think you and the army might just need each other."

She turned her attention back to the road, and Tesla settled back into his seat, content to rest his back before exploring the next twist in his fortunes.

Savannah drove them to the main gate at Fort Hamilton. A long line of cars waited to be inspected, but Savannah steered around them and drove to the front of the line. The military police waved her through on sight. Tesla cast a sideways glance at the woman, but she said nothing.

She led them through the military base, and they soon came to a stop outside a sprawling complex of low, gray cinderblock buildings.

"Well, here we are," she announced, stepping out of the car.

He looked around. The buildings were all large, but nondescript. In yellow stenciled block letters, a small sign read "Auxiliary Operations."

"And this would be…?" Tesla asked.

"Where the magic happens!" She beamed and ran for the wide double doors. "I simply cannot wait to see your face."

He caught up to her and followed her into the building.

They passed two armed soldiers standing at attention as she led him down a corridor. Ornately framed portraits of military figures watched impassively as he followed Savannah.

"We have a lot of really smart people here, but I think you will fit in particularly well," she said. They turned a corner and came to a wide, steel door, flanked by two more armed guards. They nodded at Savannah as she approached.

She rested her hand on the doorknob. She paused, then turned back to Tesla. "Are you ready?" Her high-wattage smile gave away her anticipation.

"You *are* a spirited woman." Tesla had no idea what lay behind the steel door, but he now very much wanted to step through and see.

"Thanks!" She laughed. "Now come on. The Rabbit Hole awaits." She opened the door, and Tesla followed her inside.

They stepped into the room, and Tesla stopped short. There was nothing inside but a small ramp leading up to a circular platform in the center of the room. Just inside the platform, a small panel extended from the floor to waist height, and Tesla saw the blinking of indicator lights and a metal throw switch.

Savannah strolled up the ramp and stepped on the platform, waving him to follow her.

"You're in the army's research and development lab, Mr. Tesla."

He joined her on the circular platform. "Please, call me Nikola. But I thought that was in Maryland. The Aberdeen Proving Grounds."

Savannah smiled. "That's where the meat and potatoes work gets done, yes." She rested a slender hand on the throw switch. "But here we focus on more… unbridled creativity."

She pulled the switch toward her, and an electric hum rose from beneath them. The floor vibrated, and Tesla looked at his guide in concern.

Then the platform sank into the ground. Like an open-air elevator, the floor descended, carrying them with it. They sank lower, the walls of a carved concrete shaft rising around them.

"My God," whispered Tesla, reaching out to let his fingertips run along the shaft wall. As they continued down, the rough stone tickled his fingers, confirming he wasn't dreaming.

He turned and found Savannah studying his face, which was agape in delight and awe.

"Lovely," she said.

"This is amazing. So, we are traveling to an underground workshop then."

She nodded. "Seven of them, actually."

His eyes went wide, and she chuckled.

"Damn, I love showing this place off. We have seven labs, each on its own floor. We're doing work on everything here, Nikola. Electricity, robotics, atomic theory, exotic munitions, computing, even the nature of light and gravity. For someone with your talents, it's a playground."

Tesla was speechless as he struggled to catch up with the news. All his life, he'd taught himself. Years of solitary, quiet study in libraries had been difficult, but had fueled his inventive spirit. The thought of such advanced collaboration was heady.

"No words, hmm? I hear that doesn't happen to you so often," she said, chiding him.

"It really is... incredible," he admitted.

"Just you wait."

As the platform descended, a wide slit of light appeared in front of them, then grew taller. He realized they were arriving at the first of the lab's levels. As they continued, he got a view of the activities going on. Multiple long rows of metal cabinets lined the room, each with a face of blinking lights. Technicians milled about, tending to the humming machines. He recognized the devices as computers, but on a vastly larger scale than he'd ever imagined existed.

"This is Herman Hollerith's lab. Computing," she said as they continued. "He's doing incredible work on machines that can think faster than a human."

They continued down, and the lab disappeared, replaced by the blank wall of the shaft again.

"I am fascinated by computers!" he told her. "In fact, I have a working prototype of a mechanical brain!"

"So you have it working now?" she asked. "That's very, very good. We've been following your work, Nikola. That's why you've been invited here today."

Before he could respond, a second level appeared before them. He stepped forward to the edge of the platform for a better look.

He instantly recognized huge electrical generators. A wide circuit switchboard covered one wall. Metal and ceramic towers towered over the researchers. Then, with a startling roar, a spider web of lightning branched from one tower to the other. The unmistakable smell of ozone reminded him of his own lab.

He turned to her, his face aglow. "Those are my coils! I designed those!"

"Yes, you did. We just scaled the design up a bit. They're a favorite of the staff, I can tell you."

They continued lower, and each level gave a tantalizing slice of fantastic technology, the sort Tesla had never before seen, even in his most fevered dreams. Everywhere, men and women in uniforms and lab coats were dealing with ideas made real.

He saw an atomic reactor, large-scale chemical experiments, solid shafts of light burning through steel plates, even a test subject floating in midair. At one point, he swore he saw a mechanical man walking haltingly toward an encouraging researcher, like a mother would beckon her child.

"And here, we are, level seven," she announced. The final level opened before them, and he saw this level was much taller than the others, perhaps sixty feet, and the sounds of sparking metalworking were loud even from this distance. Like the other levels, technicians and military observers milled about in groups, some in front of large blackboards filled with equations. But the centerpiece of the vast room caught his attention and didn't let go.

On a slightly raised platform was a steel tank, bigger than most houses. It rested on twin treads, which rose a good two feet taller than the workers standing beside them. The main body was a dull steel-gray, like a sloped pyramid with the top sliced away. Housing the treads, the base was wide, thick, and imposing. A dozen weapon barrels were visible, tucked back within recessed ports. The midsection was a rotating turret carrying the main cannon, and the apex of the beast bristled with various antennae, sensors, and smaller weapons.

"What a monster," Tesla exclaimed, his eyes taking in every detail. He wanted to believe that such a force of destruction didn't exist, that men would never put their energies into such a machine. But the sheer audacity of the thing was impressive, he had to admit.

The elevator settled on the lab's floor and stopped.

"This is it," she said, stepping off and leading him toward the tank. "It's a bit to take in, I know. Hey, Sophia," she said, waving to an attractive brunette.

"This your boy?" Sophia asked.

"We'll see."

Sophia smiled. "Well, good luck!" she said, joining a group of officers.

He followed Savannah through the lab, and they grew closer to the intimidating machine. Several men and women in military uniforms and lab coats walked in and out of banks of computers, worktables, and cordoned areas with smaller machinery within. The smell of oil and diesel mixed with the chatter of excited voices and arc welding.

As they neared the tank's treads, Tesla felt small. A tickling chill of vulnerability ran between his shoulder blades. He craned his neck to look up at the machine of death looming over them. In his mind an image flashed and persisted, a newborn babe staring up at a well-muscled lion.

Savannah turned and waved her hand at the monstrosity.

"Nikola, meet Beowulf," Savannah said.

"I'm… glad it's on our side."

Deep laughter boomed from behind him, and Tesla turned. A tall, barrel-chested man in blue uniform and medals was approaching, all smiles. "Damn right," the man said. "I bet the first Crowns to come face to face with Beowulf will soil their linen britches!"

"General, please," Savannah said.

"General Sam Houston," said the man, grabbing Tesla's hand in a vise grip. "I'm the base commander."

Tesla squirmed as he always did when politeness required him to shake hands with someone, but the general's grip was tight, so he forced a smile and waited for his hand to be released.

"Savannah has told us a lot about you, Mr. Tesla. We're excited to have you." He broke the handshake and studied the inventor with intense blue eyes. Tesla thought the man belonged in a painting, riding a horse into battle, sword drawn and yelling a battle cry.

"A pleasure, General," he replied, grateful when he got his hand back. "But I'm still not sure of the details for my visit here today."

"Sure, sure," the general said, clapping him hard against the shoulder. "Savannah is our civilian liaison, so she's the one to bring you up to speed. I have a meeting topside, but I'm sure we'll catch up again soon." He turned and headed for the elevator.

"Thank you, General," Tesla called after him, then looked at Savannah. "We have much to discuss, I assume."

"Do we ever. First, the basics." She began a slow walk around the tank. "Beowulf is a coal-fed, steam-powered, autonomous tank. It has an eight hundred and thirty horsepower engine, driving twin treads of woven steel."

"Did you say autonomous?"

She raised a hand. "We'll get to that in a second." She pointed to the recessed ports above the treads. "Anti-personnel shredders. Lethal out to three hundred feet. Up above, the main cannon fires eleven-inch shells. Behind that, twin mortar tubes. The upper tower holds sensors, multiple frequencies. From visible light to infrared. Also, radio antennas for the two- and six-meter bands."

"Amazing," whispered Tesla, walking around the huge tank. He was tempted to run his hand over the burnished hull, but kept his hands close. "So much ability in one device."

"Uh-huh," agreed Savannah. "But the real magic is under here," she said, walking under the massive machine. Tesla followed her between the treads, astonished that he didn't have to stoop to fit under it.

She pointed overhead to an access hatch, which hung open. He stood below it and looked up. He saw an open space, large enough for a small car. Secured within it, a metal cube hung in the space, connected to the tank by a flurry of hoses and cables.

"Autonomous," she said. "That cube houses a mechanical brain. Hollerith's team upstairs designed it."

Tesla searched her face, certain she was joking. "This machine has no crew?" The idea frightened and excited him. Such a machine without proper control would be a nightmare. But with the right guidance, it could be put to glorious use. He instantly imagined a world where war no longer ground men into the dust.

"I know that look," she said. "You see the potential, don't you?"

"Why yes, of course! Technology is the best tool we have for improving man's lot. Though I haven't invented weapons before. At least, not on purpose," he added, remembering the debacle at the Academy.

"I know. And while you'd be free to pursue such things here, we really are interested in one invention in particular."

"My mechanical brain? But you already have—"

"It doesn't work. At least, not the way we need it to. Sure, it can handle fire control and navigation. If we give it a target, it can shoot it. Put it on a navigation course, and it will get back home just fine. But it can't fight effectively. In a simulated battle, it just can't process the variables quickly enough to react the way a person would."

"I see," he replied, stroking his cheek. "But my device is hardly superior. It can be trained to recognize items, yes, but —"

"I know. Here's where that unbridled creativity comes in."

Tesla's brows furrowed, wondering where this discussion was about to go.

Savannah paused and took a breath. "We want you to expand your design. Radically. To the point that an actual human mind can be placed within the computer."

Tesla cocked his head, waiting for her to laugh, and ask forgiveness at teasing him. But she didn't laugh. If anything, her silent questioning look implored Tesla to respond positively.

"My design is patterned after the neural network of the human brain, yes. But my invention has two hundred and fifty-six connections. A real brain has billions. It's just not possible."

Savannah held up both hands. "I know, it sounds

impossible. Maybe it is. But this project is dead in the water without a breakthrough. Hollerith is a genius, but he couldn't do it. I'm thinking if anyone can, it's you. Am I mistaken?"

Tesla laughed nervously. He had expected military interest in his wireless communications, or his work with oscillating vibrations, but this was madness.

Seeing the thoughts in his face, Savannah tried another tack.

"Just… think about it. Let's have coffee in the morning. The Empress at nine. You've seen the resources we have here. Someday, someone will figure it out. I'd just as soon that person be you."

Tesla bit the inside of his lip and stole another look up into Beowulf's brain housing.

The dark metal cube had no advice for him.

A DEBATE WITH PIGEONS

Tesla enjoyed two things above all else. One was the thrill that raced through his heart when he saw some creation of his brain unfolding to success. The other was feeding, and spending time with, pigeons.

The whirlwind morning and the sights he'd witnessed, not to mention the impossible task asked of him, had set his mind spinning.

Savannah had returned him to the city, but he found the walls of his room confining and claustrophobic. He quickly ran outside and went straight to Central Park.

He found an empty bench and pulled an old loaf of bread from his jacket pocket. The birds immediately congregated around him, but their demands were singular and easily satisfied. He pinched off chunks of stale bread for them and tossed the bits around, ensuring everyone got some of the meal.

In one day he'd gone from toiling in a ditch to witnessing the pinnacle of human inventiveness. He realized he was mostly right earlier. God may not be cruel, but He *did* have a sense of humor.

An attractive young couple walked by, holding hands. The man whispered in her ear, and she giggled, clutching his hand to her chest.

The thought of working for the military gave him deep

pause, though. A pacifist by nature and by training, he hated war for its ability to derail human progress. When nations chose to fight, more was lost than men. Resources that could fuel new discoveries instead went to bullets and bandages. Time that could be spent investigating the universe was instead squandered on espionage, conflict, and empty political promises.

For a moment he thought he could change all that, but his father's voice chastised him for such hubris. Man was a violent creature, and always would be.

Tesla agreed that violence was a potent ingredient in man's makeup, but that didn't mean it must dominate. After all, men had created the rule of law. It wasn't always that way, but it was now. Progress was possible, even if maddeningly slow.

Perhaps technology had an important role to play on the military stage? If nations could settle their differences with machines rather than men, wouldn't that be a vast improvement? And didn't he have a moral duty to further that cause, if he could?

The pigeons were enjoying their meal, he could tell. They were single-minded creatures, and in that moment, he envied them their simplicity. No wrestling with moral dilemmas. Just enjoying their bread.

The work would be well paid, he was sure. He could repay Mrs. Harrison's kindness with welcome cash. And the job would be a resounding response to Edison's smear campaign against him. In a flash he would leapfrog over the engineering jobs he'd recently begged for.

But he would still be working for the government, and he had rarely known governments to act honorably. Individually, a country's leaders were typically good men. But when brought together as a collective, moral accountability had a way of fading away, like morning fog under the sunrise.

The bread was almost gone. He tore it into three last

pieces and offered it to the pigeons. They gulped the pieces down quickly, then idled about, content to keep him company even without enticement.

He shivered, realizing the late-afternoon air was turning cool, and pulled his jacket tighter around him. The weight of his options pressed upon him, and a small frown formed on his lips.

He ran a hand through his hair and saw a military man approaching him. Older, but walking with a deliberate grace. The man smiled as he neared, then called out.

"You seem a man with much on his mind." The officer grew closer, and Tesla recognized the rank insignia of colonel.

Tesla stood. "And you must be Savannah's father, the strategist." He stuffed his hands into his jacket pockets to avoid another handshake.

"That I am," said the man. He seemed kindly, more grandfather than military officer. He noted Tesla's reluctance to touch, and nodded his greeting instead. "I was told you come here to think. Sorry I didn't catch you back in the Rabbit Hole. I imagine you have a lot to think about after your visit."

Tesla drew a deep breath and released it. "A fair assessment," he admitted. "To be honest, I'm not sure how I feel."

Colonel Browning nodded sagely. "Something we have in common, as far as this venture is concerned."

At Tesla's questioning look, the colonel wrapped his arms around himself. "Getting cold. My bones could do with a shot of whiskey. Don't suppose you know a good place?"

Tesla guessed this man already knew much about him, including where he liked to drink.

But the idea did have merit.

MAJOR THOMAS ARRIVES

Major Archibald Thomas lay in his rack, unable to sleep, staring at the small cabin's ceiling. Thankfully, the wild heaving of the ship had calmed considerably as they neared land. The captain predicted landfall today, and the men were beyond restless. They'd been crammed together at a density the ship wasn't designed for. He'd kept them as busy as he could, cleaning and repairing the ship alongside the captain's crew, but they yearned for solid ground again, and he mirrored the sentiment.

The ship's crew had taken the worst of the attack, but his army had lost seven men also. In the lower holds, the twenty horses had escaped any injury, and their supplies were completely intact. It could have been much worse, he mused.

He sat up and moved to the small desk built into the cabin's bulkhead. Pulling out a US map, he rolled it out again, for the hundredth time this journey. They'd sail along the coastline, then slip behind Long Island. Moving the beef tallow candle closer, he found New Haven, Connecticut, and placed a finger on it, blotting it out.

Twelve miles north was Branford, a sleepy town of no note, but a perfect landing site to unload the men and supplies. He slid his finger up to it. A few hours to get everyone off and a few more for the gear. Then he'd finally be ready to march his men south and take New Haven. With a decent port city under control, reinforcements could arrive. They should be a few days behind him, so controlling the port was key.

Then once their strength grew, it would be Boston to fall next, with its deep water port, allowing a steady stream of heavier ships to dock. A perfect foothold in this treacherous country.

He heard shouting and cries of celebration from above. The happy mood spread through the ship, and he knew they must have arrived.

"Thank God," he said.

STALKING THE ARTEMIS

ELSTREE, ENGLAND

Lucas led Morgan and Eliza through the Aerodrome base, working their way to the hangar that housed the airship HMS *Artemis*. Their uniforms were a perfect match, and no one had looked twice at them. Once past gate security, everyone assumed they were supposed to be there. They approached the massive hangar and found an entrance.

"Here we go," muttered Lucas and threw the door open. They slipped inside.

The vast building was empty.

Bug-eyed, Morgan stammered, "So much for luck."

"What does this mean?" wondered Eliza. "Could they know-"

"Not a thing," said Lucas. "They've probably just moved it out early for the launch. Let's cross through to the airfield."

The group walked against the wall inside the huge building, their steps echoing in the cavernous space. At the far end, they found an exit in the hangar doors. Stepping outside again, they saw it.

The HMS *Artemis* was moored on the airfield not five hundred feet away. Thanks to their spy, they'd received blueprints of the massive ship and had memorized the major features. But walking toward the floating leviathan, they felt awe at the scope of the ship.

Soon they were walking under it. Even though only fifty feet off the ground, it blocked out the sun, casting a shadow across an area the size of a large farmstead.

Workers ran back and forth, hauling crates, electrical equipment, supplies, and huge coils of line. They began seeing more crew members now, recognizable in their dark-blue uniforms with gold piping.

"Best to look busy," said Lucas, pointing to a nearby pile of crates. They headed to it, then waited while Lucas looked the pile over. He read lot numbers on the crate sides, moving the boxes around.

"You looking for something in particular?" asked Morgan.

"In fact, I am," he said. "But it's not here. Goddammit." He stood, looking around the airfield, his face fallen.

"What's going on?" asked Eliza.

Lucas started to answer her, then held his hand up as a man approached them.

He was dressed as they were, but had been working hard, as his face was caked with sweat and dust. Short and thick, he moved with an ungraceful rhythm as if walking were painful. He carried a briefcase-sized wooden box, and was coming straight for them.

"Lucas," whispered Morgan.

Eliza scanned the area for escape routes, noting areas of cover she could shoot from.

"We're good," he told them. "Relax, and say nothing."

The man approached Lucas and nodded with a tight, thin smile that held little humor. "You are Lucas?"

"Yes. You have a package for me?"

"It's right here." The squat little man patted the box. "Might I trouble you for a cigarette?"

"My sister convinced me to give them up," replied Lucas.

The man nodded curtly and handed the box to Lucas.

"Good luck, my friends." Then he turned and walked away.

"What the hell was that?" asked Eliza.

"Let's get aboard," said Lucas.

Morgan and Eliza picked up their own cargo and followed Lucas toward the ship.

The silver zeppelin was a huge cylinder with tapered ends. The airship's shape and strength came from a duralumin skeleton made of rings and longitudinal girders. Inside, sixteen hydrogen gas cells provided lift. Tanks of Blaugas were used for heating and lighting.

A central corridor ran the length of the ship, with another corridor fifty feet above that, joined by six ladder gangways. Along the outer belly, eight diesel prop-engine nacelles gave forward thrust. Between them, an extruding passenger compartment hung low.

The group saw five hatchways along the underside of the airship, but only two were currently open. Wooden towers had been positioned under the open hatches, providing stairs for workers to board the airship. A steady stream of men and women came and went at both towers.

Lucas steered them toward the nearest tower, and soon they fell in line with other workers hauling supplies and gear aboard. They climbed five stories up the stairs, and then they were aboard the *Artemis*.

As they stepped off the support towers onto the metal flooring of the ship, a foreman checked the crates they were carrying and barked orders at them.

"This goes to front mooring hub. That, crew quarters aft." He looked over the electrical gear Eliza had brought aboard and frowned. "I have no idea what that is. Better take it to Einstein's team. Axial corridor, room seven," he said, pointing.

Eliza nodded agreement and headed in the direction he'd indicated. The foreman quickly lost interest in them and was scanning the new crates being brought aboard. Lucas and

Morgan followed behind Eliza, lugging their cargo.

Once out of sight, they found a storage room and slipped inside. Setting down the cargo, they took a moment to regroup. Morgan checked the corridor.

"All clear," he said.

"Room seven is one level above us and then forward," Eliza said. "Chances are, that's where Einstein is."

"Agreed," said Lucas. "But that's not where we're heading."

"What?" she asked.

Morgan raised an eyebrow, but held his tongue.

"Our mission isn't just to kill Einstein. We're taking out the whole damn ship too."

Eliza sat down hard on a crate. "Um, that's an important detail to not share with us."

"Need to know. Sorry," Lucas said.

"And now, we need to know," said Morgan.

Lucas nodded. He waved them forward and pried the lid from the small crate. They looked inside. Fourteen sticks of dynamite rested within, wired to a timing clock.

"My God," said Eliza.

Lucas nodded. "This is one ship that will never bomb an American city."

ROSABELLE, BELIEVE.

Colonel Browning raised his whiskey glass. "To the end of war. Or at least its mitigation."

Tesla raised his glass and clinked it with the colonel's. "Well said."

The Petal & Thorn was busy tonight. John Roberts held court behind the bar, and several busty young women wove through the crowd, fetching drinks and bowls of hot lamb stew.

Tesla sipped slowly, enjoying the new brand of whiskey. "I like this," he said. "What was it called again?"

"Jack Daniels. Young fella makes it in Tennessee."

"He does good work."

"That he does. So, tell me Mr. Tesla, what has you in knots over this thing? Is it the idea of contributing to the war machine?"

Tesla shook his head. "Not directly. If my work can make war less bloody, I am all for it."

"Good, good," said the colonel.

Tesla wasn't ready to dive into his reservations just yet. He paused, looking around the tavern. *So much fun others were having*, he thought.

The colonel was a crack poker player, which meant he read men well. He knew pushing the issue would only delay things.

"I made colonel down in Mexico City," he offered.

Tesla's brows rose, and his sympathy for the man climbed. "By all accounts, that was a horrible situation."

"Was a goddamned mess. We ended up saving South America from the Crowns, but it cost us bad. 'Course, we wanted the buffer state, so it wasn't totally altruistic." He shrugged. "Nothing ever is, in war." His eyes went glassy, and Tesla knew he was revisiting Mexico City.

The colonel blinked. "Anyway, I lost a lot of boys there. And now we've got Crown forces landing on our mainland. So, I'm with you. If Beowulf takes men out of war, it's worth anything."

"I understand. The technical challenge is mountainous, of course. I have no idea how it could be done."

The colonel waved dismissively. "Sure, but if it could?"

"Then I suppose we come to the real issue that bothers me, though it took some time to surface."

"Which is what, exactly?"

A waitress appeared beside him, all smiles, in a low-cut green velvet dress. "Bring you anything?" she asked.

Tesla frowned and waved her off. "No, no, please. Thank you." She slipped away in the crowd.

Tesla set down his glass. He leaned forward to keep his voice low, despite the noisy atmosphere.

"Say I can do it. Say I figure a way to put a man's mind into a machine. What would that mean? Am I playing God? Would he even be a man any longer? And what would it do to him? He would have no body, at least in the traditional sense. His body would become a machine. No man has ever experienced such a thing. What if it drove him insane?"

"Oh, I've given much thought to the very same questions."

"You have? Why? What's your role in all this, anyway?"

"Me? My role is easy. I just have to die. *You* have to resurrect me."

"What?" Tesla's spine went straight as an iron rod.

"I'm the logical choice. I have the military strategy up here," he said, tapping his temple. "And I have the cancer." He tapped his chest.

"You mean you're…"

"Going to die. Yes, I am. Fairly soon now."

"My God. I had no idea."

"Course not. But now you see why I'm asking the same questions you are. I'm the one going into the machine. If you can do it, of course."

Tesla held his head in his hands, staring at the table. "I don't know if I can."

"None of us know what we can do, until we do it."

Tesla looked up. "I don't know what to say to you."

"Buy me another round then."

Tesla waved the waitress over, and they got another set of whiskeys.

The colonel took a sip. "Doctor told me no drinking or smoking. I got weeks to live, and he tells me that. That's what I call a complete lack of situational awareness."

Tesla chuckled at the gallows humor.

"Good man," said the Colonel. "You'll be OK."

Tesla grew silent, then asked, "What about Savannah? I assume she knows?"

The colonel nodded. "She does. And her little girl, Madelaine, too."

"Oh, I didn't know she was married."

"She was. We don't talk about him."

Tesla heard the warning tones in his voice and didn't pursue the question.

He rubbed his cheek, feeling the stubble of a long day. "I didn't realize this project was so personal for your family."

"You play the hand you're dealt, right? Don't get me wrong, I'm not thrilled with the idea of crossing over into… whatever it is. Or even worse, not crossing over completely."

"How do you mean?"

"There's not exactly a field manual for this kind of thing. What if some of me comes over, but not all? What if it's not truly me anymore? Gives me the creeps."

"I hadn't thought of that yet. You're right, that would be a macabre situation."

The colonel stared down at the table. A hint of a scowl appeared on his lips, then disappeared. "My sister was close with that magician, Houdini. Before he died, he was worried all sorts of charlatans would come to his wife, pretending to be in contact with him from beyond the grave. So they arranged a secret phrase. If anyone came to her and used that phrase, she'd know her husband really was there, talking to her."

"Clever. I'm sure given his fame, the con men must have come out of the woodwork."

"They did. My sister said dozens came to Houdini's widow, all claiming to speak for her dead husband. But not one of them said the phrase. They were liars, just after free publicity. After a few years, she made the secret public and said she was done looking for ghosts."

"What was the phrase?"

"'Rosabelle, believe.' From a play they both enjoyed, I think."

The men both grew silent. The talk of death had brought the mood down, and despite the raucous environment around them, they sat brooding on the heavy subject.

Tesla sensed the spark go out of their evening and felt responsible for it. If this man was to die soon, he shouldn't have to spend that time poorly.

"Your granddaughter is how old?" he asked, hoping to steer the conversation into happier waters.

"Madelaine?" The colonel's face lightened, and Tesla knew he'd hit the mark. "She's twelve. A very precocious twelve. Her mother's girl, for sure. She's at the lab pretty often, so I'm sure you'll meet her."

The colonel sat back in his chair. "Assuming you take the job, of course."

Tesla felt the spotlight intensity of the unasked question. "Your confidence in me is extremely gratifying, Colonel. It really is. But the weight of the thing… you are putting your life in my hands, as it were. I am completely unaccustomed to such a thing." Tesla realized the irony was that his father, as a parish priest, would be better suited to such mortal issues.

"Nikola, despite my chosen profession, death scares the hell out of me. But since the reaper isn't under my chain of command, I figure I better maximize the benefit while I can. And my gut is telling me you're the man we need."

Tesla gulped the last of his whiskey. "I wish we had met under better circumstances, Colonel. I like you."

"Me too, son. Me too."

TAKING SHUNT CONTROL

ELSTREE, ENGLAND

"So we're blowing the whole ship with that?" asked Eliza.

Lucas indicated the ship around them. "This ship is filled with hydrogen. Once we start it off, those gas cells will do the rest."

"And the best place to do that?" asked Morgan.

"The boys in Washington say we want the lower corridor, room twelve. It's far aft, directly below the petrol tanks. From there the hydrogen lights up like a match."

Morgan checked the time. "We've got a little over an hour before this beast flies."

Lucas gathered up the box and checked the corridor. "We better get on it then."

The three headed aft, each carrying a load of cargo as before. They found the third ladder gangway and carefully made their way down to the lower corridor.

Looking about to gain their bearings, Lucas thought back to the blueprints they'd memorized. He pointed. "This way, about two hundred feet." They nodded agreement and followed him.

There were more workers and crew on this level, and they frequently had to turn sideways to pass them in the narrow corridor.

Lucas passed an open bulkhead, then stopped and went back to look again. He felt Morgan and Eliza join him, looking over his shoulder. The room inside was large, with black steel racks suspended above a hinged double door in the floor.

"That's the bomb bay," Lucas whispered. They nodded silently, each feeling the determination mount.

Lucas's hands grew slick with sweat, and he swore the box felt warm to the touch. He wiped his hands on his pants and continued down the corridor with a tighter grip on the box of dynamite.

Outside at the base gate, Lieutenant Dowers caught a glimpse of something down the road. A shimmering, mirage-like blur. He realized it was a dust cloud, kicked up by a large number of vehicles coming towards him. His eyes narrowed and he barked at the nearest marine. "Get me dispatch on the line. Right bloody now!"

The marine ran into the guardhouse and spun the crank powering the telephone handset. "Dispatch?" he called. "This is Elstree Aerodrome, main gate. Stand by for Lieutenant Dowers, please."

He held out the handset as the lieutenant snatched it from his hand. "Dispatch? I have a large convoy approaching my position, and—" The lieutenant's face went white. "Why the hell wasn't I notified? No, I—never mind. Arghh!" he yelled, slamming down the handset. He burst from the guardhouse, pointing with both hands.

"Jameson! Open the gate this instant! Peterson, form the men up! Now, now, now!" he yelled.

They scrambled to obey the hasty orders as the convoy approached rapidly. The long row of motorcars was flanked by twin lines of marines on horseback, galloping in formation. They each bore Imperial colors.

"God in heaven, someone is going to pay for this!" the lieutenant cursed. He turned to his marines. "It's the king! Present…arms!"

The marines snapped to rigid attention, rendering a crisp salute, just as the convoy arrived. The marines carrying submachine guns held them out in front, underside to the honored dignitary. Not slowing, the procession blew through the gate, a blur of horse, dust, and motorcar. And then they were gone.

The lieutenant broke his salute. "Order… arms!" he bellowed, and the marines returned to attention.

"Someone is going to pay," he muttered.

Lucas led the team down the corridor toward the aft of the airship. As they approached a sealed bulkhead, the floor beneath them shifted.

"That was a guide wire being loosed," he told them. "We don't have much time before this ship is in the air."

They crowded together against the bulkhead. "This is our room," he said. "Be ready."

He turned the lever and pushed the heavy steel door inward. Stepping inside, the three hoped for another empty compartment. Instead, they found four men in dark blue uniforms with gold piping. They were examining an open crate of whiskey bottles and didn't appreciate the interruption.

"What is this, then?" one of them asked, standing and blocking their sight of the theft in progress. "No workers allowed in this compartment, you know that. Out with you!" The man strode forward, arms out, to push the three back into the corridor.

Lucas set down the box and raised his hands in apology. He smiled a warm, apologetic grin and noting which wrist the man wore his watch on, decided he would be right-handed.

"Beg pardon, we had no—" Lucas grasped the man's outstretched wrist, and stepped sideways, then around the man, twisting his right arm viciously behind the startled man's back.

"What—" the crew member began.

Lucas wrapped his other hand over the man's mouth, then wrenched the arm up hard between the man's shoulder blades. The shoulder dislocated with a hollow *pop*. He screamed in pain, but Lucas had effectively gagged him already.

The other crew members leaped to their feet, still unsure at what they were seeing. Two of them had their mouths open, shocked at the scene. The third, a large brute, cracked his knuckles and stood slowly, ready for combat.

Lucas still held the first man and kicked his toe into the back of the man's knee, bringing him to his knees easily as the support went out from under him. Lucas reared back and drove a punch into the man's neck. The crewman went down like a felled ox.

One of the smaller crew found his wits and darted to the side, reaching for an alarm switch on the wall. Eliza ran at him, her knives already in her fists, points held down. Like a great cat, she leaped upon him, landing against his chest, and wrapping her legs around his waist. In the same movement, she drove the twin blades down into the startled man's collarbone. He went stiff, mouth working furiously to scream, but finding no air to carry the pain he felt wash over him. He staggered, then crashed to the floor, Eliza still wrapped around him in a murderous embrace. She knew he was finished and rolled off him, easing back up to her feet, both blades wet and red.

"Dear God!" cried the remaining little one, frozen still, hands raised.

The big man only smiled and crouched, circling. Then he came at them, swinging a thick ham-fist through the air, to connect with Lucas's jaw.

Time slowed for Lucas as it always did in these moments. He watched the fist roaring toward his face. Seeing the ragged scar that ran down the length of the man's thumb, Lucas wondered what made the injury. Probably a wood saw, he guessed. But the thick fist was closer now, and it was time to act.

Lucas brought his left hand up to intercept the punch. With unnatural speed he placed his palm over his attacker's fist, and with the slightest of pressure, guided its trajectory away from his face. He pushed down gently, sending the attack toward the floor, but at the same time, Lucas raised his right arm, bending it tightly to bring his elbow forward. He guided the brute's fist directly into his elbow, the sharpest bone in the human body. Letting the two connect, Lucas felt pain, but nothing like what he had delivered to the brute.

The man's fist smashed against the sharp bone, and the power behind the punch was channeled into the bones of his own hand. The bones in the fingers are not so durable, and the brutal force meant for Lucas quickly overwhelmed them. Lucas heard four distinct cracks as they shattered.

The man howled in agony as he ruined his own hand. He gulped air, in shock from the sensations flooding his brain. His vision swam and then cleared. Enraged and flushed with adrenaline, he launched an attack with his remaining good fist.

Morgan stepped forward into the man's path, bringing with him a hammer blow of a punch into the man's temple. The giant's head rocked back, and he staggered, mouth agape. His eyes raced around the room, then blinked, then went dim. He collapsed at Morgan's feet, unconscious.

"Couldn't let you two have all the fun," said Morgan.

Lucas smiled in agreement.

The final crewman gasped in astonishment, his eyes darting between his friends on the floor and those who defeated them so easily.

"Who are you people? What are you?" he cried. He made no movements, freezing like a rabbit before three wolves.

Eliza sided up close against him, and he struggled not to run away.

"We are Americans, dear," she told him.

A GOOD NIGHT'S SLEEP

Under a bright, full moon, Tesla carefully made his way down Post Street. The evening with the colonel had run late, and there had been perhaps too many whiskeys. He deliberately placed each footstep, careful not to trip on the uneven cobblestone.

Overhead, the city's new electric streetlights glowed warmly. Demand for electricity and its comforts had proved considerable, and city planning hadn't yet caught up. A rat's nest of dozens of power lines ran overhead, sagging on wooden poles. Every few weeks someone stepped on a downed line and got himself electrocuted. Tesla kept a wary eye out for such dangers as he crossed the street. The papers would inevitably chortle with ironic headlines, should the inventor meet his maker by stepping on a live wire.

Stepping up onto the sidewalk, the world tipped to one side with a disorienting lurch. He reached out for the nearby building, jamming his palm against the wall. The steady, unmoving brick was comforting and reminded his equilibrium which way was truly vertical.

When the moment of dizziness had passed, he pressed on, eager for his pillow and the delicious surrender of sleep. The streets were quiet, with only the occasional couple returning home like himself, and a ratcatcher, carrying his wire cage and poking through trash piles in search of his quarry.

He finally came to his current home, the house of Mrs. Harrison, where he rented his room.

Not wanting to wake anyone, he entered quietly and slipped into his room. He stripped off his overcoat and draped it over the back of a chair, then sat heavily to remove his shoes. He'd just slipped them off when a powerful banging knocked at his door.

He groaned and called out, "Mrs. Harrison, please. I will pay you tomorrow. Right now, I must sleep."

There was a pause, then the knocking resumed. Tesla brought a hand to his forehead, realizing he had a headache.

"Fine, fine!" He stood and opened the door. "Mrs. Harrison, I—"

The hard face of Clay Bracken greeted him, and he knew the evening was turning for the worse. The throbbing in his head increased, and he winced.

Clay flashed a jackal grin. "Owe money to someone else too, huh? I'm not surprised."

"Not tonight, please. I can find you tomorr—"

Clay shook his head and pushed his way into the room, knocking Tesla back. "Nah, don't think so. Think we need to settle things tonight. Right now, even."

Tesla stumbled back, falling over the chair and knocking his coat to the floor.

Clay stood over him, shaking his head. He looked around the room. "Genius inventor, hmm? Not much to show for it. Maybe you should invent yourself a better life, eh?" Clay laughed.

Tesla closed his eyes, willing the room to stop spinning, then opened them and clambered to his feet. Standing only in his socks, he was still as tall as Clay, but he didn't feel it.

"There's no money for you here, Clay. But there will be soon, I promise."

Clay finished his survey of the room. A bed, a table,

books, and a lot of mechanical junk. "Yeah… I believe you. About the first, anyway. Which is a shame. Man who collects gambling debts like you ought to be more careful. Otherwise, people get hurt."

"There's no need for that, Clay. If you just give me a few more days, all will be—"

Casually, Clay brought his thick fist up and swung it into Tesla's face.

Tesla's world exploded into stars. The room swam again as he fell back, landing hard on his back. He opened his eyes and stared at the ceiling panels.

Then Clay's face slipped into view. "Few days won't be good enough, buddy-o." He grabbed Tesla by the collar and pulled him up, standing the inventor on his feet again.

Tesla blinked hard at the vertigo of the sudden movement. Clay's face was inches away, and he smelled the man's breath. The close physical contact was distressing, and Tesla struggled to step back, but Clay's grip was strong and held him in place.

"Going to give you something to remember me by. And then I'll be back tomorrow. I'm not paid then, things get bloody. Are you hearing this?"

Tesla felt his pulse racing, and he admitted to himself he was afraid of this man. He thought of Mrs. Harrison upstairs, unaware of the intruder.

And of her sleeping children…

"Just get out," he said. "Get out of here!"

Clay grinned. "You got it, Professor."

He hauled his fist back, and Tesla flinched. The blow slammed against Tesla's jaw, and a blossom of pain raced through his brain. Then the room grew dim.

Clay's voice went distant, with an odd echo. "See you tomorrow, chum."

Tesla slid to the floor and finally found his slumber.

A SIMPLE TEST FLIGHT

ELSTREE, ENGLAND

The Royal procession blew through the main security gate, then turned and veered around and behind Hanger Seven, home of the HMS *Artemis*. The lead motorcar traced a wide curve toward the floating airship, and slowed as workers scrambled to run out of the way. It settled to a stop just past the first wooden stair tower.

Behind it, the rest of the procession slowed and stopped. Eight dark motorcars rolled to a stop. The twin lines of horsemen spaced themselves apart, leaving a wide gap beside one car. It was a large, heavy-looking black cruiser with flared wheel wells, silver running boards, and purple pennants flickering in the mild breeze. The V-12 Rolls Royce engine rumbled with a throaty purr, then went silent as the driver killed the ignition.

The entire base seemed to freeze, struck by the unexpected spectacle. Dozens of workers and crew members stood frozen, staring at the impressive sight. For almost all of them, it would be the first time they'd seen the king. Then several remembered the stories of the king's fickle mood and sadistic nature, and decided they were needed elsewhere. Just last week the king felt an unlucky gawker was staring too hard, so he had the man's eyes removed.

The driver stepped from the motorcar, opened the rear door, and stood still as a statue, eyes cast down.

Inside the *Artemis*, word had spread like a brush fire, and Einstein was bolting down the stairs to meet the monarch. Right behind him, Captain Stevens raced to catch up.

"Always a pleasure to see the king," muttered the captain. Einstein laughed at the jest, careful not to trip down the stairs.

The two men stepped off onto the ground and hurried to the king's motorcar. The door was held open, but no one had exited the fine vehicle yet. Just as they arrived, the king stepped from his car.

He was tall and unlike so many before him, had not let his body go to fat. In his perfectly tailored Saville Row dark suit, leather gloves, and silver-tipped walking stick, he could be mistaken for a wealthy industrialist or perhaps a very successful banker. But in truth, he was far more. He was the God-appointed supreme ruler of the Commonwealth, with all the weight and privilege such a role bespoke.

Einstein and the captain stood at attention and bowed at the neck as the king approached them. "Welcome, Your Majesty," said Captain Stevens. "Hello, Your Majesty," echoed Einstein.

"How goes my airship, gentlemen?" asked the king.

"In fine shape, sir," said the captain. "In fact, we are preparing for a flight test just now."

The king's smile could wilt flowers. "Yes, I know. Why do you think I am here?"

"It would be a delight to have you observe the—" began the captain.

The king waved his hand dismissively. "No, no. I am here to take to the skies, good Captain. Make that happen."

Einstein stepped forward. "Sir, that is not possible. The ship is not ready for a passenger of your importance. We have many systems still under development."

The king turned to his head scientist. "Professor, I have brought my friends here," he said, waving toward the twenty men and women stepping from the motorcars behind him. "And we will see my country as the birds and God see it. Are we understood?"

"Yes, of course, sir. But—"

"Has the passenger compartment been furnished?" interrupted the king.

"The… well, yes, sir."

"Is there tea aboard?"

"Tea? Ah, I don't—yes, I believe so."

The king nodded. "And, is there… champagne?"

Einstein's eyes went wide at the question. Several subsystems were in disarray, and the King asked about champagne? "Your Majesty, I don't see what—"

Captain Stevens put a hand on Einstein's shoulder. "But of course there is champagne, sir. Please follow my steward, and we'll have you properly situated at once."

The king clapped his hands. "Excellent! Forward, my friends!" he called out and strode up the stairs into the *Artemis*, his retinue in tow.

Einstein leaned into the captain and whispered. "Are you mad? The ship is not ready for him! And there's no room in passenger compartment for his group."

The captain nodded. "I know. That is why you have five minutes to pull your team off the ship. We take off in ten."

"What!? We have all sorts of tests to run. We can't possibly—"

"It's done, Professor. Let's make the most of it. Who knows? You may get more funding out of this. Now, if you'll excuse me…" He turned and headed up the stairs after the king. Along the way he called to a crew member. "You, Harrison! Find me some champagne, now!"

Morgan knocked the last crew member unconscious and bound him, while Lucas brought out the box and retrieved the dynamite. He looked around the room for the first time. It was an electrical relay station. On the blueprints it had simply been labeled as "Shunt Control," which meant nothing to him.

Thick electrical cabling fed into the room from several directions, each as wide as his wrist. A central board held several large fuses, to prevent excess power from flowing through the system. It seemed a fine place for an explosion.

He set the dynamite bundle down and set the timer for ten minutes. Enough time to get airborne, but not too much to risk discovery. He slipped it inside a crate of bananas.

"Help me with them," he told Morgan, pointing to the four bodies. Together they pulled the four men into the small storage closet and locked the door. Eliza frowned at the bloodstain on the floor, then shoved a large crate over it.

Lucas looked around the room and was satisfied. "All right, let's get off this damned ship."

"I second that plan," said Eliza.

They slipped back out into the corridor, retracing their steps. "Let's go back to the same staircase we came in on. With a little luck—"

BRANG, BRANG!

A brass bell mounted on the wall rang twice, loudly. They froze.

"Alarm?" asked Morgan. Then it repeated.

BRANG, BRANG!

"I don't think so," said Lucas. "But it could be something worse."

Just then the floor beneath them shifted and rocked gently. They all reached out to steady themselves against the nearest wall, and the swaying motion told them all what the bell indicated.

They were now airborne.

In the passenger compartment, the king and his party marveled at the view as the *Artemis* took flight.

The compartment was mostly furnished, with dark mahogany tables and lushly upholstered chairs. The oval-shaped room had wraparound glass panels, giving the occupants a clear view in all directions.

The king leaned against a brass rail and pressed his forehead to the glass, looking down. Already, the workmen on the airbase seemed small and ant-like. He could see Einstein, surrounded by his scientific team and no doubt fuming mad.

Behind him, the king's friends murmured their amazement at the experience of flight. The excited rush of chatter and laughter pleased him immensely.

"It seems a shame to waste such a craft in war," said someone. "As a pleasure ship, it has no equal."

The king turned around. "It's true. But after the war, we can always have her again."

A display caught his eye, and the king crossed the room and discovered the rack of maps, all rolled in tight tubes and labeled with brass plaques. He ran his finger along them, then stopped at "USA-Eastern Seaboard." Pulling out the rolled tube, he brought the map to a nearby table and spread it out. As his group crowded around him, he placed two ceramic statues in the corners to hold the curled map in place.

"Here," he said, stabbing the map with his finger. "Washington, DC. Our very first target for Einstein's new bombs."

The crowd tittered and applauded the news.

"Our previous colony has grown arrogant and willful. Very soon we will remind them of their rightful place."

"Do we abort?" asked Morgan.

Lucas shook his head. "Mission's too important. Who knows when we get another break like this." He checked his watch. "Six minutes. Plenty of time to figure something out."

Morgan and Eliza waited for the promised plan, but Lucas just ran his hand through his hair and looked around the corridor. He began running through options.

"Once started, the timer can't be reset. Blueprints showed no escape mechanism. There's no time to commandeer the thing. That just leaves one bad idea."

"I seriously doubt we can survive a jump from here," said Eliza.

"Yeah, no way," agreed Morgan.

Lucas nodded. "I know. But if we drop a line down, we can cut a hundred feet from the altitude. It's that, or we stay here." He looked at the time again. "Five minutes."

"Let's do it," said Eliza.

"Agreed," Morgan said. "But where? That access hatch was pretty public. We can't just shimmy down a line without attention."

"I know, I know." Lucas turned and looked down the corridor. "Follow me." Not waiting, he ran down the narrow hallway. Morgan and Eliza sprinted after him.

Lucas led them down the corridor, slipping past surprised crew members. He slammed shoulders with a large worker, but didn't stop running, despite the man's cursing. Morgan and Eliza caught up and stayed right behind him. As they bolted forward, Lucas scanned the room names, then stopped suddenly right before an open bulkhead. He peered around the corner into the room, then pulled back.

"The bomb bay," he told them. "Just one worker in there. Guess they're not worried about dropping many bombs today.

Eliza, take him out, fast. Morgan, figure out how to get those bay doors open. I'll find the longest rope I can."

Eliza nodded and stepped softly around the corner. She saw the man across the bay, his back to her. He was checking a meter on the wall, and flipping through pages on a clipboard.

She padded forward and reached for the blade tucked into her boot. She gripped the knife hatchet style, with the sharpened edge out. The blackened metal quivered slightly, and her lips pulled back in a grimace of uneasy anticipation.

She crossed the bay silently, coming almost within striking distance. He dropped the clipboard on a worktable and turned aside to a valve fitting. He tried to turn the gray steel wheel, but it was frozen. Only his focus on the valve kept him from turning around.

Eliza stepped forward, now within arm's length.

The man grunted and pulled on the wheel with both hands. The valve gave loose and spun freely. He opened it to the maximum, then began to turn back around.

Eliza crouched and slashed her blade forward, level with the worker's neck. Something warned the man, maybe the glint off her knife's edge, maybe a whisper of air movement. His head spun around just as her blade sliced across the side of his throat. Their eyes met as the blade opened skin and severed the carotid artery. Eliza felt the subtle vibration of rough texture as her blade's edge slid over his vertebrae.

He opened his mouth to scream and Eliza whipped the knife back, opening his throat below the Adam's apple. His lungs pushed, but the scream escaped only as a puff of air from the severed windpipe. Sliding quickly into shock, his body went slack.

Eliza stepped forward and wrapped the man in a bear hug, stopping the body from hitting the floor. Arterial spray coated the side of her face with warm, coppery blood, but she ignored the grisly fountain. She bent to ease the body quietly to the floor, when a voice brought her head up.

"Hey, Johan, I have the—" A young crew member was stepping from behind a large support column, holding a heavy silver wrench. He froze, mouth open at the morbid scene.

Eliza dropped the body, and it landed with a heavy thud on the steel floor plates. Without thinking, she reversed the blade in her hand, bringing the knife into throwing position.

The junior officer was young, but fast. He dropped the wrench and sprang for an alarm switch behind him.

Eliza drew back and threw the blade hard. It sliced through the air before slamming into the officer's back. It slid into his right kidney, throwing his nervous system into hysterics as his hand fell across the alarm. His fingers clenched, and the switch tripped. A red light on the wall flared. He hit the floor, twitching. A moment later, the klaxon blared, a high-pitched whine of alarm.

Lucas burst into the room, scanning for a coil of line. "Christ, that's loud!" he yelled, the sound ringing in his ears.

Eliza shot him a look of apology, but he waved it off.

Morgan was at the bay doors, looking over the hinges and release mechanisms. He ran his hands over the metal as if to pull their workings out through osmosis.

Lucas darted around a corner and found a wide rack of tools, various metal fittings, and a wide assortment of pipe in differing sizes. Then he spotted it. A thick coil of woven rope. He threw it over his shoulder.

Eliza retrieved her knife from the unlucky officer's back and took the sidearm from his holster. She posted herself at the corridor entry, peering around the corner, waiting for the guards sure to arrive any second.

Lucas joined Morgan at the bay doors. "We need this open now, my friend."

Morgan nodded. "Almost have it. The hydraulic lines run this way," he said, following the black rubber hoses to a panel with two levers. He put his hands on them and pushed. Nothing.

"We have company!" yelled Eliza. "Four, at least!"

The king pressed his hands against his ears, and he saw everyone else was doing the same. The wailing klaxon was distressingly loud.

He looked about the room, and finding a crew member, yelled above the alarm. "What is happening? Bring me the captain!"

The king's scowl told the officer all he needed to know, and he nodded, then ran off for the bridge.

Eliza risked another look around the corner. She peeked her head around the corner, saw a bright flash, and jerked back as a lead slug slammed into the bulkhead, barely missing her eye.

"Make that five!" she yelled to Lucas. "Royal Marines. And they're not happy."

"Guess not," offered Morgan. "Reckless bastards shouldn't be shooting on a hydrogen ship."

Eliza swung the officer's sidearm around the corner, firing blindly twice down the corridor.

Lucas tossed the heavy rope coil on top of the bay doors. He found an end and began tying it off to the overhead bomb rack.

"How about we get out of here, hmm?"

Morgan tried the hydraulic levers again. He pushed them forward. Nothing. He pulled them back. Nothing. He punched the panel, screaming. "Dammit!" He looked around the bay for a solution.

Lucas cinched a fast bowline knot to the bomb rack.

"Eliza, we are leaving!"

She fell back, joining them, but kept her sidearm trained on the bulkhead door.

Lucas turned to Morgan, yelling over the alarm. "Now, Morgan!"

Morgan raised his hands in surrender, then froze. An idea came to him. He slipped a knife from his boot and grabbed the twin hydraulic hoses in a tight fist. He slipped the blade under the rubber hoses, and slashed upward through them. The blade cut cleanly through, and the hoses leaped from his grasp, writhing like two angry snakes, spewing thin, brown liquid over him, Lucas, and half the bay.

But the doors fell open. With the pressure released, gravity drew the doors down. They hung barely halfway open, but it was more than enough for a man to slip through. The coil of rope fell through the gap, streaming out to its full length. Cold wind ripped through the gap, blowing Lucas's hair back.

Lucas flashed Morgan a thumbs-up. He leaned over the gaping doors and looked down. Vertigo made his stomach clench, and he grabbed hold of the bomb rack frame above the open doors. He guessed they were two hundred feet off the ground. The rope covered maybe half that.

Morgan came up with the same math. "That's a hundred-foot fall, Lucas…"

Lucas checked his watch. "You've got one minute to find your courage, my friend."

Before he could reply, two marines burst through the door. Like the gate guards, they wore the striking scarlet jackets with white chest band. And they carried Vickers submachine guns.

The marines squeezed the triggers, and a lethal flood of lead rounds screamed toward the intruders.

Lucas was behind the bomb rack, and the heavy guide rails caught most of the bullets headed for him. Several rounds slammed into the wall behind him, but many struck the rails, and ricocheted crazily in the bay.

Then one slug found its way through the framework and tore through Lucas's calf. He cried out from the trauma and pitched sideways toward the open bay doors.

Morgan yelled for him. "Lucas!" He reached for his friend, but was just out of reach. Lucas stumbled, then fell through the gaping bomb bay.

Eliza saw Lucas fall, but forced herself to focus on the most critical threat. She crouched low, turning sideways to present the smallest possible target and lined up her first shot. The first marine was moving quickly. She led his movement, and smoothly squeezed the trigger. The marine's jaw exploded and he collapsed. She swung her aim toward the second marine, as her peripheral vision told her three more had entered the bay.

Morgan's eyes were locked on the open bay doors where Lucas had fallen. Then he turned to those responsible. With a guttural roar, he charged straight at them, both fists eager to pound bone and brain. He saw one marine go down with a shattered jaw, then saw the other one lift his Vickers.

Morgan surged forward to close the gap, but it wasn't enough. The marine opened fire. One round ripped through Morgan's bicep. He screamed as another bullet tore through his shoulder, then another hit him in the chest, shredding his lung. He slumped to his knees, blood frothing in his mouth. He fell forward, then went still.

"No!" screamed Eliza. She took aim at the marine who'd killed Morgan, and sent a round into his chest, then another into his temple. The three new marines saw her, and she dove for cover as they brought their guns to bear on her.

Outside, below the airship, Lucas was falling. The cold air roared around his head, even louder than the alarm klaxon had been. He twisted in the air, slipping closer to his death by the second. The massive airship flashed above him, then he spun and saw the airbase and the nearby forest. The rope he'd secured whipped past him, and he reached out, frantic. His arm caught, then lost, then caught the line.

He spun his arm around madly, wrapping the line around it. Then he pulled hard, clenching his arm against his chest. The line tightened like a python, biting deep into his forearm. The friction burned through the thin worker's uniform, then continued burning through his skin. A vise grip clamped down on his forearm, and the line dug itself into his fragile arm, but it caught.

He stopped with a sickening jerk, and the tendons in his shoulder and elbow screamed in protest. The pain blinded Lucas, and he blinked repeatedly, working the tears from his eyes. The roaring wind wicked them away, and he realized with surprise that he was hanging from the floating airship.

Eliza scrambled away from the three marines as they opened fire. A blistering hail of lead tore through the bay, and she screamed, covering her head as she crouched behind a heavy winch motor. The bullets ripped and shredded the wood shelves above her, and a dozen technical manuals rained down on her. The shelves disintegrated into splinters, and she knew the bullets would do the same to her flesh. Unconsciously, she ran through her tactical options, and came up short. She checked the sidearm. The magazine held five more rounds. More than enough, she figured. She got ready to launch one final assault.

Just then, inside a crate of bananas, a timer's clockwork clicked. An electrical connection was made, and with one small spark, fourteen sticks of dynamite detonated. The explosion blew through the shunt control room, ripping through the room's ceiling, and rupturing three of the six petrol tanks stored there. The additional fuel added its energy to the blast, and the explosion grew into a fireball.

The detonation rocked the *Artemis*, and knocked Eliza

back, landing hard on her bottom. She recovered and slid around the winch, gun raised. The three marines had also been thrown to the floor, and she sighted the first. She fired, and he fell back, clutching his eye. She fired again, and the man next to him took a round in the gut. She swiveled for the last marine, but he wasn't there. She scanned the room, but he was gone.

She jumped up and ran to the bomb bay doors, ready to power slide down the line. Looking down, she saw Lucas swinging on the rope like a distant pendulum, and her heart lifted.

Lucas dangled from the end of the line, hanging a hundred feet below the *Artemis*. He saw a flash of movement and saw Eliza in the bomb bay, her hand up in greeting. He waved his free arm frantically. "Come on!" he yelled, but the wind stole the sound away.

The petrol tanks had given their all to create the fireball, and it tore loose within the HMS *Artemis*. The petrol storage room disappeared in a blinding flash. The force channeled into the main exhaust shaft, racing upward, then the shaft exploded, sending shrapnel tearing through the lower crew compartment, auxiliary control, and the aft-most hydrogen cell.

The ruptured cell began bleeding hydrogen into the ship's upper chamber. Emergency fire suppression systems snapped on, but rather than dousing the flames in a heavy shower of water, only a weak trickle dripped out. Without water pressure, the system was impotent.

The expanding fireball surged through the ventilation shafts, spidering out throughout the ship until it found the upper chamber. The flames touched the hydrogen gas, and the fireball became a monster.

Eliza grabbed the line and looked down, the cool wind whipping her hair back. Lucas was still there, dangling above a small pond. She started to leap onto the line, when something forced her to look up.

Hot, searing air washed over her. She knew the shock wave would be right behind it. No time, and no chance. Before even deciding to, she had her blade in hand.

With one last glance at Lucas, she sliced the line and watched it fall away. She looked up to see a solid wall of furious, roiling fire sweeping toward her.

Lucas felt the sudden lurch of gravity as he fell again. The line was loose in his hands, but he grabbed it with white knuckles anyway. He fell backward, looking up at the doomed airship. In the bay doors, Eliza waved, then was engulfed in flames.

With a deafening boom, the shock wave hit Lucas next, propelling him down to earth even faster. He spun through the air, then crashed into the pond, driven down to the bottom. Above him, the HMS *Artemis* went nova.

The monster rampaged the length of the ship in the blink of an eye. Even twenty-five feet under water, the glare was blinding, and Lucas squeezed his eyes shut tight.

He still saw Eliza.

MADELAINE BROWNING

Tesla realized he was drifting back to consciousness.

He couldn't see anything, then decided that was to be expected, since he hadn't opened his eyes yet. His fingers moved, and he felt the tight-knit carpet of his room. He sensed someone else in the room with him. He smelled something pleasant. Perfume?

He willed his eyes to open, and the sudden light stabbed into his sore head. "Ohh," he moaned and shut them again.

"Come on, you can do it," a female voice coaxed.

His forehead scrunched, wondering if the voice understood how badly he felt.

But he looked again and saw a cute, blurry female kneeling over him. Her long blonde hair was familiar. "Savannah?" he whispered.

"Ha!" The girl laughed. "Hey, Mom, he isn't dead after all."

His eyes focused, and he realized the girl above him was around twelve. That would make her...

Savannah walked into sight, standing behind her daughter. "You gave us a real fright, Nikola."

Tesla stared at Savannah, then at the cheery face right above him. The resemblance was quite strong.

"Madelaine Browning," he said. "Despite the circumstances, it's a pleasure to meet you."

She smiled, and he saw that her mother's infectious smile had been inherited, along with the blonde hair.

"Aw, what a gentleman. Flat on your back, and all polite still." She took his hand and pumped it twice. "A pleasure to meet you too, sir."

Savannah crouched beside him. "When you didn't arrive for our coffee, I grew concerned. Mrs. Harrison let us in. She's off calling for a doctor." She reached under his shoulder to lift him from the floor. "Here, let me help…"

He rolled forward and sat up. The headache was now a railroad spike through his brain, and the left side of his face felt thick and swollen.

"Ugh," he muttered.

"Indeed," said Savannah. "I'm guessing it wasn't my father who hit you."

He started to shake his head, then decided against it. "No. The colonel and I had a lovely evening, actually. This was… something else."

Savannah frowned. "Something else related to your gambling debts?"

"So you know about that."

"Of course, Nikola. You don't get cleared for the things you did without being checked out."

That made sense. "Yes, quite right. Of course," he agreed. "I'm afraid I'm not exactly at my best."

"You got that right, brother," offered Madelaine.

"Be nice," said Savannah.

With a hand from the two women, he got to his feet, then paused, making sure he could stand unassisted. So far, so good.

He set the overturned chair back upright and retrieved his overcoat from the floor. Hanging it back on its hook, he turned and found Madelaine inspecting his equipment.

Savannah still focused on him, her wary look telling him

he must look fairly rough.

"I'm fine, Mrs. Browning, really. I just need some sleep, is all."

"Uh-huh."

"Is this it? Is this the thing?" asked Madelaine, standing by the mechanical brain.

"That is my prototype neural net array," he told her, thinking instead about climbing into bed.

The answer didn't satisfy the girl, and she waited, eyebrows raised in question.

"That's the thing," said Savannah. "And you got it working, you said?"

He nodded, slowly. "I just did yesterday." The interest in his inventions pushed the throbbing pain back slightly. "Here, watch," he said.

He threw the browning apple into the trash can, and set a water glass where it had been. Then he flipped the power switch, and the machine snapped to life. Relays flickered back and forth, then the teletype chattered the machine's decision: "GLASS."

Madelaine clapped her hands enthusiastically. "Yay!"

"You really did it. A learning machine," said Savannah, one hand on her hip.

"I've trained it to recognize about a dozen items so far. I'd guess it could handle up to thirty. Not enough bandwidth for more than that. I'd have to increase the number of relays and connections."

"Still. It's an amazing breakthrough. And a necessary first step to our goal."

"Which is the reason for your visit."

"We're on a merciless schedule, Nikola. As you now know."

He remembered his night with her father. Despite his weariness, and the knowledge of the colonel's cancer, he smiled at the memories.

"Yes, I do know. And I'm very sorry for the news."

"Thank you. But I'm hoping you can offer us a lot more than sympathy. Can you, Nikola?"

Tesla sighed. His bed was beckoning him like a siren call. So tired…

And yet a glimmer of something hopeful welled up within him, rising to the surface. Was it pride? Arrogance? Optimism?

He'd always seen technology as the way to improve men's lives. Now he was being offered the chance to demonstrate that ideal, and on a momentous scale.

To build a machine capable of actual human thought. His ego savored the thought. His love for the excitement of a huge bet enjoyed the idea also. But the most convincing voice in his mind spoke to him of the joy of seeing such a creation come to life, having been born from nothing but his ideas.

"I will do it," he said.

Savannah beamed, rushing to hug him. "You will?"

"I will. If," he said, holding up his hand to thwart the embrace, "I can get some sleep first."

Savannah stopped short, her face glowing. She remembered his aversion to touch and dropped her arms. But knowing she'd secured Nikola Tesla to work with them filled her with happiness. She'd known they'd be losing her father soon, but today she felt more hopeful that in a sense, he could deny death and stay with them.

"You got it, Nikola. Get your rest. Because we have a lot of work to do."

He nodded, already shambling toward the bed. "And we will succeed. Tomorrow."

Savannah hustled her daughter to the door. On the way out, she called back, "I'll ask Mrs. Harrison not to disturb you. And don't worry. I'm going to have an MP posted outside your door, so you won't have any more unwelcome guests."

He stopped, surprised at the idea. "You can do that? Yes, I suppose you can."

Savannah peeked from behind his door. "You're a government asset now, Nikola. Which has its perks. Sleep well."

She closed the door gently, and Tesla fell into bed.

Before the women had even reached the street, he was asleep and dreaming of a vast open field of mechanical relays.

Under an electric sun, they stretched for miles, switching back and forth like wheat waving in the wind.

FIRST, NEW HAVEN

Under a waning crescent moon, Major Thomas stood on dry land again, for the first time in forty-three days, atop a sloping bluff. His mind told him the ground was rocking, but that would pass soon enough. A cold October breeze swam around him, and he pulled his coat tighter. The wind wove through the nearby tree line, forcing a soft rustling roar from the dried leaves. It would be dawn soon, and the early-morning chill gave him a shiver.

The bluff provided a fine view of the shallow harbor where the *Glasgow* waited at anchor. She couldn't get as close to the beach as he'd have preferred, but this frustration was a necessary first step. Things would only get easier from here.

His army of seven hundred soldiers had been coming ashore in longboats over the past several hours, and they were massing just over the bluff. He had allowed campfires to be built, and several men had already shot deer, soon to be skinned and roasted.

The men could use a good rest before attacking New Haven, but he didn't want to spend the time. Doubtless, some peasant had already reported their arrival.

So let the men have some warmth and good food while the supplies came ashore. He anticipated another six hours for the last of the men, the twenty horses, six cannons and their supplies of food and ammunition.

Two of his officers approached, leading a thin, slight man between them. *And this must be the traitor.*

"Welcome to America, Major," said the man. "Good journey?"

Major Thomas looked down, taking in the man's unkempt appearance. He was unshaven, with hollow, sunken eyes, and his shirt boasted an orange patch of dried soup.

"You have maps for me?" the major replied.

"I do, yessir." He reached into his jacket and withdrew a thick folded document. "The city layout, complete with important sites marked. The armory, city hall, church, mill, even the tannery, the oyster beds, and the clockworks factory. I also circled the richest homesteads," he said, proud of his thoroughness.

The major took the map from the toad.

"Pay him in full," he told the officers. They nodded, understanding, and led him away as he called back, "Good hunting, generous sir!"

A moment later a single gunshot rang out, and the toad was dead. The major's aversion to disloyalty was strong, despite the circumstances.

He turned and headed over the bluff, eager for a taste of American venison.

The rest of the day was long, filled with screams, gunfire, dirt, bayonet attacks, cannon explosions, and sweat.

But that evening the township of New Haven was theirs.

The Major had lost only fourteen men, to the Americans' ninety or so. Of course, they weren't soldiers. They were simple townsfolk defending their homes and business. *And rather badly, at that.*

He'd ordered a dozen of the resisters hanged and left to swing. A strong, visual reminder for those who may still harbor treachery in their hearts.

The major formed detachments to secure and search key buildings. A proper perimeter was established, and scouts were sent into the surrounding area. Census records were being checked for land holdings, and where the best farms lay. The port defenses had been pacified, and his men were preparing for the arrival of their reinforcements.

A total success, thought the major. He guessed Boston would not be as easy.

But he was eager to find out.

BOSTON MUST HOLD

WASHINGTON, DC

Inside the State, War, and Navy Building, President Roosevelt paced as if the movement would somehow erase the news he'd just been told.

"I can't believe it. How did this happen?"

The long table was circled by a dozen generals and policy experts, but none had a ready answer for the commander in chief.

General Houston spread his hands and spoke. His singsong Tennessee accent was disarmingly charming, and appreciated, given the situation.

"Mr. President, all we know so far is what our man in the airbase saw. The team picked up the explosives and successfully boarded the *Artemis*. Shortly after that, Einstein left the ship, and the king went up instead. It's probable that our team didn't even know the situation had changed."

"This complicates things considerably," Roosevelt said, wearing a path in the thick carpet. "England's population wasn't entirely behind this war. They could have lost a scientist, and that wouldn't change. But this?"

"I know, sir."

"You don't see your country's ruler assassinated and stay on the sidelines. They'll rally now, behind whoever takes over."

"Absolutely," added General John Pershing. "And our guess is, that man will be Winston Churchill."

"The alcoholic prime minister? He doesn't seem the type."

"I've seen him speak, sir. I think you'd be surprised. He has a real talent for uniting people behind a banner."

"Well, we've given him one hell of a cause."

The general's eyes fell. "That we did, Mr. President."

Roosevelt caught the man's shift in mood.

"I know you didn't approve of the action. This was my decision."

General Houston cut in. "Water under the bridge, sir. What matters now is how we go forward. How's the Asian empire taking all this?"

Roosevelt shrugged. "They're staying out of it, letting us and the Crowns beat our brains out. Smart."

He gestured to a file folder laid open on the wide table. "We've lost New Haven. That English major has a full battalion, and he is gathering his forces. He won't be content to sit still for long."

"I know."

"The Joint Chiefs and I have ordered three companies to move in, but it will take some time to mobilize a larger force."

"Tell me about that. What's the plan?"

Secretary of War Elihu Root stood and walked to a large chalkboard on the wall, covered with a rough sketch of the Eastern Seaboard. New Haven was marked, as was New York City, Yonkers, Providence, and Boston.

"Mr. President, as the general said, the military intelligence division tells us the English have a full battalion, that's seven hundred men, stationed in New Haven. If we—"

"I'm quite aware of military organization, Root," the president said.

"Ah, yes, sir. We assume that Boston is their goal, so we're bringing the Second Cavalry over from Albany, the Seventh

Infantry up from Yonkers, and the Third Artillery Battery in Providence is already well positioned."

"Good. But not exactly overwhelming force. Sounds like an even fight."

"Roughly, it is, sir. We have more options out of Columbus, Ohio, but that will take time."

The president frowned. "If they take the deep water port in Boston, we'll have a hell of a time getting them out of there."

General Houston nodded. "Quite true, sir. Their land force will get resupplied by sea. And the city is defensible, being half surrounded by water."

"Then it must hold. How's the garrison there?"

"At half strength. They sent a lot of boys into the fight before the Armistice, and funding pressures have held back a full recovery of enlistments."

The president scowled at the bad news. He turned away and walked the length of the room, lighting a thick cigar. He pulled the hot smoke in, and let it linger before blowing it up at the ceiling.

"Well, goddamn," he said.

The room waited in silence as he took another long drag.

"Forgive me, General," he said, turning back to the men. "How is your team? Did they make it out all right?"

"Only one, I'm afraid. Our man in the base saw the team leader fall from the *Artemis* just before the explosion. Managed to pull him from a lake before the Crowns covered the area. He's recovering on a steamer now, heading back home to Tennessee."

"Back to your neck of the woods."

"Yes, sir."

"Well, that's something. Keep me apprised of his condition, will you?"

"Certainly, Mr. President."

"What about Beowulf? About now, we could use a force multiplier."

"Savannah did get Tesla to join us, but not even he knows how to build what we need. At least, not yet. It's going to take time."

"Not a lot of that to go around."

"Rarely is, Mr. President," General Houston agreed.

A FAREWELL TO KINGS

LONDON, ENGLAND

The night had been a fine, fun affair for newly appointed Prime Minister Winston Churchill. A fund-raising dinner in the country had gone long, and there'd been excellent champagne and scotch before, during, and after the meal. Despite his reputation, he rarely drank to excess, preferring instead a consistent minimal amount of alcohol in his system. Tonight was the exception to that rule, however.

His bodyguard had helped him to the car, and as ordered, brought Churchill back to the office, rather than home to bed. There were always reports on his desk of great interest, and he found it difficult to stay away, especially after such a fine evening.

Arriving at the office, he allowed his man to provide some balance as they climbed the steps together. As soon as they swung open the door to his secretary's office, he knew something had happened. The room was filled with various officials and military officers.

"What is it? What's happened?" he demanded.

The room was silent, each person looking to another.

"Come along!" he yelled.

General Taylor stepped forward. "Sir, there was an incident aboard the *Artemis*. The king is dead."

"What?" he bellowed. His mind rejected the notion as simply not possible.

He scanned the room and now saw fear on faces wherever he turned. They'd lost their king in war. It would knock the wind from anyone.

He nodded acceptance of the fact. Their world had changed.

"In ten minutes I wish to see Generals Cornwallis and Taylor. Also, Home Secretary Nelson and a typist," he told the room, then walked to his office door unsteadily, waving off offers of help.

"You're drunk!" said Bessie Braddock, the bulldog-faced vice-chair of the Labour party. Her abrasive nature had clashed with Churchill many times before, and he was in no mood for it. The country had lost a king, and he had no plan to calm their anxiety, besides taking ten minutes to develop one. And this woman was wasting his time.

He stopped and turned to her. "Bessie, my dear, you are ugly, and what's more, you are disgustingly ugly. But tomorrow I shall be sober, and you will still be disgustingly ugly."

Not waiting for a retort, Churchill entered his private office and slammed the door.

A FATHER RETURNS

"All this is for me?" Tesla asked.

He stood on the sidewalk outside a colonial-style house. It was white, with green shutters and comfortably set back from the street. Near the center of the wide front yard, a willow oak rose majestically seventy feet high. It predated the military base, and had given shade to the surrounding land for over two hundred years.

"Visiting dignitary housing," said Savannah. "I'd say you qualify."

"I'm touched. Thank you."

"Come on, let's get you settled in." She strolled up the winding driveway and let them inside.

The home was spacious, well appointed and already furnished with anything an important guest may desire. Savannah gave him a quick tour of the main rooms, and he saw his things had already been delivered. Each room held several boxes of his belongings, waiting to be unpacked.

The house felt far too large for him, coming from a rented room. Mrs. Harrison had wished him well, and he knew the feelings to be genuine. While pleasantly surprised to be paid in full by the army, she was also wistful at losing her eccentric guest.

Savannah finished their tour in a small library, and Tesla was delighted when he leaned in to scan the book titles.

"Marconi… Kelvin… Einstein… even Theodor Wulf?" He looked up, beaming.

"Yeah, I took the liberty of stocking the shelves a bit. Some of your books are in there too."

He looked at the wall of ceiling-high bookshelves, shaking his head in amazement. "This is an impressive technical library, by any standard, Mrs. Browning. And you place it in my new home?"

"I told you, Nikola. This project has to work. It just has to. So whatever you need, you'll have."

"I'm flattered," he said, now beginning to feel the weight of the task expected of him.

He stepped to the window, overlooking the yard and the graceful old oak. "I've been working the problem around in my mind," he said then grew quiet.

Savannah slid into a leather-upholstered club chair and waited.

He blinked and continued. "My previous estimation was not hyperbole. It would take billions of connected relays to simulate the structure of the human brain. Even with a government's resources at work, it's just not possible. Not to manufacture, nor to maintain. Not to mention the size requirements."

"Then we must be as clever as nature."

Tesla nodded his head once, staring out the window. The moment drew out, and she was content to be patient.

After several minutes he sighed and turned to her. "Someday, it will be practical to run street cars in California using power from Niagara Falls."

"I believe you."

"Or wireless communications around the world. These are the types of challenges I have set myself to. But war interrupts progress. Today the most civilized countries of the world spend a maximum of their income on war and a minimum on education. I think the twenty-first century will reverse this order."

She admired his optimism, but couldn't decide if she shared it. "That would be a good world to live in."

"It will be," he said. "It will be more glorious to fight against ignorance than to die on the field of battle. The discovery of a new scientific truth will be more important than the squabbles of diplomats."

She smiled, wanting to touch him. "I'm surprised you never married. That kind of talk sounds like a man wanting a better world for his children."

"I do not think you can name many great inventions made by a married man," he told her. "I don't believe an inventor should marry."

"Why's that?"

"Because he has so intense a nature, that in giving himself to a woman he might love, he would give everything, and thus take everything from his chosen field."

She saw the truth in his words, but they also made her sad. Being a parent was an amazing experience, one she wished everyone could enjoy. But some people were made for other things.

He continued. "I do, though, want that better world. And I think my inventions will in some way help bring that about. I think we have that obligation, to make things better."

"I agree. Having Maddy meant I worked even harder for that. You just want to happily do anything for them. It's amazing, and humbling."

"I do envy you that, I admit."

"Well, who knows? You're still young."

Tesla grinned. "Anything is possible, I suppose. Forgive me, but the colonel alluded to Madelaine's father. Is he—"

"He's alive. But… it's complicated."

"Such things often are."

114

"Not like this," she said. "I wasn't always a liaison officer. Before that I worked in the field."

"Not in battle," Tesla said.

"No, certainly not. But I was behind enemy lines, so to speak. I was sent to England by the intelligence division. My Mother was English, so I fit in fairly well. My mission was to marry an English officer, and to gather what information I could."

"My God," said Tesla. "That's incredible. You did that?"

"I did that. Landed in London and met an infantry captain right away. He was handsome and ambitious, everything a girl could want. We were married within six months."

"So Madelaine is…"

"Yes. Her father is an English officer. We were together for five years before he found out I was sending intel back to Washington. He was never a kind man, but after that… I grabbed Maddy, and we ran for it. I started overseeing scientists instead."

"Astounding. I'd have never guessed!"

"That would be the idea."

"Yes, right. So, her father?"

"Extremely bitter, as you'd expect. I think it broke his heart, honestly. I felt badly over that, I really did. But I saved a lot of American lives with the reports I sent back. It's just a balance I had to deal with. Still do some days."

"Will you ever see him again?"

"Until last week I'd have said no. But now? Maybe so. He's made major now. Archibald Thomas. And he's recently landed in New Haven."

X-RAYS

"Dally, I've told you repeatedly, those X-rays are dangerous!" Edison told his assistant.

Clarence Dally grinned and nodded. "Ya, ya. I know. But what isn't these days?" His smile was handsome, even aristocratic, as many ladies had indicated to him over his twenty-seven years. But he'd happily settled down and had two wonderful children to show for it.

At Edison's lab in Menlo Park, scores of men worked on a dozen projects, but one of the most bizarre involved research into the strange nature of X-rays. For months Dally had led the group and had developed a fascination with the beguiling invisible light.

"The price of opening new frontiers," said Dally's brother Charles, as he unsealed another canister of calcium tungstate, which they'd found to be superior to barium platinocyanide as the main emitter source.

He had accurately described their work. Together the brothers had greatly advanced Rontgen's work on a X-ray focus tube.

They'd improved the fluoroscope, and the cone-shaped device was able to see right through solid objects, with remarkable sharpness. Doctors and surgeons were especially giddy with the possibilities.

As was his habit, Dally was holding his hand on top of the

scope, allowing the invisible light to pass up through his skin, blood, and bones to then be collected and made visible through a specially coated eyepiece. He wiggled his fingers, and never tired of seeing his bones move about.

After an exposure of ten seconds, he pulled his hand back. A sore, red patch had developed along the back of his palm, but it wasn't terribly painful. He scratched at it absently.

"A little itching is a small price to pay, eh?" asked his brother.

"You said it." The brothers knew a good thing when they saw it. Once perfected this invention would make them all wealthy.

Edison had good reason to fear the new technology. Using a smaller scope than the brothers currently worked with, he had exposed his left eye to the rays, and come away with that eye considerably out of focus. An optometrist told him the damage put his eye twelve inches out of focus, and he couldn't say if the change was permanent or not. He shied away from the technology after that, but the Dally brothers were adamant the work was worth the risk.

"Just be careful, please," said Edison. "Frontiersmen often died young, you know."

Dally waved his hand at his mentor. He did love to worry.

A VEXING CHALLENGE

Tesla and Colonel Browning watched as Bertram scratched a long formula on the blackboard. Before he'd finished, Tesla leaped up.

"No, no!" he said, snatching the chalk from the R&D chief's hand. "The squashing function of the output values must be done this way." He found a clean section of board and whipped out a differing formula for the math needed.

"Ah yes," said Bertram. "I see that now. A very useful methodology."

Shooting pain ran from the colonel's chest down to his thigh, and he winced silently. He leaned against the table for support, careful to not let the others notice.

"Useful, but not sufficient," said Tesla, tossing aside the chalk. He banged his palm down on a worktable, startling three nearby technicians.

"Easy, son," said the colonel. "We'll get there."

Tesla had been working in the lab for a week, enjoying the resources available to him, but still no closer to a solution than when he'd begun. He had a staff of eighteen researchers, access to Hollerith's computer research, and the freedom to explore any line of thought he considered worthwhile. So far none of it had mattered. The colonel's presence reminded him just how much was at stake. And how little time remained.

Seven days of failure. The hulking mass of the Beowulf

118

tank still sat quiet, awaiting Tesla's work to bear fruit. He turned and looked up at the steel war machine. Without a human mind to drive it, the beast was inert, a sixty-ton pile of organized steel, coal, bullets, and wiring.

Beowulf had a comfortably sized crew compartment and could carry a half-dozen men within it, but this compartment had been built for observers or special operations, not general usage. No human crew could operate at the speed needed to fulfill Beowulf's potential. There were too many weapon systems and variables involved for a disjointed crew to handle effectively. The machine had been designed to be controlled by a single brain, one that could compute strategy and tactics at lightning speed.

In front of Beowulf, a set of massive steel doors reached the lab's ceiling. They were just wide and tall enough to allow the tank to drive through, and they opened to a long concrete corridor, built especially to let the tank leave the Rabbit Hole.

The lab was dug into the side of a large hillside, and down here at their bottom level, the corridor extended out to the base of the hill. There, another set of huge blast doors protected the lab, capable of stopping anything, up to and including a radiological bomb.

Tesla glanced at the massive steel doors, hoping he'd get to see them open.

"What about the other side of the problem?" Bertram asked.

"You mean reading the impulses from the colonel's brain?"

"Yes, precisely."

"I spent a few days on that, when I was making no progress here." He pointed to a far table with an assortment of gear strewn on it. "I believe I have that side of the problem solved. Measuring such minute electrical signals was tricky, but much easier than this."

"I fear I'm not being of much help to you Nikola," said Bertram. His glasses were sliding down his nose, and he pressed them back up.

"The fault isn't yours. I appreciate the attempt."

Tesla surveyed the board, then swept his eyes over the worktables. His prototype brain had been expanded and pushed to its limit, in order to better understand the potential of his network of relays. The device had turned out to be capable of recognizing forty-eight items, after some additional improvements had been made. The training cycle for each object had been reduced from several minutes down to seven seconds.

A mechanical brain that learned so quickly would have been a marvel and cause for celebration, but compared to Tesla's true goal, it fell short by a laughable margin.

Madelaine approached and hopped onto a tall work stool beside Bertram. He tousled her hair, which she hated, but put up with.

Bertram knew he had nothing more to offer and decided to take his leave. He collected his clipboard and pile of books. "I will leave you to it then," he said.

As he left, Madelaine looked up at him. "Can we continue our chess lessons tonight?" she asked.

Bertram smiled. "Absolutely. Tonight, we discuss the Knight and his cunning reach."

"Cool," she said.

Tesla waved good-bye. "Thank you."

Bertram returned the wave and headed off, wondering if the mess hall was still open.

Madelaine sat quietly, spinning herself on the stool.

The motion drew Tesla's attention. "Shouldn't you be in school, young miss?"

"It's Sunday, Mr. Tesla," she said.

"Oh. Is it?"

"For the whole day."

He smiled, glancing at the colonel and saw his knowing smile. *Precocious, indeed.*

She looked like a smaller version of her mother, he thought. In a few years, when boys became interesting, her mother would have one more thing to worry about.

"Are you close to fixing it?" she asked.

"I am not, sadly."

"What's the problem?"

How to explain such a thing to a child? He thought for a moment. "There's just too much complexity in a human brain to fit within any device I know how to build."

She looked at his prototype. "That's a lot bigger than someone's head."

He laughed. "If only it were that simple."

"Hmm," she said, then turned to Beowulf. "They should paint it red and black. My favorite colors are red and black."

"That would be something," he agreed. "Like American Indian war paint."

"Yeah!" she cried. "My Mom said Beowulf was a warrior, a long time ago."

Tesla nodded. "From a very old poem. He saved his village by slaying the monster Grendel."

"So the British are our Grendel?"

"An apt analogy, yes."

"Why do they want to fight us?" she asked.

Tesla looked to the colonel, but he shook his head. "Let's hear your estimation, Nikola."

"Like most wars, I imagine it's over resources. The oil in Texas, and now the gold being found in Alaska. We have a lot of things other countries want."

"Don't they have their own?"

"Not enough, I suppose."

She thought about that for a moment. "At school Rebecca

had a chocolate bar I wanted. When she wasn't looking, I took a bite. A big one."

Tesla studied the young girl intensely. "Then you are a wicked, wicked girl."

"Am not!" she cried. "Take that back!"

"Yes," the colonel jumped in, straight-faced. "A wicked, warmongering little girl." He nodded in solemn agreement.

"It was just a bite, Mr. Tesla."

He shrugged his shoulders. "A big one, you said. This is how such things begin."

She scrunched up her face, fairly sure they were teasing her now.

"In fact," he continued, "I wouldn't be surprised to hear of armed conflict down at Fernwood Middle School any day now."

She perched on the stool, arms folded over her chest, pouting. "You're mean."

"At times," he agreed, then returned to his work.

A POOR LIAR, BUT A BRAVE ONE

NEW HAVEN, CONNECTICUT

Young Paul Harris had been inside the city hall once before, when his father sought permission to expand his grazing pasture, but on that day, he didn't wonder if he was about to die.

Two Redcoats pushed him forward into the mayor's office. He tripped over the rug, but caught himself before falling. He didn't want to give them anything to feel smug about.

He looked up to see a highly decorated British officer behind the mayor's desk, reviewing papers. The officer smiled without looking up, then continued focusing on the reports of confiscations his men had made.

Paul stood tall and shrugged off the restraining hand on his shoulder. He wished he had something sassy to say, but nothing came to mind.

At length the officer made some notes on the reports and set them aside. He stood and walked around the desk, facing the young man. Paul met his gaze, and a mutual dislike was instantly formed.

"I'm Major Archibald Thomas," said the officer. "I've brought you here because the city records indicate your father was stationed in New York, at Fort Hamilton, six months ago. Is that accurate?"

Paul wondered what the major was after. Sure, he knew the general layout of the base, but he certainly didn't know any military secrets. He began to tell the major to ask his father, if he wanted to know so badly.

But then he remembered his father was dead, killed in the attack on the city. Even after a week, he couldn't believe his father was gone. Unless he walked by the West Gate, where his father's body still hung.

"My father was stationed there," he said, holding back a tear. "What about it?"

"There was a Colonel Browning there? Second-in-command?"

That was public knowledge. "Yeah."

The major leaned forward now, his dark eyes open wide, taking in everything Paul said or didn't say.

"And his daughter? Savannah?"

Paul's breath caught in his throat. It wasn't a military secret, or anything like that, but it was so unexpected. He remembered the kind, beautiful blonde and her little girl. What was her name? It was a cookie of some sort. Florentine? Rosette? Madelaine! That was it.

"Haven't heard of her," he said.

The major's mouth stretched wide, turning up into the grin of a jackal watching the antelope fall. "So she *is* there!" He ran his hand over his chin. "Outstanding…"

He stood lost in thought for a moment, already imagining Savannah brought before him, then turned back to Paul.

"You Americans are no better at telling a lie than you are at telling the truth."

The major thought about what to do with the boy. He was young, strong, and brave. Three traits not desired in an enemy. And the years after Savannah had hardened the major beyond mercy.

He looked at the Redcoats. "Hang him with his father."

HELPFUL APPARITION

"I didn't see you at dinner."

Tesla looked up, surprised to see Savannah, and no one else, in the lab with him. She carried a tray with a large silver dome on it. *Women seem to always be bringing me food.*

He looked around. "What time is it?"

She set the dinner down beside him, sliding aside a coil of twelve-gauge wire. "Ten o'clock. Can't have you wasting away, can we?"

With a flourish she lifted the silver dome, revealing a large sandwich.

He lifted the top slice of bread and peered inside.

"Chicken, mustard, and cheese?"

She shrugged. "I never said I could cook."

"It will be fine, thank you." He took a bite of the sandwich to back up the words. *Interesting.* He set the sandwich back down.

"Any progress?" she asked.

He threw up his hands. "I don't know. Sometimes I think yes. But now… I just don't know."

He had taken over an entire workstation, covering it with hundreds of relays. The wiring that interconnected them was a blizzard of insulated wire. When the relay network was active, it reminded him of his dream, which was not unusual. Many ideas came to him from dreams or otherwise altered states of consciousness.

"This model is eight times more complex than my first prototype. I thought it would be a more suitable sandbox to experiment within. It works well, in that it is capable of learning eight times more objects than before."

Savannah waited for the summation.

"Which is to say, I am no closer now than before," he admitted, his shoulders slumping.

"You'll get it, Nikola, I know you will."

He flashed a half grin of thanks. "This is interesting though," he said, pointing her attention to a section of the connecting wires. They were not insulated, just bare copper wires. Now that she looked, she saw several other patches of bare wire across the table.

Tesla placed his hand on a patch of the naked wires and with his other hand, flipped the power on.

"Nikola!" she cried, reaching to pull his arm away.

"It's fine. The amperage is quite small. See?" he said, holding his hand on the wires, with no distress. "What's intriguing is how the human body can serve as a measuring device. Each differing pattern of current running through this network has a different feel."

He pulled his hand away. "Here, try it," he said.

Savannah looked sideways at the inventor. Live current wasn't something to trifle with. But Tesla quite possibly knew more about electrical forces than anyone else on the planet. She placed her hand on the bare copper.

"Oh wow!" she exclaimed, feeling the prickly forces running along her skin.

"Now, wait, and notice the difference."

Tesla slid a teapot out of the device's field of view. The electricity flow changed, minutely. She scrunched her forehead as she leaned in, trying to identify just how it had changed.

"Try something else," she told him.

He picked up a heavy book on the aurora borealis and placed it where the machine could see it.

Savannah smiled, delighted by the subtle shift in the electrical flow. "It's like it changes flavor."

"Indeed. A helpful diagnostic tool, isn't it?"

"I can see that." She took her hand away. "Just so long as you're careful."

"Yes, yes. Of course. With amperages this low, extremely high voltages are still safe."

Savannah took in the relay network. "I love the way you play with the current. It's like water for you, flowing here and there."

He nodded. "That's not a bad analogy. In some ways electricity does behave like water." He waved his hand over the large table. "It sloshes this way, then—"

His head cocked to the side and he froze. "I—" he began, then went silent. In his mind, he pictured the liquid-like flow of current running through the network, then smashing into the end of the network. If the current really were like waves of water, they could rebound, and crash back in the opposite direction. And in that moment, the answer came.

Since childhood a curious phenomenon would visit him at unpredictable occasions. He would see a new idea for an invention, but not just roll it around in his mind like other people. He would actually see the device floating in the air before him, completely rendered in three dimensions, down to the smallest detail. And once this happened, his memory captured every aspect, as if he'd instantly sketched all the diagrams needed to recreate the idea in reality.

Savannah's mention of water triggered such an episode, and the answer sprang into being, just inches in front of him, floating in the space above his workstation. He saw the current being bounced back and forth across the relay network, and his understanding of radio waves provided the final missing key.

"I see it," said Tesla.

Savannah felt a chill, watching Tesla have one of his famous visions. "The answer?" she asked.

He sat still as a marble bust, only moving his lips to respond. "Yes. It's all here. It adds an elegant layer to the existing work, so it shouldn't take long. I know how to make this possible now."

Savannah brought her hands to cover her mouth. The sense of elation filled her and threatened to break out. She knew her feelings about this man had been correct. The justification was warm and comforting.

She gave no heed to the chance of his idea not working. If he said it would solve their problem, then it would.

"What do you need?" she asked.

Tesla reached out his hand to touch the floating device. His fingers passed straight through it as if he'd dipped his hand into a pool of reflective water.

"Fascinating," he said.

He blinked, and the apparition vanished.

Turning to her, he said, "I need quiet. Please let no one else in here until eight o'clock tomorrow morning. I think I will have your machine ready by then."

"Eight o'clock," she confirmed. "The lab is yours, Nikola."

She left him alone and posted a sign forbidding anyone to enter.

Then she headed home to Madelaine and to lay in bed for a joyous, sleepless night.

The following morning the entire lab was abuzz with speculation. Most recognized the inventor's genius, but the size of the task was considered impossible by many. Still, a hopeful ripple of anticipation ran through the small crowd gathering at the Rabbit Hole's upper level.

General Houston, the colonel and Savannah were there. Thomas Edison had been cleared for the lab and was on hand. Bertram, Sophia, and a half-dozen other senior researchers were milling around, checking the time repeatedly. Madelaine was with them also, nearly lost behind the group of taller adults.

Savannah paced, unable to contain her enthusiasm. If he had really cracked the mystery, this was a world-changing event. Of course, such things were the raison d'être of the lab, but this was special. This could save her father's life, in a sense. She checked her watch.

"It's time," she announced to the impatient group. They all crowded together on the elevator platform, and she brought them down to Tesla's level.

As they neared the bottom of the elevator shaft, Bertram addressed Edison.

"You're in for a treat today, I think, Mr. Edison. Tesla will come through, I know it."

Edison wore a slight frown for the occasion. "I hope you're right, Bertram. There's a lot riding on a man with impossible dreams and who dresses like a Parisian."

The elevator had just opened into the final floor of the lab, and Edison's words carried.

Tesla stood, waiting for the group. He was tall, dapper, and in command. In a glance Savannah knew he'd succeeded.

Tesla called up to the crowd, still descending to the lab's floor. "The ladies seem to appreciate my stylish dress, Mr. Edison."

Edison felt his face flush, embarrassed at having been overheard.

"As for my impossible dreams," Tesla continued, "my imaginings have often proved equivalent to realities."

Edison merely smiled in response.

The group reached the lab's floor and stepped forward, milling around Tesla in a semicircle.

While often quiet and brooding, when Tesla wanted attention, he gained it easily. He stood ramrod straight, hands folded behind his back, and in a clear, strong voice, started his explanation.

"The device is complete," he began, and the group broke into applause and hearty shouts. He waited for them to subside, then continued.

"Today's scientists have substituted mathematics for experiments, and they wander off through equation after equation, and eventually build a structure which has no relation to reality."

He pointed behind him to the relay network. It looked much as it did the night before, but now thick metal boxes sat at either end.

"For this, I began with basic mathematics and then refined the idea mechanically, through tuning the resonance the network requires. As you all know, it would be impossible to build enough connections to mimic the brain and allow for consciousness. The trick therefore was to use the existing network we have, but to use it repeatedly."

He stepped to the table and pointed out the new metal boxes.

"These phased reflectors bounce the impulses back through the network, but at a slightly different frequency. The impulses reach the far side, and the process repeats. This back-and-forth reflection multiplies the effective number of connections."

"Damned clever," said Bertram.

"So while we only have two thousand and forty-eight wired connections here on the table, this back-and-forth action is repeated millions of times, each on its own frequency, making it complex enough to support sentience, at least in theory. It is now an empty vessel, but one with the same storage capacity of the human mind."

Savannah couldn't hold back anymore and grabbed Tesla in a quick bear hug. "You did it. I knew you would!"

In a mild panic at her physical intrusion, he smiled awkwardly and raised his hands up, waiting for her to release him. "I call it the Reciprocating Cascade Array," he offered.

She broke the hug, but held him by the shoulders. "RCA," she said. "I like it."

"It will have many uses, both within the military and without. After the war we should form a company to market it."

General Houston stepped forward. "So what's the next step, Mr. Tesla?"

"The device is ready for testing. We just need to reconfigure it to fit inside Beowulf's brain cavity. It will be tedious work, but fairly simple. I think by dinner tonight, my team and I can have the relays remounted and integrated inside Beowulf."

"That's fantastic news, Mr. Tesla. Well done, sir," said the general. "Apparently, your reputation was genuine."

Madelaine stood off to the side, with a wide grin plastered across her face. She gave him a thumbs-up sign.

Edison broke in. "Well, let's see if it actually works first."

Savannah turned and gave him a withering glare, then her sense of office politics returned, and she forced a smile. "Of course, Mr. Edison. Proof is in the pudding."

Tesla clapped his hands twice loudly. "I need all Beowulf technicians now. Paulson, you take six men and remove Hollerith's device from Beowulf, please. The rest of you, assist me in remounting the relays into a cube structure, and the rewiring. It will be a long day, but a rewarding one. Let's begin!"

Technicians dispersed throughout the lab, all eager to dig

131

into their tasks. Within a minute the dignitaries were forgotten as workers discussed details of the needed work.

General Houston turned to the remaining VIPs. "I suppose we are dismissed," he said with a rueful grin.

While they headed back to the elevator to let the technicians do their work, Edison held back and sided up beside Tesla. He leaned in and whispered into the man's ear.

"I don't want to see Colonel Browning die, but this is an abomination of technology, Tesla. It is just plain wrong."

Tesla coolly met Edison's glare.

"I doubt the colonel would agree. Now get out of my lab."

EMPIRES OF THE MIND

LONDON, ENGLAND

Churchill entered his private office, stunned by the news of the king's death. Adrenaline had already sharpened his focus, but he wanted more. He unlatched the window and swung it open, enjoying the brisk night air. He drank in a deep lungful of the coldness and released it.

How could the king be dead? What did it mean? What did the country need to hear? What did their enemies need to hear?

With no heir, the rule of law fell to the prime minister, which placed Britain as close to a democracy as they'd ever been. Churchill had sometimes said the best argument against a democracy is a five-minute conversation with the average voter. But those average voters were whom he needed to speak to now. They must be calmed, reassured, and then inspired.

It would be a long night, and his body would benefit from more water. He splashed a smidgen of Johnnie Walker in a tumbler, just enough to cover the bottom, then filled it with water. His time in British India had taught him the trick to "purify" bad water, and he'd learned to enjoy it. His daughter called it a Papa Cocktail.

There was a soft knock at his door. "Come," he called.

His top generals entered, followed by the home secretary,

and a pretty girl carrying a typewriter. He waved them in and leaned against the windowsill, letting the air cool his back. The typist got set up and nodded when she was ready.

"Go ahead," he told her.

He addressed the officials, all still standing. "Tell me what you know."

General Cornwallis spoke first, a tall, thin man with a family heritage most would kill for. "Hours ago, the HMS *Artemis* went airborne for a scheduled flight test. A few minutes into the flight, an explosion occurred that ignited the hydrogen cells. The ship was destroyed in seconds."

The typist worked her keys, recording everything the men said.

"Why was the king aboard?"

"That we're not sure of, sir. The base staff tells us a large party of friends joined the king aboard the ship. It did not appear to be a planned event."

"Didn't it? That's interesting. Do you think—"

A quick, insistent rapping at the door interrupted Churchill. "What is it?" he yelled.

The door opened, and Albert Einstein entered. He looked pale and furtive.

"Perfect timing, Professor Einstein. Join us," said Churchill. "The general tells me the king may not have been scheduled for the flight?"

"He most certainly was not, sir. I was. The flight test was solely for me and my team. The king arrived and surprised everyone. Ordered me off the *Artemis* and took off."

Churchill looked at the leaders in the room, and they all understood the situation. The true target had been this scientist. Their king had been murdered by accident.

Instinctively, Churchill committed to memory the names of everyone who knew this fact, then he stepped across the room and pulled the paper out of the typist's machine.

"Thank you, my dear. We won't be needing you, after all."

The girl nodded and made her exit as Churchill found his cigar lighter and lit the paper on fire.

Einstein continued. "Someone went to a lot of trouble to kill me. So I came straight here, I don't know where else is safe. I can't very well go home."

Churchill dropped the burning paper into a fruit bowl, where it curled and blackened.

"Certainly not, Professor. It seems you are America's biggest fear, which is good."

"Good?" asked Einstein.

"You have enemies," Churchill said. "That means you've stood up for something, sometime in your life."

Einstein found little comfort in the words, though he appreciated the sentiment.

"I've read the reports of your work with great interest. These new radiological bombs, they can make an entire city uninhabitable?"

"Yes, sir. The radiation fallout can do just that, for many months or years."

"Incredible. I can see why they want you dead," Churchill said, sipping his water. "The empires of the future are the empires of the mind. Scientists like yourself are a national resource."

General Nelson spoke up. "We can put him in embassy housing for a day or two, until a more permanent solution is found."

Churchill nodded. "Yes, do that." He turned to the scientist. "How many of these new bombs do you have?"

"Operational? Only six. But seventeen more are in process."

"And how many zeppelins capable of reaching the US mainland?"

"Having lost the *Artemis*, we have three long-range airships now, sir."

Churchill nodded. "All right then, I suggest we split the new bombs between the ships, and load on as many conventional warheads as possible. Then we get those birds in the air and on their way over the Atlantic. Generals?" he asked.

They both nodded. "Yes, sir," replied General Nelson. "That was the plan, after successful flight tests of the *Artemis*."

"Well, gentlemen, our schedule is pushed up," said Churchill. "I want those ships in the air by sunrise."

DEATH AND LIMERICKS

Tesla's lab was buzzing with activity. His team had worked all day, stripping wires from the relay network, then remounting the small switches onto a series of sixteen square boards. They were sized such that when sandwiched together, they would all fit within the steel cube of Beowulf's brain cavity. Rewiring the two thousand relays was tedious, as Tesla had predicted, but if they went carefully, the work was not difficult.

The boards were currently on Tesla's workstation, held in place by temporary ribs. They already formed a cube, and they fit inside the outline Tesla had marked on the table.

"Looking good, Mr. Tesla!"

He smiled, recognizing Madelaine's cheerful voice. "Why, thank you, young miss. I do believe we are getting there." He picked up a screwdriver and tightened down the restraining rails on an outer board.

"I'm thinking you're… an hour away from being done," she said, hopping onto a stool.

"I'm thinking you're about right. Where's your mom?"

"Upstairs in a meeting. The nuclear reactor had some problem."

Tesla raised an eyebrow. "Anything I should be worried about?"

"Nah, probably not," she said.

"That's a comfort."

"Not to worry, Mr. Tesla. They haven't had a serious problem in… oh, at least two months."

"What?" said Tesla, dropping his screwdriver.

"Just kidding!"

"Very amusing," he said, retrieving the lost tool.

"Hey, I've got something for you," she said, looking left and right to make sure no one was nearby. The furtive action drew his attention.

"Yes? Do tell."

"I know some great limericks," she whispered.

"Do you now? All right, let me have one."

"It's British," she said, then stood and cleared her throat, as if she were about to perform at Carnegie Hall.

"There was a young tart from Moss Side.

Who charged three pound sixteen for a ride.

For four twenty one,

You could enter her bum,

And a tenner would make her your bride."

She covered her mouth and burst out laughing at her own joke. "Told you it's good!"

Tesla tried to hide the smile that crept across his lips, but could not.

"It's a good one. I bet Mr. Edison would appreciate it, you should go tell him."

"I doubt that!" she said. "He's a bit stuffy, if you ask— oh," she said, getting his prank late.

She wagged a finger at him. "Naughty. Going to have to be careful with you."

"Nikola!" yelled Savannah.

Tesla's head snapped up at the urgent tone in her voice. She was descending on the elevator platform, along with the General, Edison, and several men he'd not met. Then he saw Colonel Browning, lying on his back on a gurney. Savannah was holding his hand and whispering to him.

She stood up and cried to Tesla again. "We're out of time! We have to do this now!"

"Oh God," said Tesla. "Madelaine, stand aside, dear."

She stood frozen, mouth open, then said, "Save him, Mr. Tesla." Without waiting for a reply, she bolted out of the way.

The elevator settled to the floor, and two medical staff lifted the gurney over the small steps, setting the colonel down gently. They wheeled him over to where Tesla stood, waiting.

"Can we do it, Nikola?" asked Savannah.

He looked at the cube on his table, not fully assembled.

"The mechanics are in place. I was just going to run some final checks before integrating it with Beowulf."

He looked down at the colonel. The man was awake, but his eyes fluttered. He was struggling to breathe. The nurse held a finger over his wrist and called out, "Pulse down to forty-two!"

Tesla nodded. "Yes. Yes, we can do this now."

He swept his arm across his workstation, clearing an area. Tools, fuses, and papers clattered to the floor. He called out to a young man working closer to the huge tank.

"George, bring me the reader, hurry!"

While Tesla disconnected testing circuits, the technician sprinted to a nearby table and scooped up a large metal sphere. A thick bundle of wires trailed from it, like the nerves from a huge eye. He brought it over and set it down carefully in the space Tesla had cleared.

"Hang on, Colonel," Tesla said. "I just need another minute…"

Savannah stood beside him, wanting to explode, but just squeezed her father's hand.

Tesla took the cable bundle up in his hands, finding the ending connectors. He snapped them into a dozen fittings at the base of the unassembled cube.

"OK... help me get his head inside."

He took the metal sphere, and Savannah saw one side of it was open. Inside, the helmet-like thing was studded with hundreds of electrodes.

Savannah reached under her father's shoulders and lifted his head off the gurney. Tesla slid the reader into place, and the steel device reached down to just above the colonel's eyes.

Edison grunted, but said nothing. *This is unnatural*, he thought.

Tesla looked around for Madelaine, but couldn't find her.

General Houston stood back from the group, his face a mask of stone.

Still gripping her father's hand, Savannah placed her other hand on the colonel's chest. She stretched her neck around. "Chaplain?"

The base chaplain came forward to deliver last rites. "I'm here, Mrs. Browning."

"I'm sorry. I can't really explain—"

"I've heard rumors. And that's all I care to hear."

Savannah blinked, but let it go.

Her hand suddenly hurt, and she looked down at it. Her father's grip had tightened, and his knuckles were white from the pressure.

"He's squeezing my hand, hard," she said. She leaned down to him. "Can you hear me, Papa? I'm right here. We're all right here."

She looked around for Madelaine and cocked her head, inviting her to come closer, but the little girl shook her head.

The chaplain stepped forward, beginning the last rites.

Colonel Browning's eyes opened then and focused on Savannah. A slight smile began to form, then was gone. His chest sagged, and his grip on Savannah went slack.

"No pulse! It's now or never," said the nurse.

Tesla felt a fine sheet of sweat along his back. His heart

was racing as he reached for the large main breaker switch. His hands were wet, so he clamped down hard, then threw the breaker.

The cube's temporary power supply hummed, then whined to life. They could all smell the familiar tang of ozone in the air, and the area was bathed in static electricity. Savannah felt the hairs on her forearm rise.

The colonel's hand slipped out of his daughter's grasp and fell off the gurney.

"No," whispered Madelaine.

They all waited, frozen while the chaplain finished his words. "…On behalf of a man whose soul is departing, and who cannot speak."

Savannah's mouth worked, but no sound came forward.

Then, beside the cube, a single mono-filament light bulb glowed. Edison realized it was one of his new designs, then wondered why he noticed such a thing now.

Tesla pointed to the warm, orange light. "I rigged that up as a signal. It means the RCA is fully loaded."

"So he's OK?" asked Savannah.

"I can't say for sure. This has never been done. But it's a good sign."

Savannah looked from the cube to her father's body, then back again. Which was now really him? Did he even still exist?

The nurse pronounced the time of death, and the chaplain stepped back, biting his lower lip.

Edison whispered into the chaplain's ear, "I wanted no part of this."

"Nor I," he sighed. "A mockery of a good life."

Everyone looked to Tesla for an answer, but he had none to give. His heart still raced, and his muscles felt weak, like he'd just run a great distance. He wanted to sit down.

George brought over the teletype and connected it to the cube.

Tesla nodded his thanks and found a microphone. He set it on the table, wired it up, and waited to see if anyone wished to try first. When no one stepped forward, he leaned down to speak to the colonel's consciousness.

"Wait," said Savannah. She took her father's dangling arm and placed it back on the gurney by his side. Then she came forward, and Tesla moved aside.

She pressed down on the transmit switch and bent down, her mouth an inch from the microphone.

"Papa…?" she whispered.

The lab was utterly silent. No one dared move or disturb the heavy sense of dread and hope that settled over them all.

Everyone's eyes were fixed on the teletype, which sat still and quiet.

"Papa? Can you hear me?" she tried again.

There was no response.

Savannah's face was wet before she realized she was crying. The tears slipped down her cheekbones and fell from her jawline. She wiped them away, shaking her head.

"We're here. Say something to us. Just… tell us anything. Please."

She turned to the teletype, but it gave no sign of life.

The knowledge of her father's death hit her then, and a racking sobbing doubled her over. The general wrapped an arm over her shoulders and led her away. The sounds of her heartache tore at Tesla, but he was powerless to help her.

"You said you could save him!" cried Madelaine. She was standing behind Tesla, and he turned to her, his arms outstretched.

"Maddy, I'm so sorry. Come here," he said, but she backed away. Her face was tight, and her fists clenched by her sides. She turned and ran away from him.

The heavy sense of dread in the room was broken, replaced by a grim realization they'd lost the colonel. Tesla

142

stood by his table, but everyone else began filing out.

As they stepped onto the elevator, Edison's voice could be heard.

"We gave Tesla his chance. Now let's move on."

COMFORTABLE BITTERNESS

NEW HAVEN, CONNECTICUT

"If any harm comes to them, even a small amount, I'll have you hanging out there with the Americans. Am I understood?" asked Major Thomas.

Lieutenant Danvers stood at attention. His blond locks and gray eyes had made him a favorite with the ladies, but he rarely had time for such distractions, preferring to focus on gaining his commission. "Extremely, sir. My men will take the base, but Savannah and Madelaine Browning will be brought safely to you."

The major nodded. "All right then. At ease. Let's go over the approach."

Danvers relaxed and joined his commanding officer at the desk. A large map of the area was spread out.

"The base is about forty miles southwest. I want you to stay away from the coastline. Head to Trumbull first, then on to New Canaan. From there, make your assault on the base. Reports say there's a research lab of some kind there, but your primary goal is to secure the prisoners and return them to me unharmed."

Lieutenant Danvers nodded agreement. "We should not explore this lab?"

"Not yet. I want these prisoners as soon as possible. We

can send another detachment later. But really, what level of technology could they possess?"

The major's mocking smile gave the lieutenant permission to laugh along. "Quite right, sir."

"I'm giving you the Second Infantry Company, lieutenant. Two hundred men is your largest command to date, yes?"

He nodded. "It is, sir."

"I knew your father well, Danvers, and I was very sorry to hear of his passing. The army misses him."

"Granite Danvers," they'd called his father. Made major in short order and racked up a string of victories, leading men into the battles other commanders shied away from.

"Thank you, sir. I appreciate that. And the trust you're placing in me."

The field radio buzzed, but the major ignored it for the moment.

"I'd be going with you, but our reinforcements arrive tomorrow and I have to meet with their commander," said the major, standing up. "But I think you're up to it. All right. See it done."

The lieutenant snapped into attention and saluted smartly. "Yes, sir."

Major Thomas returned the salute, then answered the radio. "This is Major Thomas."

The lieutenant spun and left the office. He had a lot to do and less than an hour to get the men headed south.

The major listened to the report from field headquarters. The zeppelins were en route from England, loaded with Einstein's bombs.

As one of five officers in the field given authorization to order a bombardment, the required command codes were given and verified twice. A thin smile appeared as he was told they'd be over American soil within twelve hours.

He signed off and sat back, thinking of what the following

days might bring.

Alone now, the major catalogued the emotions he was feeling. Anticipation, certainly. For years he'd imagined seeing Savannah again and asking her how she was capable of such betrayal.

There was a gloomy bitterness too. They had begun a life together, made a daughter together. When she left that night, running away with their girl, his life took a sudden departure from the future he'd always assumed. She'd deprived him of that, and when word spread, her actions had chipped away at his career also. He'd done well to make major, but he knew he'd be further along by now, if not for the whispered stories and muted laughter at his gullibility.

The knowledge he'd be seeing her again had made him melancholy. He walked to the mirror hanging on the wall and studied himself. He was an attractive man, even handsome in an intense way. He'd given her and Madelaine a good life. They'd never wanted for food or security. Every few months there was even the pomp of the military balls, where Savannah could wear her flowing dresses and dance until her legs ached.

He missed her body too. The memories of her nakedness still visited him in the night. He'd dream of her pressed against him, her long blonde hair falling upon him as she closed for a kiss.

He blinked and remembered where he was.

And where she was.

The bitterness grew, rising up inside him, assuming a larger shape. He hated the sight of his face then and punched the reflection. His Academy ring caught the glass, and the mirror shattered, falling to the floor in shards.

In the vicinity of his heart, the bitterness settled in and made itself comfortable.

ONE-SIDED CONVERSATION

Tesla sat alone in the lab, kept company only by the body of Colonel Browning. The room was huge, but it felt doubly so when empty of life. He thought of the tons of stone and earth above him and felt the weight of it, threatening to collapse upon him. Claustrophobia had never been an issue for him, but he began to sympathize with those so afflicted.

Deep underground, it was easy to lose track of the time. He checked his watch. Ten minutes after nine. He'd forgotten dinner, and no one had brought him anything. There was no appetite anyway, but the absence made him wonder and worry about Savannah. His presence would be a painful reminder, not a comfort, so he stayed away.

The still-glowing lightbulb held a tether on him also. If the RCA was fully loaded, there was still a chance the colonel was in there somewhere, his consciousness racing along copper wires and silver-coated relays. Was he conscious in there, perhaps in shock and unable to speak? Was he dreaming? Or had the electrical impulses been lost, scrambled in the transfer, so all that remained was garbage data, no more resembling a mind than a vast collection of gibberish?

The coroner had come for the body hours ago, but Tesla had run the man off, threatening to strike him if that was required. In truth, the physical body was no longer part of the experiment. But releasing the remains felt like an admission of failure, and he couldn't do that yet.

He looked at the old soldier, lying peacefully on the gurney.

"I do wish you'd say something, old boy," he said to the corpse.

The colonel's face was calm and unmoving.

Tesla felt the room's high ceiling pushing down on his shoulders. "Fine then. To work."

He spent a half hour rechecking all the primary connections, looking for the mundane answers first, like loose wires or blown fuses.

When they all checked out fine, he realized he wanted someone to talk to. He pressed the transmit bar of the microphone and locked it place.

"Maybe you're in there, maybe not. Either way, you're keeping me company tonight, Colonel."

He spent the next six hours meticulously touching every connection in the RCA cube, closing his eyes and focusing on the subtle patterns and flavors of current he detected. In the sections where capacitors evened out the flow of power, he felt the expected smoothness to the flow of electrons. The diodes were serving their function well too. On one side of them, the current felt full and complete, while on the other, it had been whittled down to the frequency range the diode permitted to pass through.

In fact, over the next hours, everything he checked seemed right and proper. He spoke to the colonel frequently throughout the night, like a loved one talking to a coma patient, unsure if he was being heard, but taking comfort in the possibility.

"I wish Dane could be here, Colonel. He may have had an answer. He was truly the gifted one of the family."

Tesla paused, remembering playing with his older brother back in Serbia. The day was gorgeous, full of sunshine and warm breezes. At twelve, Dane was already comfortable on horseback and cut a gallant young figure leading his horse in a gallop. The boys were romping in an open field when five-year-old Nikola spooked the horse.

"The horse bucked and threw him," Tesla said. "I… he didn't survive the fall. That day my parents lost their brightest child."

Melancholy gripped him then, but he shook it off, remembering the task at hand and that the newly dead took precedence over the old dead.

"Any sign of life, Colonel. Give me something."

The teletype sat still.

Tesla had forgotten anyone else belonged in the lab when the elevator ground to life. The cleaning crew came in and went about their duties, emptying trash cans and sweeping the floor. Having movement and life around him seemed odd after the long night. While the quiet and stillness were at first unsettling, he'd soon found the solitude relaxing and conducive to good thinking.

Tesla scrubbed at his face and rubbed his tired eyes.

"I don't know what to try next, Colonel. Your connections are good, the current feels right, and the boards are fully loaded. You should be talking to me, you stubborn goat."

A cleaning woman frowned, watching the scientist talking to himself.

"So perhaps it isn't the mechanicals at fault here. Maybe the issue lies in the math. What do you think, Colonel, shall we revisit the formulas?"

Tesla wheeled over a large blackboard, filled with formulas. He wiped the board clean and took up a stick of chalk.

"Let's go through it all, Colonel. Step by step, together."

A NEW DAY OF FAILURE

A few hours later, Tesla had reworked every formula that had gone into the RCA. The board had been filled, then wiped clean, then refilled several times over. His legs were fatigued, as were his shoulders, neck, and eyes. His right hand had cramped a few times, but he set the chalk down and rubbed the pain away, then continued.

He sat, slumped forward, staring at the chalkboard. Everything seemed as correct now as it did days ago. Whatever had caused the colonel to be lost to them, Tesla had to admit he couldn't find it.

"He died, Nikola. You didn't kill him."

He'd never heard anyone enter. He jumped to his feet and turned around. Savannah was there and looked like she'd had a rough night as well. Her eyes were still red and puffy, but she held herself together well. Better than Tesla felt in that moment.

Madelaine stood beside her. He couldn't determine the expression on her face.

"I can't find the problem," he said. "I've gone over everything, I swear."

She looked down at her father's body, still lying on the gurney. During the night Tesla had pulled a sheet over his face.

"I know, Nikola, I know."

She pulled the sheet back, looking at her father's face one

last time. She let Madelaine see, then pulled it back up.

Bertram and Edison were there too, along with the coroner. Tesla realized he must have arrived with them purposefully, knowing he'd get no interference this time. He and his assistant rolled the gurney away, and Tesla never saw the colonel's body again.

"It's OK, Nikola. You fought hard for him, I know you did." She wrapped her arm around her daughter's shoulders, pulling her to her side. "We all do, right, Madelaine?"

The little girl nodded, her lips pursed together.

Savannah ran her fingers through Madelaine's hair, sweeping the bangs out of her eyes. "We spent the night saying good-bye to him. It's time you did too. Sometimes we need to listen to what the universe is telling us. He's gone."

Tesla stood unsteadily, his eyelids heavy with exhaustion. He heard her words, and after they'd bounced around in his head for a moment, he understood them. He'd done his level best, but to continue further would be unnecessarily cruel to the colonel's family. He knew the value in grieving and closing the door on a painful tragedy.

"You're right, of course," he said. He crossed to the workstation where the RCA cube and its single glowing light bulb still stood. He put his hand on the breaker switch.

One pull, and the power supply would stop sending current into the RCA. The oscillating waves of power would fade, then bleed away to nothingness. Any usable pattern would be gone forever. The capacitors would hold a minute charge for a few minutes, but then they too would go dark, and the RCA would return to being nothing more than a collection of wires and switches.

Tesla wrapped his hand around the breaker switch and looked to Savannah for permission to throw it.

She pulled Madelaine tighter against her and nodded.

He pulled, feeling the breaker's spring tension resisting

him. Then he froze. He released the breaker and stood still, processing some partly formed thought.

"Nikola?" Savannah asked.

There was something she said… He rubbed his fingertips together, coaxing the thought out.

"That's enough, Tesla!" Edison shouted. "You put this family through hell. End this now."

Savannah watched him, knowing how the man sometimes hooked onto an idea, but still needed to fight and drag it out into the light.

"Is there something you missed?" she asked him.

"I don't know. Maybe. What you said, about the universe."

Edison barged forward and faced off against Tesla. "You're done. Mrs. Browning gave her consent to end this charade, and it will be ended now."

He reached for the breaker switch.

Tesla placed a hand against Edison's chest and shoved, sending him staggering back. He crashed against a table, knocking a stack of books to the floor with a clatter.

"You son of a bitch," muttered Edison.

"Wait," said Tesla. Then he looked up at Savannah, and his face was no longer tired. He looked spry and energized again. "I think the colonel's been here all along!" he cried.

He ran to the table Edison had crashed into and grabbed a linear tuning power amplifier. He brought the bulky device over and dropped it on the table with a loud thud.

"We just couldn't hear him. The power of his response doesn't reach the level where the teletype would detect it." He wired the amplifier into the line feeding the teletype. "If we strengthen his signal, we may hear him."

Savannah's hand flew to her chest. "You mean he could have been answering us all this time?"

"It's possible. Everything else has checked out. It must be this!"

Edison glared at Tesla. "If you give this woman false hope again, Tesla, I will ruin you forever."

Tesla met his gaze. "Yes, I believe you would."

He took a screwdriver and adjusted the amplifier, then spoke into the microphone again. "Colonel, are you there?"

The room was oppressively silent, and everyone's eyes were locked onto the teletype, which sat obstinate and unmoving.

Then it chattered into action, startling them all. Everyone crowded around it, straining to see the paper it fed out.

"XJdh5vce uIikkas," it read.

"Hold on," said Tesla. He made another adjustment and tried again. "Colonel, this is Tesla. Are you there? Can you hear me?"

Again the teletype chattered, and Savannah whispered, "Oh my God."

The paper read "Rosabelle, believe."

Tesla felt a chill as he saw the words as if a spirit had just whispered to him from beyond the grave.

"He told me that story," Savannah said, pointing a shaking finger at the paper. "It's him. It's him!"

Tesla raised a hand. "We can do better, now that we have his signal amplified," Tesla said. He brought over a loudspeaker and connected it to the RCA's outputs. A low growl of static hissed from the box.

"Colonel, you should have a voice now. Can you hear me?"

The colonel's voice was metallic, but recognizably his.

"Tesla? This is Colonel Jack Browning, US Army. Can you hear me?"

Savannah wept, celebrating how close they were to losing him, but hadn't. She gulped a lungful of air.

"Papa!" she cried out.

Madelaine was agog, her eyes wide. "No way," she whispered.

Tesla let his tired eyes close. The effort had paid off, in full. He took a moment to savor the victory, then looked to Edison. Now faced with Tesla's victory, he wanted to see the man's face.

But Edison was staring at the loudspeaker, his mouth clamped shut, his lips white and thin.

EAGER FOR ACTION

"Get the men ready. We head out in twenty minutes," ordered Lieutenant Danvers. His staff sergeant saluted and went to get the company ready to move out.

The cooking fire had died down, which was fine. The lieutenant was eager to keep going. He knew Fort Hamilton was a smaller base and not a strategically important target. But it meant much to the major, so it was a good opportunity. With luck they'd be there tomorrow morning.

His advance scouts had reported back, and he didn't anticipate a major fight. With the element of surprise and their new rifles, he expected to lose only thirty men.

He'd given his snipers the Ross MkII long guns. While slow firing, they were deadly accurate out to six hundred yards. The scouts had found several good firing positions, and the snipers had them marked on their maps of the area. His main force carried the new P14 Enfields, which were heavier versions of the previous production runs.

He stood and surveyed his company. The men were well trained and well fed, eager for action and glory. Tents were being broken, and horses loaded.

Several platoons of infantry were already forming up on the main road, and his dozen cavalry were ready, their horses clomping at the packed earth.

A heavily laden merchant's cart came down the road then,

driven by a small horse team. When the American saw the British troops, he yanked hard on the reins and whipped the cart back where he'd come from. He disappeared in a cloud of dust.

The lieutenant laughed. Today would be a good day.

FIELD TESTS

"Tesla, this is the strangest thing I have ever experienced," said the colonel.

"It's the strangest thing *any* man has ever experienced," Tesla replied, pushing a large cart of ammunition cartridges underneath the huge tank.

The RCA had been finalized and sealed in its metal housing, then hoisted inside the Beowulf tank. Once connected to the tank's systems, the colonel had *become* the tank.

His legs were now twin woven-steel treads, six feet wide. His heart no longer beat with a steady rhythm. Instead, it hummed with the pressure of steam driven to blistering temperatures by coal fired in his furnace.

His eyes were a dozen viewports, each holding a camera that fed visual data to his brain.

While he couldn't reach out with hands, he did have instant, intuitive control of antipersonnel chainguns, twin mortar tubes, and an eleven-inch cannon.

His hearing was also superhuman. Recessed microphones collected auditory signals from the standard range of frequencies, but at a sensitivity no human ear could match.

The colonel had been overwhelmed by the saturation of stimuli assaulting his mind, and Tesla had been forced to disconnect most of the systems, giving his mind time to adjust before adding them back, one by one. All basic systems now checked out, and the colonel was ready for the next step.

"I want to get outside!" he said. Beowulf had four loudspeakers mounted under its superstructure, and the commanding boom of its voice was startling.

"Like the voice of God," joked Tesla. "Easy on our ears, hmm? The rest of us aren't so invulnerable."

"Sorry. I'm just eager to try more of this out."

"And you will, Papa," said Savannah. "As soon as we think it's safe for you. And us!"

"Actually," said Tesla, "I think we're about there. Hang on." He turned to the six workers busy underneath Beowulf.

"George, Sophia?"

They both turned and flashed the thumbs-up. "All set for the first round of tests," he said, pointing in the direction Beowulf was facing. "We rigged up the targets downrange."

Sixty yards away a makeshift gun range had been set up. Multiple stationary bull's-eye targets were mounted on the far wall, some as high as fifty feet from the floor.

A series of moving human-sized targets was set on a moving chain, able to slide back and forth behind several fixed panels. On the panels, images of peaceful noncombatants had been painted, their hands up in surrender.

"We're ready to send rounds downrange. Once we have the gel-rounds loaded, that is," George continued.

"Got them right here," said Tesla, patting the large metal canisters on his cart. It wouldn't do to have Beowulf firing live ammo inside the lab, so training rounds had been created. They were the exact size and shape of standard rounds, but made from a stiff gelatin that was just firm enough to survive Beowulf's muzzle velocity, but soft enough to not tear chunks from the lab's wall.

Tesla positioned the cart just under Beowulf's center.

"OK, Colonel, please open the crew chamber for me," he

called out.

Overhead Tesla heard a soft click as the heavy steel panel was unsecured. A hydraulic piston pressurized, and the panel swung inward, exposing the cavity. A vertical ladder descended to the lab's floor.

Tesla climbed the ladder into Beowulf's crew compartment. The space was about as large as his old rented room at Mrs. Harrison's, which made him smile, thinking of how much had changed for him since his days there. The hatch was about seven feet wide, with a chrome railing encircling it to prevent accidental falls.

To the rear five heavily padded crash chairs were welded to shock-absorbing mounts. Two faced Beowulf's left, one faced forward, and two more faced right. They all sported five-point restraint belts. The four chairs facing the sides looked into observation ports, giving a clear view outside through a four-inch-tall slit that ran for two feet along Beowulf's sides. When going into combat, a sliding panel of armor would be slid into position, protecting the crew.

Tesla stepped off the ladder and thumbed a green button on a control panel built into the railing. Directly above the open compartment door, a motorized winch whined, and a steel cable descended to the lab's floor below. A heavy snap hook dangled from its end.

George secured the hook to the centered ring on top of the first gel-round magazine, and Tesla brought it up. The eighty-five pound magazine rose through the access hatch, then hung in the air, swinging slightly. Tesla shoved it over until it cleared the hatch and hung over a small, temporary worktable. He lowered the winch, and the steel magazine settled heavily onto it.

A weapons technician released the hook, then scooped both arms under the ammo magazine and lifted it from the table. While Tesla lowered the cable to repeat the process, the technician wrestled the magazine over to Beowulf's ammunitions stores, and slid it into an empty port.

Twenty minutes later they'd loaded eight magazines of the gel-rounds, totaling 1,600 rounds.

"Damn peculiar," said the colonel. "I could feel it every time you loaded a magazine. Like I was putting food in my belly."

"You've got sensors that report the presence of each magazine. How much each one weighs too," said Tesla.

"Well, I guess I just had dinner!" He laughed.

The weapons tech scanned the bank of magazine ports. They were secured, and green lights glowed under each one. "We're all good here," he told Tesla.

Tesla nodded. "All right, let's get everyone behind the blast shield and see what you can do."

Nonessential workers took a break and headed upstairs for an early lunch. Tesla, Savannah, Bertram, and General Houston huddled together behind a wide, transparent sheet of bullet-resistant glass.

"Care to do the honors?" Bertram asked Savannah.

"Definitely," she said. She raised her voice. "Dad, can you hear me?"

The colonel responded, his amplified voice booming through the lab.

"Sure can, honey," he said.

Sixty yards downrange, the far wall had been decorated with five bullseye targets. Arranged like an X, each one was four feet square.

"OK, let's start easy. Can you see the upper-right target?"

The colonel's view ports allowed him to see in 360 degrees at once, but he focused his attention forward. When he was merely human, his two eyes would have given a decent sense of depth, but he now had four forward view ports, and the two extra eyes gave his brain additional angle data to work with.

"Yep, I see it," he replied.

He visualized pointing a finger at the distant target. Three of his antipersonnel chainguns twitched and swung to aim downrange.

"Hang on," he said. "Still trying to remember I'm not running a human body anymore."

He focused, reminding himself of the new appendages he controlled, and shifted his attention to only one of them. Two of the chainguns went slack and relaxed. He adjusted the remaining one and called out, "Firing!"

With a single *THWAP*, one gel round raced downrange. It struck the target and splattered into a one-inch patch of orange.

Bertram studied the target with binoculars. "Quite good," he said. "No bull's-eye, but you're in the three ring."

"OK, I can adjust for that," the colonel said. He re-aimed the chaingun up and right by a tiny amount and fired again. The orange splat landed dead center in the bullseye.

"There we go," he said. "Just needed to get the hang of it."

"Which you did rather quickly," Bertram said. "Outside, you'll have to compensate for windage and changing terrain as you move, but that shouldn't be a major challenge for you, I think. How about a single burst? Say all five targets."

The three forward guns swiveled up, trained on their targets independently, and fired. Two guns then twitched to secondary targets and fired again. In all, less than a second had passed.

Bertram whistled as he scanned the wall through his binoculars again.

"Three bull's-eyes and two in the four ring. That's really impressive, Colonel."

"Thanks. Always was a good shot. But this is amazing. You

boys have really created something here."

"We created half of it. Beowulf is a hybrid now, half man and half machine," Bertram replied. "Give yourself some credit too."

"Well, let's just wait and see. Target practice is one thing, combat is something else entirely."

Tesla spoke up. "Maybe the colonel would like to combine moving targets with some basic navigation?"

"Damn right," the tank replied.

"Fine, fine," said Bertram. "Colonel, please engage any moving target. Let's say two shots constitutes a kill. Avoid firing on the civilian targets, and do this while advancing forward at three percent speed. Proceed when ready."

"Now we're talking," he said.

A low whine filled the lab as the Beowulf tank engaged power to its treads. Gears wound, then clicked into place, and the massive tank edged forward. The woven steel treads inched along, propelling the house-sized tank at a man's walking speed.

Bertram clicked a stopwatch to begin timing the exercise.

The colonel took a moment to sight the rows of moving targets parading by at the far side of the lab. They disappeared behind the friendly stationary targets, then exposed themselves again.

"Firing," the tank announced.

Beowulf's forward chainguns twitched and found their targets readily. The movements were sure and precise. Two rounds went screaming downrange, then the guns reoriented for the next victim. The *BRAPPP* of firing rounds was painfully loud, and everyone stuck their fingers in their ears.

Downrange, the targets were taking a beating. Each impact left a ding in the sheet metal, and each target was quickly colored in twin patches of bright orange.

Beowulf's forward left chaingun trained on a target

painted like a British trooper. As it slid behind a woman carrying groceries, the gun followed the motion, but held its fire. As the trooper emerged on the other side, the gun spat twice, and the trooper's face and chest went orange.

Beowulf scanned for hostile targets, but they were all dead, by the rules of this simulation. The tank stood down, and all guns relaxed.

"Ceasing fire," announced the colonel.

Bertram clicked his stopwatch again. "Wow," he muttered.

"I know *how* he did," said General Houston, "but how fast was he?"

Bertram looked up. "While moving, the colonel dispatched nine enemy combatants. No civilians were touched. He took six seconds to do this."

"Incredible," said the General. "I believe you will get the go-ahead for the Mark Two, Bertram. I'll speak to the president right away."

Bertram nodded, then looked from his stopwatch to the array of painted targets.

"Thank you, General. The British won't know what hit them, that's for sure."

"They'll be telling themselves campfires stories about the boogeyman called Beowulf," agreed the general. "I'm glad I could see this before I head out."

"Head out?" asked Bertram.

"The Brits are massing near Boston. I'm to get out there and take command of our land forces."

Bertram extended his hand. "I'm glad you're the man running the defense, General."

They shook hands as General Houston laughed and hooked a thumb toward Beowulf. "Thanks. Now get him ready. There's a good chance I'll need him in Boston."

"Will do, don't worry."

"OK then, I'm off." The general said his good-byes and

headed for the elevator.

As Bertram and Tesla discussed the next steps, Savannah walked over to the tank and ran her hand along the tread.

"I'm proud of you, Papa," she said.

"Thank you, honey. I'm just glad for the chance to be useful again."

"How do you feel?"

"Invincible," he said, laughing.

"Yeah, well, that's not a bad description."

"Back at your age, I thought I was tough. Now? I could level a building, literally."

Smiling, Savannah pointed a finger at her father. "Don't enjoy it too much." She realized how silly she must look, chastising a tank that towered over her.

"OK, honey, I'll remember my place."

He laughed with her. The moment felt good, like they had reconnected despite the bizarre circumstances.

"Sure wish I could hug you again, though," he said.

She smiled sadly. "I know, me too. But if it's this or losing you to the cancer, I'll take this and call myself lucky."

"Not exactly how we pictured spending my retirement with you and Maddy, is it? But who knows? It could be a blessing. Lord knows how long I can live in this thing. We'll have more time than we ever thought possible. I'll even get to watch Madelaine grow old."

"The silver lining," she agreed.

A pinprick of worry tugged at her attention, but she ignored it. The moment felt nice, and she wanted to focus on it.

X-RAYS II

"Sweet God in heaven," whispered Edison, his face gone white.

He'd been away for a short time and wanted to check on his apprentice, Dally. The sight that greeted his return horrified him. He thought of the scary picture books Marion enjoyed, full of ghouls and monsters. With a cold tickle climbing up his back, he realized his old friend resembled the fictional creatures.

Dally's handsome, aristocratic face was now grotesque. Radiation damage had eaten away at the fragile tissue, leaving behind craggy ravines and sagging, misshapen skin that appeared scalded. His hair had fallen away, even the eyebrows. His left hand bore the scars and puffy redness of multiple skin grafts. While no doctor, Edison knew at a glance Dally's body was rejecting the attempt to repair it, determined to slough off parts of itself, and fall apart.

Edison resisted the urge to step back.

"Dally," he whispered, afraid to speak louder. The entirety of the man before him looked fragile and precarious, as if a loud noise might cause him to break apart and tumble to the floor, a pile of human pieces.

Then the monster spoke in a rough, grating tone like a rasp pulled along metal. "You were right, Mr. Edison. I'm sorry."

"Dally… I don't know what to say."

"It's all my fault, sir. You don't have to say anything."

"Is it…Are you in pain?"

Dally nodded. "Hurts like the devil. I sleep with my hand in a water bath, which helps some."

Edison reeled. He prided himself on exploring the boundaries of science, but never to put others at risk. He'd even turned down work on devices designed to kill. And now this…

"Your wife and children?"

"They are supportive, of course. What else can they be?"

Edison ran his hands through his hair, turning away. "You are on paid leave, of course. As long as you need. Just try to relax with your loved ones."

Dally pursed his lips, and the sight revolted Edison, though he stifled the reaction.

"Thank you, Mr. Edison. I do appreciate that."

"And have your doctor send his bills to me. The lab will pay them all."

"You are very kind," Dally replied, which only made Edison feel more guilty. "However, my medical bills will soon escalate."

Dally held up his left hand, showing Edison the gnarled fingers. "The good doctor wants to remove four fingers. I'll have just the thumb left."

Nausea washed over Edison, and his balance swayed. His stomach clenched, wanting to vomit, but Edison focused, denying the impulse.

"All will be well, Dally," he said, turning aside. He had to get out of there. He needed some air. "All will be just fine." He clamped his hand tightly over his mouth and strode stiffly for the exit.

COMBAT OPERATIONS

"Major? Did you hear me?"

Major Thomas had not heard the man at all, since his mind was forty miles to the southwest. Lieutenant Danvers should be in position at the US base by now. He'd probably launch his assault at first light. Could he penetrate their defenses? Would he properly organize the search for Savannah and Madelaine? Could he get them out unharmed?

He really should have gone and overseen the assault personally. But the three ships filled with reinforcements needed his attention. Nineteen hundred men had landed that morning, and a lot of logistics needed to be handled, getting them ashore. Their commander sat across from him, and the major remembered he'd been asked a question.

"Forgive me, it's been a long day. You were saying?"

"For us all, Major. I said, my personal staff requires a proper house for billeting. Have you one set aside for them?"

Housing assignments. I stayed behind for this?

On a fast horse, he could catch up to the assault force, maybe even reach them before they attacked.

The lieutenant was a good officer. He'd doubtless consider the major's arrival to be a critique.

But if I held back and observed? If the boy does well, no need to step on his toes. And if he needs help, he'd be glad to have it.

The major's decision was made before he stood and made an empty excuse to the confused commander.

He raced outside and called for the fastest horse available.

Occasionally, personal needs trumped official duty.

"It's not a major base," the staff sergeant said. Even in the pre-sunrise dimness, his tanned, leathery face declared him a veteran of the colonial wars in India.

Lieutenant Danvers nodded. Beneath him, his pale horse shifted restlessly, sensing the upcoming battle. He pulled gently on the reins and leaned forward to pat his stallion on the neck, calming it.

"No, it's not. But Major Thomas has a need for these prisoners, so we will go pull them out. Safely."

"And if we have to kill a few Americans in the process?"

"Then we shall," replied the lieutenant. Unlike the major, he held no personal animosity toward the unruly Americans. Truth be told, he admired their spirit. But his orders were clear, and sentiment had no place on the battlefield.

"Very good, sir," he said, saluting. "The snipers are in position, ready to fire as we crest the hill. I'll have the men ready to go on your order."

"Good man." Danvers returned the salute, then surveyed the terrain below. From the top of the bluff, he had a good view of the base's entrance. A single road led into Fort Hamilton, which covered several acres. Toward the far side of the base, the land dropped down into a ravine, providing natural defense from attackers.

Fort Hamilton wasn't a large base, but it did have a garrison of 140 soldiers. His advance men had found the Americans' perimeter patrols and had taken them out quietly. Now, with sixty more men, the element of surprise and their modern weapons, the day should go well.

He turned and looked over his shoulder at the company hidden below the bluff's ridgeline. These men had performed remarkably well at New Haven. They were brave and battle-tested. And now he had the chance to lead them in an assault. With luck, this would be the first in a string of bold victories, just like his father's legacy. He sat up straighter in his saddle and enjoyed the moment.

The sun was just breaking over the horizon, orange tendrils reaching up into the sky. He turned his horse to join the men, when a single rider on horseback caught his eye. He approached fast, staying hidden from the base's view, pushing his animal hard and coming straight for the lieutenant. No American would approach this way, so curiosity held him in place until the man grew closer.

As the rider closed, he saw it was Major Thomas. *He lost confidence in my command.* Well, there would be other battles, no doubt about that.

"Danvers!" the major cried, approaching and pulling his exhausted horse beside the lieutenant.

"Is something wrong, Major? We were just about to begin our run."

The major shook his head and held up a hand. "No, nothing. But I realized I needed to be on hand. To observe."

He saw the junior officer relax as he realized the major wasn't here to assume command of the charge.

"Besides," said the major, "I didn't want to miss your first major victory." He smiled at the lieutenant, whose face brightened at the compliment.

"Yes, sir!" He glanced at the company. The staff sergeant had formed the soldiers into four platoons of fifty men each, and they stood ready.

"The company is prepared, sir. Shall we begin the assault?"

The major cast his eye over the men and nodded. "Begin your charge, Lieutenant. I will watch from here."

"Thank you, sir," he said, saluting and steering his horse down the bluff and in front of the assembled company.

He called the order to the platoon leaders, and the four platoons marched forward, rifles at the ready. The lieutenant led the way, and as they crested the bluff, the four snipers opened fire.

They'd each found hidden positions with clear fields of fire on the base, and each had chosen his initial target based on distance and how meaningful it would be to the battle.

Just inside the base gate, a raised watchtower sat perched fifteen feet above ground. Inside, a young corporal finished checking the list of today's scheduled events.

"Nothing major today," he told the private assigned with him.

"Nice. First quiet day this week."

The corporal stood, lit a cigarette and looked through the large glass window at the base entrance. Movement along the bluff's ridgeline caught his eye.

"What the hell is that?" he asked, reaching for his binoculars.

Private Harland followed his gaze, but saw nothing in the dim early morning. "What? I don't see any—"

In the darkness to the side of the bluff, a brief flash of light flared, then disappeared. A moment later the glass pane in front of them shattered with a piercing crash. A single .303 round found its target, hitting the corporal in the forehead, and killing him instantly. His mouth went slack in surprise and the cigarette fell from his lips. Then he collapsed, dropping the binoculars.

A second flash, and another round screamed for the private's head, but missed, whispering an inch to the right. As the round slipped past his head, the private heard the soft whistle of air, then felt a sharp pain in his right ear. He clapped a hand over it, then held the hand in front of him, amazed to see blood on his palm. The bullet had clipped his ear, tearing off a marble-sized chunk of cartilage.

The sniper swore, seeing he'd missed so narrowly. For a shot of five hundred meters, it was still damn good, but not enough. He cycled the bolt-action Enfield and aimed again at the stunned private who stood frozen, gaping at the sight of his own blood.

Harland looked up and saw another flash. This time adrenaline worked for him, and he threw himself to the floor as the next round slammed into the wall behind him. He crouched down low, protected by the masonry of the tower, and looked over at his corporal. The man's head had been punched like a melon, and the sight made him turn away and retch, filling the small room with the smell of vomit.

At ground level, the four MPs manning the gate heard the shots, and reacted. They each bolted for cover, but snipers had already sighted them as targets. Three shots rang out from the darkness, and two of the MPs fell to the ground, dead. A moment later the shots continued, and a third MP went down, clutching his side to stop the dark blood that seeped between his fingers.

The last MP raced to hit the alarm switch in the gatehouse. Two sniper rounds screamed to intercept him, but went wide. Running hard, he launched himself into the gatehouse, landing hard on his side. Ignoring the cracked rib that radiated hot pain through his chest, he rolled over and reached up, triggering the base alarm.

Klaxons mounted high on buildings throughout the base wailed, and now the whole base knew they were under attack.

General Houston had just finished his exercises and was

getting dressed when the alarm rang out. "What the hell?" he muttered, throwing his jacket on and racing to the base phone. He dialed the main gate and was relieved to hear someone pick up.

The last MP stayed on the floor, but reached up to answer the phone. "Sergeant Miller here!" he yelled over the sound of bullets impacting the wall between him and the enemy.

"Miller? This is General Houston. What's happening, son?"

"Snipers, sir. Walters, Abbott, and Paulson are dead. I think the watchtower got hit first. I don't know about them."

"Goddamn. OK. Do you see the ground force yet?"

"One second, sir." The MP slid along the floor toward the gatehouse door. Keeping his face low, he peered around the doorjamb, then pulled his head back.

"Yes, sir. A quarter mile out. A hundred men, maybe two."

The general ground his molars hard. This base had been built as a supply and research depot, not for combat operations. He thought of options. It was a short list.

"OK, Miller. If you can, get your men and fall back into the base. We'll make our stand a hundred yards back, beside Admin Building B. Got that?"

"Got it, sir!" He hung up and wondered how the hell he was going to dodge those snipers with a busted rib.

General Houston rang Operations and gave them the intel. In minutes the garrison's men would assemble and do their best to push back this force. At least by choosing a spot a hundred yards within the base, he would force the opposition to funnel themselves through the narrow gate entrance. Like the Spartans at Thermopylae, his strategy studies reminded him. *Let's not think about how that worked out for them.*

In the lab, red alarm lights flared, and the klaxon howled,

making everyone yell to be heard.

"What the devil?" yelled Tesla. He'd been focusing intently on soldering a bundle of wires to a delicate seismic detector, and the sudden cacophony made his hand slip, sending too much solder into the joint, ruining the expensive sensor.

He looked up and disliked the look on Bertram's face as he went pale. *Like a white fish*, Tesla thought.

Savannah ran to them, hands over her ears. "The base is being attacked!" she yelled over the alarm. "Where's Madelaine?" She scanned the room, panicked at not having her daughter beside her.

Tesla set down the soldering gun and leaned closer, cupping his hands to be better heard. "She was going to my house for a book."

Savannah nodded and ran for the elevator.

"What does this mean for us?" asked Tesla.

Bertram was distracted, scanning the room. Most of the technicians had never experienced an attack, and he saw the nervous twittering spreading through the room. He crossed the lab and hit the alarm button to shut off the room's klaxon, to everyone's relief. On the other floors of the lab, the alarm continued, wailing faintly through the ceiling.

Edison had been consulting upstairs with Hollerith's team and had just stepped off the elevator platform when the alarm was raised. He prided himself on remaining calm during adversity, and his years of running his own lab at Menlo Park had instilled a natural leadership role. Seeing the building confusion, he raised a hand and began to address the crowd.

"Don't worry," he began.

Then Bertram returned from silencing the klaxon and jumped on a table, waving both hands. "Can I have your attention, please!" Bertram called out.

Edison was caught short, interrupted. He lowered his hand, his eyes burning into Bertram's back.

Throughout the lab everyone dropped what he was doing and moved toward Bertram, clustering around for info.

"The base appears to be under attack. What this means for us is that we will remain right where we are. This lab is the most secure point in the entire base, and we are in no danger here. OK?"

Many in the crowd were nodding and calming down. A moment ago, the lab was lurching into a flurry of chaos but now was calming down and focusing on the tasks at hand.

Bertram projected his voice to the far sides of the lab. Despite his bookish appearance, his booming voice and confident tone had great effect.

"In an abundance of caution, however, we will begin our overrun protocol. All sensitive lab books will be collected and readied for incineration, if necessary. Let's focus on what we must do, and let the soldiers upstairs do what they do best. Let's go," he yelled, clapping his hands once.

The crowd dispersed quickly, now strengthened and purposeful. Bertram hopped off the table as Tesla approached.

"Well done, Bertram. You gave them exactly what they needed." He raised his voice just enough to ensure Edison overheard. Tesla knew he had when the inventor suddenly went stiff, then turned and walked away.

"Thanks," Bertram replied. "Now let's just hope we don't have to destroy our work down here."

That thought instantly filled Tesla with sorrow, and a scowl turned his aristocratic face sour. Losing people would be tragic, but destroying research was an even deeper loss. The human race improved, bit by bit, with the help of science and the pushing back of unknown frontiers. To throw away their efforts would be like turning their backs on the future. And that idea was unthinkable.

He ran to Beowulf and looked up at the massive blast doors that opened to the outside world.

He pointed to them and called out to the colonel. "Can you open those doors?"

"I certainly can," the booming voice declared.

"Get out there, Colonel," said Tesla. "Savannah and Madelaine are running around at ground level. I'll take responsibility."

"Good enough for me," said the colonel. He scanned his data banks for the command codes to the blast doors and broadcast them over short-range radio.

Twin lights over the massive steel doors flared, and the multi-ton doors swung open silently. Beowulf powered up all systems and moved forward.

"Tesla, what the hell are you doing?" yelled Bertram. "He's not checked out for combat yet."

"I have no doubt he soon will be," Tesla said.

Miller held a hand against his cracked rib, pressing firmly. He leaned around the gatehouse door. The ground force was closer now, just a hundred yards away. He pulled his head back just before a sniper round tore into the doorframe where his head had been. Splinters of painted wood sprayed over his face.

"Jesus!" he cried.

He looked up at the watchtower and saw the smashed front window. These snipers were good. If the tower had been their first target, it was likely both the men up there were already dead. Still, that ground force would be here in minutes.

"Hey! You guys alive up there?" he yelled. He strained to hear a response, but the dull roar of the approaching horde made it hard to hear anything. "Corporal!" he tried again. He heard nothing, so he started thinking about making a run for it. Zigzag pattern. Change directions randomly, but keep adding distance. A shitty plan, but it beat waiting here and feeling a pistol muzzle against his forehead.

"Corporal's dead, but I'm here!" yelled Private Harland from the tower. Miller breathed a sigh of relief. *Thank God. At least I'm not doing this on my own.*

"Let's go, Private! We got about one minute to fall back!" he yelled back.

"OK!" said Harland. He opened the door to the narrow staircase and peeked out.

A round dug into the door two inches from the private's head. He flinched and jerked back inside.

"Watch it!" yelled Miller. "Sniper's got your exit zeroed in. You want out of there, you need to go the hard way. Now!"

In the tower Harland glanced at the shattered window and muttered. "That's just fuckin' great."

He crouched down beside the dead corporal and snatched the man's dog tags from his neck. He tucked them into his pocket, took a step back from the shattered window, then launched himself out sideways. As he cleared the shattered window, he twisted and grabbed hold of the window's base. Shards of glass sliced into his palms, sending a sharp wave of pain that took his breath away. His momentum continued, and his body sailed out into the air. With his feet splayed out, fifteen feet over the ground, his grip on the window stopped him, and he fell, swinging down into the tower's outer wall.

He held on to the ruined window frame, gasping at the agony in his hands as he hung there, his blood coating the window's base. *Snipers are aiming in now. Three… two….*

He glanced down. He'd saved himself six feet by hanging, but still had ten more feet to the hard-packed earth. He let go and fell from the tower. Three shots hit the wall above him as he dropped, and he grinned, cheating the bastards of their prize. *Didn't expect that, did ya?*

He fell, then landed on his feet, but was off balance. His body leaned to the right, and his foot rolled. A blossom of pain sprang from his ankle, and he screamed. He rolled over in the dirt, then scrambled awkwardly toward Miller and the gatehouse.

Looking back, he saw what looked like a thousand Redcoats roaring down on him, barely twenty yards away. He saw rifles, swords, bayonets, and lots of screaming faces. An officer was charging forward on horseback, urging the men on, sword raised high.

A warm wetness told part of his brain he'd just pissed himself, but he didn't care. He felt hands grab his shoulders. Miller had run out of the gatehouse, joining him, and hauled the private to his feet. Miller spun him toward the base entrance and screamed in his ear, "Move it, Private!"

Together the men lurched and ran into the base. The private's ankle howled with every step, and he sucked air like a beached fish, clutching Miller's arm with a white-knuckle grip.

Miller didn't look back. He didn't need to. The sounds told him how close the British were. The British were forced to bunch up as they entered the base, but they piled in. Rifle shots rang out, but they weren't sniper fire. *They can't fire now. Their own men are too close to us.* Miller grinned.

Another rifle shot cracked, and Miller gasped at a hot, searing pain in his left shoulder. He stumbled, but the private held him up. As best they could, they sprinted forward, lurching awkwardly as they held each other up. They'd made it maybe sixty yards inside the base when Miller looked up and saw the garrison's infantry running toward them. A flush of elation welled up within him, and he laughed madly.

The American troops were forming up in a skirmish line, fifty men wide, with a second row behind them. They were all armed and swung their rifles up to meet the oncoming British. Miller decided he'd never seen a more beautiful sight, not even that dancer back in Paris.

"Get down!" a sergeant was yelling at them. *Sounds like a*

fine plan.

Miller took a tight hold on the private. "Good enough!" he yelled and rolled them both down into the dirt. They landed roughly, sliding along the rough ground, adding multiple abrasions to their injuries.

"Fire!" screamed the sergeant, and fifty American rifles exploded, sending a hail of lead shot ringing over Miller's head. He and the private lay flat, face down in the dirt, arms over their heads.

The Redcoats were massed together tightly, and the wall of lead slammed into the group, killing many instantly. Men screamed as metal shot tore into the bodies. A dozen British fell, and the forward surge faltered.

Lieutenant Danvers had hoped to run his men straight into the base, continuing his momentum, but the quick response of the Americans required a new approach.

"Take cover!" he yelled, just as his horse was shot from under him. He tumbled to the ground, losing his sword, and rolling to a stop on his back. The air had been solidly knocked from him, and he stared up at the sky, gasping.

The British broke formation and scattered, finding protected positions to fire from. They crouched behind supply trucks and hid around the corners of buildings. Danvers knew his snipers were repositioning now, and would be back in the fight momentarily. So now the need was to encircle the Americans. He rolled to his belly and clambered to cover with his men.

Miller saw their chance. He yelled to the private. "Let's go!" They both jumped and ran hard for the American troops. They got within five yards when Private Harland took a British round through the back. His momentum carried him forward, and he collapsed into the arms of a startled sergeant, then fell to the ground. He flopped onto his back, gasping once, twice, then went still. A sharp rock dug into his shoulder blade, but the pain was fading. His vision blurred, and he slipped quietly away.

Miller didn't break his speed as he approached the firing line. Instead, he leaned back and kicked his feet forward. He found a gap between two firing soldiers, and like claiming home base, he slid along the ground between them. He rolled over on his belly, finally getting a good look at the British force he'd escaped. Then he grabbed a dead man's rifle and joined the fight.

From the bluff Major Thomas watched the assault through binoculars. It had been a splendid run, and the snipers did a fine job. Getting his force bunched up in the gate entrance was worrisome, but he saw the lieutenant was now working on a flanking position. The boy was doing very well, and there would be a commendation for him.

For another ten minutes, the two forces traded fire. Danvers called for men to push around the side, to flank the Americans' position and set up a cross fire. But the American captain in charge of the tightly massed soldiers was mindful of the attempt, and kept the British at bay by sending extra men to strengthen his side. Both sides had lost another dozen men, but the fight was grinding into a stalemate.

Then the British snipers found new positions, and the tide turned quickly.

The Americans began dropping, killed by shots from unseen assailants. Another ten men screamed and fell within a minute. The four snipers had arranged themselves at cross angles, and the Americans could find no safe position from the murderous fire. Seven more soldiers collapsed, and a tinge of panic ran through the men. When the captain went down, his chest stained red, the Americans felt the cold hand of defeat reaching for them.

Beowulf raced down the corridor cut into the hillside. As he approached the outer blast doors, the colonel ran an inventory of his armaments. A tenth of a second later, he was satisfied. Two hundred gel rounds, fifty armor-piercing, and four hundred standard antipersonnel rounds. Not enough for a full battle, but he'd make do.

He broadcast the access codes again, and the outer doors opened for him. Bright sunlight spilled into the corridor, and he increased speed. He burst forward from the hillside into the valley's base and took his bearings. A magnetic compass gave him instant readings, and said he was headed northwest, but he realized just how superhuman he'd become when he calculated the angle of the sun, checked an almanac, and came up with the same data redundantly. And all in the space of a heartbeat.

The ravine's walls were too steep to climb here, so he tore down the valley, his woven-steel treads throwing rocks and dirt up in twin sprays behind him. After a mile the valley's sides grew shallower and he swung to the left, racing up the valley's side. He needed to gain 228 feet of elevation to reach the level of the base.

With an odd sense of knowing, the colonel realized he needed more power. His steam pressure tank was capable of driving him forward easily, but the added strain of racing fast up a 17 percent incline was taxing his energy stores more quickly.

He needed more fire in his coal-fed furnace, so he willed the conveyor rig to increase speed. The belt obeyed and scooped coal into the furnace at twice the normal rate. In seconds the colonel felt the increase in combustion. His furnace temperature soared, boiling water into high-pressure steam.

Satisfied, he turned his attention to the radio bands. He scanned the two-meter and six-meter frequencies, but the only chatter he heard was American. If the British were using radio to coordinate the attack, he couldn't hear it.

He crested the valley's wall then, leveling out to flat ground again. He eased back on the coal conveyor and surged forward for the base entrance. With the flat ground, he approached his maximum speed of thirty five miles per hour. He concentrated on his antipersonnel shredders, and they flickered to life, swinging about and eagerly seeking targets.

Then he saw the main gate and aimed straight for it.

Major Thomas had enjoyed watching the battle. Danvers found a tougher fight than he'd first imagined, but the snipers had made all the difference. He smiled as he scanned the base interior through his binoculars. The sniper's angles had pushed the Americans into a tight ball. Now unable to defend against a flanking attack, the lieutenant was moving his men around to surround the defenders. Once in place, things would end quickly for the Americans. Then they could begin the search for Savannah and his daughter.

He brought the binoculars down, seeing the wide scene of the battle. Movement in his peripheral vision turned his head, and he was unsure if what he saw was real.

It was a tank, fast approaching. But not like one he'd ever seen. The monster was the size of a house, easily five times bigger than normal. It was damned fast too. It must have come around from behind the base, up the valley's wall. It tore up the earth as it raced for the main gate, and the major stared bug-eyed.

"My God," he whispered, suddenly worried for the lieutenant. He cursed his lack of foresight to not keep a radio with him.

Then the massive tank suddenly ground to a stop.

The colonel's increased sight showed him a single British officer at the bluff's peak. He saw the man's eyes go wide, then the colonel startled, recognizing the officer who'd married his daughter. *I see you too, Major Thompson.*

But the single distant rider wasn't the reason for Beowulf's abrupt stop. He'd detected four sources of gunfire nearby, and the firing signatures told him they were snipers. Instantly, eliminating them became the colonel's top priority. He turned toward his new objective and moved forward, listening for more shots.

Within a minute he found them, scattered far apart. They had excellent angles to fire within the base, and they'd been so focused on that task, they hadn't turned around to see him approaching. He closed to within one hundred yards and stopped.

"Snipers like head shots," he said to himself. He focused his attention on the closest sniper's head. Beowulf's forward left shredder twitched. A moment later the head disappeared in a cloud of pink and gray. The headless body fell and three snipers remained.

The colonel found the next enemy in line and fired again. Like his friend, this one went down headless, his blood pouring into the dry earth.

The sound of the second shot carried to the remaining two snipers. They turned, gaped, and swung their Enfields around at Beowulf. The rounds both struck solidly, but clanged off Beowulf's forward armor, leaving only twin scratches.

The colonel moved forward, gaining distance quickly. With limited ammunition, he saw no reason to risk a bad shot. Apparently, rifle rounds weren't much of a concern for him anymore. The two snipers continued firing, and inwardly the colonel flinched slightly with each impact. He chided himself at the response. *Going to have to get used to this new body*, he thought.

Beowulf ground over rough scrub and knocked aside small trees as he closed on the remaining British shooters. He wanted to try a simultaneous kill, so he'd chosen an approach vector to bring him within equal distance of both snipers. As he closed the distance, he came to within forty yards of them, then slowed.

The one on his right threw down his rifle and dug into a pouch. A moment later, he lobbed a small steel sphere at the colonel. As it flew toward him, the colonel focused on it. Sized like an oblong baseball, the device was grooved like a pineapple. He recognized the grenade as a Mills bomb, recently invented by the British weapon designer William Mills.

The man's throw was remarkable, or lucky. The grenade hit the ground in front of Beowulf's right tread, and his momentum carried him over it. The device detonated with a horrendous boom, and a sideways geyser of dirt exploded out from the tank's tread. The colonel noted that his right suspension took an impressive amount of force from the explosion, even momentarily shifting Beowulf's weight slightly. But he could detect no damage from the explosion. *I can run over grenades now. Amazing.*

He saw the men's eyes go wide as he ignored their grenade. They watched in dawning horror as the massive tank ground onward toward them. While snipers typically hunkered down outside the active combat arena, these soldiers had also faced the enemy directly, and lived to carry on. But this was something entirely different. While separated by a hundred yards, the snipers were united in their sheer terror at seeing this mountain of steel descend upon them.

The colonel brought to bear both of his forward shredders and fired them as one. The snipers died instantly, the image of Beowulf blazed on their panicked minds. As the bodies fell, the colonel spun within his own axis and resumed course to the base gate. In minutes he reached it, but realized he had a serious problem.

He was too big to fit through the main gate. His width exceeded the entrance by several feet. The colonel cursed. He could see the battle being waged not one hundred yards away, but he was powerless to get in there and help. He scanned the thick masonry of the gatehouse and the watchtower and swore again.

He checked his inventory and was disappointed to find he had not been equipped with any mortars. From this close, it would be a simple matter to land the explosive clusters on the British's heads.

He focused, singling out British soldiers, hoping to at least pick off a few, but they appeared and withdrew behind cover too quickly for a clean shot. His steel treads churned the ground as he maneuvered back and forth for a good angle, but he came to realize he would be of little help to the desperate Americans.

Lieutenant Danvers knew the day was his.

The American force was quickly being whittled down. And with every man lost, their combat strength dropped further, accelerating their decline. The snipers had been key, and he made a mental note to see them properly recognized.

Now that he thought of them, he realized they'd stopped firing. *Perhaps they're repositioning?* In any event they'd done their job well. His men could handle it from here.

The British troops had found cover behind several military transport trucks. The windows had all been shot out, but they still provided good firing positions. His men's boots stepped over the shattered window fragments as they fought, adding the crunch of broken glass to the sounds of rifle shots and screams.

He crouched low behind a transport truck. Kneeling

beside a large tire, he peered under the truck's flatbed at the Americans' position. He guessed they had sixty men left, bunched together into a tight ball by the sniper fire. He paused, watching them carefully. A dozen men had rifles, but were no longer firing. *They're out of ammunition!* And the rest would be running low.

He sprinted away from the truck and joined the staff sergeant, who crouched behind a steel water tank, lining up a shot. He fired, and another American went down, clutching his belly in shock and surprise.

"Yes, Lieutenant?" he asked, looking up. Without missing a beat, he ejected the five-round magazine, snapped another in place, and chambered the first round. Then he paused, expecting orders.

The lieutenant appreciated the man's military bearing, and his respect for an officer who had seen far less combat than the grizzled NCO.

"I want you to take fifty men. Circle around and push into the Americans from the east. I will lead the remainder, and we'll crush them between us."

The staff sergeant saluted crisply. "Yes, sir!" He slung the rifle over his shoulder and ran through the British ranks, slapping men on the back, calling them to follow him. In minutes, he'd assembled his group to the east of the beleaguered Americans, and waited for the lieutenant's move.

Danvers knew the major was up on the bluff, watching the battle unfold. Well, let this be the first chapter in his military legacy. He looked around at the tired, eager faces waiting for the command to charge. They tasted victory and wanted to end this now, decisively. Still one hundred or so men strong, they would hit the Americans hard.

He raised his hand, then brought it down. "Charge!" he cried. The men rushed forward, yelling as they stormed out of cover. Rifles were raised and fired as they ran. The British stayed low, but surged forward in a wave.

On the far side of the battle, the staff sergeant saw the lieutenant charge, and led his fifty men forward to join them. They rushed to hit the Americans first, but the larger group had less distance to cross. Running, he brought his rifle up. He saw a beefy corporal taking aim at the lieutenant. Sighting for the man's gut, he squeezed off a round. The shot went wide, impacting the mess hall's outer wall. Without breaking pace he cycled the bolt to reload and fired again, this time hitting his target. The muscular corporal fell against the man standing beside him, then collapsed.

The lieutenant hadn't seen the corporal aiming for him, but he was elated to see the staff sergeant's men approaching. Both groups would hit the Americans and crash around them like a wave striking a rock. This battle would be over in minutes, and the base would be theirs. They were close now, twenty yards and closing fast. He clearly saw the Americans' panicked faces and felt pity for their fate, but also the thrill of conquest. *If only my father could be—*

A tremendous crash ripped through the air, like an avalanche or a ship running hard aground. The sound turned the head of every man on the field, and they all gaped at the sight that caused it.

A monstrous steel tank was roaring through the main gate. It was too big to fit, but with high speed and the mass of a building, it plowed forward. The gatehouse exploded in a cloud of brick and mortar as am eight-foot-tall tread punched through it. The other tread gouged a jagged truck-sized chunk from the watchtower's cement pillar. The thousand-pound mass of stone fell onto the tank, then rolled back and fell to the ground behind as the tank surged forward.

Beowulf was in the base now. Both British and American forces stared in astonishment as the tank roared toward them. Behind it the watchtower tilted, then crashed to the ground in a mound of rubble. A cloud of dust billowed into the air with a loud *whumpf* and served as a dramatic backdrop as the steel beast raced straight at them.

The colonel scanned the three masses of men and quickly found his allies. He mentally marked each of their faces as friendly, then willed his guns to kill every other man standing. One hundred and fifty-one hostiles. Detaching a small part of his mind, he assigned it the task of managing firing solutions and confirming enemy status before firing.

Satisfied that ballistics would be handled properly, he swung his main cannon to bear, but realized the force would be too great with friendlies nearby.

He adjusted course, swinging left twenty-seven degrees, bringing him on a collision course with the larger of the two British groups. He'd covered sixty yards already, since smashing through the gate. In another three seconds, he'd be upon his enemies.

With his electronic mind, he had the leisure to ponder thoughts in milliseconds. What used to be minutes of internal debate in his mind now happened in the blink of an eye. For him, everyone else had slowed to a crawl, but he knew it was he who had changed, not the universe.

He scanned the British and identified their ranking officer by insignia. Large command for a lieutenant, he mused. He wondered why the major stayed back on the bluff. Thomas was no coward. If anything, he loved the thrill of a fight. Especially one against Americans, given his history with Savannah. This must be a proving mission for a protégé. It would be his last.

The colonel checked his internal chronometer. His musing had used up fourteen-hundredths of a second. Again he marveled at how radically different his life had become. He closed on the lieutenant's group at twenty-seven miles per hour. Smashing through the gatehouse had slowed him down a bit, but this speed was sufficient. At twenty-three yards out, his shredders sprang to life.

As he bore down on the stunned British, both forward shredders spit rounds in a nonstop beat. With American lives at stake, he allowed himself two shots per kill. Twin rounds ripped through British soldiers before the shredders would twitch slightly, realigning for their next target. All around the lieutenant, his men dropped like leaves from an autumn tree.

Beowulf roared into their midst then, and the British found the will to tear their eyes away and dive aside as the tank burst through their line, stopping their charge instantly and dividing the group in two.

Around the tank's outer edge, the lieutenant saw eight shredders rise up, eager to send metal through flesh. They swiveled smoothly, mechanically, seeking targets and firing in 360 degrees around the huge tank.

Danvers couldn't quite process how deadly this machine was. In all directions, his soldiers continued falling and accumulating on the ground in morbid heaps. Nothing killed this fast. Even crack gun crews needed more time to fight this effectively. In seconds a hundred men were dead. The horror of the macabre spectacle froze him in place, and his breath caught in his throat as he watched the machine do its terrible work.

The stunned Americans had dived for cover at first, having never seen the top-secret tank before. But when they realized it fought for them, they stood and cheered as it brutally engaged the British.

The staff sergeant was equally appalled at the force tearing them apart, and his men were dropping as quickly. But years of combat had trained his nervous system to react without waiting for commands from his mind. He knew the battle was lost, even as men fell around him. He ran for cover, sprinting to reach the brick mess hall. If he could get behind it, he might be able to slip back out of the base unseen. Besides saving his own life, he knew Command needed to hear about this machine. He pumped his legs as hard as he could and threw down his rifle, letting his arms swing widely. Behind him he heard someone else following him, someone who also had fast instincts. *Good for him*, he thought, not taking his eyes from the safety of the building.

In the small, reserved part of the colonel's mind that handled firing solutions, British faces appeared, were checked against the database of allies, and condemned to die. Their faces were added to a queue for elimination, and a second later, a shredder swung and executed the sentence.

At times the colonel saw an opportunity to save ammo. By delaying firing for several tenths of a second, he was able to line up multiple targets. His rounds would cut through the closer target and pass through, killing the more distant one. He appreciated the efficiency possible by processing the tactics so extremely.

The lieutenant's face appeared in the kill queue, but the colonel placed an override on it, saving his life. If possible, he wanted to capture the man for interrogation.

The staff sergeant's lungs were screaming. The battle and his frantic sprinting had exhausted him, and he sucked the air hard for every bit of oxygen it held. He reached the corner of the mess hall, surprised by not feeling twin rounds rip into him, like his fellow fighters. As he whipped around the corner, he slammed his back against it, desperate for a quick breather. A moment later a skinny private raced past him, then joined him against the wall. Panting, they shared a silent look of congratulations as they caught their breath.

All around the lieutenant, his men fell in droves, until he was the only one standing. He stood alone, surrounded by piles of the dead. The morning sun on his face was warm, but he felt a deep chill spread up from his gut. His entire command, a full company. All gone in less than a minute. It simply was not possible.

Beowulf's guns ceased fire. The eight barrels each glowed a dull red, and Danvers saw the distortion of superheated air wavering above them. Simultaneously, they all retreated back within recessed ports, and the deadly machine was still.

The colonel scanned the area. He confirmed no friendly casualties had been targeted. He counted 148 British dead, plus the stunned lieutenant. With a sharp prick of alarm, he realized he was two men short. It had been a chaotic fight. It was possible two British had slipped out while he was otherwise engaged. He was already growing accustomed to machine-like efficiency, and loose threads annoyed him greatly.

Then he realized he had powers of sight beyond normal men. By default he preferred to see the world with eyes that saw light as he did as a mortal, in the 380- to 700-nanometer range. But now he could choose what frequencies his eyes saw. He shifted his visual receptors, allowing light in longer wavelengths to be detected. As he did so, he began to see the world of infrared light, which let him look through walls.

He scanned the area again. The heaps of dead British were quite hot, though slowly cooling. The standing lieutenant was brightly visible, of course. Then he saw two thermal masses, hiding behind the mess hall. They were resting, leaning against the wall. From his current angle, he guessed there was seven inches of brick between him and the two British. Too thick for a standard round. And if he moved, the sound would spook them. The colonel mentally smiled as he remembered he carried a magazine of armor-piercing rounds. He told a subsystem to load them into a shredder.

The staff sergeant was getting his breath back, and he clapped the private on the shoulder.

"Good instincts," he said. "Now let's get back and report this."

The private grinned and rested his head back on the brick. "Damn right, Sarge. We'll—"

He never finished the thought. Instead, he looked down, amazed to see a hole blasted through his stomach. Beowulf's armor-piercing round had sliced cleanly through the bricks and punched its way through the private's digestive system.

As the dying private slid down the wall, the staff sergeant threw himself to the ground. He heard a concussive crunch and saw a second fist-sized hole appear in the wall, right where he'd been standing.

He scrambled along the ground, crab-like, diving behind a shipping container, then standing to run like a man with the forces of hell behind him.

Beowulf saw the first shot connect, but the rapidly fading heat signature of the second told him he had a single runaway. He threw his treads in opposite directions, spun about in a fast 180, then tore after the fleeing staff sergeant.

He was limited in his mobility, as he didn't want to destroy the base for a single hostile, but he drove back along the main entryway, scanning in all directions. He came across a dozen Americans, mostly clerical workers who were coming out now that the fighting had stopped. But no British.

"You lucked out today," he muttered, terrifying an older admin woman peeking her head out of her office. She hastily slammed the door shut.

He thought of Major Thomas on the bluff, but knew he'd be gone before he could reach him. The colonel reversed course and returned to the grateful Americans.

Many were tending to the wounded. Tourniquets were being wound, stretchers were brought out, and a makeshift morgue had begun to separate the dead from the living. Beowulf ground to a stop beside the sole remaining living British, Lieutenant Danvers. The man wore a brave face, but knew he was in a bad spot. To run the point home, he had to crane his neck up to see the top of the battle tank standing over him. At that moment a lifetime free of combat seemed sweet indeed.

The stunned Americans crowded around, awed by the scale of Beowulf and what he had just accomplished. Some reached out to touch him, to convince themselves the past few minutes had actually happened.

Beowulf spoke to the intimidated officer. "Who are you?" he demanded, fully knowing the effect his amplified voice would have.

Danvers flinched, but was interrupted before finding his voice.

"Forget him," Sergeant Miller said, stepping forward and gently running two fingers along a woven-steel tread. "Who are *you*?"

He paused before replying. Now that the threat was past, what should he say? He was a top-secret project that had just been extravagantly exposed to the world. Should he let them know he was their colonel, just in a new form? Would that only shock them more? He struggled with the dilemma for a full five-tenths of a second, before finally deciding his best option was silence.

The Americans had taken Danvers into custody, and there was nothing more he could do here. Ignoring the question, he slowly turned and cautiously drove out of the base. Once outside, he accelerated, then curved around, heading for the valley and the home of Tesla's lab.

Major Thomas had seen the fleeing staff sergeant escape.

He'd known to avoid the main gate, and instead climbed atop a building near the base wall and gone over it, landing a good distance away from the base entrance. From there he ran for the nearest tree line.

The major kicked his horse up to speed and raced to intercept him. The jittery sergeant was spooked by a rider after him, then greatly relieved to see the major.

"Sergeant!" called the major.

"Major. Thank God!" the exhausted man replied. "You saw that thing?"

"I did, and I've never seen anything like it."

"I don't think anyone has," said the sergeant, leaning one hand against a tree and breathing hard. "I think the lieutenant was captured."

The major nodded. "He was." The disgrace of being taken alive would be the first entry in the lieutenant's military career. And maybe the last. The major's effort to find Savannah had cost him his lieutenant and a full company of men. He hated her even more for it.

He saw the sergeant eyeing his canteen, and he offered it. The sergeant raised it to his lips and eagerly gulped down the water. He was sloppy in his thirst, and half the water ran down the man's front, soaking his chest.

He paused to continue speaking. "That thing was alive, Major." He tipped the canteen back again and drained it.

"Alive? What do you mean by that?" The tank was monstrous, yes. But alive? He narrowed his eyes, wondering if the man had finally snapped from years in the field.

The sergeant saw the look. "Call me insane if you like, sir. But that thing moved like a person. It fought like a person. My brother drives a tank, and I am certain no human crew could do what I saw. Not possible." He pointed back at the base. "That thing is a new invention, and a game changer. That's my report, sir," he said, handing back the empty canteen.

Major Thomas accepted it and thought about his words. From his viewpoint, the thing was brutally effective. He decided he had no opinion on the sergeant's more fantastic claim of a living tank. But he'd heard of crazy new devices being invented by Einstein and his team of scientists. Was it possible the Americans had a similar magician?

It struck him then. That machine responded to the British threat because it had to. If they had never attacked this base, Fort Hamilton would have continued as a quiet, overlooked backwater. Which is precisely where you'd put your advanced research projects.

His passion had overridden his judgment in attacking Fort Hamilton, but by dumb luck, he'd uncovered a vital base for the Americans. Suddenly, the loss of one company seemed a fair price for such intelligence.

He rubbed at the stubble on his jaw. Even with the remainder of his force in New Haven, he couldn't take this base. Not with that thing guarding it. And if he waited too long, the Americans would redeploy it elsewhere. Maybe even to protect Boston.

He weighed his history with Savannah and the craving for revenge against the good of his country. Destroying that abomination had to come first, no matter the cost. Savannah, his daughter Madelaine, and the lieutenant had to be considered expendable. Sometimes official duty trumps personal needs.

He and the staff sergeant would ride back to New Haven, where he would order an immediate zeppelin bombing of this base. Before the next sunrise, that tank and everyone living near it would be ground to dust.

CAMARADERIE & BOMBS

The colonel sent the command codes for the outer doors and drove through the long, dark tunnel that led back to the lab. He'd grown more concerned about the security breach he and Tesla had committed. Not to say he wouldn't make the same choice again. He saw firsthand that the entire base garrison would have been slaughtered if he hadn't engaged the British.

Still, military and political brass weren't always known for their common sense. He chuckled, realizing he'd just included himself in that assessment. Part of his arrangement with the government had been that he retained his full rank and privileges as a colonel.

He approached the inner doors with a growing sense of worry. The downside of processing thoughts at the speed of a computer meant he had more time to grow anxious. He commanded the inner doors to let him pass, and they obeyed. Scanning carefully for any technicians in his path, he motored forward into the lab.

"He's back!" someone yelled, and the room erupted in a standing ovation. All around the lab, dozens of people stood and clapped, cheering his return.

"Not the response I expected," he said to the room.

Everyone laughed, and he was pleased to see Tesla run forward with Bertram. "The general called down and told us all about it," Tesla said. "You're a war hero, Colonel."

"And you just proved the viability of this project," added Bertram. "Conclusively."

"Well, I—" he replied. "I just reacted."

"Damn right you did!" yelled Savannah from the far side of the lab. She ran forward, Madelaine struggling to keep up with her. She slid to a stop in front of the tank and looked up, beaming.

"You saved them, Dad," she said. "You saved all of us."

Madelaine caught up to her mother. She raised both arms wide in the air and squealed, "You kicked ass, Papa!"

"Kicked ass. A fair assessment," agreed Tesla.

"I was worried about breaching project security—"

Tesla waved the concern away. "I made the call, Colonel, for right or wrong. Besides, with British troops on the ground, you would have been cleared soon. I spoke to the general, and he agreed. We're in the clear on that issue."

Tesla leaned in. "And the thrashing you gave the British certainly didn't hurt our case."

"It was incredible!" replied the colonel. "I felt invincible. I could process so much information. Like child's play! Multiple firing solutions were trivial. Honestly, I felt like the god of war out there."

"That's my dad," quipped Savannah. "Ever modest."

"Well, I mean—" he said.

"I'm kidding!" She laughed. "A hundred and fifty dead, with no friendly fire? That's kinda godlike. Just don't let it go to your head."

Tesla joined in. "Agreed. You're damned tough, but not invincible. A company of infantry is one thing, but there will be much worse out there."

"You still have to be careful, Papa," said Madelaine.

"I know, honey," he answered. "And I will, don't you worry."

Tesla turned to Bertram. "Shall we see how his systems fared in the battle?"

The lab director nodded vigorously. "Absolutely. Our first combat trial! Damn exciting!"

"I'll go over the RCA to begin with," said Tesla.

"Right," said Bertram. "Sophia, could you inspect Beowulf's armor? Catalog any hits, what caused them, and the resulting damage?"

"Be happy to," she replied.

"And George, get some help and check out the shredders. Sounds like the colonel put a lot of rounds through them. I'll have a look at the drivetrain and furnace."

For most of the day, the team went over every inch of Beowulf, recording any damage found and verifying all systems were still within desired parameters.

Sophia found dozens of impact marks along the hull armor, but none were more than scratches. The Enfield rounds had bounced off harmlessly, even the dozen impacts she found in the treads.

The shredders had been given a thorough workout, and the black powder buildup in the eight barrels proved it. George personally cleaned each one meticulously, spending four hours on the job. It wouldn't do for Beowulf to have a jammed gun out there.

The colonel had burned through a good amount of coal, Bertram saw. Getting his mass up the valley's slope at speed was energy-intensive. But coal was plentiful and cheap. While the nuclear boys upstairs were making great strides, they hadn't yet gotten a reactor scaled down enough for powering a tank.

Bertram had the coal reserves refilled, and the steam tank's gaskets and fittings checked. A few copper fittings had worked loose, letting some pressure escape. They were resoldered, and Bertram figured Beowulf would have an extra 6 percent power on his next outing.

The day passed smoothly, with everyone preoccupied on his assignments. Through it all the colonel felt humbled by their diligence and efforts. He supposed some hero worship was unavoidable, given the circumstances. But he continually felt his recent success against the British was very much a shared victory.

UPSTATE NEW YORK, USA

The British zeppelin *Orion* cruised at 7,300 feet, just above the cloud layer. Captain Mary Francis Montgomery loved looking out the wraparound windows and seeing only sunlight and clouds. She was pretty, in a severe manner, with long dark hair tumbling past her shoulders, but the expression of serenity on her face made her seem calm and approachable.

Zeppelins typically cruised much lower, at 650 feet, but could go as high as 24,000 feet, if needed. To avoid rough weather, it was customary to stay low and observe cloud patterns before entering them. But wartime had other demands on the great ship. Over hostile terrain, staying hidden took priority.

It was surreal to look down on a bed of clouds, she thought. Flying this high made navigation more difficult, certainly. There were no landmarks to spot, only miles and miles of white cotton clouds. But the inspiring view made it worthwhile. Besides, that's why God invented dead reckoning navigation.

She fixed her long hair in a ponytail and ran her fingers over the navigation chart of the Eastern United States, then checked the wood and brass command dashboard and saw their course of 177 degrees held steady. Their current run of four hours on this heading at eighty miles per hour was coming to an end. With a ruler she drew a course line, then used a divider to plot their current position. Twenty-eight miles north of her target.

She'd never heard of Fort Hamilton, and after doing some quick research, she still wasn't clear why Major Thompson ordered her to bomb the area so thoroughly. But he'd been exceedingly clear on the importance of her attack.

She'd spent time in New York City before the war and remembered the Broadway shows warmly. Dropping bombs near that city made her uncomfortable, and she had more sympathy for the Americans who fought in their Civil War. Attacking an unfamiliar enemy was hard enough, but when your adversary was familiar, even liked, it would be truly horrible. She had pushed back on the major's order at first, until he made it clear her officer's commission was on the line.

It hadn't been easy, gaining the captain's status as a woman. Years of whispered jokes and condescending smiles had begun to wear on her. But the king was more open-minded about such things than his predecessor, and made it known he wanted to see more balance in troop assignments. Within reason, of course. She knew this was as close to combat as she'd ever see. But cruising over the clouds was a damn sight better than hauling cod out of the North Atlantic, which her father had done and which she was destined for, before joining the air corps.

And so she'd accepted the orders and would carry them out. She would saturate the base with conventional warheads, then station her ship over Fort Hamilton and stand by for the order to release one of Einstein's new radiological bombs, set for airburst. The radiation would spread for miles, rendering the area deadly to all living things. It would be months, maybe years, before the area was fit for human life again. Whatever that base contained, Major Thomas wanted it dead in a bad way.

She looked around the bridge at her young flight crew.

Lieutenant Leeson was manning the rudder controls. He stood tall, both hands on the large rudder wheel. He was focused intensely on the gyro compass in front of him, occasionally flicking a glance at the twin pointers that showed the angles of the upper and lower rudders.

Running the rudders was considered an easier job on the bridge. Once officers gained experience there, they'd be moved to the elevator controls, responsible for maintaining the ship's pitch. Lieutenant Roberts had recently gained that honor. He stood before the elevator wheel, facing to the ship's port side. Scanning the elevator panel constantly, he took in the angle of their twin elevators, the ambient temperature and humidity, their altitude, rate of climb, and the temperature of the lifting gas cells.

Beside him, the ballast board showed how much water was in each of their seven 4,400-pound ballast tanks. Below that, the gas board displayed the pressure within the sixteen hydrogen cells, and each had a corresponding valve for releasing the gas, to allow the ship to descend.

She glanced at the chronometer. In less than an hour, it would be time to bring her ship below the clouds and carry out her orders. She hoped the radiation wouldn't carry over to the city. Someday she hoped to see more shows on Broadway.

As the day wound to a close, the lab turned from inspections on Beowulf to celebration. Clipboards were put down and bottles of beer taken up. The lab team had never been terribly formal, and as the evening began, the combination of victory and alcohol gave rise to a lively spirit of camaraderie.

Worktables were cleared as people sat on them, chatting and laughing about the day, and then about the future. Everyone had been worried about the war of course, but

Beowulf's performance today gave them deep satisfaction. The work had been worth the effort. The base was safe again, and they were poised to make major contributions to the war effort. Maybe to the nature of warfare itself. Even without the drinks, such a thought was dizzying.

Tesla was working on his second beer, enjoying the feeling of the ice-cold glass bottle in his hand. "Beer is fine, but it lacks a certain intensity," he mused.

"It does serve well as a lead-up," replied Savannah, clinking her bottle against his.

He cocked his head, questioning her. "Have you held out on me?"

She smiled mischievously. "I might know where Bertram keeps a bottle of rye whiskey. If you're interested in such a thing."

Tesla studied the beer in his hand. "This now seems insufficient," he said, setting it down.

Savannah knocked back her bottle and finished her beer. "Be right back," she told him, then got up and wove her way through chatting lab workers.

Tesla eased back in his chair, resting his hands behind his head. He closed his eyes and listened to the chatter all around him.

George was chatting up a young woman behind him, and by the sound of her warm laughter, he'd be enjoying her company later that night.

He heard Sophia explaining why the works of Dickens should be required reading in school. Someone told her they generally were.

"Oh," she replied. "Well, that's good then. The kids will love it. They really will. What a journey they have in store for them!" Tesla chuckled. Sophia must have started drinking before he did.

"Fall asleep on me?" Savannah asked.

His eyes popped open, and he sat up. "Not at all. Just taking the pulse of the room." He saw she carried a half-full bottle of whiskey and two shot glasses, and smiled.

"Yeah? And your prognosis of the room?" She sat and began pouring for them both.

Tesla took his glass and raised it in toast to her. "All will be well," he said, taking a deep sip.

7,300 FEET ABOVE FORT HAMILTON, NY, USA

"It's time, Captain," said the young bridge officer of the *Orion*.

Captain Mary Francis Montgomery looked up from her book, *The Rise and Fall of the Roman Empire*, and saw Lieutenant Roberts standing over her.

She glanced at the chronometer and confirmed it was time to begin their bombing run.

"Very well, Lieutenant," she said, rising. She lifted the telephone handset from its cradle and spoke to the engineering room.

"Engineering, bridge. Make your speed one-half," she ordered.

"One-half, aye!" came the reply. She felt the four engines slow, their vibrations growing softer.

"Helmsman, down bubble five degrees," she said.

Lieutenant Leeson spun his wheel, watching the indicator carefully. Within a glass tube, a thick liquid held a single air bubble. As the ship responded to the change, the bubble slid to one side, indicating a good dive.

"Down bubble five degrees," he confirmed.

Behind her, Lieutenant Roberts was back at elevator control. Watching the altimeter, he called out, "Seven thousand feet, Captain."

Captain Montgomery nodded. With rudders down, the thrust from their engines was driving them lower. She could bring the ship to attack altitude this way, but it would take too long. She wanted to be at eight hundred feet for the bombing. They needed to release hydrogen from the cells to make the ship heavier.

She turned to face Roberts. "Release lifting gas for eight hundred feet, Lieutenant," she ordered.

He nodded and slowly twisted valves along the length of the gas board. The ship vented hydrogen into the atmosphere, losing a small portion of their buoyancy. He worked to keep the ship in balance, venting equal amounts along their length.

"Ship is coming down, Captain," he reported. As they neared the target altitude, he would release water ballast to hold them at eight hundred feet.

"Very good," she said. She picked up the phone again. "Bomb bay, bridge. Attack run will be at eight hundred feet. Saturation bombing, conventional warheads. Stand by."

Along with Lieutenant Roberts, she watched the altimeter click steadily lower.

Six thousand feet…fifty-six hundred feet…

The lab had quieted considerably as dinner approached. Most everyone had cleared out for the day, leaving Tesla and Savannah lounging in low chairs beside Beowulf's right tread. The bottle of whiskey sat on a nearby table, but held quite a bit less than two hours ago.

Tesla had sunk low into his chair, and his feet were up on Savannah's chair. For her part, she'd matched him drink for drink, but seemed more composed, sitting forward with her elbows resting on her knees. The colonel had joined in their wandering conversation, but lamented the fact he couldn't drink anymore.

"Are you religious, Nikola?" Savannah asked.

He shrugged. "Religion," he said, "is simply an ideal. It is an ideal force that tends to free the human being from material bonds. I do not believe that matter and energy are interchangeable, any more than are the body and soul. There is just so much matter in the universe, and it cannot be destroyed."

He drew in a deep breath and let it out, pondering her question further. "As I see life on this planet, there is no individuality. It may sound ridiculous to say so, but I believe each person is but a wave passing through space, ever-changing from minute to minute as it travels along—finally, some day, just becoming dissolved."

Savannah stared at him wide-eyed as his answer rolled through her brain. She closed her eyes to focus, but that didn't help, so she opened them again.

Before she could form a response, the colonel interjected. "And that, my daughter, is why I wish I could still drink."

"You're better off," said Edison. He approached the group, carrying a tall stack of notebooks.

Of the three of them, the colonel was the only one not startled by Edison's arrival. Savannah's head jerked up, but she flashed a welcoming smile by habit. Tesla raised an eyebrow, but gave no other outward indication of surprise.

"You disapprove of alcohol, Mr. Edison?" asked the colonel.

He dropped the stack of books on a table beside Tesla. "I have better use for my head. To put alcohol in the human brain is like putting sand in the bearings of an engine."

Tesla rolled his eyes. "Sanded many engines, have you?"

Edison ignored the question and pointed to the notebooks. "Bertram asked me to bring these. The after-action findings of your tank's status." He turned to leave.

"You don't approve of Beowulf," said Tesla. "Why are you

here?"

Edison turned back with a huff of impatience. "The president asked me to assist the lab's work. One doesn't disappoint a president."

Tesla nodded sagely. "Right. Could be bad for business."

"You're rather pure, aren't you?" asked Edison, his lips curling in a humorless smile.

Tesla poured himself another whiskey. "The scientific man does not aim at an immediate result. His work is like that of a planter for the future. His duty is to lay the foundation for those who are to come and point the way."

Edison scoffed. "Very easy to say, working with other people's money. This facility cost a fortune. Capital isn't free, Tesla. It's an engine to be put to work. It has value on its own."

Tesla sipped his drink, content to let Edison make his speech.

"In fact," he continued, "anything that won't sell, I don't want to invent. Its sale is proof of utility, and utility is success."

Tesla scowled. "Men like you are an impediment to progress. The frontiers of the mind won't be pushed back with safe, conventional thinking." He slowly downed the shot of whiskey, enjoying Edison's disapproval even more than the burning flavor.

Edison knew when he was being goaded. "Do you require whiskey every day to be productive?"

Tesla shook his head. "Not at all. Vodka, beer—any type of alcohol, really—is perfectly acceptable."

The colonel chuckled. Savannah stifled a laugh, her hand clasped over her mouth. She was pleasantly drunk, and the warm buzzing in her head made her forget her manners.

Edison recognized he was the outsider in this group and was eager to rejoin Bertram upstairs. He nodded toward Savannah.

"Mrs. Browning," he said, then spun and walked away.

"Good evening, Mr. Edison," she called after him, with a touch of guilt. When he was out of earshot, she swatted Tesla on the shoulder. "You should be nicer to him. He means well."

Tesla grunted. "His kind…more concerned with market forces than the workings of the universe."

She smiled. "Well, 'his kind' help good things happen too."

"Hmm." He looked around. "Where's Madelaine?"

"One floor up. The physics team is trying out a new approach to anti-gravity."

"Fascinating. And she is interested in physics?"

Savannah shook her head. "Not that much. But the team leader has a daughter two years older, Tracy. They've become a terrible twosome. At twelve, life is all about peer approval."

"It's good to have a hobby," said Tesla.

Savannah couldn't decide if that was the whiskey talking, or just classic Tesla. Either way, she nodded.

"Uh-huh," she agreed.

The colonel had been listening, but also replaying the day's events in his mind. He found several instances where he could have optimized more effectively, but overall he was satisfied with his performance.

"Tesla, what you have done will change the face of war as we know it," he said. "Do you realize the gift you delivered? No more foxholes or trenches. No more mustard gas, gangrene, or field amputations. This is a major step forward for mankind."

Like all inventors, Tesla enjoyed having his work appreciated. "Let the future tell the truth," he replied, "and evaluate each man according to his work and accomplishments. The present is theirs; the future, for which I have really worked, is mine."

"Well said—"

THOOMP. A muffled explosion came from above them,

and a slight tremor ran through the floor, then faded away.

"What the hell was that?" asked Savannah.

Tesla sat up straight in his chair, now more alert. His eyes narrowed as he guessed at the unexpected noise. "Colonel?"

"My seismic sensor picked it up loud and clear. Some type of impact, quite close. I believe it came from one floor up."

Savannah looked at Tesla, and they shared a concerned worry. "Madelaine," she said, leaping from her chair and running for the elevator.

Before she reached it, the platform began descending. She and Tesla stood waiting for it to arrive.

"Hurry up!" she yelled, pounding her thigh with a clenched fist.

Finally, the platform slipped below the lab's ceiling, and she saw Madelaine coming down with Bertram. A wash of relief flowed through her body, knowing her daughter was safe.

"Bertram, what's going on? Is everything—"

He raised his hands. "Everything is fine. The gravity test had a small issue, but no one was hurt. I figured I better get Maddy down to you right away, though."

The lift settled, and Savannah ran up to grab Madelaine, clutching her in a tight hug and lifting her from the floor.

"God, Maddy," she said. "I was so worried. Think I aged a year in a minute."

"I'm fine, Mom. It was fun," she said, but she buried her face in Savannah's shoulder anyway. They were having less of these moments as she grew older, but Maddy admitted they still felt good.

Unconsciously, Savannah stood Madelaine up and ran her hands over her, ensuring she wasn't hurt. "Bertram, that sounded like an explosion." The statement came out more accusatory than she'd intended.

He nodded. "Technically, no. But we did experience a

rapid release of energy. Like I said, though, no one was injured."

At her raised eyebrow and silent look, he continued. "The experiment involved manipulating gravity waves by use of a localized field of anti-graviton radiation. Basically, we tried to destroy the subatomic particles that carry the force of gravity."

"You destroyed something, all right," said Madelaine.

"Unfortunately, the experiment worked too well. The lead cannonball we tried to levitate was instead fired into the ceiling at great force."

"You shot a cannonball into the ceiling?" asked Savannah.

"Not *into*, per se…"

"Bertram!"

"It went through three floors. I'm told it's currently lodged in the wall of level three."

"That's fantastic!" exclaimed Tesla.

"One word for it," said Savannah. "And no one was hurt by that thing ripping through the floors?"

"We were…quite lucky in that regard," admitted Bertram. "Although we may have some structural damage to repair."

"Lovely," she said. "Well, the price of knowledge. Right, Nikola?"

"Absolutely," he agreed. For a man whose experiments brought down buildings and generated lightning, the lab had been a rather tame affair. Runaway cannonballs added spice to the day.

1,400 FEET ABOVE FORT HAMILTON, NY, USA

As the zeppelin *Orion* descended lower, Captain Montgomery could now make out the details of the base. The main gate seemed to have already taken damage, which was odd. She scanned the ground, tracing the perimeter of the base in her mind. There were no specific targets in the major's order. Her instructions called for a full saturation bombing, so she focused on where the base's outer limits were. Everything inside that ring would be decimated.

She glanced at the altimeter. Twelve hundred feet…one thousand feet…

"Level us out, helm," she ordered.

Lieutenant Leeson spun his wheel and watched the bubble slide back to the center of the indicator. "Level bubble, Captain."

Nine hundred feet…

"Drop ballast for eight hundred feet," she said.

Lieutenant Roberts nodded and spun four wheels. He watched the levels of their water tanks drop, then checked the rate of climb indicator.

Eight hundred and fifty feet…

As their rate of climb settled toward zero, he closed the ballast wheels. Releasing the water had given the ship more lift, just enough to stay level at their desired height. The huge airship soon found its balance in the cool evening air and became neutrally buoyant.

"We are now level at eight hundred feet, Captain," he called back.

"Engines ahead one-half," she said, then called the bomb bay. "We begin our run now, gentlemen. Full saturation. Space twelve conventional bombs across the base. Fire at will."

The order was acknowledged, and within the bomb bay, a junior captain patted the first bomb, already set in the attack rails.

He went to the release console and opened the bomb bay doors. The sudden howl of cold air was always a shock, even when you knew it was coming.

He watched his board, leaning down to look into a sighting eyepiece. The black rubber cup shut out everything but the view directly under them. Watching patiently, the bombardier watched as the ground below slid along his view.

Then the base came into sight. He'd already calculated for the delay at eight hundred feet, and at the right moment, his finger pressed a red metal button.

Nearby, in the attack rails, a latch released. The large steel bomb hung in the air momentarily, then fell free.

"God in heaven," whispered Sergeant Miller, leaning against the doorframe that led to the sick bay. The flood of wounded and dead Americans had overwhelmed the medical facility, though three doctors and a dozen nurses scrambled to deal with the onslaught.

Miller had been shot in the shoulder, but the sights, sounds, and smells of the chaos distracted him from the pain and the slick wetness of blood coating his arm and chest. The cries and screams came in different flavors, some muffled and suffering, others bright and clear. The worst came from the back, where behind a white curtain, a surgeon removed limbs, a necessary horror to prevent a bigger loss.

The large square windows were closed, but light streamed in, shooting through the bay's dust-filled air in dramatic shafts.

Miller had no medical training, but he could offer comfort. Pushing himself off the doorframe, he shuffled into the hectic, terrible scene. He found a bed nearby with a young corporal in it, lying on his back with a thick field dressing strapped to his midsection. His eyes were glazed, fixed on the ceiling above, but flicked to Miller as he approached. The corporal's mouth opened, then closed. His eyes blinked once, slowly.

Miller sat on the man's bed and took him by the hand. The corporal's grip tightened, and the pressure told Miller he'd done the right thing. He smiled, encouraging the injured man.

"Not to worry, Corporal. A cute nurse will be back for you soon. Till then, you just lie there and keep goldbricking."

He got a small smile in reply, and the corporal nodded slightly. "I'll…wait here," he said.

Miller's response was drowned out by a deafening explosion outside. Nothing like the high-pitched clap of fireworks, this was a deep, rumbling, in-your-gut boom that said *don't fuck with me*.

"What the—" he said, instinctively turning toward the sound. A warning rose up in his brain, but didn't quite get there in time.

Four buildings away, the bomb's shock wave raced out from the point of impact, throwing people into the air and sending them spinning like unwanted dolls. Trees older than Miller were grabbed by the wall of force and ripped from the ground, only to be tossed back down forty yards away.

As the shock wave struck the outer wall of the sick bay, the pressure slammed against the brick wall, bowing it in. The windows immediately lost the fight and exploded inward, pelting everyone inside with a rain of shattered glass.

Miller saw the windows disintegrate and turned his head aside, already diving to throw himself over the corporal's face. His reaction was fast, but couldn't beat the spray of razor-sharp glass racing at him.

The shards washed over him, slicing the side of his face and neck a dozen times. The cuts hurt sharply, and he gasped at the sensation, already feeling the too-familiar awareness of wet slickness covering his hands and face. *How much blood can a man lose before passing out?* He opened his eyes and focused them on the corporal.

He'd taken a nasty gash across the forehead, and a thick rivulet of blood was already running into his eye, but otherwise he'd not been badly hurt. Miller pulled at the bed sheet and mopped the blood away from the corporal's eyes.

"You OK?" he asked.

The stunned corporal opened his eyes. They swam around the room before settling on Miller. His grip tightened again.

"Good man," said Miller. "Hang on, I'm going to check outside." He pulled his hand free and headed back to the doorway. Behind him the chorus of cries had quieted since the blast. He hoped that was just from the shock.

He pushed the sick bay doors open and stepped outside, looking around for answers. Men and women were running in all directions, many screaming. He turned toward the explosion's direction and ran out into the street for a clearer view. The sight made his skin grow cold.

A black, smoking crater had opened up where the mess hall used to be. His mind refused to accept the news, and he stood frozen, his imagination still seeing the large two-story building where hundreds of people had met for meals and laughter. But it was gone, obliterated in a high-explosive blast. But the only thing that could do that—

He looked up into the sky and saw the zeppelin. It floated peacefully above him, eight hundred feet up. Moving forward at thirty knots, it seemed to be ponderously lofting its way across the sky. But it could carry bombs. A lot of very large bombs.

He saw something fall from the zeppelin then. It was dark and large, but growing closer by the second.

"Oh Christ," he muttered.

The second bomb landed just outside the sick bay front door and detonated.

Sergeant Miller was the first casualty as the shock wave roared outward, and he disappeared instantly. The explosion tore into sick bay, stripping the walls off the building in a flash. Some of the roof was blown backward by the force, but most of it collapsed in place, crushing the wounded men and women in their cots.

The surrounding structures fared no better. Three administrative buildings disintegrated in the blast, killing the sixty-two occupants before they knew what had happened.

The *Orion* continued on, and as the base continued sliding into view within the bombardier's eyepiece, he continued pressing the red metal button.

In the lab the colonel was enjoying taking a catalog of the new stored data Tesla had installed. He'd included several hundred books in digital form, which should make the evenings a bit less lonely.

As the first bomb fell a half mile away on the base above, the force rippled through the earth. This far from the blast, and deep underground, the effect was too minute to be felt by humans, but a subroutine monitoring Beowulf's seismic sensor detected a strong pulse that didn't fit any expected parameters. It processed the signal for several tenths of a second before deciding to report the discovery.

The subroutine filed a summary report in Beowulf's main awareness queue and attached a priority code. Milliseconds later the colonel became aware of the incoming data.

"Hey, guys," he began. "I think something's happening on the surface."

"That covers a lot of ground, Colonel," said Tesla.

"An explosion of some kind. Maybe a fuel tank? I don't have a library of seismic data to check against, sadly."

"That's a good idea, though," said Tesla, scribbling a note. "We should ask the general about that."

Savannah came closer. "How far away, Dad?"

"About thirty-eight hundred feet from my position. That's diagonal to the surface, of course."

"Within the base then, for sure," she said.

"Correct."

Bertram frowned. "I'll call Operations, see what they know about it." He headed for the lab wall and the phone to the surface.

Just then the colonel spoke again. "Another one, Bertram. About four hundred and sixty feet from the first one."

The lab's klaxon wailed, and Madelaine stuck her fingers in her ears, grimacing.

"Another attack?" yelled Tesla. Savannah shrugged her shoulders, but made sure she could see Madelaine.

Bertram ran to the lab's wall, silenced the alarm, then called Operations. His face grew tense as he listened, then quizzical when the line went dead. He hung up and returned to the group.

"What's happening now?" asked Savannah.

"I…we're being bombed."

"What?" she yelled.

"Operations said a zeppelin was bombing the base. The line went dead before I could get anything else."

"I'm detecting a third detonation," said the colonel. "Given what Bertram said, this is probably the start of a prolonged bombing run."

"So we're stuck down here," said Savannah.

"You mean we're *safe* down here," corrected Bertram, throwing a glance toward Madelaine. She was doing a good impression of a brave young girl, but he saw the fear in her tight lips.

Savannah pulled her daughter close and wrapped her arms around her. "We're fine down here, honey. We'll just wait it out. No problem at all."

"I know, I'm not scared," she said, clutching her mother's waist tightly. Savannah stroked her daughter's hair, letting her have the final word on the subject.

She hated the idea of being out of touch with the base. Ever since they had fled England, Fort Hamilton had been their home. The garrison here had become extended family, and the base was a great place to raise a child. Until today.

The colonel's voice boomed. "Well, there's no need for me to hide out in here. I've got a hell of a main cannon, and haven't been able to try it out yet. If I can get an angle that high, I'll blast that gasbag out of the sky."

Tesla and Savannah shared a look. Beowulf's cannon could get the job done, but the bombs falling out there could kill even the heavily armored tank.

"He's your father," offered Tesla, reluctant to send the colonel into a truly dangerous situation.

Savannah nodded. She stared at the floor, thinking it through, then looked up.

"There's no choice," she said, looking to Bertram. "That zeppelin is killing our home."

"Agreed," he said.

Savannah turned to the massive tank. "Go get it, Dad."

"Will do." Beowulf's power system surged, and the tank slid forward slowly on its huge treads.

The colonel accessed his records for the door codes and was about to throw them at the door access in a tight radio burst when the lab's lights flickered, then went dark. Beowulf stopped, analyzing the situation.

The lab went black as a bottomless mine. Madelaine's grasp on her mother's leg grew tighter, and Savannah was grateful her daughter had been against her when the power failed.

"Mom?" she said, her voice trembling.

Savannah patted her head gently. "Don't worry, honey. We're fine."

Tesla intuitively reached out into the darkness. The sudden blindness was disorienting, but he stood still.

"What the hell?" muttered Bertram in the dark. "Must have hit the power relay station. Nobody move, backups will be on—"

Around the large room, eight dim backup lights snapped on, not enough to cover the whole lab, but they weren't blind anymore. Mounted high on the walls, the lights cast shallow pools of light, surrounded by wide expanses of darkness.

"That's a bit better," said Tesla.

"I can improve on that," said the colonel. Across Beowulf's front, five recessed lights flared, bathing the far wall in white light, and raising the visibility in their half of the lab.

"Nicely done," said Tesla.

"Unfortunately, that's all I can do. The doors aren't responding to my codes."

"Quite right," said Bertram. "When we lost main power, we lost the tunnel doors. Backup power isn't sufficient to open them."

"Damn!" yelled the colonel. "And I can't blast them open —"

"Without blowing out our eardrums? No," said Bertram. "The overpressure in the room might even kill us."

"Damn!" he said again. "I guess we are stuck down—"

The fourth bomb from the zeppelin *Orion* landed then, directly above them.

The bomb's pressure-trigger was designed to detonate upon impact with the ground. The bomb fell from the *Orion* and landed on the Rabbit Hole's entry building. It hit the roof and very nearly triggered the explosion then, but the roof failed under the huge weight, and the bomb punched through. It fell another twenty feet, then struck the floor inside the secured building and detonated, exploding the building from within. Tons of brick, steel, and wood were blasted away in a millisecond.

The lab's top level was destroyed by the blast. It had been dedicated to computing machines, and under Hollerith's leadership, was making great strides in processing information rapidly. The long banks of computers were smashed against one another, and every technician on the floor died instantly, Hollerith among them. America had just lost one of the finest minds in the field, but the devastation was only beginning.

"Jesus!" cried the colonel. "Right on top of us!"

Bertram ran to the elevator shaft, while Tesla yelled at him to get back.

"The elevator platform is here on our level. If we can get it above us, it might shield us from further damage. There's a counterweight system," he said, throwing open a panel in the elevator base and digging inside.

Tesla ran for Savannah and Madelaine to pull them away from the open elevator shaft.

Seven floors above them, the force from the zeppelin's two-ton bomb dug into the computing lab, ripping several tears through the floor, and sending thousand-pound slabs of flooring crashing into the level below.

Level two was Electrical, where Tesla had seen the huge steel and ceramic towers he'd invented. A slab of concrete fell against one of the "Tesla coils," toppling it like a twenty-foot tree. The device was designed to take current and greatly increase its voltage. At the top of the tower, a conductive steel ball served as an exit point for the electricity. There was no current flowing through the device currently, but the tower itself was a danger, ripping loose thick wiring as it fell. It smashed against a beefy power generator, then slid off, collapsing onto the floor with an ear-assaulting crash.

The force of the fall pressed against a man-sized capacitor, still fully charged from before the blackout. As the storage device was torn from its foundation, it fell over, rolling across the snarl of wiring from the downed coil. Two elements touched, and the capacitor released its energy in a blinding flash. The current roared into the coil, and the voltage quickly shot up until it reached the point of arcing off the coil's steel ball.

A dazzling snake of lighting leaped from the conductor, sizzling through the air, seeking a path to ground. The coil's collapse had brought it perilously close to the generator, and its steel fuel tank. The arcing current reached out with tendrils of blinding current that approached the temperature of the sun. The blazing tendrils stroked the fuel tank and ignited the fuel within.

Six hundred gallons of gasoline exploded with a force comparable to the zeppelin's bomb. The shock wave killed everyone on the floor, and a fireball shot up into level one and broke through into level three below.

The Robotics lab was next to fall. A dozen mechanical creations resembling dogs, birds, and even men were engulfed in the ferocious orange flames. There were only seven workers on the floor at the time, but they were all instantly burned to death, crouching away from the fires.

The structure had been heavily built, and the damage would have settled down at level three, not penetrating deeper. But earlier that day, an anti-gravity experiment had gone awry, sending a heavy steel cannonball punching through the building. Among the damage had been a structural support beam in the floor of level three. It had been cleanly snapped through by the shot, which had sapped much of the cannonball's energy, so it finally stopped, lodged in the wall nearby. But the damage had been done.

The fuel explosion slammed down into the floor, and with a main beam crippled, the floor gave. A single large split formed in the floor, like a ragged gash running the length of the lab. The wound sagged open, and the weight of the flooring slumped down toward it. Desks, chairs, bookcases, and bodies slid along the slanting floor and fell through the gash into the lab below.

The energy from the fuel explosion raced in all directions,

seeking release. Most was directed up and down, but a portion of the force was channeled sideways, into the elevator shaft. As it moved, it collected debris. Chairs, iron rebar, and chunks of concrete were all scooped up and blasted along by the force into the elevator shaft.

At level four, workers dove under their tables, seeking cover from the macabre rain of furniture, debris, and dead coworkers. In seconds the rain stopped. The flooring settled and stopped groaning. A cloud of dust was still hanging in the air, but the worst seemed to be over. Tentatively, they began to pull themselves out and take stock.

Bertram had succeeded in raising the elevator platform two feet when the explosion ran down the shaft. The force crashed down into the platform, now at the height of his belly. A horrible mix of debris was driven down by the explosion, and a fist-sized piece of brick ricocheted off the platform, then punched into Bertram's chest. Orange flames roared down the shaft, then retreated.

The air in his lungs was pushed out in a single huff, and his hands came up. The world grew hazy. He blinked to clear his vision, but the lab only grew darker. *I never taught Madelaine about the Knight*, he thought.

"I—" he said, then fell sideways, landing hard on his side. He saw Savannah running to him, but before she reached him, his eyes closed.

"Bertram!" she screamed, sliding to her knees beside him. She rolled him onto his back and stifled a sob when she saw the wound. The brick had partially embedded into his chest. He was unconscious, but his chest still rose and fell.

"Savannah—" said Tesla. Something about his tone was off. It carried an undercurrent of panic, even hysteria, she'd never heard from him. The fear of Bertram dying gave way to a new chilling awareness. Her mind told her not to look, but her body acted anyway. She turned back and saw Tesla standing beside Madelaine.

Her daughter stood, unsteady and dazed. A three-foot section of iron rebar stuck out of her belly.

"Mom," she said, then fell to her knees. Tesla grabbed her shoulders, keeping her from falling forward.

"No!" Savannah screamed. The world fell away. Nothing else existed then, except the sight of her daughter. Madelaine's eyes were wide, the whites clearly visible in the dusty glow from Beowulf's lights. Her mouth worked, but no sound came. The wide eyes blinked, slowly.

"Maddy!" yelled Savannah, scrambling along the floor, reaching for her girl. She took Madelaine's face in her hands, holding her up. "Maddy! Stay awake, honey. Just stay awake!"

The colonel could see what had happened, but felt helpless to assist, even to offer comfort. He stayed silent.

Savannah's face was flushed and hot, despite the tears running down her cheeks. Together they'd fled a cruel man, crossed an ocean, and made a new home. If God chose to take her this way now, he was a crueler bastard than Thomas had ever been.

Tesla held a hand to his mouth, aghast. The bar had run her clean through, with ten inches of it sticking out her back. He knelt behind her, touched the clothing around the wound, and looked at his fingers. The blood was dark.

He was no medic, but he knew a spleen rupture meant death was all but certain under these circumstances. It meant her blood was no longer being filtered, and that she was bleeding internally at an alarming rate. At her small size, she had minutes to live, if that.

He'd never been religious, not like his father. The concept of asking for desires, rather than working for them, seemed odd. Despite that he willed a silent prayer to any god who may be listening.

Madelaine's eyes were drooping. She was fighting to stay

conscious, but the lure of sleep was wrapping her in a soft, final embrace.

"Love you, Mom," she whispered.

Savannah was nearing hysterics. She raged with the need to do something, but was impotent to help her daughter. She kissed Madelaine's cheeks, now going pale, and whispered in her ear. When she pulled back and saw the iron bar puncturing Madelaine's belly, she shook uncontrollably, mumbling in denial.

A wild, irrational idea came to Tesla then, born of desperation. He eased his grip on Madelaine's shoulders, letting Savannah take the weight.

"Hold her," he said. "I have an idea." He leaped up and ran to his workstation, assembling pieces of hardware together quickly. "OK," he muttered to himself. "This can work."

He returned to Savannah. "Help me get her to my table," he said. Savannah didn't respond.

"Now, Savannah!" he yelled, shaking her. Her head snapped up, and glassy eyes found his. Barely comprehending, she nodded.

Together they lifted the young girl, Savannah holding her feet and Tesla wrapping his arms under her back. They sat her up on the edge of the table.

"I need to lay her down," he said. Savannah blinked at him absently. "I need to remove the bar first."

Savannah's pretty face turned ugly, and a deep scowl carved into her features.

"There's no time," he said. "I'm sorry for this."

Tesla stood in front of Madelaine and took hold of the bar. As gently as he could, he pulled. The iron bar slid forward an inch, and Madelaine's eyes popped open wide. She screamed in pain, then vomited.

"Nikola!" yelled Savannah. "Stop!"

Tesla ignored her and pulled again. The bar slid forward,

and then it was out of her. Madelaine's eyes flared wide, then shut. Mercifully, she'd passed out.

She slumped forward. Tesla dropped the bar and caught her in his arms as the bloody iron clattered to the floor.

"What are you doing?" asked Savannah.

"Saving her life." He laid Madelaine on her back, then picked up the consciousness transfer gear.

"But…we can't," said Savannah. "There's only one RCA."

"That's true," said the colonel, understanding Tesla's plan. "And I had seventy-two good years. It's her turn now."

Savannah was drowning in the storm of emotions and decisions being thrown at her. "I don't know, I just…" She watched Tesla attach the reader to Madelaine's unconscious head. "Will this—" she began.

Tesla was running a thick cable to Beowulf and stood on a table to connect it to a socket in the tank's brain cavity. He nodded once, curtly. "The array can only hold one pattern. This will kill your father. But save your girl."

On the table, Madelaine's chest heaved, then fluttered rapidly, hyperventilating.

He jumped down and pointed at her. "There's no time! Once the spark leaves her brain, we can do nothing!"

Savannah looked at her beautiful daughter sprawled and bloody on the table, then tore her eyes away toward Beowulf, then back again.

Tesla's hand rested on the switch. "Savannah?" He saw she was barely hanging on, but there was no time for pity.

She squeezed her eyes shut and nodded once.

The Colonel's voice boomed out one last time. "Do it, Tesla. Do it now!"

"Forgive me, Colonel," he answered. He threw the switch, and Madelaine's consciousness was copied into Beowulf.

In a flurry of cascading relays, the Colonel was gone.

800 FEET ABOVE FORT HAMILTON, NY, USA

Aboard the *Orion*, the bombardier released his final conventional bomb. Watching the explosion through his magnified eyepiece, he thought he saw a secondary explosion caused by the bomb, but couldn't be sure. Regardless, his role was complete. He called up to the Bridge.

"Bridge, bomb bay. All conventional bombs are released. Standing down."

"Acknowledged, thank you," replied Captain Montgomery.

Major Thomas had been explicit in his orders. Full saturation, then stay on station until he had personally surveyed the base. She couldn't imagine anything was still alive down there. Even eight hundred feet up, she'd heard every detonation. The base had been reduced to dozens of piles of rubble. But if he wanted his confirmation, so be it.

She got on the long-range radio, tuned to the frequency he'd specified, and called for him. In New Haven his radio operator had answered the call, then went to find him.

He was outside, sitting with two other officers beside a campfire, a steaming mug of coffee held in both hands. They'd been trading stories and lies, and having a raucous time of it. He reluctantly set down the coffee when the radio operator approached, carrying the bulky device. He accepted the radio and stood, moving away from the fire.

"This is Major Thomas," he said.

"Captain Montgomery here, sir. Our run is complete. Standing by for phase two."

Though he'd stepped away from the fire, hearing the delicious news gave him a warm glow. "Thank you, Captain. And what have you seen?"

She paused. "I saw Fort Hamilton laid to waste, sir."

"No survivors?"

"We see no evidence of any. The area is completely dead."

"And no tanks?" he asked.

"Tanks?" She'd not been told of any heavy armor at this base. Regardless, they'd seen none on the move, and if any had existed, they were buried under tons of rubble now. "No, sir, there's nothing down there now but bricks and dirt. We all agree on that point."

The major wore a smile like a leather glove. Within him, grim satisfaction mixed with sadistic joy.

"You've done well, Captain, and I won't forget it."

"I appreciate that, Major. And phase two?"

The major rubbed his chin and mused on that for a moment. Using a radiological bomb would be a highly satisfying nail in the coffin. Like salting an enemy's fields, preventing anything from growing there again.

But such weapons were extremely valuable. And useful elsewhere. To use one for his own satisfaction would be almost criminal.

And yet, to allow that tank to survive and join the resistance in Boston would be disastrous. It's even possible such a machine could alter the outcome of the war.

He thumbed the radio's transmit button. "Captain Montgomery, you are ordered to deliver one radiological bomb on the Fort Hamilton base. You will then set course for Boston. Understood?"

She'd hoped this order wouldn't come. But she trusted there was a good reason for it.

"Order understood, Major. Phase two will occur in five minutes. *Orion* out." She turned and saw the bridge crew watching her closely. Everyone aboard knew what those bombs were, at least in theory. None of them had ever seen a nuclear reaction, and now that they had their chance, a sense of nervous apprehension ran through the bridge.

She checked the cloud level. Changing barometric pressure had lifted the level to about 7,300 feet. From her readings about the one-megaton device, she preferred to be higher than that, but they would still be within the safety limit.

"Take us to seven thousand feet," she ordered.

Tesla took his hand from the switch and moved to Savannah, wrapping his arms around her. She buried her face in his shoulder, sobbing. Her legs went slack, and he had to tighten his grip on her to keep her standing. The close physical proximity was difficult, but he pushed aside the thought and focused on Savannah. She was normally strong and unflappable, taking on any situation gracefully. To see her this way pained him, but also bolstered his desire to support her.

He heard voices coming from the elevator shaft and was pleasantly surprised to know others had survived the attack. With the colonel gone, Bertram badly wounded, and Savannah distraught, he needed help. He sat her down on a chair, making sure her back was to Madelaine's body.

"Wait here, OK? I'll be right back. Just one minute."

She slumped forward, her head in her hands. "OK," she whispered.

Tesla crossed back to the elevator platform. He knelt beside Bertram and felt for a pulse along the side of his neck. It was faint, but there. The jagged piece of brick protruding from Bertram's chest made Tesla wince, and he knew he couldn't move him without help. Frothy pink bubbles had appeared around the wound. *Punctured lung.* For now, letting him lie quietly was the best he could do.

Bertram had raised the platform only two feet before being struck down. Tesla saw the open panel that worked the counterbalance system, and thought Bertram had the right idea, if the wrong timing. Getting that steel platform above them made sense, especially if more bombs were to fall.

He stepped up onto the platform, looking up the dark shaft. The voices of several men were clearly audible now, though he couldn't recognize them. They were climbing down the emergency ladder recessed into the shaft's wall. As they came lower, he made out a white lab coat on the lowest man.

"Hello," Tesla called up. "How many are you?"

The lowest man looked down. "Mr. Tesla? It's George. Sophia is with me, and we've got three more. Hang on," he answered, and shuffled down the ladder faster. He jumped the last few feet, landing solidly on the platform. Straightening up, he smiled broadly. "Damn good to see you, Mr. Tesla."

"Thank you, I feel lucky to still be here," he said, watching the others descend the ladder behind George. Someone above was feeding down crates from a rope, and they began stacking the supplies on the floor just off the platform. Sophia slid down the ladder and flashed a smile when she saw Tesla. George went straight to her, and he wondered if the two had begun a relationship. Two more men descended, but Tesla hadn't met them before. As the last person stepped off the ladder and turned around, Tesla was unkindly disappointed to see it was Edison.

"As we all do," Edison said. "What's your situation here?"

Tesla pointed to Bertram. "Bertram is badly hurt, but alive. We'll need to get him to a hospital quickly. Savannah is unhurt physically." He paused, unsure how to explain the rest.

Edison stepped off the platform and frowned, seeing Savannah crying. He looked around. "Is Madelaine…"

"I'm here," said Madelaine, her quivering voice amplified through Beowulf's speakers. Savannah jumped as though electrically shocked. She leaped from the chair and stood frozen, staring at Beowulf.

Edison whirled to look at the tank, his mouth gaping. "My God," he muttered. "Tesla, what—"

"Mom? Mom, it's dark. I can't see you. I can't see anything!" Madelaine's voice was rising in urgency.

"It's OK, honey," said Savannah. "I'm right here, right next to you." She looked down at Madelaine's body on the table. Her daughter's chest was still heaving, but the movements were slowing, with longer pauses between each breath. Savannah raised her voice to carry over to Beowulf, but her eyes were fixed on her daughter's body. "How do you feel, darling?"

The voice from Beowulf was Madelaine's, just bigger and more powerful. "I feel...I don't know. For a minute, I was drowning. Now, I'm just...here. In the dark. Why can't I see you?"

"You can, you just need to focus. Open your eyes, honey."

A moment passed, then Beowulf's twelve view ports snapped open. The inputs from twelve cameras fed into her mind at once, giving her a 360-degree view for the first time in her life. The flood of stimulation overwhelmed her mind. She wanted to gasp, but she felt no lungs, and no air. That scared her even more. Then Beowulf screamed.

Everyone clapped their hands over their ears against the amplified wail. Tesla ran to her and shouted, "Madelaine? Listen, focus on my voice!" The piercing scream wavered. "Can you see me? Look for me, I'm right next to you." The scream faded away as she concentrated.

Beowulf's cameras brought in a wraparound view, and her young mind couldn't process it. She imagined closing one eye, and half of the view ports snapped shut. Now dealing with half the input, she began to calm down. She found Tesla's familiar face and focused on it. He smiled, and the image comforted her.

"I see you, Nikola," she said.

"Good. That's very good," he said. "Now, let's—"

Behind him Madelaine's body convulsed, the muscles

clenching hard and lifting her chest off the table. She hung there, gasping silently, then collapsed. She exhaled one last time and went still. Her head rolled to one side.

Savannah brought a fist to her mouth and bit down hard, stifling a scream. She tasted the sharp tang of blood, but the pain was necessary.

The body's motion caught Beowulf's attention, and she shifted her focus from Tesla's face to the familiar body behind him on the table. In a stunned flash of recognition, she saw herself die.

"Is that me?" she squealed, a sharp edge of juvenile panic in her voice. "Did I just die? Mommy!"

"Dammit," yelled Tesla, grabbing a lab coat from the floor and throwing it over the girl's body. "I'm sorry for that," he said.

"I just died!" she screamed. "I'm dead, I'm dead!"

Edison strode toward Tesla, getting in his face. An accusatory finger jabbed at his face.

"What have you done?" bellowed Edison. He gestured to the covered body. "This is your fault. You want to play God? Well, now you've made an abomination!" he yelled, glancing at Beowulf.

Tesla felt his face grow hot, just as he did in Edison's home months before. The same urge to strike out rose to the surface. His jaw tightened, and his teeth ground together.

"He's right," screamed Madelaine. "I'm a freak now. What am I? I should have died!"

Edison turned back to Tesla. "See? Even a little girl knows —"

Tesla's clenched fist swung and smashed into Edison's jaw. The crunch was audible, and his fist lit up in pain. Edison's head rocked back, a look of total, pained surprise on his face. Then he fell back, falling over a chair and crashing to the floor. His vision swam for a moment before seeing Tesla standing over him, his fist still clenched.

"Call her that again," Tesla hissed, "and I will beat you unconscious, so to spare us your foolishness."

7,000 FEET ABOVE FORT HAMILTON, NY, USA

"We are at seven thousand feet, Captain," said the helmsman.

She nodded acknowledgement. "Bomb bay ready?"

He checked his board. "Bomb bay light is green, Captain."

As far as she knew, she was about to make history. The first radiological bomb dropped in anger. Not the entry in the history books she would have chosen, but in war how much really goes according to plan?

She lifted the phone. "Bomb bay, bridge. This is the captain. Release the weapon."

She watched the board as the green light flickered off. The bomb was away, now falling beneath them.

While the ship was now 2,200 lbs lighter, Captain Montgomery felt a heaviness settle on her shoulders and knew she'd carry it the rest of her life.

"Take us up," she ordered. "Get us over the clouds again."

The airship dropped water ballast and rose up through the cloud layer, breaking through at 8,100 feet.

With the comforting blanket of cloud below them, the *Orion* turned northeast and sailed for Boston.

Edison sat alone, nursing both his bruised jaw and ego. When Tesla came near, Edison's eyes tracked him hard, but the two men had nothing to say to each other yet.

It had been agreed that Beowulf was their best chance of escape. The upper floors were destroyed, and even the ladder was useless above level three.

George had organized the team in getting their supplies down the shaft and loaded into Beowulf. They had one box of emergency rations, but the gear mainly consisted of data records and handheld instruments. Still wrapped in a white lab coat, Madelaine's corpse was gently brought aboard by Tesla and Sophia for a proper burial later.

Tesla had rigged a generator to power the tunnel doors, and they were ready to load Bertram inside the massive tank and make their way out of the destroyed facility.

With everyone else inside Beowulf, Tesla and George carefully lifted Bertram on a makeshift stretcher. They got him inside the tank, and Tesla paused on the ladder before joining the group inside Beowulf.

The lab was in disarray, but held strong recent memories. Running away didn't sit well with him, but he understood a strategic retreat was sometimes required before a final victory.

Then, from the open elevator shaft came a tremendous roar. It sounded far away, but hideously powerful. The roar grew quickly, and a hot wall of air pushed against his face. The heat and the intensity were jumping up fast. Already, his forehead grew slick with beads of sweat.

"Another bomb!" shouted Savannah. "Get in here!"

He turned and scrambled up the ladder, hearing the approaching shock wave chasing after him. At the top of the ladder, he sprang forward, diving into Beowulf's crew compartment. Savannah slammed the heavy steel hatch shut and punched the locking mechanism.

The nuclear shock wave hit full force then, originating from an air blast a quarter mile away, channeled down the shaft and ending in their lab. A tsunami of blistering air slammed against Beowulf's side and shoved the huge tank, its woven steel treads grinding and screeching against the lab's floor. The tank was slammed sideways twenty feet before hitting the lab wall and punching a dozen gouges into the concrete.

Within Beowulf, anyone not strapped into a crew chair was thrown violently against the left side of the compartment. George sailed through the air, then slammed against a bulkhead before falling to the floor plating, a deep gash already bleeding over his eye.

Tesla, Bertram, and Savannah slid crazily along the floor, bouncing off equipment crates. Two other workers were carelessly thrown against the fire control dashboard, and tumbled on top of each other.

Edison had just secured himself in a crash chair, and his head lurched from the movement, but stayed safe.

Sophia had thrown herself into a chair and held on tightly. She tried to ride out the crash, but she lost her grip and fell. She sailed out of the chair and struck the safety railing, doubling over on it, then slipping to the floor, the air knocked from her lungs.

Madelaine's body had been knocked to the far side also. The lab coat had come loose, exposing her face and long blonde hair. Her head rolled with the motion, then settled, her eyes open and staring blankly toward Edison. Strapped into the crew chair, he squirmed under the morbid gaze until Sophia pulled herself closer to Madelaine's body and recovered her, tucking the fabric under her shoulders. Edison made a mental note to thank her later.

The tank settled then, smashed against the lab wall. Outside, the pitch of the shock wave shifted and drew down. At the point of detonation, the expanding shock wave had created a vacuum, and air was now rushing back to fill it in. Within seconds it was over.

Tesla opened his eyes and saw the steel floor plating. He rolled over and cautiously sat up. Nothing felt broken.

Beside him, Savannah was doing the same, running her hand over her head. She found some blood, but not enough to be concerned about, given the circumstances.

Everyone was pulling themselves to their feet and helping one another. A young man who'd been tossed against the fire control dashboard wasn't moving, and Tesla saw his neck was bent at a disturbing angle. He felt for a pulse, but found nothing. The man's neck had been broken by the impact.

"He's gone," said Tesla. "Quickly, at least." He looked around the crew chamber. George and Savannah were on their feet, and Edison was unlatching himself from the crew chair. George checked on Sophia, and Tesla smiled at the one researcher he hadn't met before.

"I'm Nikola Tesla," he said, extending his hand. The young man picked himself up and stepped forward. With his bright red hair and wholesome country smile, Tesla would have placed him as a farmer or maybe a small-town doctor.

"Of course I know who you are, Mr. Tesla," he said, shaking Tesla's hand. "Nicholas Terrine. I'm assigned to level four, helping Dr. Klein with the carbon-dioxide laser. But today I was on level six, assisting with the antigrav tests."

"A pleasure," Tesla said, then he turned to the group. "So assuming we can open the blast doors, where shall we go?"

"Another army base, preferably," offered Edison. Tesla nodded agreement.

George raised his hand as if they were back in grade school, making Tesla grin. "And we need a building large enough for Beowulf. Of which there aren't that many."

Edison grunted. "I'm not sure that's our priority. We need to report back and be debriefed on what's happening."

"We certainly do," said Tesla. "But we may as well choose a destination that can support ongoing work, with our best chance to push the British off our shores."

Edison's sour smile communicated his low opinion of that statement.

"We should head for Hanscom," said Savannah.

"The air force base?" asked Edison. "Why there? We could join the general in Providence instead. It would be closer."

"We could, but the fight is moving to Boston, and he'll probably be gone by the time we get to Providence. Hanscom is ten miles outside of Boston. It's a natural staging point. I'd guess that's where the army's center of gravity is moving. Plus, they have several large hangars, all big enough for Beowulf."

"Sounds reasonable to me," Tesla agreed.

"So it's your intention to put this device into the fight?" asked Edison.

Tesla was incredulous. "What do you think we've all been working toward?"

"Research is one thing, and maybe when we had the colonel's experience to control this thing. But now…"

Savannah's eyes bored into Edison's skull, but then she softened and sighed. "He makes a valid point, Nikola. We don't know how effective Beowulf is now. Our previous tests aren't relevant anymore."

"Hanscom is…what, a hundred miles northeast?"

Savannah nodded. "About that."

"Then we shall have time along the way to determine Beowulf's readiness. I'm sure we'll come across some British forces, yes?" said Tesla.

"Wouldn't bet against it," agreed George.

Sophia and Nicholas nodded, but Tesla could tell they'd be fine with having an uneventful trip. He understood their hesitation. A life of theory and experimentation in a lab did nothing to prepare one for possible combat. He liked the idea no better than they did, but put on a brave face and bluffed through it.

"We'll be fine. How about you, Madelaine?" he asked. "Think you can get us to Hanscom?"

She laughed, but the pitch was a touch manic. Tesla suddenly remembered he was inside a hideously powerful weapon of war, controlled by a twelve-year-old girl. The thought was sobering. But these were the cards he had been dealt, so he would play them out.

"Nikola…I don't even know how to move. Or open the big doors. I could barely handle the cameras. I have no idea what I'm doing! This isn't fair! I can't do this. Papa was the one for this."

"He was," agreed Savannah. "But now you are. We have no idea what's out there. You're our best chance to get out of here in one piece."

"I know," she whined, "but—"

"But nothing," her mother interrupted. "We're together, and we're going to do this together. Right, honey?"

Madelaine paused, but could find no other reason to object. "OK, Mom."

Savannah smiled, for the first time in hours. "That's my girl. Now find the door access codes."

Madelaine thought about the codes, not knowing what she was looking for. Slowly, her mind's eye showed her a vast, deep blue ocean. *Is that my memory? It's huge. How can I find anything in there?*

"There's too much," she said.

"Maddy, your memory is very large," said Tesla. "But the actual input and output of data is handled by lower level processes. You don't have to do it yourself."

"Then how can I get what I want?" He could almost see her, standing there pouting and throwing her arms down in protest.

"You need to concentrate on *having* the data you want. Your subroutines will notice the desire, and step in to fulfill it. Just relax and let them work for you."

She sighed, but said, "OK, I'm trying again."

She stood at the edge of the blue ocean again and tried not to think of how big it was. *It's just a bucket. And I need a drop from the bucket. I need the door codes that—*

And there they were. She had what she needed, without knowing how.

"I have them!" she yelled. "I have the door codes. Now what?"

"Now, you need to radio them to the door control. Again, just think about the reaction you want."

"I want the doors open," she said.

"And you have the keys to open them," Tesla encouraged her.

A moment went by, then the access lights over the huge doors flared. The doors cracked open and slid away.

"I did it!" Madelaine squealed. "They're opening!"

Savannah smiled in pride at her daughter's accomplishment. No matter the circumstances, a mother always enjoyed seeing her child succeed.

"You did it, honey," she said.

Even Edison felt the need to say something. "Well done, little one," he offered.

"Think you can drive us out of here?" asked Tesla.

"I know I want to try. Let me think…"

The huge treads surged forward, grinding gashes into the lab wall with a horrendous shriek.

"Shit!" she yelled, and the tank ground to a sudden stop. Everyone found something sturdy to hang on to.

"That's OK," said Savannah. "We were pushed into the wall. Just steer us away from it, then through the tunnel."

"Right, sorry," said Madelaine. She focused again, and realized she could see the lab around her, but not only in the normal way. She had the ability to see through walls if she wanted to. That confused her, though, so she shut that ability out and concentrated on moving slowly away from the wall.

Her treads ground to life again, but she added just a touch more power to the one on the left. The tank lumbered forward, and again there was the terrible shrieking of grinding concrete, but after a few seconds, the sound went away. She had cleared the wall.

"Good, good," said Tesla.

She added more power, just a little bit. The massive tank rolled forward, approaching the open door. She told her left tread to slow, and her right one to go faster. The tank turned smoothly until she was aligned with the tunnel's entrance. She balanced out the power to the treads again, and they moved forward, heading into the tunnel.

"That's great!" yelled Tesla. "Just keep—"

CRASH!

Beowulf hadn't been lined up perfectly, and her right front corner slammed into the tunnel wall. They stopped instantly, everyone clinging to a handhold to stay standing.

"Dammit!" she yelled. "Sorry, guys." She backed them up ten feet, straightened up, and tried again. This time she cleared both sides of the tunnel.

"And we are on our way," said Tesla.

"You're doing great, honey," Savannah said.

"Thanks, Mom," she said, trying to monitor their progress and not swing into the wall again. The tank weaved slightly, at times coming within three feet of the tunnel wall, but she kept adjusting, coaxing the steel monster back on a straight path toward the outer doors.

As they approached, she again thought of having the door codes. They came again, but she realized she'd drifted off course. With eight inches to spare, she jerked the tank back to the center of the path. No one said anything, so she kept that little mistake to herself.

She closed to within twenty yards of the outer doors and slowed to a stop. *Better to take things one at a time.* She sent the codes and smiled inwardly when they too obeyed her and opened wide.

She drove them through the outer doors and came to a stop just outside, in the valley's floor. She told the doors to close behind her, and they did so.

I have no idea where to go. Where's north? How do I get out of here? Can I climb those walls?

"OK, guys, now what?" she asked. George walked over to a view port, and slid the steel panel aside. A thick slit of sunlight shone into the cabin, and everyone cheered at the welcome sight.

"Something is stinging me," she said. *What is that? It's like mosquito bites, but all over everywhere at once.*

"Stinging?" asked Tesla.

"One second," said George. He turned and flipped off the cover of a crate. Rooting around inside, he found a small yellow and black device. He brought it over to the open view port and flipped the switch. Instantly, the needle jumped into the red. An audible clicking sound rose and fell in speed.

"Damn!" he yelled and slammed the view port shut. The clicking sound grew much fainter, but was still audible.

"Radiation," said Tesla.

George nodded. "A high dose outside. That last bomb was radiological."

Edison leaped from his chair. His experiments with Dally into X-rays had taught him to fear and respect the invisible particles.

"How much dosage in here?"

George frowned, watching the needle as he swung the Geiger counter around. "This armor is pretty good shielding, actually. But we should leave the area as soon as possible."

Savannah spoke to Madelaine. "Darling, that stinging you feel is your radiation sensors. It won't hurt you, but we need to get moving now, OK?"

Madelaine heard the undercurrent of worry in her mother's voice. "OK, which way?"

Savannah closed her eyes, visualizing the layout of the valley. "Turn to your left, and go fast. After a bit you'll see the valley walls get less steep. Then you can climb us out of here. I think the left side will be easier, but I'm not sure."

"Got it," she said, even as Beowulf spun and accelerated. They reached cruising speed quickly. Beowulf's suspension was designed for navigating most terrains, not necessarily for crew comfort. The five crash chairs were quickly filled, and Tesla volunteered to stand. He braced himself like an *X*, with his arms up and wide, grabbing the overhead railing and letting his legs absorb the bumps and sways.

After a few minutes, Madelaine announced they'd reached an area where the valley walls leveled out.

"There's something else," she told them. "I can see the marks from where Papa went up this slope already."

Savannah smiled warmly and felt a tear form, pooling in the corner of her eye. "Follow his trail, honey."

Madelaine steered toward the twin tread marks and followed them precisely, enjoying the knowledge that she was following in his footsteps.

LONDON, ENGLAND

"A tank as big as a house?" asked Einstein, looking up from the report. "That lives somehow? Is this to be believed?"

"Apparently so," said Churchill, trimming the end from a fresh cigar. "That major was well regarded by the king. And I know the staff sergeant who corroborated the story. We both fought in Eastern India. I believe them."

"So the major using one of my bombs on that base…"

"Was a prime example of the quick thinking we need in the field. If he'd pushed that up through channels, some overcautious bureaucrat would have dismissed it. And we'd have never known of this. I've already promoted him to lieutenant colonel."

"I see," said Einstein.

Churchill struck a match, then saw the musing expression on Einstein's face. He blew out the match.

"What are you thinking? That the promotion was a mistake?"

"Hmm? Oh no," he replied, waving his hand. "I'm sure the major deserves it, and more." He frowned at the report. "I'm just wondering who was behind this. The technical challenges are immense."

"I've made enquiries about that. Our people in the States say Nikola Tesla was in that base."

"Tesla?" exclaimed Einstein. "Ah yes, that would be about right."

"Did you know the man?" he asked, relighting his cigar.

"Not well. But we had dinner once after a conference in Vienna. Brilliant man. Eccentric. Visionary, even."

Churchill nodded. "Fits the bill, I would say."

Einstein grew silent. "I'm sorry to hear he was killed. He had a very fine mind."

"Good men die in war. It is a shame, though. One of those truths that never change, I'm afraid."

Churchill opened a wooden box on his desk and tossed a cigar to Einstein. "Here, try one of these. You'll feel better."

Einstein caught the cigar and smiled, but slid it into his jacket pocket. "Thank you. I'll save it for later."

When news of his promotion reached Major Thomas, he was in his office with his staff, reviewing plans for moving the men out of New Haven and marching on Boston. His original force of seven hundred had grown considerably as the reinforcements were off-loaded from their ships. His garrison had swelled to four thousand, two hundred men, a full brigade.

He had five captains to serve under him, managing the force, but he'd been wondering when a colonel would be sent out to replace him, as no major had ever led such a large group.

And then, welcome news.

With the higher rank, he was now directed to lead the force north to Boston and take the city, something he'd been eager for since leaving Portsmouth.

But more than that, he realized, the promotion meant his report had been believed and valued. Maybe the damage from Savannah's betrayal was fading? The thought was heartening, and he felt a brief flash of guilt for her death.

The grizzled staff sergeant appeared in his doorway, carrying a thick book. "I have the inventories, sir," he said, and the major forgot his guilt.

"Excellent," he said, taking the book and thumbing through the pages, skimming the numbers. "We're in good shape."

"That we are, sir. It's a three-day march to Boston, and we'll be well supplied to attack the city and hold it."

"Perfect."

Colonel Thomas looked at the five officers around his table. "Get your men prepared. We march in two hours."

Beowulf cruised forward, following the trail left by the colonel. As they cleared the top of the valley, Madelaine swung northeast, carrying them away from the ruined base. She ground over hard-packed earth roads at about a horse's gallop. She came upon farmers hauling carts, groups of civilians walking together, and the occasional Model T automobile. Each time she slowed and hugged the side of the road, allowing them to pass by. The gaping mouths and wide eyes that tracked her movements made her chuckle inside.

The stinging from her radiation sensors grew fainter as they put distance between them and the nuclear detonation site. Soon she could feel nothing at all from the sensors.

"I think we're out of the radiation area," she told everyone.

George slid the view port open and confirmed her finding with his Geiger counter.

"She's right. Just background radiation now. We're good."

The crew cabin had grown hot from the steam furnace, plus the warmth of six people in the enclosed space. George went around and opened view ports, letting in a welcome cool breeze.

"Thank you, Madelaine," said Tesla. "If we had gone out there without your armor, we'd be dead. You saved us."

"He's right, darling," agreed her mother.

Madelaine didn't know how to respond to that. *Did I really? I just did what came naturally. It's not like I'm a hero or anything.*

"Glad to help," she said, keeping things simple.

She thought more about heroes, what it meant to be one, and what they all had in common. The musing set a subroutine into action, and before she knew it, a collection of historical novels had been assembled for her, pulled from Beowulf's data banks.

She glanced over the titles. Homer's *Odyssey*. Virgil's *Aeneid*. The epic poem *Beowulf*, that she'd been named for. The tales of Gilgamesh, Hercules, Perseus, Havelock the Dane, and Robin Hood.

She split her attention between driving and reading the books. Seventy-eight seconds later she'd absorbed the material, but felt discomforted by the new wisdom. Heroes typically led hard, lonely lives. And with few exceptions, their defining quality was sacrificing themselves for others. *They get the glory, but not much else.*

She pushed aside the thoughts for another time and focused on a new sensation she couldn't identify at first. She pondered the distracting feeling, then realized what it was.

"I'm hungry," she announced.

Tesla's eyebrow rose, and his lips pursed together as he puzzled that out.

"Did you say you're hungry?" asked Savannah.

"Yeah, I'm starving!"

Everyone looked at one another in surprised silence, then Tesla broke the quiet.

"Maddy, I think what you're feeling is phantom pain."

"No, it doesn't hurt, I just really want a grilled cheese sandwich. Two, maybe."

He smiled. "I wish we could satisfy that. But I mean, for example, the pain that a soldier feels after he's lost a leg. Many men swear the missing foot still hurts. It's the brain not catching up to the physical reality."

"So I'm not really hungry?"

"My dear, you no longer have a stomach to feed."

"She does have a furnace, which requires being fed by coal," offered George.

"Yes, but those reserves are filled," Tesla said. "I suspect this is a habit that must be broken. Maddy, you must unlearn some things, while learning much about your new abilities."

"I don't like that, Nikola. I liked eating. A lot."

"I know, but we must play the hand we are dealt, yes?"

"I don't want these cards. I want a new deal."

"Doesn't work that way, honey," said Savannah. "We'll get through this together, OK?"

Madelaine sighed. "Fine. I'll try not to think of food."

"Good girl," said her mother.

The next few hours passed quietly. Madelaine kept her

focus on the road, and everyone else got as comfortable as possible.

George had pulled out several technical manuals on Beowulf's operation, and was reading up on the subsystems he hadn't worked on. He'd selected some of the more basic manuals and offered them to Nicholas, who was eager to study up on his new ally.

Edison had found a small leather-bound notebook and had been busily writing in it. Tesla casually walked over behind him once and tried to catch a glance at the writings over his shoulder, but Edison felt the intrusion and closed the journal until Tesla went away.

Savannah had been drawn back to Madelaine's body. She wiped the hair from her face, then cleaned the blood and vomit from her. When she looked presentable again, Savannah lay down beside her daughter's body and nestled her head on Madelaine's shoulder. Soon she was asleep, lulled by the noise and motion of the road, dreaming with a soft smile on her lips.

To Tesla the sight was macabre and yet very human. *We all grieve in our own way.* He saw no reason to disturb her.

Instead, he sat cross-legged on the floor beside Bertram. The lab director had regained consciousness, but was deathly weak and only partially responsive. At times he was lucid and questioning, but often he muttered unintelligibly before going silent again. Tesla kept him comfortable, reassuring him that the Hanscom base would have an excellent hospital.

Madelaine kept one subroutine focused on listening to Bertram's mutterings. During a lucid moment, she spoke to him.

"Hang on, Bertram," she said. "You still have to teach me the rest about playing chess."

Lying on his back, Bertram laughed, then winced. "My dear, I'm sure there's a book on chess in your library. You could learn the game in a second."

243

"There are three, actually. But I'm not reading them. I'll wait for you to teach me."

Bertram smiled, clutching a hand over his chest wound. "You're a sweet girl, Madelaine."

She said nothing, but kept them moving. As they headed farther north, she saw the trees had lost more of their leaves than back at home. There were still vibrant splashes of red and gold, but more and more, the trees were bare, preparing for winter.

She heard something then and reduced her speed by half, then came to a stop.

The change in motion woke Savannah, and the smile disappeared. She rolled to her feet, blinking away the slumber.

"What's up, Maddy?" asked Tesla.

"Gunshots ahead, I think. We may be coming up on a fight."

At that everyone sharpened up and put away what they'd been doing.

"Can you tell how far? Or how many?" asked Savannah.

"About a half mile ahead. Maybe twenty shots? Sixty? It's hard to tell."

"I've seen recent reports of a large British force gathering at New Haven," said Edison. "It's quite possible they are moving for Boston."

"Which would put them on a line that crosses this position," said Tesla.

Savannah was wide-awake now. "If it's a major force, they'll have artillery," she said. "Beowulf is tough, but enough cannon fire will penetrate her armor."

"We can't afford to be reckless," agreed Tesla. "Beowulf was designed to fight alongside infantry support, not on her own."

"Hard to hide this monster," offered George. "Not many airplane hangars out here."

Nicholas was peering out a view port. "I see a good cluster of forest up ahead. Think we could hide in there until we know what's going on?"

Tesla joined him, looking over his shoulder. "Looks pretty dense."

"Let's give it a shot," said Madelaine.

"Take us in, but be careful," Savannah told her.

"No problem, Mom." Madelaine engaged her treads and surged forward a hundred yards down the road, then turned to her right, aiming for the wide clump of forest. They bounced slightly coming off the road and traversing an open field. She knew she was leaving a distinctive trail behind, but couldn't help that.

As she approached the tree line, she slowed, inching forward, crunching over underbrush until her front armor plating pressed into the first tree, a poplar that rose narrow and straight for forty feet. She pushed forward, and with a mighty crack, the poplar snapped near the ground, falling before her. She eased forward, letting the felled tree pass under her, between her treads.

She easily took down three more trees, then stopped. While the trail of destruction was obvious if seen from behind, they were well hidden now from any other angle. She powered down her engine, and the sudden quiet was startling.

"We should be tucked inside the tree line now," she said.

"Nice work, Madelaine," said Tesla. "Please open the hatch, would you? I want to scout ahead and see what we're dealing with."

The hatch opened, and the personnel ladder descended. "There you go. Be careful out there, Nikola."

Savannah handed him a pair of binoculars, then slung a scoped rifle over her back. "We will," she said, smiling and extending her hand toward the open hatch.

Tesla knew better than to argue with her about going

alone. "Yes, we will," he said and clambered down the ladder. Savannah quickly followed him. Once they were on the ground, Madelaine retracted the ladder and shut the hatch.

They walked back along the trail of destruction Beowulf left, and stepped out of the tree line into the field. The day was cool, but the sun shone brightly in a blue sky, warming their faces as they worked their way to the road. They scouted ahead in silence, two travelers on a hard-packed dirt road.

After several minutes Savannah spoke. "I'm sorry I never thanked you. For her."

He flashed her a warm, slight smile. "There's no need."

"I couldn't have done that. Not then. But you kept your wits, even under that pressure."

Tesla kicked a rock in the road and watched it bounce off into a ditch. "I've always been good at keeping things in boxes. When there's time, I will mourn your father. But Madelaine became my priority."

"I can't imagine losing her. If you hadn't been there…"

He looked at her. "What matters is that she still lives. We'll figure out the ramifications of that as we go."

"Agreed." And there would be ramifications, she knew. Losing the colonel went beyond just her losing her father. He brought a lifetime of military experience to Beowulf, and as such was a major component of the project. While everyone loved Madelaine, she was exactly no one's idea of a competent replacement.

These thoughts pulled at her as they walked up a low hill. To push back a growing unease, she instead focused on the falling leaves on the trees around them.

As they reached the top of the hill, she heard the shots that Madelaine's more sensitive hearing had detected. She and Tesla shared a concerned glance. They continued down the road, and the sounds grew louder. Soon men yelling orders and screaming in pain became audible, and they knew they were close.

The road ahead curved to the right, and the battle sounded just around the bend. Without speaking they both ran to the edge of the forest and crouched low. They edged around the bend, wondering what sights would greet them. The sounds of battle were close now, and they proceeded carefully.

Suddenly, a subdued crashing sound came from in front of them. They looked at each other in silent questioning. Before either could speak, a young boy appeared, running straight into them. He slid to a startled stop, eyes wide and scanning them. He was young, no more than twenty, and wore the uniform of a US army private. His face was bruised and caked with dirt, and his eyes were wild with fear.

"You're not—" he began, then broke off and pushed his way around them. He ran madly back the way they had come.

"Well, that was different," said Savannah.

"Quite."

They pressed on and soon found the reason for the young soldier's desertion. Crouched low, they pushed aside some underbrush and saw a small US group fighting for their lives. Tesla guessed they had only forty men still standing, and twice that many on the ground. They were greatly outnumbered by a British force of two hundred.

A line of British riflemen were advancing on the desperate soldiers. As the guns were raised, many of the American dove to the ground, seeking cover behind the bodies of their fallen comrades. The British fired into the group, and a dozen Americans cried out. The troops broke then. As the British advanced, the remaining Americans leaped from the ground and ran, desperate to escape the field of carnage.

As they bolted, they ran away from the British and straight toward Tesla and Savannah. With a quickly growing sense of anxiety, Tesla now understood their recent encounter with the private. He'd just seen the writing on the wall a few minutes before his friends. And in about twenty seconds, they would be overrun by thirty Americans, followed by two hundred pursuing British Redcoats. Their safe observation spot suddenly felt like ground zero.

Tesla felt the urge to bolt as well. "We should go," he hissed.

"Right damn now," agreed Savannah.

They jumped up and sprinted, following the young private back the way they'd come. As they tore through the underbrush, they heard the approaching Americans catching up to them. Spiny vines scratched at Savannah's face as they ran. She raised her arms to ward them off, but that slowed her speed. Her foot slipped into a depression and threatened to send her sprawling to the ground, but Tesla caught her by the elbow and steadied her.

They were coming over the low hill now, and Savannah thought of Madelaine. American forces were running all around them now. They couldn't all fit inside Beowulf, and if they didn't do something fast, these men were all dead.

Even this far away, she knew Madelaine would hear her. She yelled out to her daughter, "Maddy! Help!"

There was no response, which Savannah understood, given the distance between them. *Still, would have been good to hear.* She pumped her legs harder, scanning the ground ahead, careful not to trip and tumble.

She heard British voices yelling then. Angry, yet maddeningly jovial. They knew the day was theirs. It was just a matter of running down the rabble.

A round of British rifles fired again, and bullets whizzed past them, tearing into the retreating troops. She heard a British bullet zip past her ear. Just in front of her, a thin branch was cut in two by the round and fell to the ground as Savannah ran past it.

The near miss spooked her, and her foot landed sideways.

She tumbled and fell to the ground, rolling into a mass of blackberry vines. A dozen cuts scratched her arms and face. "Shit!" she yelled.

Tesla looked back, horrified to see her down. He stopped and ran back to her, now seeing the approaching British soldiers clearly. He wrapped a fist in her shirt and heaved, trying to get her back on her feet, but the fabric ripped, and his grip was lost. She fell back again and cursed as she fought the stubborn vines to get back up.

Tesla looked up and saw the fastest Redcoats were no more than fifty feet away. One of them saw him and smiled as he brought his Enfield up, sighting on his chest. *He can't miss at this range.* Tesla thought of protecting Savannah, but had no way to accomplish that goal. His eyes fixed on the steel gray barrel aiming at him. The sight was bizarrely hypnotic, and he couldn't tear his eyes away, even when a tremendous crash erupted from the forest off to his right.

Madelaine had heard her mother's cry and didn't waste time backing out of the trees. Instead, she launched herself forward at full speed, gouging deep trenches in the forest floor and smashing dozens of trees to the ground. Her treads were at full power, which was crazy, considering the terrain. But she didn't know enough to worry about such things. She just knew a lot of trees were in her way, and they had to go.

The smaller trees, less than thirty feet tall, snapped easily and fell before her. She ran over them and barely noticed. The older, thicker trees, the ones that reached up into the sky, went much harder. A heavy, thick hundred-year-old oak shattered with a thunderclap, and the tree collapsed backward as she pushed through. It fell over and behind her, landing and shaking the ground for a quarter mile. The massive stump refused to be pulled from the earth, so she ran over it. The jagged, splintered shards of wood scraped and screamed against her underside as she plowed forward. Then she was past the thick trees and racing for the tree line.

Beowulf exploded from the forest like a Nordic god seeking bloody vengeance. The British instantly forgot their quarry and stared bug-eyed at the steel behemoth bearing down on them.

Madelaine saw the Redcoats and then found her mother and Tesla. She imagined the British dead, and her antipersonnel shredders sprang to life. The chainguns spat high-speed rounds toward the British, tearing up the ground around them. The aim was mostly wild, but the spectacle still caused them to freeze in panic. Here and there, Redcoats were hit randomly. Some went down with lethal chest wounds. Others had their calves or forearms hit.

Madelaine was too wound up to focus her fire, and she quickly ate into her ammunition stores. She kept a steady stream of deadly fire arcing out toward her enemy, the men who were threatening Tesla and her mother.

In her fury she felt omnipotent and righteous. Like a drug, the sense of power was intoxicating. She laughed out loud as she sprayed the field with bullets.

The British retreated, turning back and racing away. She wanted to chase them, but more important was the desire to stay close to her mother.

She kept up her fire as they ran and hit seven more Redcoats in the back. Then she saw two Americans, previously wounded, but struggling to stand and run. Her rounds ripped through them, killing them instantly. That sight made her gasp, and she shut down her shredders. The constant firing had deafened everyone around the tank, and the sudden silence was startling.

Madelaine watched the British forces, still two hundred strong, escaping from her. She wanted to reach out to them, to visit death upon them from afar. Again, the ever-helpful subroutines delivered her desires. She became aware of another weapon at her command. Twin mortar tubes, capable of firing out to 2,100 yards.

Curious, she examined the new toy. A belt fed the mortars into the tubes, and the angle could be set such that the explosives shot high in a parabolic arc, coming down almost vertically, very helpful against enemies sheltered behind cover. *Let's try it!*

She ordered the twin tubes to be loaded. She guessed the distance to the British to be nine hundred yards, and told tube one to angle itself for that range. It reported back that all was ready, so she fired.

THWUMP! The mortar launched itself into the air, soaring high over the battlefield. Gravity pulled it back to earth and soon it crested its arc, then fell back, now screaming toward the retreating British.

Her distance estimate had been off, so the tube angle was wrong. The explosive landed 150 yards short of the British. *BOOM!* The mortar hit the ground and exploded, sending a rain of shrapnel in all directions, but there was no one there.

The total miss was embarrassing. *This isn't just about me. How I behave reflects on Mom and Nikola. His work should be seen as a success. He deserves that.* She adjusted tube two for the extra distance and fired again. This range was more accurate, and it landed near the outer edge the mass of running Redcoats. *BOOM!* The mortar exploded with a geyser of dirt and grass, and three British collapsed.

They were gaining distance, and she felt content to let them run. She saw Tesla helping her mother stand, and that was most important. She told the mortar tubes to stand down.

Moving closer to Tesla, she stopped and opened the crew hatch.

"Are you guys OK?" she asked.

Savannah looked up at her daughter. *I don't know if I'll ever get used to her like this. But my twelve-year-old girl just saved our asses.*

251

She pushed the hair from her face and waved, smiling broadly.

"We're OK, honey. Hell of an entrance there."

"Yeah, that was pretty cool, huh?"

"The coolest," agreed Tesla. He gestured at the ladder. "Now let's get inside the giant tank and never do this again, yes?"

Savannah grabbed the ladder and began climbing. "If you insist, Nikola."

A lieutenant, bleeding from a gash in his thigh, caught up to Tesla, desperate for an explanation. In response Tesla raised in hands in apology.

"All I can tell you is that we're on your side. And today was your lucky day."

The lieutenant rubbed his jaw, thinking. He looked up at the monstrous tank hulking over his head, and decided to accept the non-answer.

"Fair enough. Just get your ass to Boston then. That's where we're headed. Be good to see you there."

"That's the plan, Lieutenant. Will you be OK here?"

"Should be. The detachment from Providence will be along soon. We were waiting to join up with them when we got hit."

Tesla nodded. "All right then. Good luck to you." He turned and climbed into Beowulf.

"You too," the lieutenant called up. "Not sure if you need it, though."

Tesla secured the hatch and turned, happy to see everyone again. Even Edison, he realized with surprise.

Savannah was crouching beside Bertram, leaning over to hear his whispered words.

Tesla gave them some privacy and instead sat down on a supply crate to chat with Madelaine.

"You did it again, little miss. Saved our proverbial bacon."

"Thanks," she said dully.

252

"What's that tone?"

"Nothing," she said.

"Don't be that way. It's unbecoming."

She hesitated, unsure how to express the jumble of conflicting emotions. "I loved saving you and Mom, I really did. I've never felt anything like that, not ever."

He found a bottle of water and gulped some. "Like I said, you have a lot of new capabilities to learn."

"I know. But what if I can't? I'm not supposed to be in here, Nikola. My grandfather was. He was amazing at this. And I—"

"I'd say you handled yourself quite well. Why are you beating yourself up, my dear?"

"Nikola, I just killed two Americans."

"You—" he began, then sat still in thought. "Well, if you did, it was an accident, of course."

"Yes! Of course! But I got excited and wasn't watching what I was doing. I saw them die, Nikola. It was…terrible. Like I just reached out and tore them to pieces. I can't get the sight of it out of my head."

Tesla sat down the water. "It has been my habit to treat you like a young woman, not a child. I think you've appreciated that?"

"Yes. God, yes! You're the only one who does."

"Then listen to me. Our virtues and our failings are inseparable, like force and matter. Do you understand? When they separate, man is no more."

"I guess so…"

"This is important, Madelaine. Yes, the colonel handled this tank very smoothly. And you will too, in time. Part of that is learning hard adult truths."

"Like what?"

"Like understanding that you're fallible. You have to strive to always be better and greater, but you have to also learn not to fear failure. Because you will fail. What matters is what you do after failing."

She thought on that. "But my failures kill people."

"They can, yes."

"And if it happens again? What do I do then?"

"Then we will see what you're made of."

Compared to Fort Hamilton, Hanscom Air Force Base was a flurry of activity. They had radioed ahead to explain the situation before rolling up to the gates and scaring everyone to death. Once they'd been checked out, a space had been cleared for them just off Runway Two.

The hangar was big, almost as large as the lab where Beowulf had lived. They set Madelaine up in the center of the space, and a semicircle of worktables was arrayed behind her. What little gear and supplies they'd escaped with had been put to use. Hanscom's CO, Colonel Oliver, had been curt but fairly generous in getting them settled in. He knew nothing of the project and had never heard of Tesla, but Mr. Edison's reputation was impressive. Even more so was the phone call from the White House. The president himself came on the line and asked Oliver to extend every courtesy to the unusual group.

As much as possible, Tesla and his team recreated the old lab in the empty airplane hangar. It wasn't as comfortable, but they quickly had the basics in place. They could run diagnostics on Beowulf, reequip her, and even do minor improvements.

Savannah made sure they were settled, then followed an officer to the base's radio room. She was eager to speak to General Houston, both to share news of their escape and to get the latest about the Boston offensive.

George pulled an empty magazine from Beowulf. "I'm

glad we decided on the standard NATO ammo," he said. "Would be hell to resupply, otherwise."

"Agreed," said Tesla. "We'll need to hand-fill the magazines, but the rounds themselves should be easy enough."

Truth be told, that decision had been Bertram's. There had been compelling reasons to go with custom ammo for Beowulf, but Bertram had lobbied hard that they were breaking so much new ground in its design, they would be foolish not to use standard gear where possible.

Tesla's thoughts went to Bertram then. "George, can you handle things here? I want to go check on him."

"Sure, we'll be fine. Tell him I'll be over after dinner."

"I will," Tesla said and walked out of the hangar. He turned and headed for the base hospital, mulling over the last news he'd heard about the lab director's condition. It wasn't great news.

Bertram was an odd mix of scientist and politician, two distinct skill sets rarely seen within one person. Together those skills had helped him rise from a doctoral student in nuclear fission to the director of what may have been the world's most advanced research lab. Tesla hadn't considered the difficulty of that job before, but without it, Beowulf wouldn't exist.

The thought of all they'd lost in the zeppelin attack made him feel nauseated, but he reminded himself it was a setback, not an end. It could all be rebuilt, given time and money, and there would be more brilliant researchers out there, happy to dive into such a venture. He felt the loss of the men and women he'd met there, but was comforted by the idea that scientific progress would march on, as it must.

As he neared the hospital, a group of airmen passed by, curious about the civilian in the fancy, though dirty, clothes. He nodded in greeting as they walked past him, then headed into the hospital.

Bertram had been given a private room, considering his

security clearance. When Tesla arrived, he saw his friend was unconscious. Edison and Colonel Oliver stood to one side of the room, speaking in low tones with Bertram's doctor. Tesla joined them, ignoring Edison's cool glare.

"How is he?" he asked.

The doctor shook his head. "Not well, I'm sorry to say. We got the brick out of his chest, and the lung sewn back together, but…"

"What?"

"It's the infection I'm worried about. The foreign material had a lot of time to settle into the alveoli. We're treating it as well as we can, but so far he's not responding."

Tesla leaned in, keeping his voice just above a whisper. "Are you saying he might not live?"

"I'm saying the next twenty-four hours will be critical. We just have to wait and see."

Tesla frowned at the prognosis. He caught the colonel staring at him. *I wonder what Edison's been telling him about me?*

Edison turned to Colonel Oliver. "Colonel, may we speak outside, please?"

"Sure," he answered, following Edison out to the hallway.

Tesla forgot about them and moved to stand by Bertram's side. His chest was wrapped in thick white gauze, and his face was slack and immobile. Tesla didn't care at all for his friend's thin pallor and pale lips. *He looks half-dead already.* The thought angered Tesla, and he chided himself for it. More than most, he should know that amazing recoveries are possible.

He stood, watching Bertram breath for several minutes, before deciding he was of no use to anyone mourning a still-living man. He turned and walked out into the hallway. As he came around a corner, he ran into Edison and Colonel Oliver in a heated discussion. As soon as they saw Tesla, the conversation went silent, waiting for him to leave.

He ignored them and fast-walked back to their new lab,

where he could finally be productive. He passed Sophia, who has heading for the hospital.

"He's still unconscious," Tesla said.

"That's OK. I'll talk to him anyway." She smiled.

Tesla nodded and continued back to the hanger. He strode inside, pleased to see Beowulf's comforting, hulking presence. *At least she's beyond catching her death from some infection.* He joined George at an ammo reloading station.

"How is he?" George asked.

Tesla shook his head. George let the matter drop.

"Well, I've got three magazines reloaded and back in place. She really tore through the ammo. Maybe she got lazy and just didn't want to carry the weight anymore?"

"I can hear you," intoned Madelaine.

George laughed. "Yeah, I know…just kidding, Maddy."

Tesla appreciated George's attempt to distract from Bertram's condition, and decided to let him succeed.

"I believe she chose the 'strength in numbers' strategy of enemy suppression," said Tesla.

"Hmmpf," she said. "Saved your bacon."

"That it did. But you had the advantage of surprise, bursting from the forest like that. In a pitched battle, the enemy will be steeled to your appearance. And your ammo isn't unlimited."

"I know, Nikola. I've been practicing in my mind. I can replay the fight in my head and see how wasteful I was. I'll do better next time, promise."

"I believe you, my dear. And so does George."

"It's true," he called out as he pulled the final empty magazines out for reloading.

"Thanks. Hey!" Madelaine yelled. "I've got a new limerick!"

"Heaven help us," whispered George.

"Heard that too," she said. "But I'll ignore it 'cause I like you."

"All right, let's have it," said Tesla.

"OK," she said. "Here goes.

"There was a young man named Gene
Who had a lovemaking machine.
Concave and convex, it served either sex.
And it played with itself in between."

She giggled uncontrollably. "Huh? Is that excellent?"

"Very nice," he said, chuckling with her. "Quite a talent for verse you have."

"Thank you, kind sir," she said.

"Now, that business of you shooting wild…it brings up something I've been thinking on. A way to be more precise with your shots."

"What's that?" she asked, curious. From her perspective Tesla was no less than a wizard. And if he wanted to work his magic on her, she was all for it.

"It's a new device I've been experimenting with." He went to one of their supply crates and dug around for a moment. "Here it is," he said, pulling out a three-foot panel of curved metal rods, woven together in a loose lattice.

She focused on the odd-looking thing. "What the hell can I do with that?"

Savannah had returned and caught her daughter's last question. "Language, Madelaine Browning," she admonished.

"Ah right. Sorry, Mom."

Tesla held the metal grill up, clearly proud. "This…is long-range vision," he proclaimed.

"Doesn't look like it," said Madelaine.

"Well, of a sort," he said. "See, this acts like a broadcast antenna. It takes electricity in and converts it to radio waves. It then broadcasts those waves in a certain direction." He swung the panel left and right.

"OK…"

"So then those waves hit something. A building, or a zeppelin. The waves bounce back, and are collected here again."

"OK…"

"The trick is…What if we precisely measure the time it takes for those waves to return? We know their speed already. If we then know their travel time, simple math gives us—"

"A range to target," said Savannah. "Nikola, that's brilliant!"

"Why, thank you. In any event, it should prove very helpful for Madelaine. With a precise range, her mortars can land right on target the first time. And her main cannon should be able to hit targets much farther out. I'd like to get this installed on her and try it out."

"Absolutely," agreed Savannah. "I'd say that's a great use of time while we wait."

"We are waiting for something?" Tesla asked.

"Right, sorry. I talked to the general and caught him up about our escape from the base. He's on the way to Boston right now. It's going to be a major operation, Nikola. The British will be throwing everything they have to take the city and the port. He's moving with twelve thousand men to garrison Boston now, and wants us to wait here as reinforcements until we know the layout of the attacking forces."

"Like the cavalry from medieval times," said Madelaine.

"Hmm?" Tesla asked.

"I've been reading more of the books Papa had in here. There's a bunch on strategy and tactics. In the Middle Ages, the horsemen were often held in reserve. Once a general saw how the battle was going, he could send in his cavalry as shock troops where they were needed the most."

She's growing up fast in there. Tesla looked to Savannah, not surprised to see a huge grin on her face.

259

"Mother's pride." He laughed.

"Cavalry. Armored cavalry," Savannah agreed. "Goddamn right."

"Language, Mother," Madelaine teased.

Tesla stood under Beowulf, pointing to a swivel joint in Beowulf's suspension. "Here, this is where some oil must be added. And here, and there," he said, directing Nicholas's attention down the length of the huge assembly.

Outside the hanger a plane taxied by on the runway, and he raised his voice.

"You will find similar points all the way down, about every seven feet."

He nodded, and Tesla handed him an oil can.

"Thanks. I'll have this done soon, and maybe we can go over the sensor array later?"

"Certainly," said Tesla. "And thank you."

He stepped out from under Beowulf and turned to look up. George had crawled to the high upper section to finalize the radar installation, thirty feet up. He was struggling to get a pair of thick cables in place before welding a protective barrier around the new radar panel.

Tesla yelled up to him. "I'd feel more secure if you had a safety harness roped off to the ceiling."

George grinned, a bulky welder's faceplate slung back over his head. "As would I! It's OK, I've about got it." He hauled on the cables to gain some slack, then draped them twice over Beowulf's climate sensor. He let go and was satisfied when they held in place. "All set," he called down.

"OK, on your say, I'll switch on the current," Tesla replied. He moved to a small generator they'd set up for arc welding and prepared to turn it on.

The new radar panel was currently deployed, extending on

a small hydraulic arm Madelaine controlled.

"Madelaine, please retract the panel," asked George.

"Sure thing." The arm smoothly contracted, and the hinged panel sank down, flush with Beowulf's hull.

"Thanks."

George had brought up three strips of heavy steel to weld in place around the radar panel. While the new invention was ingenious, it was also rather fragile to bullets. By surrounding it with strips of armor, it should survive firefights, assuming Madelaine remembered to keep it retracted.

George pulled the welder's electrode from his work belt and attached it to the cables. Like a handgun, it had a grip and a long extension. In this case the electrical currents flowing through the electrode were used to melt steel and make secure welds.

He shoved his hands into thickly padded leather gloves and brought the faceplate down.

"Hit it!" he called out.

Tesla turned the generator on, and George went to work adding the new armor around the panel. Heavy electrical sparks flared out, spilling down over Beowulf in a fiery waterfall. Tesla resisted the temptation to look at the welding light directly, knowing the intensity would damage human eyes.

As George applied the welds, Tesla poured himself a cup of coffee. A large bowl of fruit had been laid out, and he was tempted by a bright red apple. As he looked about for any cream, an unwelcome voice intruded.

"It has no practical benefit for wartime, you know," said Edison.

Tesla sighed, finding the cream and pouring it into his cup, watching the swirling patterns with delight.

"Clearly, we differ in our estimations of the technology," he said, looking up at Edison and taking a sip of the hot coffee.

"Oh, we played with it at Menlo Park, and it's an entertaining toy. But useful on the battlefield? No." Edison laughed.

Tesla grinned sourly. "It is fortunate then, that the costs aren't coming from your budget."

Edison's smile faded. "Yes, I meant to ask you about that. What exactly *is* the budget for this Beowulf creation? It seems to me you've burned through capital at a prodigious rate."

Tesla set down his coffee. "And it seems to me you're an over-inquisitive busybody threatened by the new and the bold. See? It's good that we have our own opinions."

Edison's face grew hard. "You'd be well advised to mind your place, Tesla."

"My place?" He laughed. "What place is that? I'm not one of your lab monkeys. You don't own me. Now get out."

"Or you'll hit me again?" Edison leaned closer, almost daring him.

"The thought has merit," Tesla replied, squaring off with Edison. "Apparently once wasn't sufficient."

"Now, boys," called out Savannah. They both turned toward the voice, surprised.

She had just entered the hangar, but even at a distance, their body language told her things were going ugly quickly. And they had enough drama already.

"Let's save all that for the British, hmm?"

Edison desperately wanted to escalate the situation. His ego demanded it. He didn't budge, glaring at Tesla.

For his part Tesla would be delighted to knock the busybody on his ass again. But he knew Savannah would be disappointed if he did. Instead, he met Edison's glare and allowed himself a mocking smile. He cocked his head toward the hanger exit.

"Have a fine evening, Mr. Edison," he said in a voice dripping with sarcasm.

Edison practically shook with controlled anger. But he swallowed it and turned stiffly, striding for the exit. He slammed the door open and was gone. Everyone paused, taking in the display.

"And I thought *I* was the child around here," said Madelaine.

"Be nice," said Savannah. She joined Tesla. "You have many talents, but the most potent of them all has to be winding him up."

"Yes, I daresay I'm getting quite accomplished at it," he said, picking up his coffee. "But practice will do that."

"Incorrigible, you are," she said, shaking her head. "All right, besides twisting up Edison, what have you gotten done?"

Tesla turned to Beowulf and pointed up at George, now making his way back down. "The radar panel is in place, and is properly protected."

"Outstanding! Maddy, how does it feel?"

"Like I can talk to things, and they tell me where they are."

"Amazing." Despite the obvious sacrifices, sometimes she envied her daughter's situation. Her new abilities were redefining what it meant to be human. When the history of their species was written, Madelaine Browning would have a prominent entry.

"What do you say we shake things up a bit?" Savannah asked. "We've had a lot of heaviness lately. I feel like having fun with this test."

"What exactly do you have in mind?" asked Tesla, now most curious. Savannah had often shown a playful side, but her focus was always on work.

With a sly smile, Savannah called to her daughter, "Maddy, please deploy radar."

The panel extended smoothly up, then rotated, pointing out into the hanger.

"Ready, Mom."

"For this test I want you to use only your forward-left shredder. And please confirm that it is loaded with gel rounds."

"Got it. Yes, gel rounds only."

"OK." Savannah casually drummed her fingers on the table. "For the purposes of this test, you will fire a single round into any airborne target. Ready?"

"Um…sure," said Madelaine, not seeing any targets nearby.

With a mischievous glint in her eye, Savannah grabbed an apple from the fruit bowl.

"Target up!" she cried, tossing the apple high into the air.

"What?" said Madelaine, but her forward-left shredder twitched to life. Through the radar panel, she spoke to the tumbling apple. Milliseconds later her voice bounced back to her: *227.8 inches*.

At the apple's apex, she put a single gel round into it. With a definitive *CRACK*, the impact vaporized the soft fruit, sending a rain of pulpy juice splattering down all over Savannah and Tesla.

"Hey!" Tesla yelled, raising his arms to shield himself from the sticky mess.

Savannah burst out laughing, pointing at the reserved scientist now covered in liquified apple. A small red patch of apple skin clung to his cheek. "Now that is a sight!" she yelled. Then she reached for a banana.

"Wait now!" cried Tesla.

"Target up!" She tossed the banana high above them.

CRACK! Yellow and white pulp sprayed down over them. Tesla's mouth hung open, not believing what has happening. Savannah caught his distressed look and doubled over, laughing.

"Very well, Mrs. Browning," Tesla said in mock threat. With both hands he scooped up the remainder of the fruit bowl: another apple, three oranges, and a clump of grapes.

"Oh my," Savannah said, her eyes wider in excitement.

Tesla swung the armful of fruit low, then cried, "Target up!" as he launched the whole batch into the air above them.

Madelaine had to hustle to speak with each target, but a series of gel rounds rang out in rapid succession.

BRRAPP!

A flood of juice, pulp, and fruit skin poured down, drenching Tesla and Savannah equally. If she minded the deluge, she gave no sign of it. Clapping her hands together, eyes bright, her white teeth flashed in delight even as her hair was wet and matted against her face.

"That was awesome!" said Madelaine.

Savannah fell against Tesla, laughing uncontrollably as she pounded his chest. "Yes, it was. Good shooting, my baby!"

With Savannah laughing against him, Tesla felt lighter and happier than he had in weeks. As he searched his feelings, he realized he also felt very fortunate.

"I'm happy to be here. Thank you, Savannah," he said, pulling a length of grape stems from her long blonde hair, and offering it to her with a grin.

She reached up to his hair and showed him the orange peel he'd been wearing.

"My pleasure," she replied.

27 MILES SOUTH OF BOSTON, MA, USA

Colonel Thomas sat high on his black stallion, enjoying the repetitive motion of the horse's gait. *Colonel. That's going to take some time to sink in.* The promotion was a genuine shock, and he'd been signing things as a major ever since. He ran a finger over the new insignia. There was a time not too distant when he'd thought making colonel was impossible.

He twisted in his saddle and surveyed the men behind him. Twin columns of fine British soldiers, 4,200 strong. And he rode at the brigade's helm. With these men he would claim the city of Boston and secure its port.

With that beachhead opened, the huge ships waiting off the US coast could land and off-load massive reinforcements and supplies. He wondered if perhaps he would be appointed mayor of the conquered city, once things stabilized.

Riding beside him, Captain Fitzwallace checked the sun, then looked at his timepiece. "Making good time. We should be outside the city by sunset, Colonel."

He nodded. A few minor skirmishes had slowed them somewhat, but that was to be expected. He had detached a company of four hundred to harass the American resistance, so the main force could press on at speed. Hopefully, they would catch up by tonight.

"Forgive me if this is impertinent, Colonel, but is this mission difficult for you?" asked Captain Fitzwallace.

The colonel had grown reluctantly resigned to others knowing his personal business. The bombshell of his marriage to a spy was an explosion heard around the empire.

"It's all right, Captain. In fact, it's a fair question to ask." Swaying with the horse's walk, he considered his next words.

"The distance of time has made it easier than it was before. But betrayal is never easy, or forgotten."

"You have a reputation for hatred of the Americans," Fitzwallace said, studying his colonel's face.

"It's not that I don't appreciate what they've accomplished. These people came to a wild, untamed land and brought the first steps toward civilization. There's a certain majesty in that, honestly. But they're also deceitful, without any sense of loyalty. If it served their ends, they would betray anyone in their way. Mark my words on that."

"I understand, Colonel. Thank you for the clarification."

Colonel Thomas nodded curtly, once. The discussion had churned emotions best left settled, and his mood had soured.

"Not at all, Captain," he replied. "Say, I believe it's time to run the line. Good for morale, you know."

The captain smiled, knowing he was being mildly sent away. "Yes, sir. Was just about to suggest it myself."

He swung his horse around and trotted back down the long line of marching soldiers, letting them see that he was checking on them. It would take a half hour to make the full trip to the end of the line and back again.

By then he was confident the colonel would be in better spirits again, and all would be forgotten.

Sophia had organized their technical manuals into a small field library, with the books arranged over two wide tables.

"OK, the manuals are all set. I'm going to visit the little girl's room."

"Right," said George. "Nice work."

She turned and left, her high heels clicking and echoing in the huge room. He watched her walk away, then turned back to the disassembled camera laid out in pieces on his worktable.

"He's shtooping her," Madelaine whispered to Tesla.

"Shtooping, hmm? How do you know that?" Tesla asked as he mopped fruit remnants off the floor.

"It's obvious. My infrared picks up his cheek flush whenever she's close to him."

He turned to look at George, oblivious to their conversation and busy rewiring the camera's output.

"Perhaps he just fancies her? She *is* an attractive woman."

"And three times now, when she goes to the restroom, he leaves the room within three minutes."

"Oh? Well, that's just coinci—"

Madelaine continued. "The women's restroom nearest us

has a loose water pipe in the corner. Two minutes after he follows her, my seismic sensors register a rhythmic pounding from that direction. At about one-point-three strokes per second, which is typical for human copula—"

"OK, I get it."

"I'm just saying. Interesting data."

"Uh-huh." Tesla picked up his clipboard and flipped through the pages. "It looks like we're in good shape, Maddy. You're all checked out to return to the field."

"Good. Now we just need to know where and when, right?"

"I'm sure the general will let Savannah know when he's ready for us. Patience."

"Easy for you to say. My brain is so much faster now, this waiting is torture."

Tesla thought about that. It's true that she was experiencing the world hundreds of times faster than any human. What would the long-term effects of that be? Tesla had no idea.

"I don't know if you'd want to, but there is one possible solution to the waiting," he told her.

"Yeah? Tell me!"

"The RCA could be placed in a 'warm shutdown' mode. The array would remain powered, but no signals would be allowed to move through the array. Your thoughts would freeze in place. Essentially, you would go to sleep until I woke you."

"I don't know…sounds kinda scary."

"I agree. I wouldn't want anyone controlling my brain either. But it is an option if you want it."

"I'll think about it, but the waiting doesn't sound so bad now."

"As you wish, my dear."

Behind them George set down the camera assembly and

headed for the exit.

"Calling it a day?" asked Madelaine.

"Hmm? Oh no," said George, still walking. "Just a quick break. Be back in a few."

Tesla watched him leave, waiting for the comment he knew was coming.

"Told ya," said Madelaine. "Shtooping."

BOSTON, MA, USA

"Well, their obvious approach would be from the south," said Boston Mayor John Fitzgerald, pointing at the large city map laid out on his desk.

General Houston and his staff were crowded around the large mahogany desk. With time short, it made sense to take advantage of the local knowledge the mayor possessed. His affable wit and warmth of character had earned him the nickname "Honey Fitz." He was also the only politician who could sing "Sweet Adeline" sober and get away with it.

Leaning over and studying the map, the general was thankful for the city's geography. The downtown core was surrounded by the Charles River on three sides. If the British wanted to enter the city without crossing a bridge, they would have to approach from the south.

The deepwater port that made this city such a vital target for the British was just to the east of downtown. He knew the British already had a dozen large ships waiting not ten miles off the coast, in Massachusetts Bay. Each loaded with soldiers and supplies, no doubt.

Previous battles had whittled Boston's navy fleet down to the point where cannons and shore batteries were keeping those ships at bay for now. But if the British got in the city and removed that obstacle, all would be lost. Whatever happened, those ships must never reach the port.

He traced his finger from the city's downtown core to the three main outer bridges that spanned the river.

"What can you tell us about these bridges, Mayor?"

"Right, well, farthest north you see the Charlestown Bridge. First bridge built in Boston, actually. Replaced a ferry that had been there since 1630. Anyway, it's not very wide. Would take awhile to get an army across it."

"OK," said the general. He ran his finger south on the map to the next bridge. "And the…Charles River Dam Bridge?" he asked, craning his neck to read the small lettering.

"That will be a better choice, but it's not completed yet."

"No way to get across?"

The mayor shook his head. "Not currently. In five months, yes, but not now."

"OK, good."

The mayor pointed out the southern bridge. "This is another possibility. The Longfellow Bridge. A hundred and five feet wide."

"So two bridges we need to cover," summed up the general. "Now, as for the land assault, I'm thinking we establish our perimeter here," he said, indicating a spot just south of the Boston Common. "We draw our line down along Arlington Street and over to the east along Essex Street."

Boston Common was a wide rectangular park, originally used for cow grazing and later public hangings, but after 1817 it was converted into a city park with a broad lake in the center.

"So you'll have the Common open behind your front line?" asked the mayor.

"Exactly. The park is wide open, giving us a lot of room to easily move men and supplies around, right behind the line. The British won't have that advantage. They'll need to flow around the city blocks, making their coordination harder. And

270

as a bonus, we get the fresh water from the park's lake, simplifying our resupply issues even more."

The general's staff nodded in agreement.

He turned to his supply sergeant. "What can we give the mayor, in terms of arms?"

"You're thinking of supplying the police force with rifles?"

"I certainly am, yes."

"We could spare four hundred, maybe five hundred rifles for them, General."

"That'll do. John," he said, turning to the mayor, "my men will handle the bridges and the flanks of the southern exposure. I'd like your police to fill in the middle, at Chinatown. They know the area, and if things get hot, they'll have my soldiers on either side to assist."

"Understood, General. I'll have them assemble here, at Harvard Street. You can issue rifles there in…say, three hours?"

General Houston nodded and glanced at the supply sergeant. "Make that happen."

"Yes, sir."

A staff member leaned over and whispered into the general's ear. "And Beowulf?"

"Not yet," he replied. "But soon."

"All right then," the general said, straightening up. "We've all got a lot of work to do, so let's get to it." He turned to one of his staff. "William, ride with me, I want to inspect those bridges before we head down to the Common."

"We have a car waiting outside, sir."

Tesla sat alone and motionless in the base mess hall, staring intently at the bowl of soup before him.

From a nearby table, Edison, Colonel Oliver, and several officers watched the strange display. When Tesla began muttering to himself, Edison turned back to his meal companions.

"And now he's gone from soup to nuts," he said, enjoying their laughter.

A quick motion caught Edison's eye, and he turned to see Savannah running through the tables toward Tesla. She carried a thin envelope in her hands, and her face was beaming.

"Nikola!" she cried as she came up behind him.

Tesla didn't turn around, but kept mumbling numbers under his breath, his eyes fixed on the bowl.

"Hey," she said, sitting down beside him. He startled, then smiled in welcome.

"What *are* you doing, Nikola?"

He grinned sheepishly. "An old game I play with myself. I calculate the cubic contents of my soup plates and coffee cups."

"And the purpose behind that?" she asked, having forgotten the envelope she carried.

"Otherwise, I would have found my meal to be unenjoyable."

"Huh. OK then," she said. "Well, forget all that, because you won't need it." She held the envelope in front of her. "This is going to be the best meal you've had in years!"

"An intriguing prediction. But that envelope doesn't look so tasty."

"Funny." She handed the envelope to him. "Just read it!"

He took it from her and pulled out a single typed letter on expensive letterhead. Unfolding it, he read the message to himself. Halfway through, his eyes went wide.

"Is this really true?"

Savannah nodded and clapped her hands. "Damn right it is. Bertram nominated you for it awhile back. It just came in today!"

"A MacArthur genius grant? For me?"

"Can you think of a more deserving genius?" she asked.

"Hmm…since you put it that way, perhaps not. I'm just stunned. It seems unreal." He set the letter down and rubbed his face. When he opened his eyes, the letter was still there.

"It means formal recognition of your work, Nikola. Around the world. Not to mention the prize money."

"Money too?"

"Enough to get your own lab started, if that's what you want. But I hope you stay with us, of course! Oh, I am so proud of you!"

"Thank you, Savannah. Truly. And you say Bertram set this in motion?"

"Yep. He meets a lot of smart folks, so his opinion carries some weight with the selection board."

"Incredible," Tesla said. "I must go thank him, at once." He folded the letter into his jacket pocket and stood. "Thank you again. Amazing!" he said, running off.

"Yes, it is," she said to herself. She glanced down at his dishes and wondered if he'd figured out the soup's volume or not.

Nearby, Edison's face burned, but he struggled hard to not let his feeling show. *After everything I've given the world, he gets a genius grant? Unbelievable.*

"Are you all right, Mr. Edison?"

He looked up and saw Colonel Oliver's concerned expression. *Guess I have a poor poker face.*

A quick smile wiped away the dour frown. "But of course, Colonel! I was just…worried about Bertram's condition, that's all."

"I understand. I haven't properly met the man, but I hear he did great work with that R&D lab. That must be a big job."

"It is," he answered, thinking of his own lab at Menlo Park. "But it's highly rewarding, directing talented people to create something great."

"I can see that," said the colonel. "I'm envious, actually. In my profession, success is usually measured in destruction. It would be refreshing to succeed in creating."

"Of course," said Edison. "You know, following up on our previous conversation, we may be able to help each other."

"Is that so?"

"You have retirement coming up later this year, correct?"

"I do."

"I imagine after a life of service, the thought of retirement is a bit…unsettling?"

"What, you can't see me playing golf all day and bridge on Wednesdays?"

"I suspect you need more challenge from life than that," probed Edison.

"I suspect you're right."

Edison leaned in and laid out his idea. By the time the Colonel had finished his coffee, he was smiling and nodding along to Edison's plans.

Tesla crossed the base, eager to thank Bertram, assuming he was awake. The lab director had drifted in and out of consciousness, and was never communicative for more than a few minutes at a time.

He had heard impertinent whispers about Bertram not making it, but he dismissed those as macabre gossip. People do love discussing other's misfortunes. *Not one of our species's better traits*, he thought.

As he entered the hospital and turned down the long hallway leading to Bertram's room, his mood was light. The good news about the award would please Bertram, perhaps even contribute to his recovery. Tesla was eager to get his friend back on his feet. There were many ideas he'd had about ways to improve Beowulf, as well as several unrelated projects he wanted to propose.

He'd never been overly concerned about money, but his lean times at Mrs. Harrison's house had taught him that when you run out of money, you run out of options. With a safe nest egg, he'd never let himself get back in that unenviable place. As long as you have choices, things can be worked out.

He bounded around the corner and strode into Bertram's room. "Bertram! You'll never guess—" he exclaimed.

Three nurses and the attending doctor were crowded around the bed, and they turned to look at him. Their long faces wiped the grin from his face.

"Oh no...Is he...all right?" Tesla asked, already knowing the answer.

"I'm very sorry, Mr. Tesla," Bertram's doctor said. "We lost him. Just minutes ago."

The words struck Tesla across the face as if he'd been slapped. His previous lightness evaporated. His hand went to his chest involuntarily, clutching at a tightness that suddenly gripped his heart.

"He can't be dead," said Tesla, looking down at the award letter still clutched in his hand. "I had news for him. Very good news."

Two nurses filed out of the room silently, heads bowed. The third nurse straightened the sheet over Bertram's body, then followed them out.

"I am so sorry," said the doctor. "The infection in the lung was just too aggressive. With the lack of oxygen, his body had less ability to heal itself."

Tesla stood still as a statue, now nervous to approach the bed.

"Was he in pain? Did he say anything?"

The doctor shook his head. "No...no pain. I prescribed morphine to keep him comfortable."

"At least there was that," said Tesla, taking a step toward

the bed.

"He said nothing while I was here, but as I came in, Nurse Smithfield was leaning over him. If he had any last words, I suspect she heard them."

Tesla nodded, his body feeling cold and sluggish. He stepped forward to the bed and looked down at his friend.

Like before, Bertram's face was pale, but now any semblance of life had drained away. His eyes were mercifully closed, and his expression seemed one of surprise as if he'd just been told some unexpected news.

Tesla fidgeted, not knowing what to do, or what to say.

"I'll give you some time alone with him," said the doctor. He slipped out into the hallway as Tesla nodded numbly.

Looking down at the former lab director, he said, "Couldn't have given me ten more minutes, hmm?" He held up the letter. "I think you would have enjoyed this, my friend. I won your award!"

The words felt hollow as he said them, and he no longer cared about the distinction or the money.

He shoved the award letter back in his jacket.

"Damn it all, Bertram," he said, then turned and shuffled back outside.

He headed back to the lab and delivered the sad news. Everyone grieved in their own way.

Savannah turned and walked away, then sat on the floor, her back against the wall. She stared into space, preferring to be alone.

Sophia fell into George's arms, crying into his shoulder. He stroked her back, pressing his face into her hair.

Madelaine searched her library for the three chess books, and devoured them in seconds. As her mind filled with gambits and strategies, she spoke aloud.

"Goodbye, Bertram"

Edison was sitting in the officer's club, reviewing a report from his Menlo Park lab and sipping a cup of strong black coffee. His latest light bulb design was proving successful, with a 30 percent longer lifespan than the previous model. The lab had been staffing up recently and had added six new researchers.

He found a personal note written into the report then and blanched when he read that his assistant Dally had taken a turn for the worse. There were no details, but Edison made a decision then to get back to the city and see his old apprentice, while there was still time.

"Bad news, Mr. Edison?" said Colonel Oliver.

Startled, he looked up to see the base CO. His expression was not one of happiness.

He nodded. "My oldest apprentice. I fear he's not doing well. Not at all."

"Sorry to hear that. And I'm sorry to add to your troubles, Thomas. I just heard. Bertram passed away."

Edison sighed. "Not a good day."

"No," agreed the colonel. "Are you still prepared to go through with this?"

Edison rubbed his forehead. "Prepared? Not especially. But I have no choice."

"Understood. I'll meet you in the radio room then? Ten minutes?"

Edison nodded. "That will be fine, thank you."

"See you there," he said and walked out.

BOSTON, MA, USA

"They are well dug in," said the British captain, surveying

the American forces encamped within the Boston Common.

Colonel Thomas nodded, sitting tall in the saddle of his horse. His men had moved into South Boston without resistance, and he now saw why. They had marched up Commonwealth Avenue easily, but as they neared the wide-open clearing of the Common, they saw the Americans had chosen to concentrate their strength there.

The colonel scanned the line of defensive encampments along the expanse of green field. The Common was about 1,200 feet wide here, and General Houston had laid out a steady line of riflemen the entire length, many hunkered down within hastily dug trenches. Behind them a cluster of cannons had been set up every two hundred feet down the line. And behind those were the support troops, efficiently arranged to resupply the forward line.

"Yes, they are," the colonel agreed with a tone of annoyance. "This commander knows what he's doing." He nudged his horse forward, slowly taking in the field of battle. *We can take him, but it will cost us something.*

Barely a half mile behind the Common lay Boston Harbor and their true goal: the deepwater port. He knew large reinforcements were waiting offshore. Within an hour of taking the port, those men could begin off-loading into the city, strengthening his hold. *So close.*

He turned and pointed to his right. "What's the situation to the east?"

"The Chinatown district," replied the captain. "Also well manned, but the uniforms are not army. I believe they have armed the city's police force."

"Interesting." His men would have the advantage against police, as they weren't trained or accustomed to field warfare. And yet the streets to the east were more narrow, and filled with turns. His visibility would be sharply reduced, and maneuverability would be cut in half.

278

"Shall we push into the police force, sir?" the captain asked, reading his commander's thoughts.

Thomas shook his head. "Tempting, but no. Once we got ensnarled in the tight streets, the enemy could flank us with these troops," he said, waving toward the Common. "We'd be trapped in a pincer."

The captain nodded. "Agreed. So make our assault here then."

"We assault here. It will be bloody, but we have the space here to fight. Tell the company commanders. We attack in ten minutes."

The captain saluted. "Yes, sir," he said, wheeling his horse around. He raced away, spreading the word to the sub-commanders.

Thomas watched him go. *I've crossed the Rubicon now. Tonight I'll either be celebrating or dead.* He breathed deep, forcing his tense muscles to relax. The butterflies in his stomach told him things were about to get intense, in the way that only battle against an enemy can be.

He knew the nerves were a perfectly normal response to the situation. Any soldier who denied fear on the eve of battle was a fool or a liar. Rather than feel shame, he'd learned to accept the failings of his human body and move past them toward victory.

He turned and looked back at his army. Four thousand British Redcoats made a formidable sight. A sea of red and white uniforms, well armed and teeming with sharp bayonets. Their appearance, combined with the famous discipline of the British troops, had struck fear into the armies of many countries, and ultimately added them to the growing British realm. *Today will be no different. The empire conquers, and grows stronger.*

As he waited for the men to make final preparations, he thought of the needs of the flesh and reached into his

279

saddlebag. He found a chunk of hard jerky and used his teeth to rip off a piece. Slowly chewing the tough, dried flesh, he made final decisions about the target of his attack.

Minutes later, when the captain rode back to him, the colonel had the battle plan settled in his mind.

"All ready for your lead, Colonel!"

"Excellent, Captain. Here's what I want." He pointed to an area ahead and to their left. "Cannon fire on that location, a dozen shots. Also, the same barrage over there," he said, pointing to the right.

"They won't know which side we're softening up for the real attack," said the captain.

"Exactly. After the cannon we will rush into the left encampment. I want four companies of infantry in there immediately."

"Very good, sir. And the cavalry?"

He had two companies, or about four hundred mounted shock troops. They were fast, highly maneuverable, and powerful. No infantryman wanted to see mounted troops bearing down on him, and many a defensive line had crumbled at the intimidating sight.

"Once I see how the infantry perform, I'll decide where the cavalry strikes."

"Understood."

"The British are massing, sir," said Lieutenant Terry. "I think it's time." He stood in the entry of the general's command tent, folding the canvas flap aside and peeking in. General Houston was sitting at his field table, writing.

General Houston looked up from the letter he'd just finished. It was an old habit, writing to his son before a battle. While his rank usually kept him away from the front lines, war was an unpredictable business, and death didn't respect seniority. Putting his words down on paper for his son helped the general clear his mind and focus on the task at hand.

"Thank you, Lieutenant, I'll be right there." He folded the letter, slid it inside an envelope, and sealed it. Across the front, he wrote "For Matthew Houston" in a broad, flowing script. He propped the letter against the brass candle holder, satisfied it would be quickly found should he not return from the day's events.

He stepped outside, joining the lieutenant. He'd had his tent placed at the far side of the Common. Two hundred feet away, he saw their defensive line. Beyond them the British were indeed assembling and organizing. *The lieutenant's right. They'll make their move here very soon.*

The general strode forward, confident in their preparations. The men were well prepared, and a solid sense of good morale was in the air. He extended his hand, and the lieutenant snapped a pair of binoculars into it.

General Houston brought them to his face and quickly found the British line. He guessed they had four thousand men brought against the city. A few hundred cavalry too, he saw. He looked for officers, usually found easily, since they were on horseback. He saw isolated officers, yelling at the men around them. *Company commanders.* He kept looking, and a gathering of three men on horseback caught his attention. Two of them seemed deferential to the third, and he focused on the obvious ranking officer. Recognition hit him like a cold splash of water. *You wretched bastard.*

"They're commanded by Archibald Thomas," he said. "Looks like the weasel has made colonel."

"You know the man, General?" asked the lieutenant.

"Don't expect an honorable fight," he replied, still focused on Thomas and watching him give orders. "He has a special hatred for Americans."

Lieutenant Terry grinned. "That's all right, General. The

men don't much care for limey invaders."

General Houston chuckled. He liked Terry. *Man always has a smile and a joke handy. That's worth a lot on the field.* He lowered the binoculars and turned to face him. "I'm glad you're—"

BOOM!

His words were drowned out by the concussive roar of British cannons opening fire. In rapid sequence a dozen explosions rang out, followed by the unmistakable whistling of cannon shot screaming through the air.

Here we go.

The heavy steel shot tore into the American line, with gruesome results. Three men were hit directly by the cannon fire, and their bodies flew apart from the force, limbs scattering a dozen yards away.

Several of the shots were low, and they struck the grassy field in front of the Americans, then continued plowing forward, bouncing in low arcs until they found something to destroy. Men screamed, but few panicked, having taken cannon shot before.

A single shot went high, racing over the men's heads. It hit the ground once with a loud *whumpf*, then arced up and landed in the small lake behind them. A white geyser of water sprung up, marking the round's final impact as it sank to the bottom.

The Americans brought their rifles to bear, but there were few targets to find in the open. The British infantry held back, using buildings and cars as cover. The cannon crews were exposed, but too far away for decent rifle shots.

There was a short lull as the cannon crew reloaded. The veterans among the hunkered-down Americans put the moments to good use, running out from cover to haul wounded men back into the trenches.

And then, all too soon, the cannons opened fire again.

"Didn't expect so many cannons," grumbled the general, watching the damage unfold. "They hauled those beasts all the way from New Haven." He scanned the field, not liking the view. "Lieutenant, get a dozen of your best shooters. Circle around to their flank and get on top of that building," he said, pointing out the Hotel Wallace. "Snipe those cannon crews. Let's make them worry too."

"Got it, General," Terry said, sprinting forward into the battle.

Both apprehensive and determined, Edison entered the base's radio room. Colonel Oliver was already there and nodded welcome.

"All right, Jones," he said to the radio operator. "Place the call."

"Yes, sir," replied the young technician. A slight shaking in his hand was the only clue to his nervousness. "Never called the White House," he said, grinning.

"Something to impress the wife with tonight," said the Colonel.

"Yes, sir," he said, checking a printed schedule of frequencies. He found today's setting and tuned it in. After a series of security challenge-response codes, the communication was verified as legitimate.

"Thank you, Jones, that's all we need. Get yourself a coffee," said the colonel.

"Will do, sir," he said, excusing himself and closing the door behind him.

The colonel sat down and pressed the transmit bar on the mike. "This is Colonel Oliver, at Hansford. Requesting a priority communication with Chief of Staff Paul Davis."

"Stand by, please."

A few minutes later, a deep voice came through the speaker. "This is Davis."

"Colonel Oliver here, Paul. It's time for that get-together."

"All right, Colonel. Send him on down, I'll get Edison five minutes with him. See him in…what? Three hours?"

"That's about right."

"OK. I'll be ready. Safe flight. Davis out."

The colonel flipped off the radio and looked up at Edison. "OK, I've done my part. Ready to go?"

Edison nodded. "Let's get this done."

The two men walked straight to the airfield, where the colonel had a plane waiting. He introduced Edison to the pilot, then wished Edison a successful trip and headed back to his office.

As Edison got strapped in, he was amazed by modern technology. Here he was, outside Boston, and within hours he would be back in Washington, sitting within the White House.

Incredible, he thought, as the pilot taxied out on the runway and powered up for takeoff.

Colonel Thomas grinned wickedly as his cannons ate into the American line. It had been difficult, bringing them so far. But the result now was worth the effort. His artillery was chewing into their line like a rabid dog, and the sight pleased him greatly.

They were reloading for their fifth salvo when the sound of rifle fire cracked through the air from his left. He frowned. The infantry shouldn't be firing yet. They were too far away for a proper shot. Then he heard yelling from his cannon crews and understood.

The rifles fired again, and he located the sound. The Americans had sent a small group into the hotel and secured the roof. It was an excellent firing position, he admitted.

"On the hotel!" he yelled, pointing. The cannon crews had determined the location of the threat also, and tried to take cover on the other side of their cannons and supply crates.

From his vantage point, the colonel guessed four of the crews had been taken out in the surprise hit.

"Damn!" he growled.

The company commander nearest the hotel had already moved into action, though. He formed a detachment, led them into covered positions, firing up at the rooftop. They had little chance of a kill shot from that angle, but they could keep the snipers pinned down, afraid to raise their heads for a shot.

The sniper fire dropped off quickly. The colonel was pleased to see twenty Redcoats charging into the hotel's lobby. Racing up the stairs to confront the Americans on the roof, no doubt.

Time for the main event, anyway. He raised his sword high in the air. His lieutenants met his eyes, nodding that they were ready. He brought the sword down with a yell.

"Charge!"

With a deafening roar, the British infantry surged forward. They sprinted hard down the double-wide Commonwealth Avenue. The men at the back of the formation lost patience and broke off left and right to the nearest side streets, then turned and ran parallel with the main force.

Together they closed the distance to the Common, yelling and with rifles up. As they neared Arlington Street, which ran the whole length of the American front line, they opened fire, raining bullets into the simple fortifications the Americans crouched behind.

After the first wave of shots, the Americans returned fire, leaping up from the trenches to take aim. The front row of British soldiers went down, tumbling to the ground and tripping up those behind them.

But the flood kept coming.

The Americans watched their enemy draw closer, despite

their best efforts to cut them down. Redcoat bodies were piling up on Arlington Avenue, but there seemed to be no end to the British troops scrambling over the bodies and gaining ground.

General Houston saw the British collecting in the street, now out from cover of the tall buildings surrounding the Common.

"Lieutenant!" he yelled, and Terry ran over.

"Time for our cannon to have fun," he said, pointing toward the open street right in front of their line. "Just make sure they aim well."

"Absolutely!" Terry yelled, already running to relay the order.

A minute later eight American cannons opened up on the street. Along the defensive line, American troops swore and dove down within the trenches as the cannon shot screamed over their heads.

The shots were concentrated and smashed into the street, gouging large chunks of asphalt from the road and sending jagged shrapnel spraying toward the oncoming British. The surge forward broke instantly under the withering fire, and the British fell back, eager to find shelter.

The American infantry rose from their trenches and cheered, firing off rounds into the retreating enemy.

"Satisfying," said the general, watching the rout unfold. "Highly satisfying."

Terry returned and stood beside his commanding officer, wise enough to enjoy the moment without needing to speak.

General Houston flagged down a radio operator. "Send this message to the Hanscom base immediately: 'Engaged British at Boston Common. Send Beowulf now. Enter city by Longfellow Bridge.' Got that?"

The junior man scribbled it down and confirmed. "Got it, sir. I'll send it out right now."

"Good."

"Bringing out the big guns," said Terry.

"Subtlety rarely wins battles," replied the general.

WASHINGTON, DC, USA

Edison entered the small waiting room for the second time in his life, waiting for the president to see him. A lot had happened since then, but if this meeting went well, those mistakes could be corrected and things set on a proper path.

He was just sitting down when the Oval Office door opened, and he stood again, ready to be asked inside, flushed with the typical nerves and eagerness that room evoked.

Chief of Staff Davis appeared and smiled toward him. He had a genial face, framed by a black, sharp beard. He stepped forward, closing the door behind him and shaking Edison's hand powerfully.

"Mr. Edison! Great to meet you. Your reputation really is amazing."

Edison smiled easily, hiding his confusion about the closed door. "Mr. Davis. Thank you so much for making this meeting possible."

"Yes, well," he said, and Edison knew he would not be meeting the president today. He'd flown down specifically for this meeting, and all was supposed to be arranged. He worked to keep the disappointment from his face.

"I understand," Edison said. "The president is a very busy man." He smiled bravely.

Davis watched him for a moment, reading him easily. Deciphering men's true feelings was in his job description, and he did it quite well. "I know it's a disappointment. And I am sorry. When the colonel and I spoke, I thought I could get the time. But this business with the British is heating up quickly. I hope you understand?"

Edison waved his hand as if the matter was trivial to him. "Of course, of course. So shall I…"

"The president has authorized me to act on this matter," said Davis. "He does have an interest in this lab and the work they do, but right now he honestly has bigger fish to fry."

Edison nodded in understanding, sensing a possible advantage here. Roosevelt had previously seemed quite enamored with the Beowulf project. Perhaps the chief of staff was less biased.

"He certainly does," said Edison, laughing.

Davis pointed toward the waiting room entrance. "Walk with me, Mr. Edison. Let's find a quiet corner and chat."

Edison let himself be led away, but not before casting a last glance at the closed Oval Office door.

Davis led him down a richly appointed hallway and into an empty conference room. "Have a seat," Davis said, pulling out a chair and sitting at the large circular table. Edison joined him, then thought how best to pitch his case to Davis.

"Mr. Davis, I—"

"You want to take over control of the lab, yes? Now that Bertram has passed?"

Edison was taken aback. "Well, I—"

Davis smiled, having confirmed his assumption about dealing with scientists. So unaware of the ways of politics. He leaned forward, smiling. "Look, I've read the file on the Rabbit Hole. Nuclear fission, lasers, this Beowulf tank, even antigravity. Obviously, I don't know a whit about science. Hell, I was a political science major. But I know the lab was effectively wiped out in that zeppelin attack, and we need our military research back up and running. And as soon as possible. That is in the nation's interest."

Edison nodded, not wanting to interrupt.

Davis continued. "I don't know this Tesla personally. He

sounds like your typical eccentric genius, which is great, but not the type to run a lab of this caliber, am I right?"

"Yes, I do believe you are."

"I know General Houston considers the lab his baby, but his main responsibility was the base itself. Savannah Browning has done great work, but I'm not putting a woman in charge up there. The whole country knows about Menlo Park and the work you've led. Personally, I think it's a no-brainer. You have the pedigree to run large research projects. You already have a facility up and running. Seems to me the smart thing to do is move the lab to Menlo Park. The PR alone would be good for the war effort."

Edison realized he was holding his breath and willed himself to breathe smoothly. He'd simply wanted control of the research. Actually moving the work to his facility was more than he'd even thought of. But it made perfect, easy sense. He'd have to staff up, of course. Which was fine. He'd prefer to hire his own team anyway. No troublesome prior alliances to worry over.

"So, to be clear. We are speaking of full control, yes?"

Davis nodded. "Absolutely. The budget's already in place. We'll just put you in at the top." He raised a finger. "Although I do know the president considers the Beowulf project important, and it should continue as before."

Edison frowned, then took a new approach. "I fear the president's information may be out of date on that particular project."

"How's that? Field tests went grandly."

"Yes. That they did. But that was when Colonel Browning's mind was controlling the tank. Sadly, that is no longer the case. When the colonel's granddaughter was injured in the attack, Tesla took it upon himself to replace the colonel with her."

Davis sat up. "Are you saying that the Beowulf tank is now

being controlled by a young girl?"

"A twelve-year-old girl, Mr. Davis. Yes, that is precisely what I am saying."

Davis rubbed his face. "My God. Things have been moving so fast around here. We didn't know that." He looked up and stared into space, turning over the disturbing news.

"And I'm afraid it's worse than you know," continued Edison. He paused, letting the moment hang.

"What? What else?"

Edison sighed as if sorry to report the news. "I know for a fact that the Beowulf tank, under the control of the twelve-year-old girl, is responsible for killing American troops."

"What?" exclaimed Davis.

Edison nodded gravely. "I heard her admit it myself. It was an accident, of course. But it does sadly illustrate the danger of putting such firepower under the control of someone woefully unprepared for it. Or of letting machines fight men's wars."

Davis's spine had gone straight as an iron bar. He met Edison's eyes. "This changes the landscape, Mr. Edison."

"I am gratified to hear you think so, Mr. Davis."

Davis took a deep breath. "All right, that hammers it home. You are hereby authorized to assume command of the lab. Any work previously begun is now yours to direct as you see fit."

Edison beamed and thrust out his hand. "Thank you, Mr. Davis. I won't let you or the president down."

Davis shook Edison's hand, standing to see him out. "I do believe that, Mr. Edison. I'm happy to have a man we can trust taking the helm. I'll get the official orders cut tonight and sent to Colonel Oliver at Hanscom."

"A pleasure," Edison said, walking from the conference room with more than he'd dreamed. He found he was looking forward to the return flight and eager to begin making changes.

As he made his way back outside and caught a taxi back to the airfield, he marveled at how things had fallen into place. Usually, success required tireless, grueling work, but sometimes all that was needed was to have patience and let victory come to you.

A warm glow spread through him, much as he imagined alcohol must do for others. He basked in the cloud-like feelings, until he remembered the other visit he must make before returning to Hanscom.

When they reached the airfield, he instructed the pilot to land in New York City before they continued north.

He had a sick friend to visit.

NEW YORK CITY, NY, USA

For minutes Edison stood outside Dally's small, ramshackle home, hesitant to knock on the door. He'd been told his apprentice's condition had worsened, badly. He tried to imagine what that might look like, but then struggled to clear the nightmare image from his mind.

Inside he pictured Dally, in bed, with his wife and children milling helplessly about, watching him deteriorate and having no way to help him. A fate not fit for criminals, let alone innocent women and children. But they would bear it, because they had no other choice.

He knocked twice, wishing he were anywhere else. A soft voice came from behind the door, and he heard someone approaching.

The door opened, and Dally's wife appeared. Edison guessed she hadn't slept much in the past week. Her welcoming smile was thin and vanished in an instant. Her eyes were puffy, and she moved with a slouching shuffle. Without a word she turned away, leaving the door open.

Edison stepped inside the dark room, struck by both the smell and the disorder. Two children were playing with blocks and other toys lay strewn around the home. Clothes and dishes had accumulated in several piles. He followed her through to the bedroom and was wholly unprepared for what had been done to his apprentice.

Dally lay on his bed, asleep, with several pillows bunched behind his back. He had been reading a book his wife had propped up for him.

The scene was quite pleasant, except that Dally had no arms.

The radiation had ravaged his body. While the doctor first took four fingers of the left hand, that hadn't been sufficient. He later removed the entire arm, up to the shoulder.

But the metastatic cancer was thorough and brutal. To save Dally's life, the other arm had been removed as well. Now his friend lay in bed, helpless to assist himself, and drowning in pain, sorrow, and guilt.

Edison had been warned, but the shock of it still made his chest hurt. He knelt beside Dally, careful not to wake him. His twin stumps were heavily bandaged, and one still bled slightly, staining the white cloth.

The scene was horrific, more suited for a battlefield than a home. But Dally's face was oddly serene.

"It's the only respite he gets from the pain," said his wife. "We let him sleep as much as possible."

Edison nodded, wanting to comfort the man. But if sleep was his only escape, then Edison wouldn't steal it from him. He stood and backed away quietly.

In the living room, Edison turned to the bedraggled woman. "Your husband will remain on my payroll for the rest of his life. I can at least do that much."

She looked up at him blankly, then nodded. She moved to

the door. Knowing he was being dismissed, Edison followed her.

She opened the door for him and stood, watching her children stacking blocks.

"Good-bye, Mrs. Dally," he said and stepped outside.

Behind him the door shut with a soft click.

The following morning Savannah's eyes snapped open. Even lying in bed and barely awake, a sense of boundless energy danced within her. She smiled and rolled up, throwing her feet over the side and pulling her comforter up around her shoulders.

The floor was cool on her bare feet, but she was excited to begin the day. She and Tesla had discussed bringing Madelaine outside for some field tests, and she was eager to let her daughter demonstrate how much she'd learned.

She rushed through a hot, steaming shower, threw on some clothes, and grabbed a banana to eat on the walk over to the hangar. There was a lot to run through today. A speed run through an obstacle course, long-range test firing with her new radar, and if they could find a suitable location, she wanted Madelaine to try out her main cannon.

As she approached the hangar, she saw Tesla, George, and Sophia standing outside the main door. From the way Tesla was waving his arms around, it looked like he was arguing with the security guards. She picked up her pace.

"I am completely uninterested in your orders!" Tesla was yelling. "You will unlock these doors now and stand aside."

"No, sir, we will not," said the beefy guard. A second guard stood beside him, coolly eyeing Tesla. Savannah realized she'd never seen these men before, and then noticed they both wore sidearms.

"Stand. Aside," growled Tesla, punching his finger into the

guard's chest to emphasize the point.

Both men's hands slid down to their belts and unsnapped their holsters.

"Hello, gentlemen! What's going on here?" she asked, smiling broadly.

"These…automatons have locked us out of our hangar!" yelled Tesla.

"Hang on, Nikola," she said, then turned to the guards. "Under whose authority was this lab locked?"

"The lab director, ma'am. Mr. Edison."

Tesla's mouth hung slack, and he began to go apoplectic. "Director? Edison!" he yelled. "That accountant is no—"

"Nikola," said Savannah, resting her hand on his shoulder. She leaned in and whispered in his ear, "This is not the way. Let me handle this, OK?"

He glared at the guards, but nodded, then turned and took a few steps away.

"Sorry about that," she said, returning to the guards and letting her Southern accent deepen.

"S'OK," the first one said. "We're just following orders, you know?"

"Of course," she replied, nodding in understanding and pleased to see their hands come off their pistols. "So…when did y'all receive these orders?"

"Last night about midnight, ma'am. We're to secure this building. No one inside without Mr. Edison's permission. That's about it, really."

"Sure, sure," Savannah said, her mind reeling. Could Edison have staged a coup so quickly? If so, she was grudgingly impressed. "So, Colonel Oliver is aware of this?"

The guards looked at each other for a moment in confusion. "Ma'am, our orders came from Colonel Oliver himself."

Savannah felt the previous excitement and joy evaporate

and a cold anxiety take its place in her belly. *I underestimated Edison.*

"What about Beowulf? The tank inside?" she asked, suddenly fearful for Madelaine.

"Don't know about that, ma'am. We just locked the place up tight, that's it."

She nodded and forced a brief smile, willing herself to remain calm. "Thank you, Corporal. I do appreciate it."

"Sure thing," he said.

She turned back to Tesla. He, George, and Sophia had huddled together, whispering together. *Hatching a rebellion plan, no doubt.* She smiled at the sight. With Tesla in his pressed slacks and starched dress shirt, and the others in white lab coats, the scientists looked like the world's least likely agitators.

There was nothing to be gained here, though. They needed to regroup, get some intel, and come up with a proper plan. While unpleasant, the fastest way to get the lay of the land was to confront Edison and the colonel.

She adored Tesla, but didn't trust him to keep his emotions reined in. "Nikola, I'm going to find out what's going on. Why don't you guys wait for me? It shouldn't take long."

His face had reddened in suppressed anger, and he paced back and forth. Savannah's forced smile told him her request wasn't really a request.

"Fine," he said. "You understand these waters better than I."

"Been swimming them a long time," she said. "Give me a half hour. I'll meet you by that big oak tree near the kids' playground. OK?" She scanned their faces and knew George and Sophia were just as upset as Tesla. They just contained their feelings better.

Tesla nodded. "Good luck, Savannah."

"It'll be OK. We'll get this figured out," she said and

headed for the base CO's office.

The short walk gave her a minute to compose herself and prepare for the worst. She felt her father's absence. The colonel would have had a good plan already. Somehow they'd need to solve this themselves.

She entered Colonel Oliver's office, feeling a bit like a sheep visiting the fox. His receptionist gave her a curt nod and spoke into an intercom. *So I'm expected. This has been well thought out.*

The colonel's door opened, and he waved Savannah inside. "Please come in, Mrs. Browning."

She followed him inside, not at all surprised to find Edison there. He stood and offered his hand. "Hello again," he said.

She smiled and took his hand. "Mr. Edison," she said with a nod. "It seems you've been a busy man."

"Ah yes," he said, walking to the window. He turned and leaned back against the sill. "Please understand this is no reflection of my feelings about you. We simply have differing opinions of how technology should be used in war. In this case the powers that be have agreed with my view."

"I see," she said, settling into a leather club chair. "And how would you summarize your view?"

Edison drummed his fingers on the windowsill, thinking. "Machines exist to serve man, Mrs. Browning. Not the other way around. And certainly not to wage war for us."

"Your vision is for machines as support only."

"Of course! We need men on the battlefield, and those men deserve our support. We're already making plans to expand our telegraph network extensively, to better get field reports and orders from place to place."

"Beowulf is a controversial project, I grant. But I was not aware the zeal of your disapproval had risen to the level of a coup."

"Please," he replied. "Let's not be dramatic. We're not

talking about overthrowing a government here, just a misguided, soulless, very expensive research project."

Dark thoughts swirled behind Savannah's eyes, but she kept them hidden away. "And your plans for us?"

"The Beowulf project is shelved. All work done by the lab will be relocated to my facility at Menlo Park. I can even offer you all positions there, on more suitable projects."

"Under your direction."

"Yes, of course."

"I see. You understand that my daughter is an integral part of the project?"

"Obviously," replied Edison. "And you do have my sympathies. But until I decide what to do with it, that tank will remain exactly where it is."

She laughed, but there was no humor in it. "Mr. Edison, you…You're about to exceed the limitations of my graciousness."

Edison smiled, but said nothing.

"And if Madelaine disagrees? You could hardly stop her."

"You're right. She will be placed in warm shutdown."

Savannah leaped to her feet. "You can't do that!"

"I most certainly can. I've studied your materials and could perform the procedure myself. As you say, I could hardly stop her otherwise. She won't be harmed, just…neutralized."

Savannah prided herself on decorum and political shrewdness, but she felt those things washing away. Beneath them, the jagged, rocky core of a mother's instinct was being revealed. She knew she was losing control, and the two men saw the change too.

The colonel leaned over and spoke into the intercom. A moment later an armed guard entered the room and eyed Savannah intently.

Savannah fought against the maelstrom swirling in her mind. She tried not to think about Edison turning Madelaine off like one of his light bulbs, but the image had stuck. Her eyes closed as she fought the impulse to rip out Edison's throat.

A hand grabbed her above the elbow. She blinked and saw the guard standing beside her. He gently but firmly pushed her toward the door. "Please come with me, ma'am."

As she was led away, Savannah felt a disturbing sensation closing around her like a hot, stifling blanket.

She had failed her daughter.

BOSTON, MA, USA

Colonel Thomas strode up to one of his company commanders. "You let your men get too concentrated!" he yelled, leaning in uncomfortably close.

The company commander stammered a reply. "I…but, sir —"

"Quiet!" Thomas yelled, backhanding the junior officer across the face. He regretted the action immediately, but sometimes his temper flared before he could control it.

"Sorry," he said as the junior man rubbed his reddening cheek.

Three other commanders joined the impromptu strategy session and pretended to have not seen what happened.

"It's all right, sir. You're right. They got bunched up, and that was my responsibility."

"Fine, fine. Now let's concentrate on the future. We hit them hard, but it cost us as well. I don't think another assault here is the answer we need."

"Circle around and come over one of the bridges?" said a young officer.

The colonel scowled. "We just got torn apart by bunching up our forces. Don't make me strike you as well."

"Ah, of course, sir," said the officer. He decided against offering further suggestions.

"No. We need the port, and we need it fast. I want to swing the men to our right. Punch through the Chinatown district."

"Where the police have been armed?"

"That's right. We can't get through here. Next best is to deal with the alleyways over there. It's tighter than I'd like, but the men there are not trained soldiers. And if we can pierce that defense, it's a short distance north to the port. Once we're there, we have the sea protecting our rear, so we can concentrate our defense efficiently."

The commanders all nodded in agreement.

"All right, let's not waste any more time here. Form your men up, and let's move quickly."

Terry's eyes narrowed as he watched the British redeploy. "They're up to something."

The general followed his look, taking in their movements. The British front line was pulling back, growing thinner as men split off from the group and slid behind buildings. In his mind a distant alarm began ringing.

When he saw the cavalry fall back and race down a side street, the alarm grew deafening.

"He's going for our flank. We need to bolster Chinatown, now!" said the general.

"Got it. I'll signal our cavalry to sweep around behind the lake and join up with the police force," said Terry.

"Good, good," said the general. He ran over to the radio operator.

"What response from Hanscom?" he asked.

"Sorry, General, I just now got through to them. It was a confusing conversation. They said…well…"

"Out with it, son!" the general yelled.

"They said no such project existed anymore. I'm sorry, sir, that's all I could get out of them."

"What?" yelled the general. "That makes no goddamn sense!" The rush of troop movements caught his eye. He needed to focus on the men here and now, however confusing this message was.

"Keep trying!" he ordered as he turned and found his horse. "We need Beowulf here, soon!" He mounted his horse and took off to oversee their movement into Chinatown.

The guard led Savannah from the colonel's office by the arm. He wasn't aggressive about it, but she got the feeling that could change quickly if she resisted. The colonel and Edison followed them out, and together they all marched down the hallway.

As they stepped outside, Savannah blinked at the bright morning sun. Then she saw Tesla, accompanied by two more guards. George and Sophia stood beside him, looking nervously about.

Savannah thought of resisting, but knew that was pointless. They were inside a military base, under the colonel's command. Fighting back now would do nothing but land them in the stockade.

Edison cast a dismissive glance toward Tesla. "You, I know, are a lost cause. Just like her," he said, hooking a thumb back at Savannah. "You're both off the base."

He walked over to George and studied his face. "How about you, George? Are you interested in making history with me? Actually helping the war effort? Or will misguided loyalty ruin your career?"

George met Edison's gaze calmly. "Tesla is twice the scientist you are, Mr. Edison. I'm only sorry you aren't a big enough man to see that."

"Very well," said Edison. "He goes too," he said to the guards.

He approached Sophia. "And you, Sophia? You've done good work here, don't throw it away, please."

She looked down at her feet, then bit her lip nervously. She fidgeted, not wanting to answer.

"Sophia?" asked George, waiting for her to join them.

"I'm sorry, George. I really am," she said, then looked at Edison. "Mr. Tesla is a brilliant man, and I'm proud to have worked with him. I wish it hadn't come to this. But if I have to choose, I'm with you, Mr. Edison."

"One out of four," he said. "Well, it is what it is. Thank you, Sophia. We'll talk about your role here in a moment. As for the rest of you," he said, turning to the three banished scientists, "your base privileges are hereby revoked. Colonel, please see them escorted off base."

Not waiting to see the result of his order, Edison wrapped an arm around Sophia's shoulders and led her away. "Now what I'm thinking is this," he said to her as they walked away.

George stepped forward after them. "Sophia! Come on, honey!"

Other than a brief pause in her step, she gave no other sign of hearing him.

George's eyes grew hard, witnessing her betrayal. "Fine then," he muttered, watching Edison lead her away.

Colonel Oliver addressed his men. "These three are off the base, right now. Their things will be sent to them later."

"Yes, sir," the guards acknowledged. They rounded the three up and escorted them away. Tesla began to resist, but with a resigned shake of her head, Savannah told him to go along quietly.

"Understand this," the colonel said, "Hanscom is a classified area, and your clearance is revoked. If you attempt to reenter the base, you will be subject to deadly force. Please don't try me on this."

Within minutes they walked through the base gate, never to return.

BOSTON, MA, USA

Colonel Thomas rode fast down Berkeley Street. He'd memorized the street map of Boston and already knew their best chance to punch through Chinatown was down Stuart Street, which conveniently opened one lane wider just south of the police encampments.

"We can't let ourselves be ensnarled here," he told his commanders. "I want four hundred men only to storm those encampments. Once they're involved in hand-to-hand, send in the cavalry, all of them. Their mission is to punch through the police line, then attack from the rear. Got that? They don't stop until they're north of the police line. Once they turn and attack, then we move forward with the entire army."

The commanders all nodded, then one raised a hand.

"We'll lose the four hundred," said an older major with dark, cropped hair. "They'll be cut to pieces before we reach them."

"I am aware," said the colonel. "We're trading some pawns now for a checkmate position later. But the game will be ours."

The major wondered if the pawns saw it that way, but gave no argument. While cold, the colonel's viewpoint was accurate. Without bold decisions their entire army could be caught here in the open while the Americans reinforced, and then the game really would be lost.

The commanders nodded and rode off to direct the action. Minutes later four hundred Redcoats ran yelling down Stuart Street, firing as they went. They bolted forward, straight into the police force, ignoring their comrades who fell before reaching the blue-uniformed Boston Police.

The Redcoats quickly closed the distance and clashed tightly with the police, falling into hand-to-hand combat. Rifle butts swung into faces, and bayonets jabbed and pierced. Pistols were drawn and fired at close range, and men even swung punches at their enemy.

American soldiers were moving to support the local police force, but they were slow to reach their position.

The mix of red and blue combatants was clear, and the cavalry rushed forward to do their part. Hundreds of stampeding mounts surged down Stuart Street, following the same path as the luckless four hundred, but they didn't stop and engage the enemy. Instead, they bore on, dodging the pairs and groups of soldiers locked in combat in the street. Like a wave they flowed around and through the many obstacles, their force splitting and re-splitting, then merging back together.

They took fire, but it was hastily aimed, and they were past before a second shot could be brought to bear. Almost before they realized it, the cavalry force had broken through. They were no longer drawing fire, since the police had more immediate enemies in their face to deal with.

While not trained for combat, the police were good shots, and they were entrenched. The four hundred British infantry kept them engaged, but Boston Police was steadily whittling down the British.

The riders eased their speed down, and the horses slowed from a full gallop to a canter, then came to rest. As they grouped together again, those riders in the rear turned their mounts around and charged back at the police. Soon the entire force was galloping back into the battle, this time attacking the police force from their rear.

The effect was devastating. With the city police forced to

deal with British infantry, their attention was directed forward as the mounted riders stormed into them. The tall riders had good visibility, and could choose their targets at will. As fast as the British cavalry could aim and fire, Boston policemen fell with bullets in their backs.

Within minutes the remaining police broke ranks and ran, abandoning their position.

American cavalry arrived, but it was too late. Few police remained on the street, and those who stayed were quickly slaughtered.

The full British army had moved in even as their cavalry was tearing into the confused police. By the time the mounted soldiers had finished their work, they were quickly surrounded by thousands of British infantry, who pushed forward around them.

The fight for Chinatown was over. Colonel Thomas directed his men to head north. With no opposition in their way, they advanced quickly.

Before the Americans could catch them, the British had taken the port.

Boston Harbor was now theirs.

"You must be feeling rather good today, Thomas," said Colonel Oliver. "Your plan has succeeded brilliantly."

"Things have a way of working out for the best," agreed Edison. "Sometimes you just have to be patient."

"And as we agreed…"

Edison nodded. "Absolutely. As soon as you are ready, you have a VP position waiting for you at Menlo Park."

"Excellent. I retire in five months, and the thought of sitting around all day doing nothing scared the hell out of me."

Edison laughed. "I know! Me too! Well, you'll have plenty to occupy yourself with at my lab, Colonel. There's still so much to do and invent. Honestly, we humans don't know a millionth of one percent about anything."

"Exciting times. I can't wait to be a part of it."

"Me too, my friend," he said. "But now I have a rather delicate matter to attend to."

"The tank."

Edison nodded.

"Do you want backup?"

"No, no. Seeing soldiers would only give away the game. This must be done softly and smoothly."

"Good luck to you then."

"Thank you. If you hear chainguns and explosions, you'll know I failed," Edison said with a gallows smile. He headed out and met up with Sophia. As they walked to Madelaine's hangar, he reminded her of the plan.

"You are a familiar face to the girl. I need you to be casual. Nonchalant. Just going about normal routine duties. Yes?"

Sophia nodded twice. "I know, Mr. Edison. Believe me, I'm well aware of what that child can do if we spook her. I'd much prefer to live through the day."

"Just making sure we understand each other."

As they neared the hangar, Edison waved the guards aside and unlocked the door. "You men stay here, please," he said as he and Sophia slipped inside. He closed the door behind them.

"Sophia!" cried Madelaine. "What's going on? Where's Tesla? And Mom? I heard them all yelling outside the door—"

"It's OK, Maddy," Sophia said in a calming tone. She tried to look casual and focused elsewhere. She found a clipboard on a nearby table and pretended to read it. "The president demanded a report on the American soldiers you killed by accident," she said. "No one was allowed inside until questions had been answered."

"Oh," she said, embarrassed that so many people knew about her mistake. "So where are they now?"

"On the way back now from Washington. Should be here in a few hours," Sophia lied.

"Good, I miss them. Hearing that arguing made me pretty nervous, you know?"

"I bet it did," Edison said, stepping closer. "And I'm sorry about that. The guard didn't explain? I specifically asked him to fill you in."

"No! No one came in. I just had to sit here, wondering," said Madelaine.

"Oh my," replied Edison. "Well, that's the military for you, hmm?" He came closer and stood beside the main worktable beside Beowulf.

"I guess so," she said.

"I've been meaning to chat with you, Madelaine. And to thank you for getting us here in one piece."

"Thanks, Mr. Edison. That's nice of you. I know my grandfather would have done it better."

"Maybe," he said, then turned to Sophia. "Sophia, were you going to run that RCA test we spoke of? I can lend a hand if you need."

Sophia looked up from the clipboard, her eyes a touch wider than they should have been, but Madelaine didn't notice. "I was just about to, yeah." She walked under Beowulf. "Maddy, please open the RCA chamber. I want to run a check on your array cohesiveness."

"Sure, Sophia," replied Madelaine. The steel panel slid open, revealing Madelaine's mechanical brain.

"Thanks." She pulled a ladder over and climbed up to connect a pair of cables to the RCA.

"Your grandfather was a great man, Madelaine. We all miss him, every day," said Edison, watching Sophia connecting the feed lines and snaking them over toward his worktable.

"Yeah, he was," she agreed. "He could do all this so easily. He's gone, and I can't do what he did. Makes me double sad, you know?"

Sophia brought the cables to Edison's table and plugged them into twin receptors. Each side was now electrically isolated, but once the proper size resistor was placed between them, it would inhibit any current flowing through the array. Specifically, it would prevent Madelaine's thought processes from advancing. She would be instantly frozen, held in stasis until the resistor was removed.

"You will, my dear," Edison told her. He found a rack of differently sized resistors. Each was a differently sized copper rod, encased in thick plastic except for the ends. He found the proper one and placed his fingers on it, looking to Sophia for confirmation it was the right one. Her nod was barely there, but was affirmative. He picked it up and placed it above the cable feed receptors.

"You will make us all very proud someday," Edison told her. "Even your grandfather, watching from above."

Her voice warmed. "Thank you, Mr. Edison. That's really —"

Edison jammed the resistor in place, and Madelaine's mind stopped, frozen in time.

It was a busier night than usual at the Blackwood Tavern, just outside the Hanscom base. The off-duty crowd had filled the bar, and the sounds of clinking glasses and laughter served as background to attempted seductions and the occasional argument.

Tesla sat alone in a leather club chair beside a blazing fire. He leaned forward, elbows on his knees, holding a half-finished whiskey. Absent-mindedly, he swirled the brown liquor in the glass, feeling the warmth of the fire against the side of his face.

Since being thrown off the base, he'd been in a shocked

daze, not knowing how things had deteriorated so quickly. He'd walked alone for hours before settling in here.

That's not true, though, he thought. *You know exactly how it happened. Edison.* It had been a fatal mistake to underestimate the man's greed for control. Or his ability to wrest it from others.

Savannah had told him about Edison's plans to shut Madelaine down. *Probably been done by now. Otherwise we'd have heard explosions as she escaped.*

The thought of Maddy alone and helpless, now frozen in place, stabbed at his chest. His eyes closed, and he felt his heart beating hard. The noise and chaos around him fell away, leaving him alone at the center of a broad, deep depression.

He'd planned to change the nature of warfare. Now he was getting drunk as his plans lay shattered at his feet, making the colonel's death and Maddy's condition seem pointless and in vain.

He gulped the last of the whiskey and waved for another.

"These too?" asked the private, pointing to a stack of supply crates.

"Everything," said Edison, nodding. "Pack it all up."

He watched the men haul away the material they'd brought from Fort Hamilton. The hangar was emptying out quickly. While he wouldn't be pursuing this line of work any further, it was classified material and would be secured in storage.

A much bigger problem was what to do with the tank. He couldn't reawaken the girl and trust her to behave. Disassembly was an option, but he didn't want to divert technicians for weeks to the job.

He stood, arms crossed, and shook his head at the sheer size of the monstrosity. He didn't want to spend any more time on it than had already been wasted. *Let's just leave the thing here, and let the colonel deal with it later.*

The soldiers were carting away the last of the Beowulf materials, leaving only the cables that snaked from the tank to the resistor block. They'd even taken out the tables, so the assembly sat on the floor. *Holding her in place, like a finger in a dam.*

"I've got the case you asked for, Mr. Edison," said a corporal, bringing a green metal box to him. It was a standard ammo box, with a hinged panel on top. Edison had requested one, with a three-inch notch cut out of one side.

"Perfect," he said, examining the box. "This should do just fine."

He sat the box on the floor beside the resistor assembly, then opened the case and carefully set the assembly inside it, feeding the cables through the notch. He closed the steel case and fed a padlock through it, locking the assembly inside. *No sense having some curious private pulling that resistor out.*

Being near Beowulf had always given Edison a sense of apprehension, like standing under something heavy hanging over him. He'd never trusted the machine itself, or the girl Tesla had put into it. Locking the resistor assembly away gave him a feeling of relief, though. *The tiger has been tamed.*

He looked around the now-empty hangar. The research material was gone, and despite the safety of putting it into warm shutdown, Edison felt acutely alone, standing in the shadow of the hulking, inert tank.

He turned and walked out, turning off the lights as he left.

As Edison locked the doors behind him, Madelaine sat frozen in the darkness, unaware she had been abandoned.

"Another one, hon?"

Tesla blinked, confused. He dragged his eyes up from the wooden table to find a young waitress smiling at him. He blinked again. Her face was pale, framed by long, rolling, red locks. *Exceptionally pretty.* He smiled dumbly.

"Another one, and he'll be snoring on your floor," said another woman's voice.

Tesla turned toward the new voice, and his eyes widened at the sight.

"Savannah!" he said, louder than necessary.

"He's had plenty," she said, sliding into the chair opposite him. "But I'll have one."

The waitress smiled and bent down to whisper to Savannah. "He's been a gentleman," she said, then slipped away into the crowd.

Savannah sat, watching the emotions on Nikola's face. When he first saw her, he lit up with delight. Given the circumstances and his inebriation, that response was the first warm feeling she'd had in hours. She held onto it, enjoying the brief distraction from worrying about her daughter.

In the next few seconds, she saw sorrow in his eyes, along with regret and guilt. All understandable, but not the one thing she was hoping to see within him.

"All these feelings you're experiencing are normal," she said. "You're suffering because you're a good man."

He smiled weakly, his lips tight.

"Maybe," he said. "But what good is that if it's paired with ineffectiveness?" he asked, rapping his knuckles against the table.

She pointed a long finger at him. "That's a choice."

"I choose to be ineffective? A dour viewpoint."

The waitress set a whiskey down in front of Savannah, and she scooped it up, taking a sip.

"You think that's depressing? Try this: It is God's will that Edison control my girl's life. That work any better for you?"

"No," he said.

She felt her pulse jump as she thought about Madelaine.

Calm down. That won't fix anything. She took another long sip, seeing Tesla was adrift.

She counted out five deep breaths, then spoke again.

"Did you hear? Marconi made the first worldwide radio broadcast today," she said.

Tesla grunted.

"By all rights that should have been you," she said. "He built on your work, didn't he?"

"Marconi is a good fellow, let him continue. He is using seventeen of my patents."

"Mm hmm," she said, studying his face. "Quite a few companies have profited from your work, without compensating you. True?"

Tesla sighed heavily. "I don't care that they stole my ideas. I care that they don't have any of their own."

Her eyes narrowed. "And that is your fatal flaw, my dear Nikola."

"What? That I—"

"You don't care! And you can afford to be cavalier, because you're a genius. There will always be more ideas, more inventions. Right?" she said, her face warming in anger. "So you walk away when people steal your work. You don't want to fight. Just go back to your lab and invent something new."

"I...I don't know. I just—"

"You just keep making more meat for the wolves, Nikola. That's what you do. And that's why I found you in a ditch."

Since locking away everything related to Beowulf, Edison felt a growing sense of optimism. So much money had been spent on the project-money that could now be channeled into useful pursuits.

He and Sophia had packed their bags and would move down to Menlo Park in the morning. Once there he would need to ramp up quickly. The government funding now coming to him would triple the operating budget of his existing facility. They would need more space, more facilities, more staff. Entire new sections could be created overnight, and would be properly funded from day one.

For an inventor, it was a dream come true.

He had made his name with the telegraph and was excited to expand on the potential it contained. Instant, accurate communication over great distances was precisely the type of technology the country needed now, especially during a time of war.

The major cities were connected by telegraph wires, of course, but that was a small beginning. Edison imagined a vast network of telegraph stations, up and down the Eastern Seaboard. Information would flow from Maine to New York to Miami as fast as electricity. It would usher in a new era of shared knowledge.

He returned to the small room he'd been assigned as living quarters and found a sealed letter half slid under his door. He examined it, pleased to see it was the latest report from Menlo Park. Settling into a chair, he took out his penknife and slit the envelope open.

There was a request to reopen investigations into X-rays, which made him frown in painful memory of Dally. There would be no further work along those lines.

He continued reading, pleased to hear of a new invention. A storage battery, capable of holding a surplus of electrical charge and releasing it over an extended period of time. Several hours, if the report was correct. *Now that's something*, he thought. He quickly thought of possible markets to approach with the new device. *Train lamps and miner's helmets. They'd be most interested.*

He found paper and pen and began writing his response. Foremost in his mind was the need to quickly secure a patent

on the device. Since he was the director of all work done at
Menlo Park, the filing would, of course, be done in his name.

Tesla considered Savannah's words, letting them roll
around in his mind. She made a good point. It was more
pleasant to create than to fight. That could very well be his
blind spot.

"Have you fully spoken your mind now?" he asked her.

Savannah's spirit was still up from identifying Tesla's flaw,
but she was calming back down.

"I believe so. For now."

"I don't disagree with your assessment. Besides, our
present circumstances would argue in your favor too."

"Thank you," she said, relaxing. "I walked back to the base
gate. I don't know, maybe I thought I could talk my way in."

"I can guess how that went," said Tesla.

"Three guns raised in my face?" she asked.

"Would have been my guess."

"We're not getting back in there." Savannah slumped back
in her chair. "We had it good at Hamilton, didn't we?"

Tesla nodded slowly. "Not much fun being homeless."

"I suppose Sophia was the practical one," she said.

"Don't judge her too harshly. George told me her father
had passed. She's been sending money to her mother. She
couldn't afford to lose her job over principles."

"Didn't know that. Well, that makes more sense, at least.
But it doesn't change our situation."

"How did you find me here, in this particular pub?" he
asked.

"Wasn't hard. I just asked someone where the officers
went to drink. Figured this would be more your style than the
dive bars that usually show up around a military base."

"Good," he said. "That's good."

"Is inventing your first love, Nikola?"

"I do not think there is any thrill that can go through the human heart like that felt by the inventor as he sees some creation of the brain unfolding to success," he said, his blue eyes lighting up. "Such emotions make a man forget food, sleep, friends, love–everything."

She smiled. "I'll consider that a yes."

Tesla's face softened. While he'd never had the time for a relationship, it did feel wonderful having someone interested in knowing him.

"Yes," he confirmed.

"So what will you do now?" she asked. "I'm not sure how much I can offer you anymore, but with your prize money, you'll be fine. Just don't let people walk over you anymore, OK?"

"I've been considering my next move all night," he said. "Whiskey is a fine tonic for rolling over a problem."

"And you've come to a decision?"

He nodded. "It took a few hours, but yes. Your tongue-lashing earlier was accurate. This time I will fight. But not alone."

"Nikola, you know I'm with you, but I don't think—"

"I know," he said. "But you're not the ally I've been sitting here waiting for." His eyes flicked over her shoulder, settling on a beautiful brunette approaching them.

"She is," Tesla said.

Savannah turned, and her eyebrows rose when she recognized the woman.

"Finally!" said Sophia, standing by their table. "I've looked through six bars already."

General Houston returned to his command tent. His letter to his son was waiting for him. He picked it up, running his finger over the envelope's creased edge. A lot had happened since he'd written it that morning.

The day had gone badly. They'd inflicted serious casualties on the British, but that meant little once Thomas's force captured the port.

Within thirty minutes the first ship docked at Boston. The HMS *Victory* was a ship of the line, and she carried 1,800 Royal Marines, all eager to get back on dry land. Twenty-two fresh cannons came off next, followed by tons of food, ammunition, and medical supplies. The reinforcements were instantly pressed into defending the port and did a fine job.

By sunset the *Victory* had completed her off load, and three more ships were in the process of putting their men and supplies ashore.

General Houston faced the fact that he'd failed in his mission. The enemy had taken the port, and more were flooding in every hour.

With the fast reinforcements, the British had managed to expand their position, forcing the Americans to fall back, block by block.

The damned zeppelin did its bit too, he thought bitterly. Like an angel of death, the thing would descend from above the clouds and bomb the Americans until they were scattering like rats, desperate for cover from the barrage.

For the hundredth time, he wondered bitterly what had happened to Beowulf. If he'd ever needed an ace in the hole, it had been today. But fickle luck had decided to withhold her graces.

The second of the three British ships was the HMS *Glasgow*, limping into port after suffering raking fire from the Americans weeks ago and being too badly damaged to return home. Captain Douglas had chosen to stay with the fleet, hoping to put into Boston for the repairs his ship so badly required.

As the mooring lines were set, the captain breathed a long, deep sigh of relief. They'd been limping along for so long, and the strain was showing, both on himself and his ship. But making the ocean crossing back to England would have been suicide, so he'd waited. He fully intended to get very drunk tonight.

He saw a familiar, if not friendly, face on the docks. *Major Thomas. No, strike that. Colonel now.* Not especially happy to see the bloodthirsty man, he smiled anyway and waved. With a moment of stunned recognition, Colonel Thomas returned the wave, and his smile seemed genuine.

Captain Douglas walked down the gangplank, saluting as he stepped ashore. "Colonel Thomas," he said.

"Captain! Excellent to see you safe. You've been biding your time until now?"

The captain nodded wearily. "That we have."

"Incredible. Really. That's truly something," the colonel said, clapping the captain on the shoulder as if they were brothers.

Victory seems to agree with him, the captain thought. "Thank you, we're very pleased to be here. So you've done it. Opened the way for the fleet. Well done, Colonel."

"We paid for it, have no doubt. But we're here, and that's what matters." He led the captain down the dock. "Things are still rough, but we're settling in. Tonight, please do me the honor of joining me for dinner?"

A true dinner of something more than hardtack and jerky sounded like heaven, despite the company.

"It would be my pleasure," said the captain.

"Sophia!" said Savannah, pushing her chair back and

jumping to her feet. "I'm not sure if I should hug you or slap you."

Sophia smiled. "Well, I'm damned happy to see you, regardless." She grabbed Savannah in a quick bear hug.

"Oh!" yelled Savannah. "Well, OK then," she said, returning the embrace. Then she grabbed Sophia by the shoulders and held her at arm's length.

"Now what's the story? Does Edison know you're here?"

Sophia shook her head. "No way. I made sure he was asleep before I left. Look, I'm sorry to be such a bitch before. I saw what was coming down the pike, and I figured we'd need someone on the inside. So, I played turncoat."

"You…that was quick thinking, Sophia," said Savannah. She turned to Tesla. "And you knew?"

"I suspected. Once I thought about it, it seemed likely. Sophia has a head for duplicitousness."

"Hey now!" she cried.

"In the best possible way, of course," he continued. "I just hoped she'd be able to find us."

"I knew if I were you, I'd be drowning my sorrows, so I've been checking every bar around the base."

Savannah grabbed a nearby chair and pulled it over.

"Here, sit!" she said, taking her own seat. The three leaned together conspiratorially.

"How's Madelaine?" asked Savannah. "Is she OK?"

Sophia thought for a moment. "She's OK. But she's been put into warm shutdown."

"That son of a bitch," she muttered. "Did Maddy know what was happening? Was she scared?"

"No, not at all," she replied shaking her head. "Edison was real smooth on that point. I think he was afraid of what she could do if she felt spooked."

"Yeah, I bet," said Savannah.

"She is still in the hangar, I assume?" asked Tesla.

317

"Right."

He didn't hesitate. "Then we need to get in there. We need to wake her up. Tonight."

Savannah nodded. "I agree. There's no advantage in waiting, and we don't know what Edison has planned for her. The sooner, the better."

She looked at Sophia pointedly. "Can you get us back in there?"

"I didn't drive to every gin joint in town to get a Manhattan. Damn right I can. My car's outside. You two hide in the trunk, and we're in."

She looked around. "Where's George?"

Tesla shrugged his shoulders.

Savannah rested her hand on Sophia's arm. "He was pretty thrown by you staying behind. After we got thrown off the base, he walked with me for a few minutes, but then wanted to be alone."

"I knew he would be," said Sophia. "I had to be convincing, though." She bit her lip. "Ugh, poor George. I'll need to find him once I get you two back to Madelaine. He's got family not too far away in Providence. He may be working his way there."

"Of course," said Savannah. "Just get us back to the hangar. Nikola and I can take things from there."

"You ready now?" asked Sophia.

Savannah looked to Tesla. He already had his wallet out and was leaving cash for the bill. He nodded once.

Sophia noticed Savannah's glass was still half-full.

"For courage," she said, then grabbed it and downed the last of the whiskey.

Ten minutes later Sophia was driving down the access road leading to the Hanscom base. She kept her speed moderate and scanned the road for other cars. With a touch of paranoia, her eyes flicked to the rearview mirror, but no one else was behind them.

Wedged in the trunk, Tesla and Savannah lay on their sides, facing each other. Tesla's dislike of personal contact made the trip feel longer than the five minutes it actually was, but the evening's drinks served to blunt the worst of his anxiety.

They hit a pothole, and Savannah's head connected hard with the trunk floor.

"Damn," she said, rubbing her head above the ear.

"Sorry!" called Sophia from the front.

Tesla found a beach towel and gave it to Savannah for a pillow. She refused until they hit their second pothole.

"Thanks," she said, accepting the towel and stuffing it under her head.

Small gaps around the rear brake lights let in just enough light for her to see his face. He wore a bemused grin that reflected her own feelings.

"Didn't plan on this when you took the job, did you?" she asked.

"A fair bet," he agreed. "I feel like a prohibition rum runner."

In the dim light, she smiled as they jostled around. "All part of the fun of serving your country."

"OK," called Sophia. "Here we go."

They felt the car slow as they approached the gate. Sophia eased forward smoothly and stopped as the MP raised his hand. As he approached the driver's side of the car, Sophia saw two other guards in the small gatehouse. A wide metal bar blocked the road forward.

"Good evening," the MP said. "Identification?"

Sophia smiled sweetly and pulled her purse into her lap. "Of course," she said, digging for it. She pulled out her checkbook and a novel and set them aside.

The MP scratched his chin, watching her search.

"Ah!" she said. "Here you go." She handed the laminated card over.

The MP took it and eyed her face carefully, comparing it to the ID. Then he checked the name against a list.

Inside, Sophia was ready to scream, but she gave no appearance of it. Her eyes kept glancing sideways to the MP's holstered handgun. *Don't be silly, they probably wouldn't shoot me. I'd just lose my security clearance and spend a few years in the stockade, that's all.* She busied herself with restuffing her purse and checking her makeup in the rearview mirror.

"Out late tonight," the MP said.

She turned and smiled. "Not late enough. But I have an eight o'clock meeting, so I'm being a good girl."

He nodded, appreciating the view of cleavage.

She smiled warmly, holding her breath.

"OK, you have a good night," he said, waving another MP to raise the gate for her.

"Thanks!" she said as the bar went up. "You too!"

Heart racing, she drove through the gate, then watched as the bar lowered behind her.

She kept going, staying right at the posted speed limit. After she'd turned a corner, she called back.

"We're through. We made it."

In the trunk Savannah grinned. "Maybe we should get into bootlegging."

"One venture at a time, if you please," said Tesla.

Sophia cruised through the base, working her way back to the hangar. As they neared the airfield, she scanned about for a dark, remote spot to park.

A few buildings away from their hangar, she pulled into a dim alley behind the base barbershop. She killed the engine and turned off her lights. Sitting in the dark alley, she waited a few moments, listening through the open window.

The night was quiet. Far away a dog barked twice, then was silent. The low croak of frogs came from an overflow culvert. Otherwise, she heard no manmade sounds.

She opened the car door, then shut it quickly to kill the overhead light that came on. Looking around, she crossed to the car's rear and popped the trunk.

Looking down at Tesla and Savannah scrunched in there like sardines, she suppressed a giggle.

"OK, we're good," she said, chuckling.

"Yeah, yeah," said Savannah, pulling herself out of the trunk. "Next time I drive." She took Sophia's offered hand and jumped out, landing on her feet and looking around the alley.

"Good. Nice work, Sophia," she said.

Tesla was following her, unfolding himself from the cramped space.

"Thanks," said Sophia. "I was sweating it there at the gate. But a little cleavage makes everything easier."

"True words," said Savannah.

Tesla joined them and quietly closed the trunk. He looked around, getting his bearings. Realizing the hangar was only a few buildings down the road, he nodded.

"You did a great job, thank you," he said.

"My pleasure. I just wish I could see Edison's face when you guys break out of here."

She hugged Savannah good-bye. "You guys be safe, OK?"

Savannah returned the squeeze. "That's the plan. Now, will you be all right?"

Sophia nodded. "I'll be fine. I'm going to crawl into bed now, in case Edison suspects I helped you and comes looking. I'll find George first thing in the morning."

"OK, good."

"Oh," Sophia said, turning back and leaning into the car. When she straightened up, she handed them a pistol.

"I hope it's not necessary, but…"

Tesla cocked his head at the sight. "I don't know," he began.

Savannah took the gun. She looked at Tesla and felt his apprehension. "It's my daughter," she said.

"I know. But—"

Savannah ejected the magazine and stripped the rounds from it, slipping them into her pocket. She turned the gun sideways and pulled the slide, ejecting the last chambered round. It sailed straight up into the air, and she caught it as it came down.

"Better?" she asked.

Tesla nodded. "For all of us, I think."

He stepped toward Sophia and offered his hand. "My thanks. George is a fortunate man. I hope you catch up to him soon."

Sophia shook his hand, knowing it was a gesture he rarely made. "You bet I will," she said, getting back in her car. She leaned out the window. "I hope we work together again soon. You guys are fun!"

They waved as her car eased out of the alleyway. She stopped at an intersection, then turned and was gone.

Tesla turned to Savannah. He indicated the way toward the hangar. "Shall we?"

"You know it," she said.

Together they walked quietly, scanning the area for guards or passing cars. They kept in the shadows as much as possible and strolled casually when they had to cross an open space.

Soon they came to the airfield's supply depot, which sat adjacent to their hangar. They crept forward and peered around the building's corner.

A single light hung above the front door of the hangar, casting a pool of illumination for twenty feet around the door. An armed guard stood near the door.

"That's the only entrance," she whispered, handing him the gun.

He nodded and took the handgun. The heavy weight was comforting in his hand, but also intimidating.

Savannah pointed to the area off to the guard's left and nodded in that direction. "Can you approach him from over there?"

"I can, and will," he whispered back. "Be careful."

He turned and eased back the way they'd come. Moving slowly, watching the way carefully, he circled around. In a minute he'd found a good spot off to the guard's left, hiding behind a shipping container. He could only get within thirty feet, which felt troublesome, but any closer, and he'd out in the open.

Savannah saw him move into position. Now it was up to her, and the plan suddenly felt very real. *That guard's gun is fully loaded. No threatening moves. Just a half-drunk girl making her way home, no problem.*

Remembering Sophia's wisdom, she unsnapped two buttons on her shirt. The cool night air brushed against the tops of her breasts, and she felt doubly exposed.

She stepped out from cover, ambling obliquely toward the hangar and making no attempt at stealthiness. She saw a small rock in the road, and kicked it absently, sending it skittering across the pavement.

"Who's there?" said the guard, now alert. He stepped toward the sound, but stayed within the light.

"Hmm?" answered Savannah, casually strolling in his direction. "*I'm* here," she said, relaxing her Southern accent. "Rather be in bed, though. Where the hell is C Block?"

He stepped toward her again, and she smiled broadly, crossing the distance. As she got close, she breathed a sigh of relief. She was pretty sure she'd never met this man. *Edison chose someone with fresh loyalty, no doubt.*

"C Block?" asked the guard, frowning. "Honey, you're a few hundred yards off." He pointed behind her. "You want to head back that way. Now."

His hand easily slid to his holster and rested on the gun's grip. Savannah caught the motion, but forced herself not to focus on his hand.

She took another ambling step forward, then stopped. She could read his insignia now. Corporal Jenkins.

Behind the man Tesla slid from behind his cover and crept forward silently.

Savannah followed Tesla's progress in her peripheral vision, but kept her eyes locked on the guard's face. He was turning less friendly quickly.

He unsnapped his holster. "Ma'am, you will turn your ass around right now and get home. Are we clear?"

"Oh come on," she said, waving her hand at him as if he'd just scolded her for jaywalking. She pointed a finger at him. "You seem really tense. Do you need a drink?"

"All right, that's it," the guard said. He drew his weapon and leveled it at Savannah's chest.

She felt her heart freeze, and her casual grin cracked. The gun's barrel looked huge and dark.

Suddenly, she forgot all about Tesla and even Madelaine. All she saw was the cold steel barrel staring at her.

"I—" she began, raising her hands automatically.

"Turn. Walk," he said. His finger tightened on the trigger. *CLICK.*

The guard froze at the sound. It came from behind him, and close. In the quiet night, the sound of a cocking hammer was unmistakable. He wanted to spin around, but he couldn't know where his assailant was, not before taking a round in the back anyway.

"I'd feel badly shooting you," said Tesla. "It would be a courtesy if you don't put me through that."

The guard raised his hands. *Who the hell talks like that?* "Easy," he said.

Savannah looked over the guard's shoulder and saw Tesla directly behind him, the gun raised and pointing at the man's back.

She stepped forward and took the guard's gun from him.

"Thanks," she said, already feeling the effects of adrenaline setting in. With shaking hands she tucked the gun into her back.

The guard's face was cold. "You two are deep in it now."

Slowly, hands still up, he turned to see who was behind him. His eyes widened in recognition.

"You're that scientist, Tesla."

"I am. Now, the keys to the hangar, if you please."

The guard dug into his pocket and pulled out a thick key ring.

"Open it up," said Tesla.

He went to the door and unlocked it. Pushing the door open, he said, "Now what?"

Savannah put her hand against his back and shoved. "Inside," she said.

Together they stepped into the hangar, and Savannah saw Madelaine there. Relief washed over her. Even if she was shut down, they were close again.

Tesla closed and locked the door behind them. Looking around the vast space, he saw everything had been cleared out. There wasn't even a rope left to tie up the guard.

With the relief, Savannah felt anger return at what had been done to her daughter. She imagined Edison sweet-talking her into oblivion, and without thinking she took the gun from her back.

She drew back and brought the butt down hard against the guard's head. There was a satisfying thump as she hit him, and he tumbled to the floor, unconscious.

"Savannah?" asked Tesla.

"I'm fine," she said, running toward Madelaine. "And he will be too."

She ran forward and saw the twin cables leading away from Madelaine, ending in the locked steel case.

Tesla verified the guard was still breathing, then joined her.

"He put a resistor block on her. The current can't flow through these cables with it in place." Crouching beside the case, he swiped at the lock. "And he doesn't want anyone removing it easily."

"What are our options?" she asked, pacing.

He pointed to the chamber that housed her RCA array. It was sealed, and without Madelaine awake to open it, they wouldn't gain access. "We can't remove the cables on that end."

"Let's shoot the lock off," she said, stepping forward with the guard's gun.

Tesla held his hand up. "Hold on. Let's not attract attention before we have to. I've got a quieter idea," he said, looking at the hangar's wall, where there was an emergency fire station, with a long, coiled hose and a fireman's ax.

Tesla took the ax from the wall and returned to the resistor case. He laid the twin cables against each other along the floor, then stepped back. With a mighty swing, he brought the ax down into the woven steel cables, cutting them clean through.

He dropped the ax and picked up the severed ends.

Nodding at the case, he said, "That resistor prevented the free flow of current through her mind. So let's bypass it altogether."

With one cable in each hand, he jammed the raw ends together, completing the circuit.

"…sweet of you to say," Madelaine said, completing her earlier comment to Edison. Then she was confused. It was as if she'd jumped in time. One moment Edison was there talking with her, and now Nikola and her mother were there.

"Mom?" she asked. "What's going on?"

"Maddy!" she cried. Both hands went to her mouth as she teared up. "You're all right?"

"Sure, Mom. I'm just confused. How did you get here? Where did Mr. Edison go?"

"It's OK, baby," she said as a tear ran down her face. "We're here now. I'll explain the rest later."

"Madelaine, please open the RCA chamber for us," said Tesla.

The hatch slid open. "There you go."

As Tesla held the severed cables together, Savannah climbed up to reach the inputs they were connected to. She found them, switched the array back to internal routing, and yanked the cables free, letting them fall to the floor.

"We need to get going, darling," said Savannah.

"Um, OK. Where to?" asked Madelaine, already opening the crew compartment for them and dropping the access ladder.

Savannah swung over, caught the rungs, and pulled herself inside the crew compartment. She smiled in satisfaction at making it back there.

Tesla dropped his end of the cables and ran up the ladder behind her. He hit the sealing mechanism, and the ladder retracted as the hatch closed.

"Thank God," he said, letting his head fall back against the railing. "I didn't know if we'd ever be here again."

Savannah grinned. "Well, we are," she said, shaking Tesla's shoulders. "And no one is hurting my girl again," she said, her voice going low and dangerous. "No one."

Tesla nodded in agreement. Looking up at her, he saw her blue eyes burning with a cold fire. He immediately knew she'd kill anyone who threatened Madelaine again.

In a comforting tone, he told her, "Let's get out of here, Savannah."

She was still seeing images of her revenge against their enemies, and paused before shaking her head and returning to the present.

"Right. Maddy, we're heading for Boston," she told her daughter.

"Southeast," she replied. "About twelve miles."

"Good," said Savannah. "Do you remember the layout of this base?"

"Mostly. At least everything I saw on the way in. I've got detailed maps of all the major cities, including Boston, but I don't have anything for military bases."

"Let's not forget, almost all the American troops we come across will know nothing about us," said Tesla.

"Agreed," Savannah replied. "Maddy, we need to get out of the base as quickly as possible, then head south on Highway Two into Boston. We need to be in that fight."

"Got it, Mom."

"And, honey?"

"Yeah?"

"Don't kill anyone, unless you have to."

Pulling late-night duty stinks, thought Private Mayfield as he quickly walked toward the airfield. He checked his watch. It was 1:58 a.m. He began jogging to make sure he reached his post on time.

He ran between two admin buildings, then cut across a runway before turning right and seeing the hangar he'd been assigned to guard. The door was closed, but no one was standing watch. He began to run faster.

As he approached the lit door, he stopped and looked about. He was on time. Why would Jenkins leave his post early? The colonel took a damn dim view of that kind of behavior. He checked the door, turning the knob and ensuring it was still locked, then walked around the side of the large building.

Looking down the length of the hangar's exterior, he strained to see in the darkness.

"Jenkins?" he called out. "Come on, man, you can't—"

SCREECH!

The private stopped, barely believing what he saw right in front of him. A fifty-foot length of hangar wall was being ripped apart, falling in tall, metal ribbons.

Painfully loud clanking, like a massive chain dragged over rocks, made him cover his ears.

Then Beowulf appeared, pushing through the hangar wall.

The private saw a tank tread taller than himself rolling in front of him. As his face drained of blood, he looked up.

Smashing through the remains of the wall was a tank bigger than he'd ever imagined. If he'd been ten yards farther ahead, it would be rolling right over him now.

The house-sized tank bulldozed on. A huge main cannon jutted forward. Ringing the outer edge of the monster were smaller chainguns. As he stood petrified, one of the chainguns swung over, aiming straight for his face.

He heard the dribble of water, then realized his urine was running down his pants leg and pooling on the runway asphalt.

As the tank rolled forward, the single chaingun swiveled, keeping a precise bead on his head.

Then it was through the wall and moving into the open space of the airfield runway. The chaingun relaxed and slid out of view. A huge pile of twisted sheet metal, the remains of the hangar wall, lay in the tank's wake.

The tank rolled forward onto the runway, then turned to the right and accelerated, following the runway.

The private watched it disappear into the night. When the

sound of wrenching metal shrieked from the far side of the runway, he knew the thing had run through the base's security fence.

Whatever it was, it was off the base.

Stunned, he gathered his wits and looked around for the nearest alarm station. He ran to a red box mounted on a nearby wall and threw it open. He picked up the phone handset inside and told a security officer what had happened.

Nearby, Sophia had just undressed and climbed into bed. She flipped on her back, thinking back on the day's adventures.

Just then alarm klaxons blared across the base, waking the dead. Security details sprang into action, but Sophia knew their adversary was already gone.

As she watched the ceiling fan spin above her, Sophia enjoyed the cool breeze and smiled.

After running through Hanscom's outer security fence, Madelaine carefully made her way through the deserted streets of the surrounding town. While her treads tore up the roads, she tried to get out of town without damaging any homes or buildings.

Tesla and Savannah were strapped tightly into Beowulf's crash chairs, which absorbed most of the bumps. They held onto the chair arms for stability and rode it out.

Once she cleared the inhabited area of the town, Madelaine found Highway 2 and kept an average speed of thirty-eight miles per hour. The night was cloudy and dark. Whenever Tesla took a look out of a view port, he could see little. Feeling how quickly they were moving through the blackness made him uncomfortable, but he trusted her abilities.

"You can see OK, right?" he asked.

"I can, Nikola. The visible light spectrum isn't much use

currently, so I switched to ultraviolet. Don't worry, I wouldn't risk hurting you or Mom."

"I'm sure," he said, but he closed the view port nonetheless.

They continued down the road that way for several more minutes before Madelaine startled them.

"We have a problem," she said.

"What's happening, honey?" asked Savannah.

"I've been monitoring the radio bands, to get any reports on the fight at Boston. Here, just listen." She turned on the internal speakers and piped the radio into it.

"—repeats. This is Thomas Edison. The research project Beowulf has escaped the Hanscom base and is now considered a rogue agent. This super-tank is extremely dangerous and has killed American personnel. All friendly forces are instructed to consider the tank a British asset and disregard any communications from it as propaganda. Good luck. Message repeats. This is Thomas Edison—"

"Wow," said Savannah.

"But I can help fight the British!" cried Madelaine.

"We know that, honey," said Savannah.

Tesla sighed. "But no one who hears that message will believe it now."

Savannah nodded. "I knew he was power hungry, but this is something else."

"It's his dislike for me, I'm afraid," said Tesla.

"What a shortsighted, arrogant, pigheaded…" Savannah fumed, letting the thought trail off.

"He would sacrifice our help just to prove himself right?" Madelaine asked. "That's crazy!"

"People often are," said Tesla. "When emotions run high, reason tends to evaporate."

"So what do we do?" she asked.

Tesla looked at Savannah. He'd come to know her

331

expressions well. Without speaking, they had agreed.

"We press on," she said. "We'll help in the fight, whether we're wanted or not."

"OK, Mom," she said.

To her right, the road had narrowed as they entered more hilly terrain.

Soon the road was running through a large hill that had been blasted away to make room for the highway. Along their right side, a sheer rock wall ran up fifty feet, nearly vertical.

She saw a broad lake approaching on their left. The highway ran between the two obstacles, and she decided to slow down to twenty-six miles per hour.

She wound her way through the carved-out hills, watching her clearance space carefully.

As she came around a curve in the road, she swore, "Oh shit."

Beowulf lurched forward as Madelaine reduced speed quickly. Soon she came to a full stop in the road.

"Maddy?" asked Savannah. "Why'd you stop?"

"'Cause we're about to feel unwanted," she answered. "There's an American checkpoint ahead."

"Perfect," grumbled Tesla. He snapped open a forward view port, seeing several large campfires burning.

"At least twenty men, blocking the road," he said. Twisting to one side, he asked, "Is that a lake?"

"Yes," said Madelaine. "I can either go through the checkpoint, or turn around and head back."

"I wonder if they heard the broadcast?" asked Savannah.

CLANG!

A bullet caromed off their front hull and dug into the rock wall beside them.

"I would guess they have," said Tesla.

"They're coming," said Madelaine. Using the natural ultraviolet light from the stars, she saw two dozen men moving toward her, all with rifles.

Another bullet struck the hull, then three more.

"Maddy, get us out of here," Savannah told her. "We'll find another way to Boston."

"Sounds good to me," she said. Her treads spun in opposite directions, and she spun around, reversing course. Heading back the way they'd come, she powered up and surged forward.

As she came back around the turn, she saw a dozen Americans had blocked her return path.

"Uh—" she said as she hit her brakes again, sending Tesla and Savannah lurching in their seats.

"What now?" he yelled.

"I'm boxed in here, guys. If I can't run over them, there's nowhere else to go."

Tesla got up from his chair and risked a quick look. A dozen men were yelling, and busy with something, but he couldn't tell—

"Maddy, is that a cannon?" he yelled.

"Two cannons, actually," she answered. "They're setting them up on both sides of us."

A cascade of bullets clanged against the hull again. Tesla slammed the view port shut.

"Maddy, cannons are dangerous, even to you. We need—"
BOOM!

The cannon directly in front of them fired with a belch of fire, and a forty-pound ball screamed toward them.

BRANG!

The shot hit Madelaine's front quarter, sending a jarring thud throughout her.

Tesla felt the impact in his bones, and the horrendous noise from the impact made his ears hurt.

"Uh, Mom?" asked Madelaine, her voice rising in fear. "I don't know what to do. That hit did something. I can't tell—

something's not right now."

Savannah's eyes searched Tesla's face, hoping for a brilliant idea, but she saw only what she herself felt: confusion.

"Honey, are your major systems OK?" she asked. "Can you move?"

"Yeah, I can move, see, and fire. Whatever that did, I don't think it was major. Not yet, anyway."

Tesla's fist beat into the bulkhead. "God, they were fast to set this up!"

Savannah shook her head. "No, this is here to stop British movements. We just got caught in the net."

"I'd rather not be the fish!" he yelled, then stroked his chin in thought.

"Madelaine, you were built to withstand chemical attacks," he said.

"That's right," she said.

"Which means that to some degree, you are waterproof."

"Oh wow," whispered Savannah.

"You mean?" Madelaine asked.

"I sure do. Those cannons are going to beat our brains out. Unless someone has a better idea?"

"No," Savannah said, shaking her head. "Do it, Maddy! Get us out of here!"

"OK," she said. She threw one tread to half-power and whipped around ninety degrees, facing the lake, then rushed forward into the dark water.

"This is so weird," she cried as they ran into the lake, sinking below the surface.

Behind them, the astonished Americans held their fire as they watched the giant tank disappear under the lake's surface.

In seconds it was gone, and the lake's surface calmed.

Madelaine drove forward, along the lake's bottom. Her

vision had been sharply reduced, and she was driving mostly blind.

"Guys, I can't see a thing. Just so you know," she announced.

"You're doing great, baby," said Savannah. "Just keep a straight course. There aren't any really deep lakes around here. We'll find the opposite shore in no time."

Hopefully, thought Tesla, eyeing the view ports. Drops of water had appeared around the seals. As he watched, the drops accumulated, running together and dripping onto the floor plating.

"Not good," he said. He stood and found an old blanket. Twisting it up, he pressed it against a row of view ports, absorbing the incoming water.

"We don't want water in the electronics," he said, pointing to the other row of view ports. Savannah nodded and looked around for something to use.

She came back holding the white lab coat they'd used to cover Madelaine's body.

"Oh no, Savannah," said Tesla.

"It's OK. Really," she said. She smiled sadly, but pressed the coat against the now-wet ports.

Within a minute the coat was saturated and dripping on the floor.

"This isn't going to work much longer, Nikola," she said.

Madelaine surged forward on the lake bottom, churning up silt and mud behind her in huge swirling clouds.

Savannah watched helplessly as water poured from the saturated lab coat, pooling on the floor plates. As they bounced along the lake's bottom, the pool ran one way, then the other, gliding over the steel plating and growing in size.

"Nikola," she said, now worried about being electrocuted.

He looked back over his shoulder. "Damn," he muttered.

Beowulf tilted forward suddenly as they ran into a shallow

depression. The water surged to the front of the tank and slipped into a control panel. It ran over a mass of wiring and components, causing a short circuit. With an angry sizzling sound, the panel lit up in a blinding flash.

"I can't tell how deep we are," Madelaine said, "but we're tilting up slightly now. It's getting lighter out there too."

"Excellent, just press on," Tesla answered, using both hands to press the blanket. He smelled something burning then and looked back. Wisps of white smoke were rising from the panel. With a sinking feeling, he realized it was the communications station.

He pulled one side of the wet blanket back and watched the bare view port. A few drops appeared, but they didn't accumulate.

"The pressure is lessening!" he cried.

Savannah tested her side and breathed a sigh of heavy relief.

They dropped the soaked fabrics down onto the access hatch, where the water couldn't get into anything sensitive.

Tesla grabbed a fire extinguisher while Savannah ran to the smoking panel and pulled it loose.

Golden flames were dancing inside the panel, feeding on the wiring insulation. Tesla could taste the acrid smell of burning plastic in the air.

He sprayed the fire, waving the extinguisher back and forth slowly until the flames had died down. White powder coated the insides of the panel and hung in the air in hazy clouds.

"Amazing," he said, coughing and smiling at Savannah. "We made it, I think."

"Yep," said Madelaine. "Take a look."

Her front edge was already climbing up the shallow shore of the lake's edge. She ground on, feeling the treads slipping in the soft sand, and then pulled herself out of the water completely.

Tesla opened the view port and eagerly stared out, while Savannah did the same on her side.

They were exiting the lake on the far shore, opposite where they'd gone in. In the distance Savannah could see the campfires from where they'd escaped the ambush.

Around them she saw only a wide beach sloping into the lake, and beyond that, a thick tree line.

She faced Tesla. "That was a crazy-ass idea."

He shrugged. "I cannot argue."

Madelaine drove higher onto the beach, then turned away from the ambush and followed the lake's edge, looking for a way back to the highway.

"Madelaine, how do your comms feel?" he asked.

"I can hear, but I can't broadcast," she answered.

"Could have been worse," said Savannah.

Tesla nodded. "Yes, easily. With Edison's message out there, we probably wouldn't have been believed anyway. We were somewhat lucky, actually," he said, opening the view ports for fresh air. Slowly, the smoke cleared out.

After an hour of trying back roads, doubling back, trying other roads, and plowing through two fields, they found their way back to Highway 2, several miles south of the ambush spot.

She brought them back up to speed, and they were on their way again.

"I've been getting radio signals on military frequencies," said Madelaine. "It sounds like the fight in Boston is going really bad for us."

"Bad?" said Savannah. "As in…?"

"The British have taken the port. There's a lot of confusion flying around, but that much is pretty clear."

Tesla looked up from checking their ammunition levels. "How much farther to Boston?"

"At this speed we'll be there in eighteen minutes," she replied.

"Ammo levels are pretty good," said Tesla. "We're lucky we got her out of there before Edison had her stripped down."

Savannah nodded, her face framed by blonde locks. She was pensive, thinking about the report on Boston. If the port was lost, things were really bad. They were almost certainly running into a desperate situation, one that she knew the general had expected them to fight in. They owed him that, and much more.

She exhaled, letting go of all her negative thoughts.

"Then we put that ammo to good use," she said. "We retake the port, no matter the cost."

BOSTON, MA, USA

"Colonel Thomas?" said the lieutenant. "You asked me to wake you, sir."

Thomas lay on his back, his cot set up in the port director's office. He wasn't asleep. He'd been looking up at the exposed wood beams of the old building, listening to the bustle of men and equipment being readied for battle. The sounds were comforting, even relaxing, but today promised to be as good as the previous one. Today he expanded his control from the port out to the entire city of Boston.

"Thank you, Lieutenant," he said, rolling over and setting his feet on the floor. He checked his timepiece. It was 6:29 a.m. He glanced out the window, confirming that sunrise was quickly on its way.

He stood and stretched, enjoying the exquisite pain of tired, sore muscles being put to use again.

He glanced at the young officer who still waited in the

doorway. "Get Roberts and Harris," he said.

"Yes, sir," he replied, dashing off.

Thomas pulled on his boots, then splashed water on his face from the basin. After brushing his teeth, he walked to the wide windows opening to the docks.

Every berth had been taken by British ships, and every pier was filled with piles of supplies being brought ashore. A hundred men scurried over the area, hauling crates, checking paperwork, or repairing ship damage.

The previous day had seen his force shift from a daring frontline vanguard to a machine of organization and stability. Tactics were now giving way to logistics.

He rubbed at the dark stubble on his cheek, watching the workers come and go. *But today will again contain tactics.*

The clomping of boots told him the two company commanders were approaching. He turned as they filed into the room.

"Come," he said, waving them in. He crossed to his work desk and indicated the map of the city.

"Here," he said, stabbing a dirty finger on the map, "is Breed's Hill. And beside it, Bunker Hill. Today we claim them both. I'm leaving the other commanders to continue pushing back the Americans. I want you to focus on these objectives."

The hills sat just north of the downtown area and offered commanding views of the city core. In 1775, during the Revolutionary War, the British had occupied Boston. The Americans hoped that by claiming these high hills, an artillery barrage might force the British from the city.

This was not to be, however. After several attempts the British routed the Americans and took the hills, in what became known as the Battle of Bunker Hill.

The colonel continued. "As you no doubt remember from your classes at the Academy, Bunker Hill has some historical significance. High ground was valuable in 1775, and more so today. We have harried the Americans extensively, and they've had little men to spare holding those hills. Within three hours I expect to see British flags flying on them. Questions?"

Harris nodded. "What resources do we have for the assault?"

"Take your pick," said the colonel, handing him a sheaf of papers. "Since midnight we've unloaded several thousand men, another hundred cavalry, twenty cannons, and tons of ammunition."

The commanders glanced at each other and smiled. Such easy victories paved the way to commendations and promotions.

As they approached the outskirts of Boston, Madelaine paid particular attention to monitoring as many frequencies as she could.

She discovered that if she concentrated properly, she could segment off a part of her mind and assign it a task. Then she could continue focusing elsewhere. The sensation was startling and a little disturbing, as if her mind were splitting apart. But when she verified she could recombine her segments again, she felt more comfortable with the idea.

She created a dozen thin slices of her mind and instructed them to listen for any news on the battle, both from the Americans or the British. Since she could guess at each broadcast's general position also, by checking the angle of the broadcast and its relative strength of signal, she tagged each new input with a location.

As the slices had something to report, the information flowed back up to her through the queue system. It worked well, so she expanded the idea and created another dozen slices.

She now could maintain a real-time understanding of all

radio traffic in the area.

"I'm getting a picture of the battle," she announced. "The port is fully British controlled, and they're bringing lots of reinforcements in from the sea."

"That was the worst-case scenario," said Savannah.

"Over the past day, they've pushed out from the port," Madelaine continued. "An American captain is retreating his men west across Longfellow Bridge, which leads me to assume the British have retaken most of downtown."

"Oh God," whispered Savannah.

"There's a British zeppelin in the area. It's been conducting bombing runs on American positions. General Houston's men are in disarray. I think they've been cut off from one another. At least three pockets of American resistance. The general's name is still mentioned in orders, so I believe he's alive."

"That's something, at least," said Tesla.

"So where can we help?" asked Savannah.

Madelaine thought about that for a moment.

"Huh," she said.

"What? Tell us!" said Savannah.

"Great minds thinking alike," she said. "I was about to propose an idea, but it looks like the British know their history too."

Tesla glanced at Savannah with a raised, questioning eyebrow. She shrugged.

"I can't do much inside the city," explained Madelaine. "I'm just too big. So I was going to suggest we take Bunker Hill, just north of the city. From there I can mortar the hell out of the city, and the dock."

"Sounds like a fine plan," said Tesla.

"Yeah. Except the British got there first. There was a token American force stationed there, but they just got overrun badly. The British have the hill, and they're digging in to keep it. They've got multiple cannons up there too."

Tesla looked to Savannah, wondering what her reaction would be. Bold words of taking cities were well and good, but charging toward entrenched cannons was another matter. He wasn't sure she'd still have the will for a fight.

She was staring ahead, not seeing, thinking about how much had been taken from them. Bertram, the Rabbit Hole, Beowulf's reputation, Madelaine's body.

Savannah's breathing was deep and steady as she catalogued their losses.

Then she blinked, and her cold blue eyes flicked to him, pinning him with an uncomfortable intensity.

"No matter the cost, Nikola."

BOSTON, MA, USA

"Move it!" screamed Lieutenant Terry. He watched with mounting impatience as his two hundred men fell back across Longfellow Bridge, retreating in the face of overwhelming British numbers.

Enemy reinforcements were flowing out of the captured dock, pushing the Americans back steadily, until they'd found themselves no longer holding the city center. Now they'd been forced back westward against the Charles River, which wrapped around much of Boston.

While General Houston was holding the southern flank, Terry's company had attempted to circle around to the north. It was a good idea, but terrible timing. As they approached the dock, a fresh wave of Redcoats flooded out of the shipyard. Three companies, at least. And they weren't tired, hungry, or wounded.

Terry had taken one look and knew engagement would have been foolish. He ordered his men to fall back. If they could get across the bridge, at least they'd be behind a choke point. They could regroup and plan a wiser course of action.

So the haggard Americans ran, dashing through the streets, dodging British bullets as they bolted for the relative safety of the bridge. Half the company had made it to the other side and were busy finding cover behind building corners, grassy mounds, low rock walls, anything they could throw themselves behind as a shield against British rifle fire.

Terry crouched low behind an overturned car. Its insides were burned out, and it still smoldered and felt hot to the touch. He rubbed his right shoulder that he'd hurt by diving impetuously over a barricade. He'd landed badly, and it throbbed now with each heartbeat.

His remaining hundred men were making their way over the bridge, harried by enemy fire as they ran or limped. He unslung his rifle and returned fire at the British. Several of his soldiers took rounds in the back and collapsed, dying in moments. But most of his force was slowly escaping the onslaught.

When he was convinced all his men were accounted for, he broke from cover and sprinted after them. He'd been strong in track back at university, and he pumped his legs madly, catching up to the stragglers.

"Run, you lazy bastards!" he yelled, catching up to them.

He cursed and goaded the men along the last of the bridge, and they each found a spot to collapse safely for a moment, huffing and catching their breath.

When he looked back, he saw the British were content to chase the Americans across the river and leave them there. *For now, at least.*

The thousand British soldiers began taking a defensive posture, reinforcing their hold on their side of the bridge.

Well, we're not getting back in that way.

"We're approaching the hill," declared Madelaine. She had approached from the west, turning off the main road and driving through open farmland, barreling straight for Bunker Hill.

Tesla and Savannah snapped open view ports, eager for a view of their surroundings. The low, scrubby land gave Beowulf the advantage, as she could see far and drive fast. They were bouncing along at forty miles per hour, and they both reached out for handholds to steady themselves as Madelaine tore across the raised furrows of a plowed field.

"Downtown Boston is a mile and a half to our southeast," she told them.

"And you can get a good firing position atop the hill?" Savannah asked.

"My records show that Bunker Hill is a hundred and ten feet tall," she said. "Earlier this morning I taught myself trigonometry and ballistics. If we can get there, I can tear them up."

"You taught yourself—" Tesla began, then stopped. He glanced at Savannah, who met his look with a mixture of pride tinged with concern. She understood. At a superhuman rate of speed, Madelaine was becoming more than what she was before. *If she can do this in a few weeks, what will she be like in a few months? Or years?*

Savannah pushed aside the thoughts. There'd be time for musing, worrying, and guessing later, assuming they lived through the next hour.

Madelaine slowed, then stopped. They'd reached the base of the hill. The incline was steep, but no worse than the valley behind Fort Hamilton had been.

Tesla found a pair of binoculars and looked through a view port at the hill. From his perspective it looked like a tall anthill, with hundreds of red and white worker ants scurrying over the top, furiously busy building their new home.

"A lot of British up there," he said. "They're digging ditches and building barricades."

Savannah came up behind him, leaning over his shoulder. "How about cannons?"

"Don't see them yet, but they're probably up there." He handed her the binoculars, and moved back to let her see for herself.

She brought them to her face and scanned the hilltop, not speaking. Then she closed the view port.

"OK, honey," she said. "This is going to be your show, I'm afraid. How do you feel?"

"Ready to kick British ass," said her daughter, regretting the choice of words as soon as she'd said it.

Savannah smiled, ignoring the language. "That's my girl. Let's go get 'em."

"You got it!" said Madelaine. "You guys better get strapped in. It's going to be a rough ride for you mortals."

"Very funny," said Savannah. But she hopped into a crash chair and pulled the restraining harness tight around her chest. Tesla did the same, flashing a thumbs-up.

Savannah took a deep breath. "We're all set, honey. Make me proud."

Before her mother had finished the words, Madelaine engaged her treads. Out of consideration for her passengers, she accelerated smoothly, so she wouldn't injure them with whiplash.

She quickly ramped up to full speed, though, and Tesla found himself clutching the armrests with increasingly white knuckles as the massive tank tilted back and rushed forward up the hill's slope.

Beowulf's huge treads tore into the soft earth, spewing twin streams of flying soil and grass behind her. She sensed the need for additional power again as she climbed, so she increased her coal burn rate. Soon the hunger for more strength faded away.

She'd climbed a quarter of the hill before the British alarm was raised. One of her mind slices reported a panicked British radio report about her, and the recognition made her feel happily satisfied. *Good. The enemy should fear me.*

She scanned the hilltop and identified 178 soldiers, with many more bound to be beyond the hill's crest. It seemed prudent to devote as much attention as possible to the upcoming fight. She recalled most of the slices she'd assigned to monitor radio chatter, leaving a handful assigned to the job. As the slices were reintegrated into her consciousness, she was already planning how best to reallocate them.

She was halfway up the hill, and the British had scrambled to orient their focus at her now. Dozens of rifle shots rang out, and many of them were good shots. Her forward armor was pelted with a rain of British bullets. While the sound of the hits set Savannah's nerves on edge, they did no real damage, bouncing harmlessly off the thick steel and leaving minute nicks as the only evidence of their impact.

Beowulf was closing on the hill's crest now, and Madelaine clearly saw the terror in the British faces. She was struck by how young they seemed, but the sympathy lasted only milliseconds. These were foreign invaders in her country, and they had brought the death from the clouds that had destroyed their home. The white eyes she saw, wide with fear, fed a hunger for revenge.

She reallocated a dozen mental processes to the shredders, assigning each to serve as independent fire control. The process of identifying an enemy combatant and sending a chaingun round through him was a fairly trivial task, and she wanted to maintain overall focus on the battle as a whole.

The hill flattened out quickly at the top, and she realized

she should probably decelerate to clear the crest gracefully. And yet it didn't seem the day for subtlety.

She knew Tesla and Savannah were safely secured, so she maintained her top speed and gave the chainguns permission to fire at will.

As one, the forward shredders sprang up from recessed ports and opened fire. She was eighty feet away from the half-finished British trenches now, and the guns had no trouble lining up kill shots at the close range.

The British faces flashed in her consciousness as each shredder chose its target and fired. Some were angry, red-faced and screaming at their compatriots, and others were grim and determined to finish whatever task they were busy with. Most were scared, mouths agape and eyes wide as a near-mythical creature roared toward them. But all of them met the end of their lives the same way: with one of Beowulf's chaingun rounds tearing through their chest or forehead.

Her guns fired continuously, the guns swiveling smoothly, seeking out their next victim. To the stunned horror of the men beside them, twenty-seven British soldiers had already fallen, not knowing exactly what the thing was that had killed them.

She reached the slope's peak then and added a last bit of power to her treads. Like a runaway train, she roared over the hill's crest. A dozen Redcoats were waist-deep in a hastily dug trench, and instinctively ducked as she bore down on them.

As the ground leveled out below her, Beowulf went airborne, arcing just over the entrenched men's heads like a massive steel comet screaming above them.

For the dozen Redcoats, the sun went dark as she passed overhead. While her approach and the deaths of their friends had been stunning, the sudden darkness was truly terrible, as such a thing simply didn't happen on the field of battle.

She cleared the trench and slammed back to earth with a

pounding that sent a shock wave through the hilltop. As she landed, her left tread tore through a pile of nine supply crates, streaming rifle bullets in all directions like a burst piñata.

Her momentum carried her forward, a mountain of steel beginning to decelerate, and she ran directly over six men struggling with a large cannon. They screamed as her treads loomed over them, then went silent as she crushed their bodies into the ground. The cannon collapsed, its wheels shattering under the weight. The cast-iron barrel survived, but deformed as it was pressed completely into the soft ground, only its aiming sights remaining visible in the low grass.

She decelerated and slowed to a stop near the center of the hilltop.

She'd made it to the top of Bunker Hill. She took a tenth of a second to appreciate the historical moment, then returned to work. Now on top of the flat-topped hill, surrounded by the enemy, her shredders had full 360-degree access and she smiled inside, delighted by the target-rich environment.

The chainguns opened fire en masse, sending rounds in all directions around her. She was the center of a circle of death, with her rounds tracing out the spokes. Bullets tore into Redcoat flesh, and men screamed and died in staggering numbers.

The British had been solidly taken aback by her arrival, but now began to regain their wits. Lieutenants and captains shouted desperate orders, gesturing wildly and pointing at Beowulf.

British rifle fire rained against her steel skin again, but the effect was trivial. Soon the riflemen realized they were firing out of fear and instinct, and not making any progress in stopping the monster among them. They fell back, seeking trenches to hide in, until bigger guns could be brought to bear.

The officers rallied quickly, organizing the cannon crews. They'd brought six cannons up the hill with them, but

Beowulf had already crushed one of them. Screaming firing orders, the officers urged their crews to line shots on the tank.

Finally, the first crew maneuvered their heavy cannon into position and loaded it. *BOOM!* The shot was deafening, but welcome to the British ears.

The shot struck Madelaine broadside, impacting heavily against her right tread assembly. Inside, Tesla and Savannah brought their hands to their ears, ringing from the sound of the brutal impact.

The tread itself was missed, but inside it, the array of support machinery was hit hard. Each of her treads ran along a long line of steel wheels, held in place by suspension joists and connectors. The sixty-pound shot was blasted from its cannon at 1,400 feet per second. It slammed into one of her tread support wheels, instantly snapping the axle of the wheel and badly twisting it out of alignment.

A moment later another cannon fired at her, striking the same side and area. Two more support wheels were wrenched out of position.

Madelaine had no sensors for such parts of herself. She only knew she'd been struck hard from that direction. She spun her treads, turning to face the assault, but the movement of the tread finished the job the cannons had begun. A terrible sound of grating metal shrieked as she turned, and three steel guide wheels ground against their neighbors, before snapping loose completely and falling to the ground.

Like a boxer's missing teeth smile, her right tread showed two gaps, one twice as wide as the other. When her tread ran over the empty space, it sagged down, showing undesired slack in the tread.

Madelaine did notice the decrease in efficiency from her right tread, and reported it.

"My right tread got hurt," she said. "You're right, Nikola, those cannons are nasty."

BOOM! BOOM! BOOM!

Three more cannons fired from the other direction, all striking brutal hits along her left armor. They all struck above the tread, smashing into her mid-side and destroying three of her cameras. Two chainguns were ripped from their mounts and bounced off her side, landing on the ground in two mangled piles.

The cannonballs carried a tremendous amount of kinetic energy. When they impacted her armor, the thick steel deformed inward, absorbing the force.

The three impacts pummeled her side, leaving three deep depressions and rocking her to the side. Inside, Savannah screamed from the sudden clamor and explosion of force.

Tesla felt his heart beating hard now, like a jackhammer in his chest. His body wanted to flee, or to help, but there was nothing to do yet. He reached out to Savannah and took her hand. She grabbed at it and squeezed hard, welcoming the warm touch.

Madelaine recovered, accelerating to present a moving target. She had a large blind spot now on her left side, and that unnerved her. She gave full priority to the cannon crews, and her shredders ignored all other targets. The first crew to hit her was also the first to die.

As the six men re-primed and reloaded their cannon, she reached out, shattering their skulls with precise hits. Almost at once the six men fell, headless. All around the cannon, six pools of blood soaked into the ground from the grievous wounds.

The nearest lieutenant yelled for nearby riflemen to step forward and finish loading the cannon, but they hesitated, staring at the horrific scene.

BOOM!

Another cannon fired, smashing into her right tread again. The shot tore into her support system, ripping three support joists into pieces. Along with the previous damage, the loss of the joists was severe. The woven steel tread sagged in several places, and part of the assembly lurched harshly as she moved.

With rising concern, Madelaine realized she could barely control her right tread now. She sought out the offending cannon crew and saw them hidden behind a thick wooden barricade made of recently cut trees, the logs stacked horizontally on top of each other. The black cannon barrel protruded out forward through a small hole.

Her shredders instinctively tore into the shield, but the wood was thick. Her bullets chewed into the stacked logs, gouging thick splinters from them, but went no further.

The cannon was hauled back, out of sight, to be reloaded. *BOOM!*

From her other side, a shot crashed against her, higher than before. In stunned horror Tesla saw one of the view ports crumple in, deformed by the force. Several small cracks around the misshapen view port now let in sunlight.

Madelaine remained focused on the stubborn wooden barricade. She swung around to face it, distressed by the awful grating sounds coming from her right tread. It took far too much power to coax that tread into action, and she knew it could fail at any time.

But for now, she pushed herself forward, lining up her good left tread with the shielded cannon. She closed to within twenty feet when the crew looked back out and saw her approaching. She heard panicked yelling from behind the barricade, with some British hoping to fire before she reached them, and others arguing to flee.

Before they reached a consensus, she was upon them. Her massive tread rolled over the barricade, splintering the thick wood as one quick-witted soldier dove aside. She pushed on and crushed the cannon and the men into the ground, grinding them together in a bloody mess of flesh, iron, and wood. The sole survivor rolled to his feet and saw the carnage happen, as well as the end result as the tank continued rolling forward off of them. He turned, fell to his knees, and vomited onto the grass.

A British lieutenant had managed to strong-arm several replacements to step over their headless comrades and man the cannon. Reluctantly, they took up the tools needed to prepare the cannon for another shot.

As Madelaine rolled off the ruined barricade, she saw the men returning to the cannon behind her. Her treads felt heavy and sluggish, especially the right one, and she didn't want to maneuver any more than necessary.

She willed two chainguns to focus on the new threat, but then realized she was running low on shredder ammo. She could kill the men replacing the previous crew, but there would be more men after them. *Better to disable the cannon.*

She instructed both rear guns to focus on the cannon's right wheel. Together, the wooden spokes of the wheel supported the heavy cannon, but individually, they were thin enough to be chewed through by her fire.

The chainguns fired, sending a burst of eight rounds into the bottom spoke, splintering it through as the crew bolted away. The guns adjusted aim, and repeated the process on the next spoke. It too was sawed through by the rapid fire.

She continued, and two more spokes were eaten through. As she prepared to fire again, a great cracking sound told her the job was done.

The heavy iron barrel collapsed, falling to one side as the right wheel disintegrated. It was out of the battle.

That just leaves the three over—

BOOM! BOOM!

From within her blind spot, two cannon blasted at her again. One shot went low, into her left tread, further reducing its ability. The other shot was higher, against her upper tower.

It missed the radar panel, but slammed mightily into her main gun turret, leaving a nine-inch depression in her armor, and throwing her passengers around again.

She tried to turn and get sight of the three remaining cannons. The gears that delivered power to her treads slipped, then caught, then slipped free again. The treads ground harshly, and she only managed to turn partially around before deciding to shut them down.

The incomplete turn was enough, though. She had eyes on the three cannons again. They were bunched close together, sharing crews and supplies.

She checked her shredder ammo level and knew she couldn't get them all.

Time to try out the big gun then. Her main turret turned slowly, swinging the massive barrel around. As it came to bear on the cannon crews, the British abruptly dropped what they carried and tried to run.

"Hold your ears," she warned Tesla and Savannah. They jammed their fingers into their ears, eyes closed.

KA-BOOMMM!

The eleven-inch barrel exploded with a belch of golden fire. The 440-pound shell smashed into the grouped cannons like God's own fist. A blinding geyser of dirt shot into the air as a deep crater was torn into Bunker Hill. The cannons and their crew were obliterated in a hazy cloud of sawdust, steel, and pink mist.

The entire hilltop froze, unbelieving, at the force of the shot. The remaining British blinked, taking in the damage and clearing their heads. As realization set in, and they saw they had no cannons left, the Redcoats broke and ran.

Rifles were tossed down, and they bolted down the hill, back toward Boston. She wanted to pursue them, but her treads were a mess, and she doubted her ability to make it down safely. She let them run.

But Madelaine had taken Bunker Hill from the British.

Lieutenant Terry cursed, rubbing his shoulder. The pain was building, coming in distracting waves. It was the last thing he needed, with the current situation.

He'd gotten his force across the bridge fairly well. The cavalry had been lost earlier, but he had nearly one hundred good men and even two cannons. A good force for taking a small outpost, perhaps, but useless against the ever-growing army occupying Boston.

He was cut off from the general, but from the sounds coming from farther south, he was giving the British a good fight still.

He had the cannons placed to cover the bridge, along with fifty rifles. If the British followed them over the narrow bridge, he intended to make them pay dearly for the attempt.

He walked over to the makeshift medical area to check on the ones who hadn't been so lucky.

Their doctor had been killed earlier in the morning, but his assistant was busy dressing a messy leg wound.

"Hey, Doc," said Terry. "Is there anything I—"

KA-BOOMMM!

Atop Bunker Hill a massive explosion sprayed dirt straight into the air.

"Gods," whispered Terry. "What the hell was that?"

He found a set of binoculars, but couldn't see anything over the hill's crest.

"That was high explosives," he said to himself. He turned and surveyed his men. They might hold this bridge if pressed to, but to what purpose? The British had the city. They didn't need to expand farther.

But Bunker Hill has the high ground.

He called to his sergeant. "Let's get the men together! We

march for the hilltop. Now!"

Madelaine scanned the hilltop, making sure there were no living British left. When she was satisfied they were alone atop the hill, she unlocked the access hatch and lowered the crew ladder to the ground.

"All clear," she said. "Bet you'd like to stretch your legs, huh?"

"Really, it's over?" asked Savannah incredulously. Her fingers worked at the restraint buckles, and she extricated herself.

She stood and stretched her arms high over her head, rising up on her toes. "Oh, that feels good."

Tesla got out of his chair and crossed to the open hatch. "Fresh air too. I could do with a little sunlight."

He stepped down the ladder, then jumped, landing on the grassy hill with both feet. Looking around, he was astonished by the carnage around them. He stepped out from under Beowulf, into the sun.

Dozens of bodies, maybe hundreds, were strewn around the hilltop like discarded toys. The tang of blood hit his nostrils.

Savannah came down then and joined him, her eyes wide at the devastation. She turned back and looked up at Beowulf.

"Honey…? You did…all this?" *It's not possible. Maddy is a little girl. A twelve-year-old girl.*

"Um—" Madelaine began, unsure what to say. "It's OK, right?"

Savannah turned back around. Wherever she looked, there was death. *And victory.*

"Yeah, honey, it's OK. I just…it's a lot to take in. You're not my little girl anymore. At least, that's not *all* you are."

"I know," said Madelaine. "I can tell. I'm growing fast. Too fast, maybe."

"Maybe," said her mother, running her fingers over the thick armor, nicked in a hundred places by rifle fire.

She leaned back and studied the heavier impacts from the cannon fire. In a dozen places, the armor was indented and deformed in the ugly manner of warfare. Savannah's hand to went her chest.

"Oh, honey…What have they done to you?" she asked.

"I'm OK, Mom," she said. "Can't really feel pain anymore. Not like before, anyway."

"I know, baby. Still…" She reined in her emotions and nodded. "You're right. It's OK," she said both to her daughter and herself.

"How about we give the general a hand now?" asked Madelaine. "That is why we came here."

Savannah smiled. "Absolutely, baby. Let's put that trigonometry to work."

"All right!" said Madelaine, already actively monitoring all radio frequencies again. As she collected new reports, she took a hard look at the British ships in Boston harbor.

She raised her radar panel from the protective armor and turned it toward the docks. Through the panel, she spoke to the large enemy ships anchored just offshore. They were the most mobile, so she wanted to take them out first. Her signal was projected through the radar panel and struck the first ship, bouncing hard off the timber decks and hull.

A second later her voice returned to her. She did the math and came up with a precise range of 2,712 feet. She looked at the trees moving slowly in the gentle wind, and guessed her windage to be three knots from the north. With that, the weight of her shells, and the known height of Bunker Hill above sea level, she created a highly accurate firing solution.

"Too far for mortars," she said. "I'll save those for the city. This is going to have to be my main cannon."

"Got it," said Tesla. He and Savannah ran behind Beowulf and jammed their fingers in their ears again.

"Ready!" he yelled.

Madelaine swung her turret right 32.9 degrees and raised the huge barrel to an elevation of fifty-two degrees.

"Firing!" she warned. The main cannon exploded, sending a massive shell arcing into the air. It screamed over Breed's Hill, continued over the Charles River Basin, and then curved down, heading for Boston Harbor.

She'd chosen the biggest ship in the harbor, the HMS *Atlas*. The 440-pound shell arced downward, straight for the *Atlas's* main deck. The sailors on board had a moment of confusion, hearing the telltale sound of incoming artillery. They looked to the sky, but never saw the incoming shell.

It hit the deck, just forward of the main mast, and punched through the heavy timbers like a stone thrown into a lake. As it smashed through the second deck, the shell detonated, tearing the ship apart from within. The thick outer hull exploded outward in a flurry of shredded timbers. Two large parts of the ship tilted toward the sky and sank below the waves, leaving behind a mess of flotsam floating on the surface. The *Atlas* was no more.

The crews aboard the other British ships anchored in the harbor stared aghast at the utter destruction. Then they obeyed the screamed orders of their commanders and dashed to make sail and escape the murderous range of Beowulf's main gun.

Madelaine fired again, and a second anchored ship disappeared in a flurry of fire, wood, and ocean spray.

She shifted targets then, focusing on the ships moored along the docks. These were secured to the docks, and their crews were unprepared for a rapid escape. She fired on them repeatedly, aiming for every other ship.

Those that didn't blow apart and sink instantly met a slower death. The shell's explosion touched off secondary detonations of ammunition stores, and soon several of the docked ships were ablaze.

Crews screamed and ran to extinguish the fires, but it was a hopeless cause. The heat and explosions fueled the fires faster than water could be brought to douse it.

Soon the fires spread, roaring high into the air above the blackening decks, racing through sails and rigging, and leaping to nearby ships.

Within minutes the entire docked fleet was sunk or furiously burning.

She scanned the docks, satisfied with the work she'd done. There would be no more British reinforcements. She lowered her main gun back down.

"I took care of the British ships," she announced.

Tesla and Savannah lowered their arms and stepped back to Beowulf's front.

"Yeah, you sure did," agreed Savannah, shielding her eyes and looking out to the docks. Even this far away, the flames and columns of rising dark smoke were clearly visible.

"That should cut off the British from their resupply line," said Tesla. "Can the general clear the city now?"

"In time, yes. I've heard there are reinforcements en route from New York. But why wait?" Madelaine said.

She directed her radar panel down, pointing at the city's core, and began taking measurements of the range to various landmarks.

"From the radio reports coming in, I've pinpointed four main British strongpoints," she said. "And I've just collected some accurate range data."

Savannah nodded. "Soften them up, honey."

"Firing," replied Madelaine.

Her twin mortar tubes slid into position, and with a loud but muffled *WHUMP*, she sent two mortars into Boston.

They disappeared into the sky, drawing out a wide

parabolic arc as they fell back to earth. Double explosions near Boston Common told them her shots had found their marks.

Just behind a wide impromptu barricade, several hundred British were arrayed in a broad firing line. They were disciplined, and their steady fire had kept a large American force from advancing. A few hundred feet behind the Americans, General Houston coordinated the American attacks, fuming at their lack of progress against the freshly reinforced enemy.

The mortars landed on the British within seconds of each other. Like grenades, but more powerful, the shells exploded, throwing shrapnel in all directions. Within fifteen feet of the explosions, Redcoats were thrown into the air, twisting and screaming, then falling back to the ground. Farther out, British soldiers felt hot steel fragments ripping into their bodies and fell to the ground, clutching their chests and faces.

Madelaine reloaded for another volley.

Tesla caught movement in the corner of his eye and turned, holding a hand over his eyes to shade the sun. Men were coming over the hill's crest.

He pointed at them. "Savannah," he warned.

"I see them, Nikola," said Madelaine. "It's OK, they're American."

Lieutenant Terry took one look at the massive tank and gasped at the sheer scale of the thing.

"Is that…a tank?" asked a private beside him. "It's huge!"

Terry nodded. It was the largest tank he'd ever seen. And with a cold sense of vulnerability, he remembered Edison's broadcast. *Secret project. Killed Americans. British agent.* He suddenly felt like a rabbit who'd stumbled onto a wolf.

He looked around the hilltop, taking in the carnage that lay strewn around the beast like discarded bones from a satisfying meal. Many of them were British, but he saw a lot of American uniforms among the dead also.

WHUMP! The massive tank fired mortars toward the city again.

It's firing on the general's men, he thought. His jaw went tight at the thought. They'd barely hung on over the past day. If this thing was shelling American positions from here, they had no chance of holding the city.

He looked behind him at the ragged hundred men scrambling up the hill to join him. His eyes flicked, cataloging their assets. *Maybe eighty rifles. Not much use against armor.*

Then he smiled. Someone had found several horses, probably running loose from losing their dead cavalry riders. Two teams of stallions were each hauling a cannon up the hill's slope. Behind them a small supply wagon was tied off behind a single horse. They were making slow progress, but were steadily climbing the hill. In a few minutes, they'd be able to set up and fire on the monster.

WHUMP! Madelaine shelled another distant British position. Again Redcoats were torn apart by the explosive mortars. She constantly scanned the city's streets, locating masses of British soldiers and calculating new firing solutions for them.

Terry had his men hide just below the hill's crest. Luckily, the thing hadn't noticed their approach from behind. He'd let the cannons arrive, then announce their presence properly.

At the docks Colonel Thomas began getting reports of the deadly shelling, which added fuel to his already raging temper. He'd watched helplessly as the fleet was set ablaze, right at the docks. Disbelief had given way to anger, then impotent rage.

Bunker Hill was mentioned as a probable source of the

fire. He snarled, knowing the guess was accurate, as he'd been unable to contact the men he had sent up there to claim the hilltop.

He wondered how his force could have been neutralized. The Americans were fighting a retreating battle in the city, and certainly had insufficient reserves to take out two British companies. *Were they reinforced from the west?* It was possible, of course, but his spies had reported no large troop movements on the roads. He frowned at the vexing mystery, then turned his attention back to the matter at hand.

His commanders were redeploying, seeking cover from the withering mortar attacks. He monitored the radio chatter, and a distressing picture soon formed. Wherever his men went, the attacks followed them, with uncanny accuracy. His army was being dismantled, and the American forces on the ground were pressing the advantage. Soon territory the British had held solidly was being given back to the oncoming Americans.

A terrified corporal burst into the room then, startling him.

"What the blazes are you thinking, Corporal?" Thomas yelled, swallowing the urge to savagely beat the man.

The junior man was sweating and gulping air as if he'd run a marathon. He snapped a sloppy salute. "Sorry, sir! But I—It killed them all, sir. I barely got away, I just ran and ran, never looked back." He leaned against the doorframe, then doubled over, catching his breath.

Thomas's eyes narrowed. "You were on Bunker Hill?"

The corporal nodded, still facing the floor.

He took a deep breath and stood tall again. "A tank, sir. Goddamned biggest tank you can imagine. Killed 'em all, every last one."

Thomas's face went white at the words. *Not possible. I killed that thing. Captain Montgomery dropped a nuclear bomb on that base.*

"It's not possible," he said out loud to himself.

"Begging your pardon, sir. I swear on my mother's grave, it's real. Like a thing out of a nightmare, it was."

The pieces clicked into place then. His lost men. The fleet destroyed. The mortar attacks. All from one cursed, unholy source. His mind felt struck dumb.

Absently, he wondered what the monstrosity was named. Was it truly alive? If so, did it feel the way men did? Did it have a soul?

He turned and looked out the windows. The Royal fleet, their only path of retreat, was a smoking ruin.

Mixed with his fury, the colonel felt a thread of fear snake its way into his heart.

Lieutenant Terry waved at the approaching cannon teams, urging them to hurry. He ran to them, signaling where he wanted them to set up. As they approached and got their first view of Beowulf, the soldiers gaped in shock, then recovered and busied themselves aiming the cannons and preparing them to fire.

Madelaine took note of the preparations.

"Um, guys?" she said to Tesla and Savannah. "I think you better get inside. Those troops are getting ready to shoot at me."

"What?" exclaimed Savannah, leaning around Beowulf's huge tread to see. "But you're helping against the British!"

"They don't know that," said Tesla. "They just see us shelling the city. And with Edison's broadcast…"

"No way," she replied. Savannah stepped out behind the cover of the steel tread and raised her hands.

"Savannah!" yelled Tesla. "Get back here!"

She ignored him, stepping into the clear, walking slowly toward the nervous Americans.

"Hello!" she yelled. "We are Americans! Don't shoot!"

Terry saw the blonde woman approaching, but couldn't make out what she was yelling. *Is this some ruse? Why bother coming out in the open? What's a woman doing out here?* It made little sense.

He'd just decided to let her come within earshot when a rifle shot cracked from his left. He spun, enraged.

"Who fired? Cease fire, cease fire!" he yelled.

"Mom!" cried Madelaine.

Savannah dropped to the grass, then turned and ran back under Beowulf.

Instinctively, Madelaine swung her main turret 180 degrees to bear down on the man who'd fired a shot at her mother.

Terry charged down the line, searching for the undisciplined shooter.

A young private lowered his rifle. "Sorry, sir. I just—they killed my brother this morning. Couldn't just sit here, doing nothing."

Terry saw the anguish in the man's face, and battled with the conflicting desires to reprimand him and also reassure him. Then he caught the motion of the tank's turret swinging toward them. *Well, the dragon's awake now.*

Tesla rushed back to meet Savannah. He helped her to her feet, and they ran for the access ladder. As they climbed it, the Americans reacted to the imposing gun swinging toward them.

A storm of American bullets rushed at them, hitting Beowulf's treads and rear armor. A dozen shots went under Beowulf, ricocheting crazily off the inner treads. Savannah made it inside, and Tesla was right behind her, reaching for a handhold to clear the hatch when a lead slug punctured his calf, tearing through the muscle.

He cried out from the hot, sharp pain and stumbled. His bleeding leg slipped from the ladder rung, and he started to fall backward. A second round ricocheted off Beowulf's underside then, and hit Tesla's already wounded leg. The round dug into his thigh, and he cried out again.

Vertigo clutched him, and he lost his balance, both hands clasping desperately for anything to stop his fall down the ladder.

Savannah heard him cry out and turned back to see his panicked face. His fingers clawed for purchase, but slid along the smooth deck plating. He tilted back and slid from sight.

She dove forward on her belly, sliding toward the open hatch, and grabbed his right wrist with both hands, clamping down as hard she could. He hung there for a moment, dangling free. Savannah fought to hold onto him, straining to maintain her grip.

He worked his remaining good leg and found a rung on the ladder. He pushed against it, taking the strain off her. She reached down and took him by the shoulder as he struggled his way up the ladder.

He cleared the open hatchway, and with her help, he fell inside, rolling to his side and reaching down to clamp his hand over the bleeding gunshot.

Savannah looked up and called out to Madelaine. "We're inside!"

The ladder retracted, and the hatch slid closed.

"Mom, what happened? Is Nikola hurt?"

She saw blood on his shoe and ripped the pants leg up to his knee. A dime-sized hole had been bored through his calf. She leaned over and verified there was a clean exit wound.

"He's been shot, Maddy."

"What?" she yelled. Her thoughts instantly turned to revenge, and a subroutine interpreted the impulse as aggression. Her main gun had finished its swing and was now aimed straight at the rifleman who first shot at Savannah. The subroutine ordered a new shell loaded into the main cannon before Madelaine became aware of it.

Savannah heard the huge shell being loaded into the cannon's breech, and yelled to her daughter.

"Maddy, no! Stand down, now! Those are American forces, and they've been misled. Don't prove Edison right!"

Tesla moaned as a wave of pain washed up his leg. Savannah turned back to him, wiping the blood away and inspecting the wound.

"The shot went clean through," she continued telling Madelaine. "Could have been worse if it had struck bone."

Then she saw fresh blood above his knee. She tore the pants leg higher and found a second entry wound, but this one had no exit. The slug was still inside him.

"Oh," she muttered, watching a pool of dark red blood accumulate on the floor under his thigh.

Only by focusing hard could Madelaine stop her own impulses from firing her main gun and decimating the American force arrayed along the hill's crest. The craving to hurt them back was so powerful, she felt lost in it. But she pictured her mother's face, and what she wanted. The urge ebbed.

CLANGG!

An American cannon ball smashed against her rear armor. The close shot impacted brutally, banging out a deep divot in her hull. *CLANGG!* A second shot hit near the first, further deforming the armor.

"They're shooting at me, Mom!" she cried.

Savannah blinked hard, trying to stay focused on Tesla. The amount of blood was startling and ominous.

"Do *not* return their fire, honey," yelled Savannah. "You cannot do that, do you hear me?" She pressed her thumb over the thigh wound and pressed down hard. Tesla screamed, then sucked a deep lungful of air and nodded for her to continue.

Madelaine watched the Americans hustling to reload their

cannons.

"I hear you," she replied dully. If she couldn't fight, she would run.

She engaged her treads and moved forward. She made it thirty feet before a horrendous screeching rang out from her left tread. The tread belt had sagged, catching against the suspension joists.

As her engine demanded movement, the tread ripped her own suspension assembly apart. The joists held to their breaking point, then exploded catastrophically. Steel shafts, bearings, and guide wheels blasted from her side as if propelled by a bomb. The tread ground on, but was no longer connected to the drive system.

She lurched suddenly to the side as only one tread was properly engaging. She could spin awkwardly in place, but forward motion was impossible. She shut down both treads.

"Get us moving," yelled Savannah, reaching with one hand for a fresh bandage.

"I can't! I'm hobbled!"

CLANGG! Another shot boomed against her hull, and the rear armor failed. The thick steel split, opening a thin jagged seam running two feet long. Just behind the failure sat her steam engine and furnace, visible from outside for the first time since her construction.

Savannah wrapped the gushing thigh tightly with a gauze bandage, but it was already turning crimson, saturated.

Madelaine became aware of the vital exposure of her power systems, and engaged her one good tread to spin the weakness away from the punishing cannon fire.

Having seen the effect their fire had on her ruined tread, the second cannon crew adjusted their aim down, to disable her remaining functional one. *CLANGG!* The cannon opened fire, sending a cannon ball into her good tread assembly. Combined with the previous damage, the shot was devastating.

The tread seams snapped, unwinding the circular tread into a woven steel strip.

As she powered up, the track stripped off the gears and lay flat on the ground as she turned and moved herself forward off it. When the length of the tread had run through the gears, they spun helplessly, with nothing to engage with.

She was helpless to move farther.

Savannah was winding a bandage around Tesla's calf and tying it off tight. His face was wet with sweat, and his eyes darted around the cabin, fighting to maintain focus.

"Maddy…" Tesla said through clenched teeth, "finish your mission."

Savannah understood. "No matter the cost," she whispered.

He looked back in her eyes hard and nodded once.

"Firing," said Madelaine. She resumed her bombardment of the British strongholds, pumping mortar after mortar into the city as quickly as she could. She knew her power plant was vulnerable, and each shot could easily be her last.

CLANGG! Another hit struck her rear-side armor. She'd managed to turn the exposed seam just out of their line of fire, but the damage to the hull was serious, and it would take little to punch through again.

Satisfied that the downtown strongholds had been neutralized, she acquired new British targets holding the port, and fired again and again, hoping to finish her task before losing power and falling asleep permanently.

In the fog of war, General Houston didn't know why his men were suddenly gaining ground more easily, but he pushed the advantage for all he could. Knowing they were holding on by their fingertips, he forewent proper advancing procedure, judging the taking of the port and the British commander to be of paramount importance.

He thought of getting a report from Terry, but events were moving too quickly. When the chance to leap forward three blocks presented itself, he snatched it up, driving his men closer to the port.

In minutes they were clashing with a British force fighting bravely to hold the port. The fighting was hand-to-hand and savage. As soon as the Americans mingled into the British lines, the mortar fire ceased, which the general thought was impressively up to date with the situation on the ground.

The British were steeled, knowing there was no retreat possible for them, and threw themselves into battle. But the Americans were grinning fiercely, having taken it on the chin for days. They finally had a taste of retribution, and they were loving it.

In the port office, Colonel Thomas heard the battle raging, and heard it drawing closer as the Americans carved out the British defenses, man by man. The panicked reports coming over the radio only underscored the losing situation.

He wondered about the American tank and what secrets it held.

Regardless, it dies here, with the rest of us.

He stood and walked to the radio station. He dialed in the local air frequency and thumbed the mike.

"Colonel Thomas calling the zeppelin *Orion*," he said. "Captain Montgomery, this is Colonel Thomas. Over."

A moment later a woman's voice crackled over the airwaves. "This is Captain Montgomery. How are you, Colonel?"

He sighed, gazing out over the smoking shells of the royal fleet. In minutes he would be shot or placed in irons and hauled away to spend his remaining years in an American prison. Either of which would be acceptable to the Crown, considering his monumental failure.

"I'm ready to go home, Captain," he said wearily.

She paused for several seconds. "Colonel? We have no ability to make a pickup here. Please explain."

"I have one last order for you, Captain. You will descend and drop a radiological bomb on the city of Boston. You will do this immediately. Thomas out." He set the mike down and poured himself a scotch.

Aboard the *Orion* the order was heard and understood. *So things are as bad as that*, she thought. *All right then, thy will be done.*

"Understood, Colonel. And Godspeed," she replied. She set the mike back and checked their position. They were still in place from the last bombing run near the Boston Common and only needed to drop below the cloud cover to find their target and fire. She turned to her bridge crew.

"Helm, make altitude six thousand feet. Take us over the city center, full speed. Bomb bay, stand by one radiological device for immediate use."

General Houston was exhausted. His men had taken the port back, and his chest was bursting with pride in the men under his command.

He marched forward into the port administration building proudly, but his legs were leaden, and more than anything, he craved sleep. But first there was a matter to attend to, one that made the suffering very much worthwhile.

Striding down the hallway, flanked by four guards, he rounded the corner and stepped into the port administrator's office, already knowing who awaited him there.

Colonel Thomas sat behind the desk, a nearly empty glass in his hand. His handgun and sword were laid out on the table. He looked up at the general's arrival, taking in the four guards and the undisguised hatred on their faces.

He looked to the general and saw a different emotion. Something more decorous, yet run through with weariness, a trait they currently shared.

He finished his drink, savoring it as his last, and stood stiffly.

He faced his adversary and saluted. "General," he said.

"Colonel Thomas," replied the general, returning the salute.

"It was a very near thing," said Thomas.

"It was."

Thomas raised his finger. "I just have to know one thing. The tank. Is it truly a living thing?"

"The tank," said the general.

In a flash the previous day's mysteries were explained. The destruction of the fleet, the uncannily accurate mortar fire. Beowulf was the reason the tide had turned so dramatically.

"My God," he whispered. His mind analyzed the information with this new addition. *Firing positions, views of the city…She's on Bunker Hill!*

"Bring him!" he ordered, already turning and running back down the hallway. Thomas was hauled away harshly, dragged along by two American soldiers, following the general.

They ran outside, where troops were taking British prisoners and putting out fires. The general waved down a military jeep and commandeered it, getting behind the wheel. He pointed to one of the guards.

"You, bring him." He looked at Thomas. "You're going to want to see this, I believe."

The men climbed in back, and the general tore away, running them down the streets of Boston, dodging bodies and burned-out cars along the way. They crossed Longfellow Bridge, then turned north and raced up the slope of Bunker Hill at an unsafe speed.

Madelaine ceased the mortar attacks as soon as the Americans closed with the British. Minutes later she heard victorious cries over the airwaves, and inside her electrical heart, she felt joy at their victory. Even if they misunderstood her intentions, she had played a large role in saving the city. She unloaded all weapon systems and retracted them.

The time for fighting was over.

Lieutenant Terry noted the tank's cease-fire, but didn't know what to make of it. A sergeant ran over from one of the cannon crews.

"Lieutenant?" he asked.

"Beats me," he said. "Maybe they ran out of ammo. Regardless, that thing was working for the enemy. Have your cannons redeploy and aim for the same area as before. I think we opened a crack in its armor. Let's tear this thing wide open."

The sergeant saluted and sprinted back. The crews began moving the cannons into position to re-engage on the tank's weak spot.

Madelaine had limited sensors inside the crew cabin, but she knew Tesla was hurt from the rapid, thin breathing she heard. "How is Nikola?" she asked.

Savannah watched his chest moving in shallow flutters. His face had lost color, and his eyes seemed to swim in their sockets, unfocused.

"Not good, honey. I have to get him out of here. He needs a surgeon. Right now, or he's going to bleed out."

"Don't let him die, Mom. I couldn't take that, OK? Save him!"

"I'm going to, baby. Don't worry. Open the hatch for me.

I'm going out there."

"They're shooting at us, Mom!"

Savannah nodded. "They're shooting at a very scary tank. I'm hoping they won't shoot at me. Now let's go," she said, watching Tesla's mouth working soundlessly. "I don't think we have much time."

"It's open," Madelaine announced.

Savannah leaned over Tesla's chest, her face just above his. "I'll be right back. Stay awake." Then she was gone, grabbing the still-wet lab coat and sliding down the crew ladder.

Her feet landed hard on the grassy hilltop, and she ran to Beowulf's front, then stepped out from behind the ruined tread, holding her hands high above her head.

Several riflemen opened fire, startled to see a human on the field. Bullets whizzed past her, and she flinched, waving the white coat back and forth, forcing a smile on her terrified face.

She saw two cannons being pulled into new positions and set up to fire again. *They're going to hit her power plant again.* She waved the white fabric frantically.

"Don't shoot! Please don't shoot!" she yelled.

Terry saw the woman step out into the open. "What the hell?" he muttered. She was unarmed and waving a white flag of some sort.

His brows furrowed together, wondering what was going on. The day's fighting had taken a decidedly bizarre turn since they'd reached Bunker Hill.

He raised his arm, turning to his men. "Cease fire, cease fire!" he bellowed. The riflemen stood down, as curious as he was.

He joined the sergeant beside one of the cannons. "Sergeant, you get your guns aimed in on that thing. If it makes a move, you unload on it. Got it?"

"Absolutely, sir."

Terry looked up. The woman was closer now, still waving the white flag.

"All right, stand by," he said and began walking toward her.

She was pretty. Beautiful, even, despite being covered in several bloodstains. Seeing him approach, she ran toward him. She dropped the white fabric, but kept her hands clearly visible.

"Lieutenant!" she called out. "We need a surgeon! Now!"

As she grew close, he realized there was something familiar about her. He strode forward quicker, meeting her halfway.

Madelaine heard Thomas's call to the *Orion*, and her joy melted. "We're about to be bombed!" she cried.

Tesla was disoriented from the leg wound, but her words quickly sharpened his thinking. "What? How do you know?" he asked.

"Colonel Thomas just ordered it. Maybe from the same zeppelin that hit our home."

"It's on the way? Now?" he asked.

"It's minutes away," she answered. "And he specified a radiological bomb."

"Oh God," whispered Tesla. *Even if her treads were intact, we couldn't outrun that blast radius, not out in the open like this.*

He glanced down at his throbbing thigh and saw a red bloom staining the white gauze. The motion made him feel lightheaded. He frowned, disliking the sight of blood, especially his own.

"Maddy," he asked. "Can you shoot down that zeppelin?"

"I think so," she said. "But it'll spook the hell out of those guys outside."

Tesla laid his head back down on the steel floor, staring up. "We're dead if we don't. Seems a worthy gamble."

"I see your point," she said.

She turned the radar panel up to the sky, sweeping back and forth for a return signal.

"Who are you?" Terry asked the attractive blonde woman.

She smiled, happy to not be shot by friendly forces. "Savannah. I am Savannah Browning."

Terry frowned. That name *was* familiar. He scanned her face and saw no deception, only earnest concern.

Then he gasped. "Colonel Browning's girl?" he asked, his brows rising.

"Yes!" she cried. "I'm his daughter, Savannah!"

"But—" he said, cocking his head to one side. This didn't add up. "You're firing on American troops. Edison said so."

She shook her head. "No way. Edison's broadcast is false." She pointed back at Beowulf. "We just shelled the British strongholds. Call General Houston. He'll confirm who we're fighting for."

"General…" he began. "My God, we very nearly blew you to pieces."

"Yeah, I know! Now we need a field surgeon immediately. Nikola Tesla is aboard that tank, and he's bleeding badly."

He took that in, then nodded. "All right, follow me. We'll get this sorted out."

Together they began running back to the lieutenant's men.

Captain Montgomery watched her bridge crew handle the huge zeppelin like the professionals they were. They worked together smoothly, bringing the airship down.

Madelaine scanned the skies for anything larger than a flock of birds. Soon she found it. Her voice had bounced off the massive airship and returned back to her, giving her a precise angle and range.

The zeppelin was still hidden in the clouds, but descending quickly. It surged forward at maximum speed, nearly directly above the city's center, barely a half mile from their position on the hill. Based on the damage to Fort Hamilton, they were well within the lethal blast area. And as soon as that zeppelin got visual confirmation they were on target, they'd release their payload.

"I found it, Nikola," she said. "It's coming down fast."

"If you move that main gun, they're going to open fire," he said, glancing up at the jagged gash of sunlight already streaming through her hull.

"Yes," she replied. "I know."

He gritted his teeth and propped himself up by his elbows. "Time to be heroes, then."

She understood the reference to self-sacrifice.

"I love you, Nikola," she said, then ordered her main turret to acquire the airborne threat.

The sergeant was watching his lieutenant talking to the woman. Things seemed to be going all right. *Maybe they're surrendering?*

Then the huge tank began moving its main gun. His eyes locked on the enormous barrel, rising and turning. *Fine, then.*

He turned to the cannon crews and bellowed, "Fire!" At each cannon a private stood ready to ignite the fuses, and they stepped forward.

Beowulf's gun continued, tracking up and away from them, aiming for the clouds.

KA-BOOM! The tank's massive gun exploded, sending its 440-pound shell skyward. The cannon crews, along with everyone else on Bunker Hill, recoiled from the deafening shock wave.

A brief second later, the sky came apart in a dazzling explosion of fiery orange streaks. The zeppelin *Orion* detonated at 6,300 feet, sending huge fireballs of flaming hydrogen gas arcing through the clouds.

Everyone turned and gaped at the display as the metal superstructure fell to earth, already twisting and breaking apart.

The sergeant realized the truth then. That zeppelin had tortured them for days. His head snapped around to the cannon crews.

"Freeze!" he commanded.

One private heard the order and stood down, nodding acknowledgement. At the other cannon, the soldier's ears were still ringing from the recent explosions, and he moved to the cannon, oblivious of the countermanding order.

As he prepared to ignite the cannon's fuse, the sergeant sprinted toward him and dove at the cannon. The private jammed the igniter forward, just as the sergeant slapped his hand over the fuse, getting a nasty burn on the back of his palm.

"I said stand down," growled the sergeant at the startled man.

His mouth open in shock, the private dropped the igniter. "Sorry," he said meekly.

Terry arranged for his doctor to climb inside Beowulf and treat the wounded inventor. The blood loss was harrowing, but the surgeon had seen much worse during the past days.

He stuck a leather wrapped piece of wood between Tesla's teeth, and working quickly, he removed the bandage, poured an antiseptic over the wound, and slid a pair of silver forceps inside Tesla's thigh, digging for the lead slug within.

Tesla's howls of pain shook Madelaine, but she stayed silent, not wanting to surprise the doctor.

In minutes the slug had been removed, and the bleeding artery sewn closed. The doctor applied clean field dressings, and gave Tesla a shot of morphine to dull the pain's edge.

He had several soldiers assist in getting Tesla down the ladder smoothly and onto a waiting gurney.

Savannah raced to his side, clutching his hand in hers. He smiled up at her, and returned the squeeze.

A jeep approached then, and the slamming of brakes made Savannah turn. Her eyes lit up brightly when she saw General Houston climbing out of the vehicle.

"Savannah!" he cried, taking her in a bear hug and lifting her feet from the ground.

"Now you show up!" she said, laughing. Then she glanced over his shoulder and saw Thomas in the back of the jeep. Her smile wilted, and she broke the hug, standing back.

"Ah yeah," said the general. "Sorry to spring that on you. We just took him into custody."

Thomas sat upright, his spine like a steel rod. His eyes darted from Savannah to the behemoth tank behind her, then back again.

"Archibald," she said, her voice coolly distant.

Thomas stood and jumped down out of the jeep, facing his ex-wife. A range of emotions played across his face. Surprise and disappointment at seeing her alive, an odd satisfaction that he'd failed to kill her, and a melancholy longing for the past they'd shared. She was still beautiful, which added to the sharpness of the moment.

"I've missed you, Savannah," he said, his voice catching in his throat.

She smiled sadly. "I know you have." She started to turn and leave, but then froze.

"There's someone you should meet," she said, waving him to follow her over to Beowulf.

Confused, he let himself be led forward as the guard kept

a pistol aimed at his back.

They stopped in front of the humongous tank, and he looked up at it, acutely aware of how small it made him feel.

"So this is the mythical beast I've heard so much of," he mused.

"Mythical?" She smiled.

"My men have sworn that the thing is alive, that it fights like a man."

"No, not a man," she said. "A little girl. Your little girl."

"What does that mean?" he said, frowning in confusion. "Explain."

Savannah looked up at the looming tank. "Say hello to your father, Madelaine."

"You're…my father?" asked Madelaine, her voice projecting strongly from her external speakers.

Thomas leaped back as if he'd been burned. He crouched, glaring up at the talking machine.

"What? What is that? Savannah!" he yelled.

"That is our daughter," she told him. "To save her life, Nikola Tesla put her mind into this machine. Otherwise, she would be gone now. Killed in your attack on our base."

Thomas paced, his eyes locked on the steel beast. "No. No! That's impossible. You're lying to me, Savannah!"

"She's not lying. It's me, Madelaine. I just have a different body now."

Thomas's mouth fell open, hearing her words, but his mind could find no way to process them.

"I have memories of you, Father. They're vague. I think I was three or four. But I remember your face, looking down at me in my crib."

"Shut up!" Thomas screamed. He jabbed a finger at her. "Shut your bloody mouth. I won't hear this!"

"Hear it, or don't," said Savannah. "The truth remains the same."

Thomas staggered backward as if the words had physically shoved him back. He felt the guard's pistol against his back. None of this could be true, not even a bit of it. His only daughter was now a monster. His military ambitions were crushed. There was no life to return to, and no freedom to even try.

He looked into Savannah's eyes, and the final, stabbing defeat was the pity he saw looking back at him.

"No!" he bellowed, spinning around. He shoved the guard's pistol to the side as it fired, missing his hip. He wrenched the gun from the man's hands and launched a vicious kick into the guard's stomach, sending him staggering back.

Thomas wheeled around, the pistol in his hands. He cocked the hammer back and swung the weapon at Savannah, aiming down the iron sights between her piercing blue eyes.

Madelaine snapped a forward shredder toward him and made ready to fire, but then remembered she'd cleared all weapons systems of ammunition. She told a subsystem to load the gun, but it would take at least three seconds to obey the command.

Thomas's mind screamed for him to pull the trigger. But he didn't. Despite their history, or because of it, he couldn't kill her. Impotently, he screamed, raging at the destruction of his hopes.

His hand quivered, and the pistol barrel danced in front of her face. Her eyes never left his, though, and he knew she was seeing him, truly seeing him, as she always had.

He felt the judgment in her eyes and knew he was being found wanting.

Without a conscious thought, Thomas snapped the gun down and jammed the barrel under his own jaw. One round, up through the mouth and into the brain, would end all the troubles.

His finger tightened on the trigger.

CRACK!

Thomas blinked, unsure why he wasn't falling to the ground dead. He looked down and the pistol was gone.

He turned and saw a fading wisp of white smoke from Beowulf's forward shredder. His daughter had shot the gun from his hand, saving his life.

He stared blankly up at the tank, disturbed that there were no eyes to connect with.

"Honestly, Father, I expected more from you," Madelaine said.

NINE MONTHS LATER
WARDENCLIFFE, NEW YORK

"Are you quite ready yet?" Savannah asked, arms folded over her chest, taunting him.

Tesla waved a hand in her general direction. "Yes, yes. Just another moment." He bent over his worktable, running his fingers over data sheets and progress reports. "Good, that's good," he muttered to himself, scanning the documents.

He straightened up and faced her.

"I think it's ready."

Savannah giggled, and her hands flew to her mouth. "I can't wait to hear her reaction, Nikola! Let's go!"

"Let's," he agreed. He joined her, and they walked together down the main hallway of his new laboratory. The bullet wounds had healed, but he still walked with a slight limp.

The MacArthur grant money had been a windfall at precisely the right time. With the sudden funding, Tesla had purchased two hundred acres of land on Long Island, New York. It lay adjacent to a rail line, and offered all the space he needed to continue his work.

After the RCA had been safely removed from the battered Beowulf, and Madelaine's safety ensured, the original tank had been decommissioned and disassembled. It was agreed that a civilian contractor of Tesla's stature could get the job done faster than the military.

The main building went up quickly, and once they were operational, General Houston had helped them secure several military contracts, each of which were lucrative enough to let him develop his ideas to fruition. Sensing a technical powerhouse developing, J.P. Morgan and George Westinghouse both invested in the new startup venture.

Edison's Menlo Park was still going strong, but focused on safer, market-driven ideas. At Wardencliffe, Tesla's lab chose to expand frontiers.

Tesla and Savannah strode through the large building, dodging the army of technicians they'd hired almost immediately after the business in Boston. With money no longer a limiting concern, they'd recreated their own Rabbit Hole, one under civilian control.

Their sole focus in the past nine months had been continuing the work on Beowulf's successor, and today was the unveiling.

As they darted around workers and scientists, a familiar voice called out.

"Hey, Nikola!" He turned and saw George racing toward him, his arm draped over Sophia's shoulders. "A banner day!"

"Very much so," said Tesla, smiling. "We were just going to get her."

"Perfect, we'll see you there," he said, wheeling Sophia through the crowded space. She grinned and waved as they dashed away.

Tesla followed behind Savannah, who was practically sprinting toward Madelaine's room. As they entered, she interrogated them.

"So today I finally see it? Finally?" she asked, with a teenager's whine.

"Only because you've been so patient," said Savannah, rolling her eyes.

"Whatever. I've been cooped up in here too long. Show me!"

The array cube had been installed at the new lab as soon as the main building had gone up. They'd done what they could to occupy her, wiring up cameras and sensors for her to stay in touch with the outside world, but life at her speed grew boring fast without heavy stimulation.

Still, they'd asked her permission to develop the Mark II privately, and unveil it as a present. Reluctantly, she'd agreed, and that room was the only one in the lab where she had no sensors or cameras to let her participate in the work.

The anticipation had been good for her, thought her mother. *It kept her mind buzzing on possibilities.*

"Today's the day, honey," Savannah said.

Tesla lowered a powered crane and moved the array to a wheeled carrier. He'd made it himself, complete with a portable power supply, just for this day. It would have been far easier to show her by wiring up one more camera, but Savannah insisted they bring her to it. Tesla agreed. Some things must be experienced in person.

Satisfied she was safely moved, he connected a "sensory box" and set it on top of the cube. The box contained a camera, microphone, and speaker, giving her basic communication abilities while they moved.

He and Savannah pushed the carrier forward, and together they steered her down the hallway. Workers made room for them as they approached, and soon they stood in front of a large door labeled "Cerberus."

"I like the name," said Madelaine. "Sounds wicked."

"Well, if you like that…" said Savannah, pushing the door

open.

Tesla wheeled her inside the cavernous room, and she got her first look at her new body.

"Oh my God," she said. Even through the small portable speaker, the awe in her voice was clearly audible.

The new class of tank, code-named Cerberus, was twice the size of the Beowulf tank and completely redesigned for the future of warfare.

"I've heard bits and pieces of conversations," Madelaine said. "But this is…"

"Yeah, we did all right," said her mother. "Your tax dollars at work."

Tesla stepped forward so she could see him, and he pointed to the gargantuan tank.

"It's nuclear powered, Madelaine," he told her. "A fission reactor. Practically unlimited energy." He walked down the side of the tread that dwarfed him.

"Your chainguns all feed from a centralized ammo source, and you'll never run out," he continued.

"Never?"

"Well, to be more clear, you can create your own ammunition from scrap metal found on the battlefield. So, effectively—"

"Wow," she said.

Savannah stepped forward. "The crew compartment is larger and more comfortable, and the entire assembly is waterproof down to sixteen hundred feet. In case you ever need to do that sort of thing again," she said, grinning.

"There's a lot of new enhancements to show you," said Tesla. "But take a look at the main cannon."

She focused the camera lens up on the mammoth barrel. "It's really big," she said.

"Big, but also completely revolutionary," he said. "No shells. It fires superheated plasma, generated straight from the reactor."

"Nikola, this is incredible! How did you do this all?"

A male voice answered from behind them. "Never underestimate the spending power of a government at war."

"General Houston!" cried Madelaine. "You came!"

The general came forward, into her line of sight. "Course I did. It's a big day for you, and us too. We expect big things from you."

"I don't know what to say," replied Madelaine. "Just… thanks. And I'll do my best."

"I do believe that," he replied.

"So we're ready to get you integrated with Cerberus," said Tesla. "We'll run tests for a week or so, then you're good to go."

"They're really sending me to England?" she asked.

He nodded. "Taking the fight to the enemy, as it were."

"A little scary," she admitted.

"You won't be going alone, rest assured," said the general. "We've assembled quite a fleet to accompany you."

"All right," Madelaine said, taking in the sight of her new body. On both sides it extended beyond the angle of her camera view. "I'm ready!"

Tesla turned to her, facing the camera lens. His smile said a lot. How much they'd gone through, and how much she had in store for her future.

"Then let's begin," he said.

The next week was a blur of systems integrations, hundreds of function tests, and dozens of calibration adjustments.

The work on Cerberus had been a priority for nearly a year, but those labors were now complete. Tesla and Savannah were now gearing up for a second grand vision.

Ground had been broken for a massive radio tower, like the world had never seen. The plans were daunting in their scope, including a fifty-five-ton steel sphere atop a huge tower and sixteen iron bars driven hundreds of feet into the ground to allow current to flow and seize hold of the earth. When completed, Tesla declared that a worldwide radio network would be possible, with instantaneous communication anywhere on the globe.

Even his investors questioned the sanity of the project when Tesla himself explained, "It is necessary for the machine to get a grip of the earth. Otherwise it cannot shake the earth. It has to have a grip…so that the whole of this globe can quiver."

By the end of the week, Madelaine had thoroughly explored her new body and its abilities. Several times she marveled at how much Tesla's lab had managed to include in the newly built tank. Her radio gear had been dramatically enhanced, and once Tesla finished his radio tower, she should be able to stay in touch with them, even from England.

The new weapons were stunningly impressive, and her ability to regenerate ammunition made her smile inside. But what truly delighted her was the digital library Tesla had personally overseen.

He'd built a dozen crude versions of her own array and put them to work scanning books for her, converting them to a digital format she could access. A lab worker would slide a new book into position, and devices would flip through the pages, scanning them at superhuman speed. In the eight months they'd been working around the clock, they had built a digital library of 148,000 books. And it was all installed in her memory, ready to be enjoyed and studied.

He'd included every book on military strategy and tactics that the general recommended, then everything he could find on Europe's geography, armies, and leadership. Then he filled out the list with a vast array of popular literature, history, science, mathematics, politics, and the arts, including one title he knew would delight her when she came across it: a compendium of saucy limericks.

Final preparations were being made for her long journey.

The crew chosen to go with her into battle had trained relentlessly for months, learning her subsystems and the details necessary to repair her in the field. While Savannah had at first pleaded to be on the team, she realized reluctantly that she didn't have the needed background, and would only take a slot away from someone more qualified to help Madelaine, in case she was hurt.

Tesla understood her fear and sorrow at staying behind, watching her only daughter go to war. He could have justified taking a crew slot for himself, but he had a backlog of new inventions to create, both for the war effort and for mankind's benefit in general. And he felt a strong kinship with Savannah. They worked perfectly together, and he didn't want to leave her side.

There was no transport ship capable of carrying Cerberus, so an oil tanker had been converted for the job. A broad steel platform had been welded over the ship's main deck, extending over each side. Madelaine would carefully drive onto the platform, and there she would be carried across the Atlantic, bound for England.

Her transport would be the centerpiece of a naval armada of smaller, well-armed ships, tasked with protecting her during the journey, as she couldn't fire her plasma cannon during the voyage without capsizing her own transport.

The lab's huge hangar doors were pulled aside, opening the room to the outside.

It was time for her to head down to the dock and then board her transport ship.

Tesla stood beside Madelaine, as they looked through the

open doors to the world outside.

"I'm a little scared, Nikola."

He nodded. "So are we."

"Rook to bishop's three," said Madelaine.

He was glad she remembered their unfinished game. He closed his eyes and visualized their board in his mind.

Tesla frowned. He'd seen this coming. Her attack was precise and relentless. Despite the impending sense of a noose closing around his neck, he'd been unable to fend her off.

"I believe that's checkmate," she offered, helpfully.

"Yes, yes," he agreed, wondering how he'd been so thoroughly trounced.

He opened his eyes again. "I thought I was good at chess."

"You are, Nikola. I've been playing against a dozen of the techs, and you lasted longer than any of them."

"Damning praise," he said. "That business with the knights was evil."

"I invented that. Call it the Bertram Gambit."

Tesla smiled. "Well done, young miss. He'd be proud of you."

Savannah joined them, looking out the huge doors.

"I guess it's time," she said.

Madelaine spun slowly in place, aligning herself with the open doors, facing the bright sunshine of an early summer morning. She pulled forward to the opening, then stopped with her forward armor just emerging from the doors. It had been nine long months since she was outside, and the vast openness of it now seemed intimidating.

Sunshine warmed her alloy skin and played across the thick steel emblem George had welded to her front quarter panel: a lightning bolt, with the words "1st ARMORED CAVALRY."

Then she drove forward, leaving the lab and stepping out into the new day. She slowly worked her way down the winding road to the water's edge and the docks, where her ship waited for her. Tesla and her mother walked behind her.

She cautiously maneuvered herself up a ramp and onto the waiting oil tanker, turning herself carefully to face forward on the giant platform.

She powered down the thirty-foot-tall treads. A ground crew scrambled around her, securing thick chains to her for extra stability. She was ready.

Savannah ran up the ramp and stood in front of her daughter. She felt hot tears pooling in her eyes, then spilling down her cheeks. She wiped at them absently, looking up at the mammoth tank.

"Be safe, honey," she said. "Please."

Madelaine had her own fears about her future. But she pushed them aside for later.

"I will, Mom. Don't worry."

Tesla joined Savannah at the ship's bow and looked up at Madelaine.

"You will do great things," he said. "And we will celebrate each one."

"Thanks, Nikola," she said, knowing that if she were in her human body, she'd be bawling her eyes out. "I'll make you proud, both of you."

Savannah reached out and stroked the steel alloy tread. "We already are, my love."

"Hey, Nikola!" someone yelled. Tesla turned and saw George racing toward him, a bottle of champagne in one hand and the other pulling Sophia behind him. He held the bottle high. "For a proper christening!"

"Of course, how could we forget such a thing?" said Tesla, smiling.

George and Sophia joined them, and he handed Savannah the bottle. She took it and looked up at Madelaine's forward armor, forty feet above their heads.

"Do the honors?" she asked, handing the bottle to Tesla.

"Delighted," he said. He took the bottle by the neck and stepped back several feet, looking up at his target.

"Bon voyage, Madelaine," he said, rearing back and throwing the champagne high into the air. It twirled as it flew through the air, clearing the high armored panel, before gravity took hold and brought it back down. The glass bottle struck the armor solidly, and it shattered in a foaming explosion, splashing champagne across her alloy skin.

The group filed back down the gangway and stood together on the dock. Dock workers released mooring lines, and her transport ship was free.

A horn blared twice. The oil tanker eased its engines forward and pulled away from the dock.

As it cleared the area, the ship increased speed, bound for a foreign shore. As the ship grew smaller in the horizon, George and Sophia slipped away, back to the lab.

Savannah stood unmoving, her eyes fixed on the distant horizon, watching the ship carry her daughter away. Tesla waited with her. In minutes the ship was a distant speck, a dark dot where the sky met the water.

And then it was gone.

They stood there together in silence for several more minutes before Savannah turned to Tesla. She smiled bravely, but her chest hurt from an invisible wound.

"Shall we get to work, Nikola?"

He nodded. The sooner they finished the radio tower, the sooner they'd be able to speak to Madelaine again.

He walked beside her, back up the winding road to their lab.

"A capital idea," Tesla said.

ABOUT THE AUTHOR

CHRIS KOHOUT LIVES in Seattle, WA but was born and raised in southern Georgia.

Word-of-mouth is **crucial** for any author to succeed. If you enjoyed the book, please consider leaving a review at Amazon, even if it's only a line or two; it would make all the difference and would be very much appreciated. Leave a review here: http://amzn.com/B00EXADAY6

Say Hello!
I love hearing from readers! Drop by and say hello on Facebook at http://facebook.com/FateOfNations.

If you want to get an automatic email when my next book is released, sign up on my site at http://chriskohout.com. Your email address will never be shared and you can unsubscribe at any time.

I hope to hear from you soon!

Made in the USA
Charleston, SC
04 October 2013